# Stalking Horse

## Terence Strong

POCKET
BOOKS

London · New York · Sydney · Toronto

A CBS COMPANY

First published in Great Britain by Hodder & Stoughton, 1993
This edition first published by Pocket Books, 2009
An imprint of Simon & Schuster UK
A CBS COMPANY

3 5 7 9 10 8 6 4 2

Simon & Schuster UK Ltd
1st Floor
222 Gray's Inn Road
London WC1X 8HB

www.simonandschuster.co.uk

Simon & Schuster Australia
Sydney

A CIP catalogue record for this book
is available from the British Library

ISBN 978-1-84739-268-8

Typeset in Plantin by Ellipsis Books Limited, Glasgow
Printed and bound in Great Britain by
Cox & Wyman Ltd, Reading, Berkshire

# FOR KEN
### godfather in a million

# Author's note

Iraq invaded Kuwait on the day I left England for Mozambique to begin research for my last book.

Subsequently I found myself in the middle of the remote African bush, trying to pick up unfolding events courtesy of the BBC World Service. And like many others I speculated as to when and how Saddam Hussein might deploy his deadly terror options – the fear of which kept the allies on edge for the duration.

That is when *Stalking Horse* was born.

A brilliant, daring type of spoiling operation or foolhardy and dangerous? Either way, members of the Washington intelligence community confirmed to me that it would have been a viable option at the time.

In the event no terrorist incidents were 'reported' within the United States during the Gulf War. Of the 164 that did occur abroad, about half were aimed at American targets.

Eleven of these attacks were mounted in Greece by the shadowy 17 November movement, who claimed that the allied assault on Iraq was a 'barbaric attack on a Third World country' engineered by Israel and Jewish interests.

But why did Saddam not deliver directly – or by proxy

– his knockout terror blow against the allies which, experts believe, would have resulted in a humiliating climb-down for the allies and victory by default for Iraq?

Was it pure good fortune? Or is there indeed a top secret file to be found in the CIA vaults at Langley, Virginia, code-named Stalking Horse?

Terence Strong
London 1993

*As always, all characters are fictitious, but in particular I should like to emphasise that Eamonn O'Flaherty and 'Big Tom' O'Grady are pure invention and I have been advised respectively by those highly respectable institutions – the Irish Livestock and Meat Board and the Turf Club – that persons of those names have not been associated with them.*

*Once more I am indebted to numerous people who have kindly given so generously their time and expertise in helping me put the pieces of this story together, including those who prefer to be unnamed for reasons of security:*

*IN LONDON: To Neil and to Leslie for helping to put an agent in place; Robin Horsfall of Immediate Response Security; Dave Reynolds of Photopress, good friend and one of the first journalists into freed Kuwait; Bob Burns of the* Liverpool Echo *for his insights into Merseyside life; Frank Dunne of Dr Barnardo's; Dave Smith of the Walton Probation Service; Mrs Freely of St Francis de Sales; the MOD Chemical and Biological Defence Establishment at Porton Down; my typist Judy Coombes for meeting an impossible deadline (again!), and Alexandros Rallis of the Greek Embassy in London for opening doors.*

*IN THE UNITED STATES: To Simone Hammarstrand – 'my man' in Washington – and 'TW' Adams for their enthusiasm and introductions; Dr Clifford Attick Kiracofe Jnr who adopted Lew Corrigan as his own, with a little help from journalist Brian Duffy; Neil C. Livingstone for outlining Washington's preparations against terrorism; Bob Kupperman of CSIS for advice on the dark arts of terrorism, unconventional warfare and 'simulations'; journalist Holly Hershfield for making it special; Bill for putting me right; Major George Rhynedance, Special Forces; Lt Commander Pietropaoli, US Navy, Norfolk; Lt Jack Papp, US Navy, London, and Lt Dave Lee, US Navy, Naples.*

*IN ATHENS: To Paul Anast of Freepress who targeted Soúda Bay; journalist Angelos Stangos for his advice and hospitality; Nelly Moucacou; Kate Smith of the British Embassy, and Colonel Vasallis Sagonas of the Anti-Terrorist Police.*

*IN CRETE: To Linda Crosby-Diamandi and her orange-picker friends who brought it all to life, and to the inspirational Lt Commander Barbara Valenti.*

*I thank you all for making this story possible.*

# Prologue

*Dateline: October 1990*

'How many dead?'

It was the President of the United States speaking.

'My latest information is two hundred dead,' the Surgeon General replied. 'And the toll of those officially reported as sick has risen to almost three thousand, Mr President. If the current trend continues we anticipate that half of those will die.'

The President's face was waxy in the harsh glare of the spotlight, beads of perspiration clearly visible on the skin above his upper lip. 'And every one was attending the Superbowl?'

'Yessir. Or else lived in the immediate vicinity.'

'Are the hospitals coping?'

A shake of the head. 'They are totally overwhelmed. Every bed in the state is taken up. All except emergency operations have ceased and all but the acutely sick have been sent home. We need help with transport to move new patients to hospitals in neighbouring states.'

There was no shortage of expert advice available from the members of the Emergency Action Committee (EAC) around the table. He turned to the Director of the National Guard Bureau. 'See to it that your people work closely with the Governor and his people on any transport that may be required. Ambulances, helicopters, whatever.'

He returned his attention to the Surgeon General. 'Do we know what this stuff is yet?'

'The Center for Disease Control says it is some particularly virulent strain of tularemia – a bacterial agent.'

'Nothing more specific?'

'It's not a type they can identify, Mr President. There is no known antidote. But the Center has been onto the British Chemical and Biological Defence Establishment at Porton Down.'

'And?'

'They confirm similarities with the type used at the Wembley Stadium in London last week.'

The President removed his reading spectacles and rubbed his eyes with his hands. 'And how many have since died there?'

'Almost two thousand to date.'

He mouthed a silent curse. 'And Paris? At the Prix de l'Arc de Triomphe?'

'Just seventy, Mr President, but that was an open race-track, not a confined space.'

He then addressed the Attorney General. 'And what is the latest about how this attack was perpetrated? Has the FBI now abandoned the hamburger theory?'

The man shifted uncomfortably in his seat. 'That was an early guess, Mr President. We are certain now that the bacterial agent was dispersed by an overflying light aircraft towing an advertising message. That's also how it was done in Paris and London, it seems.'

Then it was the turn of the CIA Director.

'And should I guess who is behind all this?' the President asked.

'I'm afraid there's no doubt at all, sir. Saddam Hussein of Iraq.'

'Do we have official confirmation from Baghdad?'

'No, Mr President. But the *New York Times* received a warning threat from a group claiming to be the Friends of the Nineteenth Province – an Iraqi euphemism for Kuwait – just prior to the Superbowl tragedy. And I'm afraid that press speculation on the point isn't far off the mark.'

At that moment Dr Melville Mace entered the lime-light and handed a sheet of paper to the US Secretary of State.

The President waited patiently while the man studied the note before looking up and clearing his throat. 'I have two messages here. One from President Mitterrand of France. He regrets that he must accept the advice of his Defence Minister and withdraw his offer of land forces to Operation Desert Shield. He reaffirms his belief that peace can only be achieved by further talks through the United Nations.'

'And the other message?'

'From Prime Minister Thatcher. She confirms her support for Desert Shield and refuses to reduce their military commitment. But public, parliamentary and media pressure since the Wembley Stadium attack has necessitated a more pragmatic attitude to be taken. The British suggest a Middle East peace conference to link the invasion of Kuwait with the Palestinian question and Israel.'

'I see,' the President said slowly, 'and what exactly does this mean for Operation Desert Shield?'

The Secretary of Defense interrupted. 'It means, Mr President, that Saddam Hussein stays in Kuwait. He has won.'

At that point the spotlamps went out and the fluorescent tubes flickered on, flooding the conference room with light.

'Right,' Dr Melville Mace announced. 'We'll stop there for a coffee break.'

There was a visible ebbing of tension amongst the experts and politicians from Capitol Hill gathered at the green baize tables – each of which represented a different player in the crisis management scenario.

Two expatriate Iraqi dissidents and a psychologist from Harvard played Saddam Hussein. A former British ambassador to the US and a British junior Foreign Office minister played Prime Minister Thatcher.

The President of the United States was a former National Security Adviser and his emergency action committee comprised specialist experts and previous holders of executive office in government. Now he returned his spectacles to his breast pocket, thankful that he did not face the decisions now confronting the real President, George Bush, as he grappled with the aftermath of Iraq's occupation of Kuwait.

He stood and stretched his legs as Dr Mace crossed the floor from the control team's table. 'Well done, Mel. That was pretty scary.'

Mace blushed, uneasy with compliments. 'Yeah, wasn't it just.'

'Thank God it isn't for real.'

'Isn't it?'

'Hell, I hope not. I mean since Saddam invaded Kuwait the CIA and the allies' security people have been leaning on every known Iraqi agent and all the Middle East terror groups. Like hard.'

Mace wasn't giving anything away, refusing to be drawn.

'So who the hell was dropping bioweapons on the Superbowl and Wembley Stadium? How the hell was it done?'

Mace handed him a coffee from the tray. 'Maybe you'll find out in the next session.'

The man nodded, smiled and drifted away to talk to the others, laughing and joking after the intense pressure of the role play simulation.

But Dr Melville Mace was neither smiling nor joking.

He knew how it had been done.

Knew how it could be done.

Was certain how Saddam Hussein would do it.

And it would be no game.

# One

There was something about the American that Max Avery didn't trust.

Something about the jokes and heavy laughter, as he dispensed anecdotes and porter from behind the bar at the back of O'Casey's barbershop, didn't quite ring true. As though the rough good humour were an act that might be replaced in a flash by a fit of unreasonable anger.

Perhaps it was just a question of bad body chemistry between them. Instinctive. But it was an instinct that Avery had learned to trust; it had kept him alive this long.

He lay back in the gloomy alcove seat and reached for the glass of Guinness. From where he sat he could see the entrance as well as his own reflection in the grubby gilt-edged mirror. Christ, he couldn't say he didn't look his age now. Although his hair was still full and dark, the sunken skin around the worried grey-blue eyes seemed to emphasise every one of his forty years. And the shadow of stubble on his chin certainly didn't help.

He sighed inwardly and tried to relax.

Perhaps he was just being bloody-minded.

He didn't want to be in this Irish backwater village,

scarcely five miles from the border with Ulster. It was fool-hardy and he didn't know why he had been summoned.

That made him nervous. Bloody-minded and suspicious.

Suspicious even of a big, jovial Irish-born American who had returned from New York to rediscover his roots. He'd just happened to find them here in rural Monaghan, and it had taken little more than the glimpse of a fat dollar roll to persuade the thriftless O'Casey to allow his back room to be converted into Corrigan's Den.

Not surprisingly, the bald-headed barber was one of only two other customers in the cramped dingy room with its all-pervading smell of malt and sawdust. He sat on a bar stool, chatting with the local farmhand next to him, laughing and drinking away the day's meagre takings. Just occasionally both men would stop talking and glower in the direction of the lone Englishman.

Avery ignored them and unfolded a crumpled news-paper from his jacket pocket. He read the headline but it hardly registered. Something about Saddam Hussein's inva-sion of Kuwait. More troops, more ships. More talk. Another world, another war. It might as well have been another planet.

The brass-faced grandfather clock struck eleven melan-cholic chimes, forcing conversation to a halt.

The farmhand stood, drained his glass, and bade Lew Corrigan goodnight.

Avery watched, tense. Observation of legal drinking times was not something for which the Irish were known.

O'Casey followed the farmhand into the front barbershop. Avery heard them exchange farewells above the hiss of the rain; then came the sound of bolts being shoved home.

O'Casey did not return. Avery shifted his position slightly until he could see the barber relaxing back on one of his own leather-padded chairs from which the stuffing was falling out. Gunmetal glinted on his lap in the light from a nearby street lamp.

The smoke-filled bar seemed suddenly stifling. Claustrophobic. Avery wiped the perspiration from his forehead. Like a rat in a trap. The words rushed around his brain and he felt his heart begin to palpitate.

'How's the room?'

The sound of Lew Corrigan's voice intruded on his thoughts and he spilled his drink. He forced an uneasy smile. 'The room? Oh, it's fine.'

The American came from behind the bar. It was too small for a man his size. Sixteen stone, Avery guessed, with huge shoulders and a powerful chest barely contained within the red lumberjack shirt. The ingrained tan suggested a lifetime under a tropical sun which had doubtless added a few years to his blunt facial features. The greying, close-cropped hair put him at about the same age as Avery. Early forties. Some just wear better than others, he mused.

'We've just the two rooms,' Lew Corrigan said. His accent was a curious mix of Brooklyn with lapses into a softer Irish brogue. 'I'm tryin' to persuade O'Casey to open up another one for next summer's trade.' He lowered his voice. 'But the guy's an asshole.'

'The room's fine,' Avery repeated.

Corrigan's lips smiled, but the Englishman noticed that the flinty blue eyes didn't. 'You spilled yer drink. I'll top it up.'

'There's no need.'

The American waved aside his protest and returned to the bar with the glass. As he worked the pump he said conversationally: 'The locals can make visiting Brits feel twitchy. Me, I'm lucky; they love us Yanks.'

Avery decided it was pointless to avoid conversation. There was no telling when his contact would turn up. He said: 'I was told you were born here.'

'True,' Corrigan replied, returning with two glasses. 'Lived about twelve miles from here till I was eight and my folks emigrated. I'm a naturalised citizen of the good ol' US of A.' The Brooklyn accent had returned. 'Started coming back here for fishing trips in the eighties. Got comfortable with the old sod. Then what? – eighteen months ago I got divorced. I thought what the shit!' He glanced around the musty room. 'So here I am. Business sucks, but it'll pick up. At least you know an Irishman'll always need a drink. Cheers.'

Their glasses clinked and froth splashed onto the newspaper that was open on the table.

'Whatyathink?' Corrigan asked suddenly.

'Pardon?'

The big hand lifted the paper. 'Ol' Saddam and Kuwait?'

'I haven't given it much thought.'

It was a lie, of course. He'd spent too much time thinking

about it, speculating. Remembering old times and old friends. It had proved distracting. But still the lie came easily. If you told the same lie enough times you began to believe it yourself.

Corrigan laughed. 'You Brits can be so cool. Half the world's goin' to war and you haven't thought about it. And they call Americans insular!'

Avery gave a grudging smile. 'All I know is it's hit the motor trade.'

'That your business? Cars?'

'Import and export, hiring and repairs.'

Another laugh. 'Still, like drink, people always need wheels.'

It was a timely statement. The squeal of tyres in the back-yard was unmistakable. It was followed by the slamming of a car door.

Avery's pulse began to race.

The American was on his feet, moving swiftly for a man of his size. Pushing aside a shabby velvet curtain at the back of the room, he unlocked the door and allowed it to swing open in the wind.

The man stood in the doorway, his lank hair and black trench coat sodden, his face pinched and white. His hunched figure was outlined by the headlights of the car in the yard, steam rising from its bonnet as the rain drummed on the paintwork.

'Inside,' Corrigan said briskly.

The man stepped in, trailing a puddle on the floorboards, and glanced anxiously around the dimly lit room. When his eyes settled on Avery the thick red gash of a mouth pulled an expression that was halfway between a smile and a sneer. He turned and waved out to the driver of the car, who then switched off his lights and killed the engine.

Corrigan closed the door and locked it. 'Filthy night.'

The man ignored the pleasantry. 'Anyone else here?'

'Just O'Casey on watch in the front.'

The tense expression on the newcomer's face relaxed and he ran both hands over his head, squeezing out the overlong black hair and leaving it plastered against his scalp. 'I'll take a large Jack Daniels,' he said, shrugging off the.wet raincoat. Under it he wore a black shirt and jacket and faded jeans.

He crossed the floor and pulled up a chair to face Avery. 'Long time, Max. Remember me? Danny Grogan.'

'No, should I?'

Another lie. Silken, convincing.

Of course he knew Danny Grogan. He'd met the man casually a couple of times in Irish pubs in London. Casually enough for him not to remember if he had no reason to. And that could raise unwanted suspicions. So he lied.

He knew Danny Grogan because he was a friend of Gerry Fox.

And Avery was interested in anyone who was a friend of Gerry Fox.

But it had been his controller at MI5 who had filled him in on the details. Grogan was Fox's second half. Together they formed a liaison cell of the Provisional IRA. A cut-out unit. Grogan received his instructions from a contact of the Army Council. He passed them on to Fox who passed them on to contacts in 'active service units' on the British mainland or Europe. Neither Fox nor Grogan knew the other's contacts. At least that was the theory.

'That's good,' Grogan said. 'But I know you, Max.'

Avery ignored the hint of menace. 'It's madness bringing me here.'

Grogan's small dark eyes viewed the Englishman with disdain. 'We'll be the judge of that.'

Avery wasn't about to be intimidated. 'I'm not going to be much use in future if I'm seen associating with you. It was decided at the start I should never come to Ireland.'

Grogan lit a cigarette, cupping the flame with nicotine-stained fingers. 'Priorities change,' he mumbled, and he let the smoke escape with a hiss. 'We're not idiots, Max. So you come here on business and spend one night's bed and breakfast at Corrigan's. Perfectly innocent. The Garda aren't given to hounding tourists. Anyway, O'Casey would swear the three of you drank and played cards to the wee small hours.' He took the offered glass from Corrigan and downed its contents in four rapid gulps. 'No one's going to know about what's going to happen. People round here know better than to ask questions.'

'Happen? And what's going to happen?' Avery didn't like the sound of it and it showed in his voice.

The Irishman belched lightly. 'You're coming with us on a little jaunt, Max. It's been decided it's time you saw a wee bit of action.'

'That's ridiculous,' Avery protested. 'I'm happy to help

out, supplies and logistics. But strictly arm's-length, we've always agreed that. For Christ's sake, man, don't you have any respect for your own security, let alone mine?'

Grogan was unmoved. 'Like I said, priorities change.' He turned to Corrigan. 'You got the gear, Lew?'

'Sure,' the American replied, placing two brown cardboard boxes on the bar.

Avery was more than mildly surprised as he realised that Corrigan was clearly and wittingly involved in the IRA man's plans.

Grogan said: 'It's time we went.'

It was cramped in the back of the Cavalier, Avery crushed between Corrigan and the Irishman. As they bumped along the narrow country lanes, a fug of condensation gathered on the windows and the wipers struggled to clear the lashing rain.

Avery didn't recognise the youth who was driving, nor the man who sat beside him in the passenger seat. No one offered the information and they weren't the sort of questions you asked. He noted that the courtesy light bulb had been removed and he guessed that it was no accident.

'This is good weather for moving about,' Grogan said after they'd been travelling for some fifteen minutes. 'The Garda don't like standing about in the rain any more than the RUC.'

The driver took a bend too fast, the rear wheels fish-tailing on a carpet of dead leaves. 'Fucken slow down!'

Grogan snapped, his nerves increasingly raw as they neared their destination.

'Is this car hot?' Avery asked.

'No, it belongs to a local doctor. He leaves it in the garage each night with the key in, just in case we have a need for it.'

'That's decent of him.'

Grogan ignored the sarcasm. 'That way he gets to keep his kneecaps.'

They crossed the border into Ulster by one of the myriad narrow lanes that was little more than a dirt track. Soon they entered a built-up area, the dank countryside giving way to the orderly terraces of a council estate with wide, unkempt grass verges. It was one in the morning now, and there were few lights in the windows. At one point they neared a heavily fortified police station, but then the driver turned off, weaving his way deeper into the urban sprawl.

At last they turned into another side street and stopped. A tense silence fell as the driver doused the lights.

Grogan jabbed a thumb over his shoulder. 'That's the place.'

It was an ordinary end-of-terrace house. A three-bedroom affair with a neat little front garden behind a white picket fence. A white baker's van stood on the driveway.

At that moment two men detached themselves from the shadows where they had been keeping watch.

Grogan wound down his window. 'Well?'

'No problems,' the first man answered. 'His alarm goes off at two. There's access from the back.'

'Let's go,' Grogan said, then placed a restraining hand on Avery's arm. 'You'll wear this.'

The Englishman took the woollen balaclava with a growing feeling of unease.

While the lookouts continued their vigil, the driver and his companion left the car first, crossing the road to a pedestrian alleyway that ran alongside the house. Then Grogan followed, ushering Avery and the American in front of him. A five-foot chainlink fence was the only obstacle between the alleyway and the back garden of the house. Once it had been scaled it took only seconds to cross the tiny lawn, with its child's swing, ornamental pond and plastic gnome, to the crazy-paved patio.

The driver was already putting the last strip of plastic parcel tape over the glass of the kitchen door. His companion produced a heavy club hammer, its head swathed in towelling. The eyes in the balaclava looked at Grogan. Somewhere in the wet night two tomcats shrieked in combat.

'Do it.'

One short muffled crack. That was the only sound.

Moments later sufficient glass held in place by the tape had been removed to allow a hand to reach in and turn the key. Then the first two gunmen were in, racing through the darkened kitchen and into the hall.

Avery and Corrigan followed with Grogan close behind. By the time they'd climbed the stairs the light was already on in the front bedroom.

The couple were sitting up in bed shielding their eyes

from the sudden influx of light. Someone had pulled aside the duvet and one of the gunmen had a revolver pointed at the white naked body of the man. His wife, her transparent nylon nightdress rucked around her thighs, began to blubber incoherently.

Grogan stepped forward, grabbed the woman's hair and forced her head back so that her mouth opened with a gasp. He shoved the muzzle of the automatic between her teeth.

'Stow it, missus!' he hissed. She gulped, staring up wide-eyed at her tormentor. 'We just want to borrow your husband. Keep quiet, do what we say, and no one gets hurt. Got it?'

The woman nodded, tears welling in her eyes, and Grogan withdrew the gun.

'Mummy?' The small voice came from the landing where the boy stood clutching a one-eyed teddy bear.

'Come here, boy,' Grogan said abruptly. 'Go to your mother.'

'Darling . . .' the woman wept, holding out her arms. The terrified child scurried past the gunmen and threw himself into her embrace.

Grogan said to the woman: 'I want you to phone the bakery and tell them your husband won't be coming in. He's got the flu. Understand?'

Her voice was quavering a little by the time she finished the call, but Grogan was satisfied. While the husband got dressed at gunpoint, the driver and his companion went downstairs. They opened the garage doors and rolled the white van silently inside. Hidden from prying eyes they began to load the fifty-pound Semtex bomb.

Avery watched on with sickened fascination as the gunmen went about their work.

One of them turned to Corrigan: 'Have you got the detector, Lew?'

The American produced one of the cardboard boxes he'd had back at the bar and extracted an oblong plastic module that resembled a car radio.

'What's that?' Avery asked, suppressing the anger in his voice.

Corrigan handed the object to one of the gunmen. 'A digital signal processor,' he replied easily. 'Or radar detector to you Brits. This is a state-of-the-art job. They're illegal here, but we use 'em to pick up the cops' speed traps in the States.'

The gunmen began drilling and screwing the module inside the rear window of the van using an angle bracket.

'And you supplied it?'

Corrigan looked at him curiously, unsure if he detected a hint of disapproval. 'Sure. Like you supply stuff for the boyos on the mainland and Europe, I do my bit for gear that's available Stateside.' He nodded towards the module now being wired into the detonator of the bomb. 'The army here's developed counter-measures against radio-controlled bombs. They can jam frequencies between 27 and 450 megahertz, but they can't do nothing against this beaut. It operates on 10,000 megs and above.'

'The wonders of modern science,' Avery murmured.

He'd heard that there were at least four American nationals helping the Provisional IRA in Ulster and Eire, but it was still an unsettling experience actually to meet one.

'Done,' one of the gunmen announced with a certain pride and slammed closed the doors of the van.

Corrigan called back into the house and a few moments later Grogan appeared with the baker and his sobbing wife and child at gunpoint.

'Right, let's get this clear. There's no need for histrionics. Your husband here simply drives his van to the border checkpoint the same way he does every day. Only this time he isn't carrying bread. At exactly four thirty he leaves the van, taking the key with him, and simply walks away. It's as easy as that.'

'My wife . . . ?' the hapless victim protested.

Grogan's impatience was starting to show. 'Your wife and wee kiddy will be safely tucked up in bed with my men keeping an eye on them until we hear that the bomb's gone off.'

The woman snivelled as her husband gave her a rough hug of reassurance. She clutched at him in desperation until Grogan prised her fingers away.

'What if things go wrong?' the man pleaded. 'What if I'm stopped?'

The muffled voice behind the balaclava said: 'Just make sure you're not. That's if you ever want to see them alive again.'

As soon as the van left the garage, the doors were locked

behind it; the two gunmen remained with the woman and her child.

Grogan led Avery and Corrigan back to the parked Cavalier. The Irishman took the wheel this time, driving at a steady thirty miles an hour until they had cleared the residential estate and were again in the countryside. Then he hit the accelerator.

He began talking rapidly with a humour in his voice that suggested he was enjoying the flow of adrenalin. 'The van's taking the scenic route. We'll be there in good time before him.'

Avery said: 'I still don't know why you've brought me here. It's bloody stupidity. If I get caught, who'll organise your cars and safe houses?'

Grogan gave a cynical laugh. 'You're not the only quarter-master we have on the mainland, Max. We don't believe in keeping all our eggs in one basket.'

'I know that.' Irritable.

'But you really *don't* know why you're here?'

'Christ!' He checked his exasperation. 'No, I don't.'

'And you don't know about O'Flaherty?'

The air in the enclosed space seemed to freeze.

Eamonn O'Flaherty was the Provisionals' commander for European Operations. An educated, deceptively charming and gregarious man in his early sixties, he was a senior official at the Irish Livestock and Meat Board in London. Snowy-haired and with a fondness for black-cherry pipe tobacco and tweed jackets with leather patches, he was the absolute antithesis of the popular concept of a major terrorist figure. His position of influence in commerce and minor establishment circles placed him above suspicion.

Avery caught himself just in time. He knew O'Flaherty socially, but his knowledge of the man's secret life had been supplied by his MI5 controller. 'Eamonn? What's happened?'

'He was lifted in London three days ago. Special Branch.'

Avery could scarcely believe what he was hearing. He'd had a long drinking session with the man and his wife only a week earlier. 'You must be joking.'

'Do I sound like a man who's joking?'

If O'Flaherty was going to be arrested, Avery should have been warned about it. It was a basic ground rule. 'Why was he arrested?'

'Why do you think? He was an important man in the organisation.'

'I didn't know that.'

'No?'

'No — and I wouldn't want to know either.' He gathered his thoughts. 'I've seen nothing about the arrest in the papers.'

Grogan was dismissive. 'Of course not. They don't announce that sort of thing straightaway. Like to make us sweat.'

And Avery could see that Grogan was sweating. But not just him. He could imagine the pandemonium that the arrest would be causing in the PIRA hierarchy. The recriminations and the paranoia. He understood now why he had received the cryptic message to drop everything and take the shuttle to Dublin.

Grogan's next words confirmed it. 'Only a handful of people knew O'Flaherty's real work for the Provies.'

'I wasn't one of them.'

'So *you* say.'

'So I'm under suspicion?'

'We've a new European commander now. The Army Council's orders are to trust nobody.'

The lane was climbing a steep wooded hillside which Avery gauged must be less than a mile from the border with the Republic of Ireland. He was proved right as the vehicle crested the hillside to reveal the stark arc lights of the British Army checkpoint glowing below in the dark distance like a disembodied filmset.

Grogan steered into a lay-by and doused the lights. The rain had reduced to a drizzle and they had an uninterrupted view of the cross-border road with its concrete vehicle traps, blockhouses and protective wire mesh fences. A handful of British soldiers in their familiar DPM smocks stood hunched against the weather, stamping their feet for warmth.

'Five minutes,' Corrigan intoned, consulting his watch.

The Irishman took the second cardboard box from the console and prised open the lid. Inside was a police radar gun which he handed to Corrigan.

'When the van reaches the checkpoint,' the American said laconically, 'we just switch this on. The army's electronic scanners won't pick up the beam, but the detector rigged on the vehicle will. As soon as it registers –'

'Boom!' Grogan interrupted; he seemed to find the idea amusing.

'What about the driver?' Avery asked.

Grogan half-smiled and returned his gaze to the border road. 'What about him? A year ago he passed information about one of ours to the Brits. His own brother-in-law.'

'So you lied to his wife? He's not coming back?'

'Let's say I was economical with the truth.'

Avery stared at the empty road in silence, drowning in his sense of utter helplessness. Forced to sit and watch as an innocent man drove to his death. A human bomb. A human bomb who would take God only knew how many British servicemen with him.

Avery found himself willing the soldiers to return to the blockhouse for one of their famous brews of tea. Praying that the driver would find the courage to stop his van on the way from his home to telephone the Royal Ulster Constabulary.

Even as Avery's hopes began to rise, the white van trundled into view, sparkling like a child's toy under the bright streetlights.

The muscles in Avery's stomach contracted involuntarily and he found himself holding his breath. Grogan made a little clicking sound of anticipation with his tongue against his teeth. The American raised the radar gun with both hands, lining it up on the rear of the van.

'Perfect line of sight,' he murmured.

Below them the vehicle slowed. Avery could almost sense the driver's reluctance, imagine the terror and confusion that must be racing through his mind.

Grogan said: 'Give it to Max.'

Avery turned sharply. 'What?'

'You heard,' the Irishman said evenly. 'Take the gun from Lew. You do it.'

'Are you crazy?'

There was a half-smile on Grogan's face. 'Crazy enough to want to be sure about you, Max. That's what the Army Council wants.' He added: 'That's why you're here.'

Lew Corrigan held out the radar gun. Avery ignored him, instead staring hard at Grogan. 'I went through all this years ago. I shot a Green Jacket in the Falls Road, you know that.'

The van was within a quarter mile of the border-post, its speed reduced to a crawl.

'As you put it yourself,' Grogan said, 'that was years ago. Times change, people change. Just look at this as renewing your subscription.'

'Take it,' Corrigan leered.

Avery glared. Last time he'd had warning. Last time he'd been able to contact his controller to set it up. Told which man to aim for, when and where. As he'd fired, just wide, a soldier fell down. It was as simple as that. The poultry blood, the panic that followed, the armoured cars and the ambulance with its flashing light, it was all window-dressing. Just like the concocted report of the assassination in the press the next day.

This time it was different. This time there was no get-out.

Reluctantly Avery took the offered radar gun, raised it slowly with both hands.

'Wait until the van's at the checkpoint,' Grogan ordered.

The vehicle was within a hundred metres of the post; the troops had seen it and were gathering, ready to do their job. Some were laughing, recognising the van, perhaps anticipating the treat of an oven-warm loaf.

It was blinding. The white-hot core of the explosion seemed to burn into the eyeballs, even at that distance. Momentarily it illuminated the surrounding countryside like sheet lightning. Fifty metres away the mesh fences of the border-post trembled in the shockwave, the on-duty soldiers blown off their feet.

Grogan's gasp of surprise was abruptly drowned out as the noise of the detonation reached them, its quaking power so deep and awesome that it made their hearts jump and set their ears ringing. Beneath their feet the very earth shook.

'Christ,' Grogan breathed, staring at the smouldering crater in the road. The van had vaporised and with it the hapless driver. A whistle blew at the border-post where dazed soldiers were climbing to their feet.

Grogan turned on Avery. 'You bastard, you did that deliberately.'

'No!' It was Corrigan, placing a restraining hand on the Irishman's shoulder. 'Max didn't touch it – his finger's not even on the trigger, look –'

Avery's hands were trembling.

Grogan was angry and bewildered. 'What the fuck?'

'It must be a fault in the mechanism,' the American said. 'I'm sorry. I'll check it out. It won't happen again.'

The Irishman could scarcely contain his fury, but the frustration quickly gave way to his instinct for self-preservation. He knew from experience that within minutes the army would call up helicopters with powerful Nitesun lamps to search the surrounding area.

'One fucken baker,' he seethed as he started the engine and swung the car into a tight turn, creeping blindly back down the hill until it was safe to turn on the headlights.

They drove back in angry silence. But by the time the Cavalier pulled up in the yard behind Corrigan's Den, Grogan's temper had subsided. Daylight was starting to break with the promise of another dismal, damp day.

'Enjoy a hearty breakfast, Max,' he said. 'Then drive back to Dublin and catch your plane. We'll be in touch shortly. Something big's in the air.'

Avery appeared not to have heard the Irishman's words. 'So have I renewed my membership?'

Lew Corrigan laughed at the look of confusion in the Englishman's eyes. He could almost smell the sweat of fear that glazed the unshaven blue skin of Avery's chin. He'd seen men break under pressure too many times not to recognise the symptoms. On the streets of Brooklyn, when the Irish gangs stood shoulder to shoulder against the mobs of Puerto Ricans, Italians or blacks from the neighbouring ghettos.

And he'd seen it under fire in Vietnam. Some silent and paralysed with terror. Some wailing like hysterical women. Others like Max Avery. Outwardly in total control. But Lew Corrigan knew when a man had lost his bottle. Knew beyond any doubt when a man was about to crack.

Grogan shared the American's mirth. 'Put him out of his misery, Lew.'

Corrigan reached inside his jacket and pulled out a .38 Smith and Wesson revolver. His thumb rested on the hammer.

Avery's nostrils flared as he felt the liquid draining from his guts like water emptying down a sink.

'If you hadn't taken that radar gun back there, Max, my orders were to kill you.'

# Two

As dawn broke over Washington DC, snakes of blue-grey mist writhed slowly above the flow of the Potomac River.

From the vantage point of his apartment window in the Watergate complex, Melville Mace viewed the new day with a mixture of relief and trepidation.

Relief because he had hardly slept that night. Apart from a few hours' fitful dozing, he had been pacing his living room, practising key passages of the report he was to make to the secret committee that morning.

Yet, as he raided the refrigerator for his umpteenth pizza slice, he knew his rehearsal had been a waste of time. Because the trepidation he felt at the prospect of addressing his peers in the intelligence community, would ensure that this delivery failed to carry the impact that it should.

And that compounded Mace's concern. Because he alone knew the extent of Iraq's terrorist capability under Saddam Hussein and the nature of the peril which faced the United States and its allies as Operation Desert Shield unfolded. It was vital he put that message across.

He stared out at the yellow glimmer of headlights through the river mist as cars crisscrossed the distant

Theodore Roosevelt Memorial Bridge. A sure sign that the capital of America was coming alive with its usual urgency and hustle.

The trouble was that Melville Mace was essentially an academic. Born on a remote farm in the vast prairies of Nebraska, his had been a solitary and studious childhood. His parents' ambitions for him were finally realised when the young Melville eventually earned his PhD at Stanford University and an MA in international security from the Fletcher School of Law and Diplomacy at Tufts.

Whilst he would have preferred the cloistered university life, his young wife Paige had taken over from his mother as the new driving force in his life. And so he stepped timorously into the rat-race world of the consultants who fed the capital's insatiable desire for information on virtually every subject known to mankind.

Each major subject had its own government department which generated endless committees and subcommittees, which in turn spawned numerous freelance institutions and, of course, the ubiquitous Washington 'consultant'.

Mace's speciality was not in economics or sociology as one might expect of the slightly built, balding forty-five-year-old with spectacles that were too heavy and too wide for his narrow baby face. Dr Melville Mace's undoubted expertise was in the area of terrorism, low-intensity warfare and crisis management. And it was in recognition of his diligence and ability to analyse situations that he had been appointed special adviser to the State Department's Office for Combating Terrorism, or ATA as it is known for its bureaucratic office symbol.

'Cometh the hour, cometh the man.'

That had been Paige's encouraging, if unthinking, response when he'd expressed his worries to her the previous night. Now she lay asleep in their king-size bed, alone with her dreams. And of one thing Mace was certain, she would not be dreaming of the world's troubles. Most probably it would be which new dress to wear to which party. Or, least likely, how to balance the growing debts on her numerous credit cards. Like so many Washington folk she really had very little concept of, or interest in, what went on beyond the Capital Beltway ringroad, let alone abroad.

Nevertheless, her words had held a certain appeal for Mace, had stiffened his resolve.

By eight o'clock he had showered, shaved and dressed in the Capitol's uniform of sober suit from Beau Monde and white shirt, set off by a Cosmos Club tie which quietly underlined his credentials.

He entered the bedroom to kiss Paige goodbye. 'Wish me luck.'

'Mmm,' she replied sleepily. 'Of course, dear. And don't forget to pick-up those lox and bagels from the deli. I'll need them for our buffet party tonight.'

So much for the imminent catastrophe facing the world, he thought, as he began the walk through the misty autumn streets of Foggy Bottom and along Virginia Avenue to the State Department building. After collecting the research papers which were kept locked in his office safe, he made his way to the front entrance where a chauffeur waited.

It was only a short drive to the Old Executive Office building which flanked the east side of the White House. The journey scarcely warranted the government limousine, but it was a measure of his new-found status and the rising paranoia over security.

His near-majestic arrival at the steps of the ostentatious French baroque façade did much to bolster Mace's self-confidence. He fairly strode through the doors and cursory security checks before taking the elevator to the third floor. A secure, 'electronically clad' room had been set aside for the SIGS meeting of Senior Interdepartmental Groups.

But, as he stepped through the carved oak door of the anteoffice, his courage evaporated in an instant. Although it was only ten to nine, the room was already milling with the familiar faces of senior agency representatives, talking earnestly and sipping coffee.

Red Browning, a florid-faced bull of a man from the National Security Council, spotted him immediately.

'Ah, there you are, Mel!' the retired colonel's foghorn voice boomed as he crossed the room. All heads turned. 'Never fails. Those living nearest the office are always the last in.'

Mace's pale cheeks coloured. 'I'm sorry, Mr Chairman, I thought . . .'

''Course you did, Mel, 'course you did,' Browning said, sweeping him towards the conference room with a broth-erly arm around the shoulder. 'But we're all eager to get this show on the road. Want to hear what *you* have got to say. Yessir. I've a briefing with the President this lunchtime and he's eager to learn what your people have come up with.' He hesitated. 'Didn't want coffee, did you?'

Mace smiled, his mouth parched. 'Not really.'

'Good. Then we'll get on.'

Even before the gathering had settled around the polished table, Red Browning was on his feet, still every inch the military man and loving his new role as Deputy National Security Adviser to the President. Clearly he was setting out to put his stamp on the meeting.

'Welcome, gents, to the first get-together of the Committee for Research into the Global Realignment of Resources.' His speech was clipped and businesslike. 'As you're aware this committee has been set up on the personal instruction of the President and the National Security Adviser. I myself shall be reporting personally to both George Bush and General Scowcroft.

'I don't have to remind you that the workings of this committee are top secret. Hence its name – to allay any suspicions as to its true nature. For "global realignment" read who's on our side? And for "resources" read Saddam's undoubted terrorist capability. Touchy stuff. So no pillow talk with girlfriends or wives – your own or anyone else's.'

He paused to allow the wave of amusement to subside.

Christ, Mace thought suddenly, these people just do not realise the seriousness of this situation. They really believe that the United States is an invulnerable fortress and that Saddam Hussein is a tinpot Arab dictator offering no real threat. He could see it in their eyes and their easy smiles.

Red Browning might have been reading his thoughts. 'Well, gents, just to get things into perspective, I can tell you that the unofficial White House view is that there *will* be war.

'And it's already been decided that we will be doubling the size of the Desert Shield forces and that an announcement will be made in a few weeks' time. In short we are merely playing for time, gents, because Saddam has unwittingly unleashed the most powerful military juggernaut on this planet.' He grinned widely at his audience. 'Saddam is already a spent force – only we haven't told him yet.'

Another undercurrent of mirth rippled around the table.

He continued: 'Now I'll ask the Federal Bureau of Investigation to reassure us with just what measures we have in hand in case Saddam decides to throw a curve and use his terrorist card against us here in the US.'

As Browning sat down Victor Weintraub of the FBI rose to his feet. He was a balding, bespectacled man in his late fifties, with a heavily lined, humourless face that looked as lived-in as the crumpled dark suit he wore. Cynical eyes suggested he had seen it all before and, even if he hadn't, nothing new would surprise him.

'The advice we've been given by the security agencies,' Weintraub drawled, his lips moving imperceptibly, 'is that Saddam had not anticipated the host'le US reaction to his invasion of Kuwait. Therefore he is unlikely to have any agents or "sleepers" in place for such an eventuality. Further, we've no evidence to suggest his operatives have attempted to smuggle in any explosives or arms to date.' He peered at his audience over the top of his spectacles as though defying a challenge. 'Although, since State saw fit to remove Iraq from the list of state sponsors of terrorism in '82, this wouldn't have been difficult to do prior to the August invasion.

'Any planned attack would most likely be on the media centres to obtain high-profile coverage. Here in Washington, New York, Chicago and LA – all of these areas are taking extra precautions, and security has been stepped up at all international airports.

'Iraqi staff at their embassy on 18th and P and at their UN mission in New York are under round-the-clock surveillance. All cars with BZ diplomatic plates are being routinely followed. And, of course, all mail, telephone calls, faxes and computers are monitored. I understand that this action is pretty much mirrored worldwide.' He looked to the CIA representative for confirmation.

Willard Frank's head of cropped snow-white hair nodded in Weintraub's direction. Ice-blue eyes stared unblinkingly from the scrubbed, open face. 'Most of our European allies have undertaken similar measures,' he confirmed. 'In any situation where we suspect a lack of motivation or expertise, our operatives have taken their own initiative. But this is mostly the case only in Third World countries which have an official Iraqi presence on their soil.' He added: 'As you can imagine it has pretty much stretched resources.'

Weintraub's lips twitched in something resembling a

smile of sympathy. 'We're having the same manpower problems, Willard, so we won't be going to full alert unless a shooting war starts. Then we'll do the works. Close down four blocks around the Capitol, dog and visual checks on cars, close the White House to the public, rooftop snipers, and have security checks on all federal buildings. When the military goes on to Defcon Two, the airports will move up to Level Four alert.'

Melville Mace listened with growing irritation, tapping the rubber end of his pencil on his notepad in a silent tattoo. This was inviting disaster, actually *planning* to shut the door after the proverbial horse. Momentarily anger overcame his reluctance to interrupt these veterans of political backstabbing and ass-watching in the safe confines of Capitol Hill.

'Pardon me, Mr Weintraub, but may I ask what happens if Saddam does *not* oblige and makes a pre-emptive attack *before* the start of any shooting war?'

He might just have broken wind. The silence was absolute and stunned, all heads turning to observe the pale unknown face. Victor Weintraub's eyes narrowed.

Red Browning cut in: 'Gents, I'm not sure any of you know Dr Melville Mace. Mel is from ATA at State. He's been co-ordinating research and analysis into the overall terror risk presented by Iraq.' He smiled uncertainly. 'It's good to have you aboard, Mel. But I think you should be aware that there's no top dog; I'm just the traffic cop here among equals, trying to keep things moving. We each have our departmental responsibilities and we all have to work within certain parameters. One of those laid down by the President and my boss here at the National Security Council is that we don't start panic amongst the general population.'

Weintraub was clearly irked by Browning's coming to his defence; the FBI deputy chief felt more than capable of fighting his own quarter. 'Trouble is, Dr Mace, once we draw media attention to this problem with a high-profile reaction, we'll be swamped. There'll be well-meaning false bomb alerts, they'll trigger deliberate hoaxers and then the copycat nuts will get the idea. And each incident will have to be investigated. Every Arab-American who visits the Smithsonian or the National Zoo will be a suspected terrorist. We'll be getting suspicious sightings all over from the public – before you know it, Saddam himself will be seen having cocktails during Happy Hour at the Jefferson. Simply, Dr Mace, we'd be overwhelmed.

'We'll have to do it if a war starts – the public will demand it. But I sure ain't lookin' forward to cancelling all leave. In the meantime I prefer the softly, softly approach.'

'Well put,' Colonel Browning added as Weintraub took his seat. 'Now, Mel, I can see you're anxious to give us the benefit of your research and findings. So if you'd like to take the floor . . .'

Mace was already regretting having publicly thrown down the gauntlet to Vic Weintraub. The FBI man's reply had been restrained and well-reasoned – a practical response to the typically alarmist predictions of outside pundits like himself. In a room full of experienced political in-fighters,

Mace had just made himself look a fool. After all, trees blow down in storms – and you can't ensure that it will never happen. He just hoped he hadn't totally alienated his audience.

'Gentlemen, I've prepared a full dossier for each of you, so I shall just outline its findings. I don't want to sound unduly pessimistic, but I must warn you that the prognosis is not good.'

As he paused he was aware of a few impatient shufflings and a knowing exchange of glances between the people around the table. They had all heard doomsday theses before; Dr Melville Mace would no doubt come up with just one more.

'Firstly, what do we know about Iraq's terrorist capability? It has an efficient overseas arm of its intelligence service, the *Estikhbarat*. It has been well-trained with some help from the British. Mostly it is concerned with the procurement of military technology – at which it has proved itself most proficient. But it also carries out more sinister operations. This mostly concerns the hunting down and assassination of dissidents abroad and co-ordinating attacks against Israel. Its agents adopt the usual covers of diplomats, businessmen and students.

'The *Estikhbarat* has a long-established relationship with the major Arab terror organisations. In his attempt to be seen as the unchallenged leader of the Arab world and champion of the Palestinian cause, Saddam has recently been dispensing millions of dollars and large quantities of arms to these radical Arab groups.

'He already has Abbu Abbas of the Palestine Liberation Front in his pocket. And although Yasser Arafat of the PLO and Abu Nidal of the Fatah Revolutionary Council may loathe each other more than they do the Israelis, both group leaders are on good terms with Saddam. Meanwhile George Habash's Popular Front for the Liberation of Palestine has been actively considering moving its headquarters from Damascus to Baghdad. And, of course, there's Ahmed Jibril. He may be considered to be in the Iranian camp, but he has no love for the US.' He paused. 'So we can see that Saddam has no shortage of allies or potential allies in the world of terrorism.'

'Pardon me, Mel.' Red Browning leaned forward bullishly. 'None of us around this table would argue with your assessment, but I think we should get this in perspective. We've been applying massive diplomatic pressure – some of it not so diplomatic – on these terror groups.' He turned to Willard Franks for support. 'Ain't that so?'

The CIA officer's voice was expressionless as he held up his left hand and crossed off one finger at a time. 'Both Jibril and his Popular Front for the Liberation of Palestine General Command and Habash operate out of Syria and President Assad is keen to rehabilitate himself with the West. He's been left in no doubt as to our response if these people react against us. Yasser Arafat sees this conflict as a way of getting the Palestinian question onto the agenda – our reading is he'll be against terror tactics. The biggest threat has to be that wildman Abu Nidal. But he's based in Libya and Gaddafi is shit-scared we'll repeat the Tripoli bombing scenario. Meanwhile every European and friendly Arab state is personally marking every goddamn known terrorist operator. And we're letting them know it.'

Melville Mace smiled gently. He could see he was going to face an uphill task. No one around this table was about to admit to their agency's shortcomings, admit that they weren't in total control. 'I'm sure the CIA is doing its best to cover every contingency. But we have to consider Saddam Hussein's *will* to win, coupled with the fact that we have no hard intelligence as to his intentions whatsoever!' His voice had crept up several octaves unintentionally. He realised too late that he was starting to sound like the university lecturer he once was.

Red Browning cleared his throat. In the silence of the room the signal was unmistakable. Dr Melville Mace was out of order.

*Cometh the hour, cometh the man.*

Mace remembered his wife's words and stood his ground. 'The truth is we need a fly on the wall in Saddam's headquarters and we don't have one. Satellite and signals intelligence aren't going to tell us what we need to know. We all recognise we've suffered from running down our "humint" – our agents on the ground – for years and now it's starting to show. Only Mossad has agents placed in the Iraqi army and near the top of the Ba'ath party although, not surprisingly the Israelis won't even confirm this. The Brits have some sympathetic friends in the Iraqi defence forces and intelligence, but none who are willing or able to tell us what is going on in Saddam's inner circle. And that's what we *need* to know.'

Red Browning said: 'You've told us, Mel, what the gaps are in our intelligence. We're painfully aware of that, but we can't change the reality of the situation at short notice. We just don't – and cannot – know what that man is thinking.'

Mace tapped the report before him on the desk. 'No, Colonel, but we can make some pretty shrewd guesses. Over the past few weeks I've been co-ordinating and analysing the research work of several governmental, university and private think-tanks on US vulnerability to terror attacks between now and the start of any hostilities in the Gulf. And frankly, gentlemen, the findings are frightening.' He stared at each member around the table for dramatic emphasis. 'As the FBI has conceded, we are wide open security-wise, either with or without moving to the highest state of alert.'

Weintraub glowered.

'And given Saddam's access to virtually untraceable explosives like Semtex, biological and chemical materials – which are needed only in the smallest quantities to wreak havoc – I have had to address myself to gauging the man's will to win.'

Willard Franks of the CIA asked: 'How've you done that, given our lack of hard intelligence?'

'The only way we could,' Mace replied evenly. 'By simulations.'

Weintraub's groan was just audible.

Mace ignored it; he was well aware the role-playing crisis management games were not popular in the national security arena. Fine as television programmes, but no politician wanted to risk details of his poor decision-making being leaked to the *Washington Post*.

'We've run through several scenarios with Iraqi and Arab friends who know Saddam, assessing his reactions and likely decisions with help from behavioural psychiatrists. Those reactions have been cross-matched with a computer database on the man's past responses to political situations to ensure consistency.'

Curiosity was overcoming Red Browning's initial scepticism. 'And your findings?'

Melville Mace took a deep breath. 'Statistically there is an eighty-five per cent chance that, given his resources, Saddam will launch a pre-emptive and undetected terror attack on the US mainland. Our pyschologists believe he will have no regard for the humanitarian or ecological damage caused by such action, even if it affects his own people. Needless to say, the same applies to our European and Arab allies. And that likelihood of action increases the more he becomes convinced of the inevitability of a war he cannot win.

'You see, his one aim is to be the leader of the Arab world and the only way he can do that is to make us in the United States stand down and start negotiating.' He surveyed his audience, satisfied that he at last had their full attention. 'Gentlemen, the sad fact is that, despite our best efforts, we can do nothing to protect ourselves from something of which we have no knowledge. Catastrophe could come from any direction, at any time, and the chances are that we will have no warning.'

He sat down to an absorbed and thoughtful silence.

Red Browning was the first to break it. 'Mel, thanks for that. But if I relay this to the President this afternoon he's going to be a very unhappy man. He's got enough on his plate just now. I'd feel more comfortable if I could be a bit more positive. Tell him what steps we're taking to find a solution. That's what he'll want to know.'

Mace felt even more awkward now that he had actually made his point. 'Solutions aren't my job, Colonel, just the risk assessment.'

Willard Franks regarded the man's apologetic demeanour with renewed respect; perhaps he should have taken more note of the Cosmos Club tie. 'Mel, I don't see what more we at Langley and the other agencies can do to protect this country from the unknown. Give us a factual threat and we can counter it. Against ghosts we're not so hot. We'll just have to hope we've covered everything. Unless you've a thought . . . ?'

He let the words hang in midair. To Melville Mace it was a bait he couldn't resist. It had not been his intention to outline the private idea that had kept him awake all night. After all, these were the experts, the FBI, the CIA, the Defense Intelligence Agency – the superspooks who lived in the real murky world. He was a mere academic, a dabbler in theories and theses, game-playing and computer print-outs.

Red Browning sensed the man's hesitation. 'Well?'

'It's just a thought,' Mace said reluctantly. 'It might not work, and I've no idea how you people could do it. But it strikes me that while you're putting pressure to hold down all the known terror groups, Saddam's fury and frustration must be mounting daily. A sort of volatile bomb – like nitro-glycerine. It will take just one gap in our intelligence shield – one opportunity to present itself – and Saddam can blow the thing apart.'

Franks allowed himself a wry smile at the analogy. 'So what are you thinking, Mel?'

'How can I put it? To open a sort of release valve, a safety valve that would be under *our* control and could be turned off when the time is right.'

'Safety valve?' Red Browning was bemused. An intense hush had fallen over the room.

'Deliberately steer Saddam our way,' Mace went on 'Like trying to dam an unstoppable river, what we do know is water will take the line of least resistance. We let him think that he has a very real opportunity to hit back at us. Something real big – I don't know, like blowing up Congress or some such. An attack so significant and so sure of success that he won't want to bother with any other plans he might be working on that we don't know about.'

Browning looked puzzled, but a gleam of intense interest was evident in Willard Franks' frosty gaze. This was his sort of territory. 'It's a neat concept, Mel.'

Mace, encouraged, warmed to his subject. 'I was thinking what we really need is a stalking horse.'

'What the hell is that?' Browning asked.

'It's what the Indians used when hunting buffalo. They'd

use a horse covered in buffalo skins to hide them and their scent when approaching a herd. Likewise we need a deception that will let us get real close to the Iraqis.'

'Ah!' Browning smiled, beginning to comprehend. 'You mean close enough to offer Saddam a dangler?'

Mace nodded vigorously. 'A totally plausible offer to do the job for him. I mean, maybe get our guys to pose as a well-known Western-based terror group offering to undertake the attack in return for funds. I thought some anarchist groups like the Red Army Faction or the ETA separatists who've the experience to do it and need the cash. Terrorists often scratch each others' backs, do stuff for each other.'

'Saddam might buy that,' Willard Franks mused, 'especially as he knows we've got all his regular Arab cronies well and truly pinned down.'

But Red Browning's initial enthusiasm began to wane. It was a good concept, but impractical. This was the fairy-tale realms of the armchair terrorist expert, the academic. 'Look, you guys, I've got to go prepare for my meeting at the White House. I'll float this risk assessment before the President and tell him we're working on a few solutions. But frankly, Mel, your idea is a non-starter. We can't just stick one of our spooks upfront pretending to be a terrorist. The Iraqis ain't fools; they'll check him out and they'll want to know chapter and verse. They and their own Arab terrorist chums all know each other, and even the European groups you mention. Your stalking horse wouldn't reach first base before he got himself killed.' He stood up from the table. 'Sorry, Mel, but there it is. Now we're due to meet this time next week, so let's try cook up some positive action to counter Mel's risk assessment. Something the President will like to read.'

As Colonel Red Browning strode out, the meeting broke up in sombre mood, old friends commiserating with each other at the impossibility of their position. No one spoke to Mace. He was an outsider. They believed he had done nothing but drive home the unpleasant facts most of them already knew but wished they didn't. And his bright idea had been publicly laughed out of court.

Mace worked his way through the lingering committee members towards the door. His earlier enthusiasm had been deflated like a soufflé to be replaced by a total sense of failure and depression. He was eager to be away.

As he stepped out into the dull, damp midday air, he heard someone close behind him. 'Say, Mel!'

Willard Franks was pulling a trench coat over his grey suit as he hurried to catch up.

'Don't be downhearted,' the CIA man gasped. 'At least you made everyone stop and think. Not an easy achievement.'

'Colonel Browning didn't seem impressed.'

Franks buttoned his coat against the chill air. 'Your stalking horse idea? Well, it has more than a few problems,' he said vaguely. 'Say, why don't you join me for lunch? We could talk it through some . . .'

Sam and Harry's Restaurant was an old-fashioned club-type steakhouse on 19th, well away from the politicians' most favoured lunchtime haunts. Vivid portraits of famous jazz musicians enlivened the dark wood panelling beneath the chandelier lighting. Franks selected a quiet corner table and recommended fried calamari with tomato aoli and peppery-sweet baby back ribs to start.

He talked almost constantly about food, the weather, his recent vacation – anything, it struck Mace, except the subject of the morning's meeting. Only later it occurred to him that the CIA man was using small talk to give himself time to think over the practical problems of his suggestion.

Mace had little appetite for the corn-fed porterhouse steak that followed and was playing with his dessert of pecan chocolate-chip pie when Franks suddenly changed tack. 'Your idea, Mel – there might be a way to make it work.'

'Yes?'

'Well, as Colonel Browning pointed out, a fake terrorist just wouldn't work. The whole project couldn't just *appear* to be genuine, it would have to *be* genuine. Right down the line.' He ordered coffee from a passing waiter. 'We'd need someone established right inside some suitable terrorist group. Someone in a position to influence events. And, of course, to stop them if they get out of hand.' He looked directly at Mace. 'Not an enviable position to be in.'

Mace could see the possibilities. 'Do we have anyone like that?'

Franks frowned his disapproval. That was not a question it was polite to ask. 'Not that I know of. But my bet is the Brits have.'

'The British?'

'They've been fighting with the IRA for over twenty

years. It's well known they've penetrated the organisation on several occasions. And the IRA would suit Saddam's purposes. Internationally recognised but with many undetected cells. Ruthless and with a proven track record. Non-Arab and free access to Europe, the UK and America – anywhere in the world, in fact.'

Mace suddenly found his appetite. Between mouthfuls of pecan pie he asked: 'Would the British co-operate?'

Franks sampled his newly arrived coffee. 'According to your risk assessment, they're in the same danger we are. Britain has always featured big in the Iraqi view of the world. I'll get in touch with our station chief in London. He's got plenty of clout with the British intelligence services. See what he thinks . . .'

Dr Melville Mace was floating on air after he left the restaurant and spent the rest of the afternoon at the Office of Combating Terrorism working feverishly on a follow-up to his risk assessment document. Into his word processor he tapped the words: *Part 2, The Solution*.

But if he were enjoying a sudden recognition of his talents in Washington's intelligence circle, on the home front he was heading for personal disaster.

On his way back that night he walked straight past the delicatessen just before the shutters came down; lox and bagels for Paige's buffet party were the last thing on his mind.

# Three

It was raining when the Aer Lingus jet touched down at Heathrow airport. The low cloud had brought the day to a premature end and the wet twilight gloom matched Avery's mood.

Bastard, bastard, bastard!

Again and again he repeated the silent curse. But still he couldn't shift the vision of the American's laughing face from his mind. Or forget that heart-stopping moment when Corrigan had mockingly drawn the revolver, clearly relishing the split second of blind terror he created.

The scene remained stubbornly freeze-framed in Avery's head throughout the return flight from Dublin.

He didn't like Danny Grogan, but at least he could understand what motivated him. Born and bred in the run-down Catholic slums, ill-educated and fed anti-British vitriol with his mother's milk.

But Lew Corrigan?

It wasn't his country now and it had certainly never been his war. Yet he'd have been happy to send a dozen innocent adolescent soldiers to their deaths, and had scarcely blinked when the baker had been blasted to kingdom come.

Whatever made a man like that tick?

Avery vowed then to do whatever he could within his power to get Corrigan dealt with. There was enough scum on both sides of the extremist divide in Northern Ireland without importing it.

The incident with the American had temporarily overridden Avery's anger with his controller for the unnecessary danger in which he had been placed.

Not that he was a newcomer to danger. That was his stock in trade. But things were different now. It had all changed with the arrival of the baby. His unplanned fatherhood put a new complexion on things, gave him new responsibilities. The security service should know that. And if they didn't, his controller should damn well make sure they did.

There was no way that Eamonn O'Flaherty, the Provisional IRA commander for Europe, should have been arrested without his controller having given him prior warning.

That would have at least given Avery time to distance himself, not leave him one of the foremost suspects in the minds of the paranoid terrorist leadership. Christ, it was hard enough being an Englishman in their midst, without giving them cause to be suspicious. It had come within a whisker of costing him his life.

The courtesy coach left him alone in the long-stay car park amid the endless ranks of empty vehicles and elongated shadows.

His nerves, he realised, were still on edge.

For six long years he had expected the unexpected. Knowing that if and when it came, there would be no warning. And no reprieve. Now it seemed that his dark world had finally closed in on him so tightly that he could hardly breathe.

As he routinely checked the underside and wheel arches of his BMW saloon he discovered that vandals had stolen the hubcaps.

Just another bad omen, he considered darkly, tossing his overnight bag onto the back seat. What more did he need to tell him it was time to get out? A broken mirror? A tarot card reading? Some things you just *knew*.

He accelerated away hard, working his way through the airport perimeter roads until he reached the M4 and took the London-bound carriageway.

The wet night settled in with determination, the wipers struggling to clear the driving rain, the windows beginning to fog. He slid a cassette into the player and forced himself to relax, narrowing his eyes against the refracted light of headlamps on the black lacquered road.

It had all begun just over six years earlier. Out of the British Army after a fourteen-year stint, nine of those spent in the elite Special Air Service Regiment. The Falklands War had been the turning point. Opened his eyes to the political and military incompetence and squabbling that the resounding battlefield victory had concealed from the public gaze.

He had realised for the first time that he was an expendable pawn in other people's power games. It had come to him like a revelation on Ascension Island as his team was stood down for the sixth time. On each occasion they had climbed aboard the C130 Hercules, ready to fly into Argentina on the brigadier's orders. Ready to land Entebbe-style on the airfield and take out the deadly Exocet-carrying Super Etendard fighters of the enemy. Not the stealthy approach that he and his oppos preferred, with an unde-tectable high-opening parachute descent then hole up to reconnoitre and choose their moment.

None of that featured in the brigadier's plan. His was high-profile. Fly in and radio that they were Argentinian transports returning from Port Stanley requesting emer-gency permission to land. Sheer bluff versus an airfield bris-tling with anti-aircraft guns and missiles. Who dares wins. 'Land, do your stuff, then get the hell out overland to Chile as best you can.'

Death or glory stuff. But whose death? And whose glory?

Thankfully the prime ministerial permission never came, and Avery's squadron was stood down for the final time. The speculation was that Downing Street had been pres-surised by the United States not to take the war to the South American mainland and upset their delicate position of neutrality.

Despite all the victories that followed in the campaign, they never quite restored the glitter to Avery's sense of tarnished pride. Mistakes were brushed beneath a con-venient carpet of ecstatic media coverage. No lessons were learned, no souls searched. He realised then that the Regiment had changed, probably for ever. It was time for him to go.

The following year, at the age of thirty-four, he was out, cold and lonely on the mean streets of civilian life. At the time the country was climbing out of recession and he had ridden on the back of the wave. Someone had suggested that he import little Citroën 2CV cars from Belgium and sell them to an eager market of cash-rich youngsters who wanted cheap town runabouts or as second cars for house-wives. The investment needed had been small enough for him to manage comfortably on his modest army savings, whilst taking out a lease on a two-bedroomed flat in the south London suburb of Streatham.

But Avery knew few people outside of his previous army life and he found the time spent between his cross-Channel ferry trips both boring and lonely. That had been his real motive for taking the beginners' course in cookery at a local night school. His days in the SAS had taught him how to make a stew using anything from snake to turtle, but beyond that his expertise was confined to unhealthy fry-ups or curry hashes. Not really the thing to turn a young woman's head at an intimate supper in his flat.

For that matter there was no young woman with a head to turn.

'That's the place to meet girls, Max,' his old SAS friend Brian Hunt had advised. 'Cookery for beginners. Full of girls who didn't take domestic science at school and suddenly realise no bloke's going to want them unless they can boil an egg.'

However, Avery discovered that most of the aspiring chefs at night school were either widowers or middle-aged male divorcees. There were only two women; one of them was Margaret O'Malley.

She was a twenty-year-old student nurse from Londonderry in Northern Ireland. It had been the toss of the cascade of ebony curls that had caught Avery's attention when he entered the room as she turned in his direction. Her green eyes widened a fraction when she saw him and he found himself responding to the hint of a grin that played on her lips.

It had been like that from the start. A magnetic and mutual attraction, impulsive and wild. As though they had known each other all their lives. In the succession of cookery lessons that followed, Maggie contrived to borrow some forgotten ingredient each week; within a month she was arriving deliberately early to ensure that the cooker she shared was his.

Six weeks after their first meeting they became lovers. Their coupling was frantic, desperate almost. She became an unleashed animal between the sheets, eager to please him in every way she knew how. And she seemed to know many. He was stunned by her lack of inhibition and her sheer wantonness. There was nothing she wasn't willing for them to do together. And afterwards, with a cigarette shared, she would bubble with good humour and witty repartee.

In short, Max Avery had found paradise, aware that he would have to look long and hard to find another woman with Margaret O'Malley's priceless charms.

But those carefree early days were to come to a shuddering and disquieting halt. It happened on the ferry out to Belgium, when Avery was travelling to pick-up another 2CV to import. He was alone in the lounge, enjoying a beer while he read the newspaper.

'Avery, isn't it? Max Avery?'

He lowered his newspaper. The man who stood before him was in his late twenties. His longish black hair was unkempt and there was a day's stubble on his chin. The grubby denims, leather bomber jacket and T-shirt suggested that he was a truck driver on a trans-Europe run.

'Do I know you?' Avery was naturally cautious. He had too recently served in the SAS to talk freely with strangers. It was an automatic reaction to listen for the trace of an Irish accent in the truck driver's voice.

But he could detect none as the younger man smiled. 'No, Max, but I know you.' Instinctively Avery had felt for the gun he no longer carried. It was amazing how naked he felt without the comforting underarm weight of a Browning automatic. 'Mind if I join you?'

Not waiting for a reply, the man sat. Close up, the face didn't seem quite so young; there was a wary look in his eyes. He didn't stand on ceremony. 'My name's Nash. I'm with Box.'

The only outward sign that Avery's heart had begun to pound was a tensing of his jaw muscles.

'Box?' Had he heard right?

'As I said, Max, you don't know me. I know you.'

It hadn't been a mistake. Box. Colloquial jargon for the Security Service, MI5, after its old Box Number 500 postal address.

'You've been seeing something of a student nurse,' Nash said quietly. It wasn't an accusation, just a statement of fact. 'Works at St Thomas's.'

Avery felt the skin on his neck begin to crawl.

'There's something you should know about her.'

That's how it had begun. John Nash worked for the Counter-Terrorism Department of MI5, which had numerous suspected Provisional IRA sympathisers under surveillance. Margaret O'Malley, brought up in the Rossville Flats in Londonderry's Republican heartland, was one of them.

'She's never struck me as the Rossville type,' Avery murmured, still trying to absorb the unwelcome news.

'That's because she left the Flats when she was eight years old. An uncle of hers was killed in the Bloody Sunday riots and her mother – her old man was a violent alcoholic – was frightened for Margaret's safety. Farmed her out to her childless sister in Hinton Park. Can't get more respectable than that. Best thing that ever happened to the girl. Decent upbringing, good education. No more filthy language. In the end the father went down for the manslaughter of her mother.' Nash raised a quizzical eyebrow. 'She's never told you any of this?'

Avery shook his head slowly. 'No, and I didn't ask. I was happy not to bring up the past, hers or mine. I gathered she was Catholic Irish and from the North, so I hardly wanted to admit I'd been with the army.'

Nash liked to be precise. 'The Regiment. In fact you're still listed as a reserve with R Squadron.'

'I was serving in Ulster just eighteen months ago. It makes you cautious.'

'And she never asked about your past?'

Avery smiled wryly. 'A bit, but she didn't press it. I was born in Liverpool and I made up a few cock-and-bull stories about my life there. Made it sound so boring I don't think she wanted to know more. Look, Mr Nash, Maggie and I have only known each other a few weeks. A couple of coffees, a few times to the cinema, a meal at my place.'

'How long have you been screwing her?'

Avery's cheeks darkened. 'What sort of question is that?'

'I need to know exactly how much she knows about you.'

'Me? Not a lot; we haven't had much time for talk.'

Nash studied his beer. 'Good in bed, you mean?' He looked up, suddenly concerned. 'Don't misunderstand, Max, I'm not prying. Believe me, it could be for your own good.'

Avery stared back long and hard before replying. 'Yes, she's good. She likes to joke around but she's not one for serious talk or for asking too many questions.'

'So there's no chance she picked you up deliberately?'

He'd thought about it before, of course. As soon as he realised she was a Catholic from Northern Ireland. But only his old oppo Brian Hunt knew of his decision to join the night-school course belatedly, and Margaret O'Malley was already there.

He said: 'No way.'

Nash appeared more relaxed. 'That's good, Max, because I've got to tell you she's been mixed up with a bad lot.

Friends of her uncle who stopped one on Bloody Sunday.
She's done courier work for the Provos. Pushed a pram
away after a shooting with the assassin's rifle in it. That sort
of thing.'

'When?'

'Last year was the last time to our knowledge. We've been
keeping an eye on her since she left the province and came
here. We check up on everyone she meets. That's how we
came across you. That was quite a surprise. Ex-Regiment.'

It hadn't sounded to Avery as though they were talking
about the same person. That the vivacious student nurse
could be the accomplice of an assassin.

He guessed what was coming. He could also see the
justification of it, but on a personal level there was no way
that he was ready to accept it. He was out now. A free man.
Free to make his own mistakes if he wanted to. 'So you're
warning me off, is that it?'

Nash looked surprised. 'Good God, Max, no. Far from
it. You see, your young lady knows a lot of people we'd like
to know better ourselves. She's well in with the Irish
community over here, including some individuals we
believe may be part of the Provos' mainland operations.
You're ideally placed –'

'Forget it, Nash. I'm not about to start spying on my
own girlfriend.'

The MI5 officer raised his hands in horror. 'I wouldn't
dream of asking you to. Just use her connections to get to
the people we really want.' He leaned forward, his voice
hushed. 'Do you know how many people we lost last year

alone? Fifteen regular and UDR soldiers and nineteen policemen. That's not counting the thirty-seven innocent civilians or the horribly maimed . . . And "Miser" Maston.'

'Miser?'

'He was with your Sabre team once, wasn't he? Died last year on an undercover operation in Armagh. I won't tell you what they did to him.'

Avery was choked. In the old days Miser, who was always the last to buy a round, had been one of his closest friends. He was still reeling from the shock of the news, hardly aware of what Nash was saying: 'You know how we're always fighting with one hand behind our back. Yellow cards, legal niceties, the RUC getting castigated every time they take a few liberties with evidence. And we all sit back and watch known terrorists walk away from the courts with fat, smug smiles on their faces. All we get for our pains is a V-sign.' He took a deep, resigned breath. 'And it gets no easier. The Provos' cell system is getting as tight as a duck's arse. Almost impossible to penetrate. And they're using more virgins, youngsters without any criminal record. We need help, all the help we can get, Max. The sort of help you can give.'

Nash had done a good job. By the time the ferry docked at Zeebrugge, Max Avery had been recruited. The first thing he did was to ring St Thomas's Hospital and leave a message for Nurse O'Malley that unexpected business would keep him away for two weeks.

He had then been driven by Nash to a private house in the Ardennes near the German border. There were three other MI5 officers there; the senior one was a serious-faced woman in her late forties who smoked incessantly.

They proceeded to debrief Avery on everything he had already told Margaret O'Malley about himself. This information would have to form the cornerstone of his new false identity.

He was questioned about his embryo car import-export business and his plans for expansion.

'It could be ideal cover,' said the woman he knew only as Clarry. 'Cars back and forth to Europe and Ireland. Get to meet a lot of people. Maybe premises somewhere a bit seedy in south London. Mix in with the lowlife.'

'Hang on,' Avery said, 'I don't have the necessary money for that. And my bank manager certainly won't want to help.'

Clarry smiled gently and it transformed the austere face into one that was quite attractive. 'Oh, he will after we have a talk to him. We'll underwrite the loans so you won't have any cash-flow problems. You know, that's what brings most companies down. And we'll get a team of commercial experts to work out a business plan for you. All you'll have to do is follow it.' She lit another cigarette. 'You know, Max, you stand to become a very wealthy man in your own right.'

Avery had been puzzled. 'This cover, the expense. It's all a bit elaborate for just an informer.'

The woman blew a perfect smoke ring. 'I don't want just any information, Max. Anyway, what would you, an Englishman, get from our Irish friends? Oh, no, I want you to *work* for the IRA.'

He stared at her. 'Are you crazy?'

'Perhaps.' She pursed her lips, the expression hinting at an allure that belied the functional pageboy cut of her hair. 'But it's been done before. Think of it, Max. You're from Liverpool, so we give you a fictitious family with strong Irish Republican links. That gives you credibility and possibly motivation. Politics, say, left-wing socialist – you've spent most of your life drawing dole. We don't really want jobs that they can check out. A lot of wheeler-dealing and some time inside. Maybe GBH. Give you a ruthless streak.' She waved her cigarette with an artistic flourish and he noticed how incongruous the chipped lilac nail varnish looked against her nicotine-stained fingers. 'You'll soon be mixing in Maggie's social circle. Irish nurses, folk clubs and Irish pubs. You put yourself about, talk to everyone. Get known. Start doing people favours, whatever it is. Cars are good. Everyone wants a bargain – and you'll be in the position to provide it. Repairs, too –' He could tell she was thinking aloud as the words came out in a gush: 'That's a good sideline, I'll make a note of that. You know, I was nearly ripped off by a garage only last week. Told me that I needed a new head gasket – lot of rot!'

It was a brave mechanic who tried to pull one over on Clarry, he mused.

'Build up their trust. Get them some hooky goods. A video off the back of a lorry. Let them know you've smuggled some stuff into the country when you've brought in cars. If you're mixing with the people we think they are, it won't be long before they try you out. What d'you think, Max?'

What did he think? He thought Clarry was one of the most remarkable and persuasive women he had ever met. She had the mind of a genius with the unusual combination of a fertile creative imagination and an eye for detail. He had seen the evidence of both the following week when they had begun the four-day indoctrination of his new make-believe personal history.

'Your cover story has been particularly difficult,' she had told him, 'because Maggie already knows your name. That's the main weakness because we have to graft you into a real family whose history can be verified. We've got numerous case files built up over the years, mostly sad little stories where children have died. In the case we've chosen for you, it was the entire family. The O'Reillys from Liverpool.'

'And the name?' he asked.

'You will become the son who, in fact, died. Instead, the boy – or rather you – will have been orphaned. That'll be our reason for the name change. Mickey-taking by other kids. Old Mother Reilly, that sort of thing. When you struck out on your own, you changed your name by deed poll. Teenagers do that sort of thing. Nash is back in the UK sorting out the official records, getting documents together.

'One other thing. I want you to come clean with Maggie about having spent time in the Army. You've known hardly any other life, and something's bound to slip. Experience shows the best lies are those closest to the truth. In fact your time in the Paras might add to your credibility – I'll explain later.' A ghost of a smile passed over her face. 'But I think we'll gloss over your years in the SAS.'

And at the end of the days of repetitious briefing he had been presented with all the necessary documentation to go with the elaborate deception. There was no need for forgeries – everything was genuine government issue.

In his time in the SAS he had served with many Secret Intelligence Service officers and a few others from MI5. Yet he had never met anyone before with Clarry's magic touch.

But despite the impressive cover, Nash had sounded a word of caution. 'Remember, Max, that we can never be certain that your cover is watertight. We can never guarantee that we've thought of everything.'

If Avery had any lingering reservations about his hesitant step into the dangerous twilight world of the double agent, Clarry had dispelled it the night before his return to England.

'How do you feel about Maggie now?' she had asked as they had after-dinner drinks by the fire.

'I don't know.' Honest.

'Earlier you implied she was the love of your life. Someone really special, perhaps for the first time?'

His laugh had been bitter. 'Perhaps I was wrong. Obviously I don't know her at all.'

Clarry studied her glass of Scotch and water. 'Don't be too hard on her, Max. She's young and impressionable. I've seen a lot of girls who've got sucked into supporting one cause or another. From the IRA to animal rights and CND.

However wrong society may view extremist actions, people often do these things from the best possible personal motives.'

'Like the murder of Miser Maston?'

'She had nothing to do with that.'

'Does it matter? Miser or some other poor bastard.'

Clarry raised an eyebrow. 'She is a nurse, Max; that must mean something.' Her eyes clouded for a moment. 'I appreciate what you're doing and I know it won't be easy. But don't think you are betraying her. Think of yourself as protecting her, ensuring she never gets involved again. And don't let it come between you and Maggie, not if you really love her. That's the most precious thing in the world, and the easiest thing to lose. I know . . .' Her face looked sad for a moment, before she made the effort to smile. 'Remember this. I'll look after you. Both of you. Whenever you want out, whenever you've had enough . . . just say the word. There'll be a new life waiting for you both.'

A new life.

The traffic slowed as the M4 filtered into the Great West Road and Avery negotiated his way through Hammersmith and Fulham Palace Road towards Putney Bridge.

Three precious words. Three words that had sounded steadily more enticing as each of the last twelve months had passed. If any doubts remained, his trip to Ireland had changed all that. He'd done his share, done enough.

He was fast approaching the slightly run-down metropolis south of the Thames that had become so familiar over the past six years. Wandsworth, Balham, Streatham. A patch he had made his own. With Clarry's help he had arrived with a full briefing from police detectives who had told him the names of all the local lowlife, the gangsters and petty villains, the egg-and-chips cafes to frequent, the pubs to drink in, the faces to mix with.

Inside six months he had been accepted by the locals; a feat that might have taken as many years without Clarry's help. And, after a year he had been able to trade up his railway-arch car mart for a large used-car forecourt off Streatham Hill.

Six years was enough. A new life beckoned.

There was little traffic for rush hour, he noted. And few pedestrians. The recession was biting; everyone was window-shopping, no one willing to buy. Used car sales were down, he knew from his own ledger. The depressing weather matched the mood of the people as they switched on their televisions for more gloomy news from Iraq and Kuwait.

He turned onto the forecourt and pulled up outside the plate-fronted office where lights still burned. A cursory glance at the front row of brightly polished cars told him that nothing had been sold in his absence. But at least the noise from the adjoining workshop suggested that his mechanics were still working overtime on repairs.

Thank God for small mercies and Clarry's foresight, he thought. Then caught himself.

A new life. Only then it occurred to him that he would actually miss all this. That had been the beauty of the elaborate cover; it really was a genuine, thriving business that had paid him well.

'I thought you'd still be here,' he said as he entered the rear office.

Floyd looked up from the pile of yellow SPECIAL OFFER tags he was filling in with a magic-marker pen. He was the third generation of a Jamaican family who had put down roots in Lambeth in the 1950s. Hard-working, God-fearing parents had steered him relatively unscathed through an endemic hard drugs scene and Rastafarian subculture of the district. Relatively. Nevertheless rap music blared from a ghetto blaster on the shelf and there was a curiously sweet smell to the tobacco smoke that coiled above the desk.

'Max! I wasn't expecting you till tomorrow.'

'So I see.'

The cigarette was hastily stubbed out. 'I thought I'd get ready for the promotion. We've not shifted a thing, man.'

'I gather.' Avery couldn't resist a smile. At twenty-five Floyd was pure gold dust with an inbred work ethic and not even the hint of a racist chip on his shoulder. He'd always scorned the popular dreadlocks of his peers and for the job of office manager had willingly swapped his shell-suit and designer trainers for a rather vulgar business suit.

'I reckon the promotion will shift some of those older models. Get the cash flow moving. I talked it over with my old tutor at the poly. You know, my business studies course. He said it was the right thing to do. He's got some other ideas too . . .'

Avery waved the suggestion aside. 'Not now, Floyd, I've just flown in. Tomorrow you can tell me.'

'And how was Ireland?'

'A waste of time. Some farmer had discovered an old Triumph TR2 in his barn. But with restoration and shipping costs it wouldn't make sense. Not now; I wouldn't find a buyer willing to pay the price.'

'TR2,' Floyd repeated wistfully. 'A shame that.'

'Thought I'd just go over this week's books on my way home,' Avery explained as he moved towards his office.

'You haven't seen Maggie yet?' Floyd sounded uneasy.

Avery turned back. 'No, why?'

'Trouble at mill, man.' He looked sheepish. 'She phoned up wanting the number of where you were staying.'

'Oh.'

'I told her it was County Monaghan but I didn't know where. I gather she thought you were in Wales. She was none too pleased.'

I bet, Avery thought.

Over the years Clarry's charitable assessment of Maggie's personality had proved uncannily accurate. In the beginning, as Avery had immersed himself within her social Irish circle in London, he noticed that she was avoiding certain characters.

One in particular was a sharp-eyed man called Fox who had a shock of unkempt ginger hair and a harelip twisting his mouth into a perpetual sneer. Avery had made a point of getting to know the character, discovering his liking for sick jokes and porter with whisky chasers. So he bought the drinks and came up with every disgusting spastic and blind-man gag he had ever heard. More and more frequently the two of them were to be seen laughing together.

Gerry Fox had always fancied an Escort XR3i but didn't have the price of a decent one. Avery found him a bargain. As a bonus he threw in a German pornographic video featuring two women, a donkey and a pig which he said he had smuggled back on one of his trips from the Continent. He had made a friend for life.

Much later Maggie confirmed what Avery had already guessed. Fox was Provisional IRA. She didn't know exactly what he did, but thought he had some sort of liaison function with Dublin.

She was surprised at Avery's reaction to the revelation. He had taken the opportunity to laugh and assure her that he had some sympathy for the Republican movement. That night he recounted in full the artificial family background that MI5 had provided for him. It had been a profound moment in their relationship. For the first time she felt able to admit to him her past association with the organisation. She had even told him that Fox had recently put pressure on her to steal medical supplies from her hospital for various Provo safe houses. With a sense of unburdening she had confessed that she now had serious doubts about the morality of the paramilitaries' campaign of violence, although not the cause itself.

As the years passed and his business boomed, Avery began doing more occasional but important jobs for Fox. Buying specific cars from Europe and bringing them in with the implication that there was contraband – perhaps drugs, arms or explosives – secreted somewhere inside. Untraceable cars were arranged and discreet lock-up garages found. Through his local underworld contacts Avery was able to supply forged documents; passports and credit cards were obtained. Two or three times an illegal revolver or shotgun was purchased. Residential properties were purchased or leased. Over the period many favours, small and large, were done in return for cash.

Avery was never told for what specific operation his help was needed and he didn't ask. But every morsel of information was passed secretly back to the Anti-Terrorism Department of MI5 to act as they saw fit.

Eventually he was introduced by Fox to Eamonn O'Flaherty at a party. Avery dutifully passed the name back to MI5. Several weeks later their undercover investigations led them to suspect his real role for the Provisional IRA. That had been Avery's biggest breakthrough when the terrorists' European commander became known to the intelligence authorities for the first time.

O'Flaherty was allowed to run, his telephone and mail monitored, all his movements closely followed. Avery made a point of developing a friendship with the gregarious O'Flaherty, whose company he might otherwise have genuinely enjoyed. But the Provisional IRA, or the Irishman's connection with it, was never mentioned. As always, business continued to be done via Gerry Fox. Over the six-year period Maggie's attitude to Avery's relationship with Fox had gradually changed. Although he never discussed such matters with her, she knew what his association with Fox implied. At first she had accepted that the money he undoubtedly earned from the Provisionals was much needed to help his struggling business. After all, Avery had joked, it was for the cause.

But Maggie's cause had changed. She became vocally anti-Thatcher, bemoaning what she saw as the rundown of the National Health Service; she worked actively for the NUPE trade union. Later she became a local secretary to an animal-rights movement in her spare time and then a fully paid-up member of the Green Party.

When Avery had once mentioned this to Fox, the man had laughed. 'I'm afraid your missus, Max, is a cause junkie.' He'd thought it a huge joke.

But at home with Maggie it had become no laughing matter. She had become openly hostile to his supposed friendship with Fox and tried to persuade him to stop seeing the Irishman. Every time there was a news report about some Provisional IRA atrocity on the television she reacted with increasing abhorrence.

Margaret O'Malley, Avery realised with a personal sense of relief, had grown up at last. And her untimely announcement that she was pregnant was the final straw. Maggie was adamant that her common-law husband should have nothing more to do with Fox. She didn't want the father of their child ending up in prison.

For the previous eighteen months the two men had met only in secret.

'I'm sorry, Max,' Floyd was saying. 'If I'd known there

was any great mystery about you flying to Dublin, I wouldn't have said . . .'

Avery forced a smile. 'No mystery, Floyd. If Maggie had known I was going, she'd have insisted I visit her folk. And I just don't have the time.'

The pat answer satisfied his manager. 'I'm off now. Will you lock up?'

'Sure.'

Avery closed his office door behind him and slid the bolt home silently. He crossed to the built-in stationery cupboard. The door was a simple hollow construction, the wooden framework sandwiched between two gloss-painted hardboard sheets. By standing on a chair he was able to remove a section of the top edge of the door which he had cut out years before. Reaching into the gap with his fingertips he pulled on a piece of string to retrieve the Jiffy bag which hung secreted in the hollow centre of the door.

He sat at his desk, switched on the lamp, and extracted the code book from the padded brown envelope. It took just ten minutes to encrypt his message into the one-off numerical code:

*From Tosca* (His codename had been chosen at a time when opera names were being used)

1. *Present at baker's van proxy bombing on border-post yesterday. Accomplices Danny Grogan and American national Lew Corrigan (Corrigan's Den, Co Monaghan).*

2. *Radar device used, believed imported by said Corrigan.*
   *Faulty mechanism resulted in premature explosion.*

He made no mention that it had been he himself who held the device, or that it had been a test of his loyalty. There was no mileage in putting his head on the block. The Security Service could choose not to offer protection if he were found out. Murder was murder, and he was not above the law.

3. *Hint of major forthcoming operation. Location and time*
   *etc. not yet known. Suspect I may be asked to assist in*
   *some way.*

There was a moment's hesitation before he wrote the last sentence. A new life.

4. *Request final recall. Repeat. Final Recall.*

He swiftly returned the code book to its hiding place, then slipped the message into his jacket pocket before picking up two library books from amongst the collection of trade price guides on the shelf. An Evelyn Anthony and a Colin Dexter. Avery's avid reading habits were something of a joke amongst his semi-illiterate staff.

After locking up, he drove the short journey to the Tate Public Library at the Brixton Oval. As usual he planned his arrival for just a few minutes before the eight o'clock closing time. He selected two new titles at random. On his way out he paused at General Fiction, Authors P–T, and removed the first Douglas Reeman novel on the left. On the rare occasion that all Reemans were out, he would merely select the next book to the left of the empty space. As he flicked the pages, he slipped the message into the flyleaf before returning the novel to the shelf.

He then hurried to the desk where the librarian waited impatiently to stamp his new books and go home.

Tomorrow a security service courier would make his regular daily visit to the library when the doors opened at nine o'clock. He too would show an interest in the works of Douglas Reeman.

He turned the key in the door of their flat. 'Hello, Maggie, I'm back!'

Nothing. The hall light was on and a Channel 4 documentary was burbling incoherently from the television in the living room.

He felt the small hairs crawl on the back of his neck, aware of the sudden sprinting of his heartbeat. The place was unnaturally quiet, not a sound apart from the indistinct babbling of the television. That same sense of unease he'd felt at the car park.

Had Grogan and the American known all the time, content to play a cat-and-mouse game?

Fully alert and ready now he edged into the hall, his back pressed against the wall.

Maggie emerged from Josh's nursery, a finger to her lips. She was still wearing her staff nurse's uniform, her sleek black hair tightly restrained by tortoiseshell clips. 'I've only just got him down,' she said in a terse whisper.

He breathed again, forcing a smile to his lips. With a sense of profound relief he entered the living room in search of a stiff drink. He'd just poured a treble whisky when Maggie came in, closing the door quietly behind her.

'Drink, love?' he asked absently.

'Don't you "drink, love" me, Max Avery. Where the hell have you been?'

He turned. She stood in magnificent anger, arms folded across her chest, legs defiantly astride. Colour flushed the cream-white skin of her cheeks.

'You told me you were going to a convention in Wales,' she challenged.

'Something else cropped up,' he lied.

Her green eyes narrowed like a cat's. 'You mean Gerry Fox cropped up. How could you, Max, after you promised me?' She frowned suddenly. 'They haven't been threatening you, have they? Fox did it to me when I first came over.'

'No, Maggie, no threats. There's a recession on. We need the money.'

She shook her head. 'Not that badly.'

'The boyos need my help.'

'I don't believe I'm hearing this. I'm the Irish girl with an uncle murdered by the English – you're the bloody Brit!'

Avery downed the remainder of his drink in one hard gulp. 'My parents were as Irish as you, woman, my family goes back a long way. Have you *completely* given up on the cause?'

She dropped her arms to her side in a sudden gesture of surrender and sympathy. 'No, you darling man, but I *have* given up on their methods. I can see the Brits won't give in to force. Not now. And I'm sick of all the violence. I don't want our son tainted by it all. If you keep messing with the Provies, it'll all end in tears. It's only a matter of time before your luck runs out.'

He turned to the sideboard and poured more drink. This time two glasses; he handed one to her. 'How d'you fancy a new life?'

'What do you mean, Max?'

'Sell up. Start again somewhere else. Abroad even.'

The clouds vanished from her eyes and an inner light danced in them for a moment. 'Are you serious? Move away?'

'I've been thinking about it.'

'And no more Gerry Fox?' she asked cautiously.

'I promise.'

A hint of triumph showed in her smile. 'Then you can tell him to piss off out of your life now. He was waiting for me when I left the hospital this afternoon. It gave me quite a shock.'

'He was waiting for you?' Avery was puzzled. Because of Maggie's antagonism towards him, Fox now only ever contacted him at work.

'Wants you to call him.'

He shrugged. 'I'll ring him from the office tomorrow.'

'And you'll tell him it's all over?'

They clinked glasses. 'I'll tell him.'

# Four

Danny Grogan's eyes were magnified like gobstoppers through the glass of the showcase, mesmerised by the disgusting sight of the grass snake devouring a live frog.

The bemused victim appeared oddly composed, its legs and torso already swallowed, only the head and forelegs showing between the snake's unhinged jaw.

'Christ, Con, it's disgusting.'

The snake appeared to be resting, the half-eaten frog blinking, stoically resigned to its fate.

Grogan ran a nervous tongue around his thick red lips and, still hypnotised by the long, slow death, straightened his back. 'Thank God I've already had supper.'

At last he dragged his eyes away from the showcase on the sill of the office window that offered a panoramic night view of Southampton's Ocean Village marina.

Con Moylan was leaning back in his leather chair, hands behind his head and his long legs resting on the desk. The jacket of the expensive suit was open, the Armani tie loose at the collar.

'You know, Danny,' he was saying, 'as a kid I always regretted we didn't get snakes in Ireland. I hated St Patrick for that. I had a collection of everything. Stag beetles, leeches, moths, you name it.'

'Keen epidermis, were you?'

'Entomologist,' Moylan corrected. 'I always did prefer the company of insects and reptiles to the other kids at school. I always promised myself I'd get some snakes one day. I've got a pond in my garden at home now, especially for breeding frogs for Hissing Sid there.'

'Yeah?' Grogan murmured. No wonder you haven't found yourself a wife, he thought silently. He knew of no woman who would put up with that sort of thing.

Lew Corrigan had said little since his arrival. While Grogan had watched the laborious execution of the frog, the American had been studying a scale model of the time-share complex that Moylan planned to build on the Turkish coast.

He had known the Irish construction entrepreneur for only a few days since being assigned to assist the Provisionals' new European commander. Moylan appeared to have taken to him. He seemed enthralled by Corrigan's experience with the US Special Forces and had inquired about the possibility of acquiring one or two American-made Barrett sniping rifles. He was fascinated by the prospect of a gun that could throw a half-inch diameter slug nearly two thousand metres and blast through the flak jackets worn by police and soldiers in Ulster.

Corrigan sensed the man knew all about sniping, and promised to see what he could do. It would be an interesting new channel for him to explore. Another way to worm his way into the secret world of the Provisionals' collaborators in the States.

'You can learn a lot about life from the animal world,' Con Moylan said, standing up and thrusting his hands into his trouser pockets. He was a tall man with striking, but unconventional good looks. He had a strongly boned face and long black hair which, in contrast to Grogan, he wore neatly cut and gelled. But his most striking features were his heavy Celtic brows and his eyes. Each was a different colour, like those of the singer David Bowie. And rather than detract, they served to emphasise his commanding aura with their intense, hypnotic stare. 'In the animal world it's all about power and control. The ceaseless fight for control of the pack or herd, the power to make others submit to your will. That's what life is all about. Yet between the male and female of the different species, it is the female who wields the real power – except, perhaps, in the case of man.'

It was over Grogan's head; he smiled meekly. 'But what about Max Avery, Con?'

'You don't trust him, do you?'

Grogan hesitated. 'I'm not sure.'

Moylan was smiling. 'But then you have a pathological hatred of all Brits, don't you? So tell me, what does the Army Council say?'

'They say it's your decision.'

'So what choice do I have?' Moylan paced thoughtfully towards the window, a slight stoop emphasising massive shoulders that were out of proportion to the long, slim body. 'O'Flaherty's being held at Paddington Green and that means everyone remotely connected with him must be considered compromised. The whole point of having you and Fox as a cut-out cell was that O'Flaherty shouldn't know any details about our active service units or other helpers. Both men ignored that rule; they got flabby and complacent over the years.'

'O'Flaherty won't say anything,' Grogan assured.

'Then it's a good job the Brits don't pull out fingernails, isn't it?'

Grogan grabbed at straws. 'At least I'm not known to O'Flaherty.' He nodded in the direction of the American. 'And neither is Lew.'

'Wonderful!' Moylan's smile was more of a snarl. 'I've now got just the two of you and the Army Council's demanding something big urgently to save face. It'll take months to know the extent to which O'Flaherty's network has been compromised, or to set up new people. So what option do I have but to use some of them – including Max Avery? From what you've told me he's operated satisfactorily for the best part of six years. And, as far as I'm concerned, the real thing he's got going for him is that he *isn't* Irish.'

Grogan narrowed his eyes at the jibe.

Moylan sat on the edge of the desk. 'Do you know who I was once, Danny?' He didn't wait for a reply. 'The Magician. Heard the name?'

The American looked up, speaking for the first time. 'Somehow I don't see you doing shows for kids.'

A slow smile crossed Moylan's face; he liked Corrigan's

dry humour. 'A *nom de guerre*, Lew. When I ran an active unit in Derry back in the early 80s I was the best, the unit was the best. Four years. Bombings and shootings, and never once did the RUC or the Brits get a sniff of our true identities. Because I did it *my* way. To this day no one outside the Council knows.'

'What happened?' Corrigan asked.

'Our success made others jealous, that's what happened. It was all down to petty feuds and rivalry amongst the local big shots. I trod on a few toes and wounded a few prides. Some couldn't take the competition. There were rows, arguments. In the end the unit was disbanded and I was virtually exiled. But the Council knew they'd found something special in me. I was sent over here to set up a money-laundering operation. Sophisticated like the Mafia. That's how the Moylan Construction Group got started. I've increased the original Provie funds a hundredfold, expanded the business into Europe. It's been a resounding success and no one has a clue as to its origins or where the new clean money finally ends up. And you know how I've done it?'

Grogan chewed on his bottom lip, finding no inclination to contradict Moylan when he was in full flow.

'I've done it by *not* using Irishmen in key positions. You'll not hear one manager or supervisor speak with an Irish accent. Yorkshire, Welsh, Brummie – anything but Irish. And if I need someone leant on, then I use a bunch of heavies from London's East End. That way no one suspects.' He paused. 'So if Max Avery's an Englishman and works only for money, I say great. Better that than some prat like O'Flaherty or Fox to prejudice security.'

Corrigan said: 'I met Avery. He's okay.'

Moylan respected the American, had already seen him at work. Corrigan's subtle black humour and frankly brutal attitude to the terror business met with Moylan's personal approval. Few outsiders could imagine a life where planning and executing bombings and shootings replaced manufacturing and sales as a daily routine. It demanded the same dedication and application as the work of any bank manager or stockbroker, if not more so.

The Provisionals could do with more people like Corrigan. Professional, dispassionate and ruthless. Men who realised that you didn't win a guerrilla war by chanting slogans and standing for elections. Men who were not afraid to do what was necessary. With no carping and no remorse. Probably brutalised and embittered in the early days by his thankless experiences in Vietnam, Moylan saw Corrigan as such a man. And instinctively Moylan trusted his judgement.

Grogan said: 'It's a mistake, I feel it in my water. For God's sake, Con, not only is Avery a Brit, but he's an ex-Para. Those bastards . . .'

Moylan waved his protest aside. 'I know, I know, and you said yourself he never made any secret of the fact, or why he got out after the Bloody Sunday massacre.'

'Surely the point is,' Corrigan interjected, 'he passed the test, he took that radar gun when the baker got blown.'

'Reluctantly,' Grogan persisted. 'And he didn't have to pull the trigger.'

Corrigan gave a snort of derision. 'He didn't know the thing would malfunction. And of course he was reluctant. He was being put at unnecessary risk.'

'It was the Army Council's orders,' Grogan snapped defensively.

The American's smirk suggested what he thought of that. 'Avery had already been tested five years earlier, I understand. Shot dead one of his own.'

Grogan slunk into a grudging silence.

Moylan stared out of the window at the forest of masts where the yachts jostled at their berths in the floodlit marina. In truth he understood Grogan's view. Ex-British troops had been used before with mixed results; there was always the risk of divided loyalties or of a deliberate plant by the security forces. Nevertheless it was *his* decision now. Superstition and paranoia were no substitutes for a proven track record. And Avery's was second to none. Almost as an afterthought, he asked: 'How did Avery get involved with us in the first place?'

'Through someone Gerry Fox knew. They met on the social circuit, some pub or other.'

Moylan sensed that Grogan was holding something back. 'What someone? Does he have a name?'

Grogan shrugged, a cornered dog reluctant to obey. He could see no way out. 'A nurse. Maggie O'Malley.'

'O'Malley,' Moylan repeated, his eyes narrowing. 'Not the same Maggie O'Malley?'

'I don't know.'

'Don't lie to me, Danny.'

'I suppose so. I'm not sure. There must be hundreds of girls with that name. This one had shacked up with Avery . . .'

But Moylan was only half-listening. Dimly lit memories tumbled through his mind, purple shadows on her arched back at his feet, the animal smell of her; the afterglow of their coupling and the beseeching eyes looking up at him. Eyes that had haunted him ever since.

'We were a team.' His words were a mumble, as though he was talking to himself. 'No one told me. No one knew where she'd gone. Just a wall of bloody silence.'

Grogan averted his head from Moylan, avoiding direct eye contact as he carefully picked his words. 'They'd heard rumours, stories from the men. They didn't like it, Con. Not some of them on the Council.'

Moylan turned on him. 'The sanctimonious pricks! What do they know about anything? The fight? Safe in their fucken ivory towers, living off the cream the boyos have earned them from the rackets and the drugs. With their posh Dublin houses, jolly wives and fucken going to Mass every Sunday! Don't tell me whose pockets all this laundered money lines. I know. And now they're running scared. And now they're happy enough to call me back. Now they're in deep shit.'

The die was cast, Corrigan knew it.

He could see that, despite his fawning manner, Danny Grogan loathed Moylan who had hardly bothered to hide his contempt for the ill-educated courier from the Army Council. But that did not concern Lew Corrigan.

The important thing was that Moylan had made his decision to use the Englishman. That satisfied the American, because he wanted to know everything there was to know about Max Avery.

In the early days of Corrigan's military career in the shadows of the world's dirty wars, he had attempted to justify to himself the actions he had been obliged to take. Actions that had seemed as distasteful to him as they had to outsiders who didn't understand the business.

At first he had convinced himself that he was working for the greater good, for freedom and democracy. That the ends justified the means. That had assuaged any lingering sense of guilt, had made it easier to live with himself. You just had to accept that the politicians and your superior officers knew exactly what they were doing and why.

But he'd given that up long ago. A contract killing or an act of sabotage might well be in the interests of the greater good. But it might just as likely be part of a less honourable hidden agenda, the result of ill-conceived political dogma, an error of judgement – or just too much unbridled power in one man's hands.

Corrigan no longer felt the flush of pride when he saw the Stars-and-Stripes and heard no tunes of glory when the anthem played. Older and wiser, nowadays he just got on with the job; it helped to pay his alimony.

Yet there was still one thing that he could not tolerate and that was treachery. The traitor who would sacrifice his own kind through cowardice or for personal gain.

Like a former soldier who would, with only the slightest

hesitation, blow up an innocent fellow countryman and would have taken out a dozen of his former comrades-in-arms.

Such a man was Max Avery.

And Corrigan felt no need to justify the action he intended to take. None at all. It was just a question of choosing the right moment.

Moylan said: 'I've already made my decision, Danny. I've told Fox to set up a meet with Avery.'

Grogan's mouth dropped. 'You? You shouldn't meet directly with Avery, Con. That's not the way we do things.'

'It's the way I do things, Danny. You forget that the Moylan Construction Group is legit. Squeaky clean. There's nothing for anyone to pin on me. And if I've got to work with Avery, then I want to know the measure of him.'

'The Council won't approve.'

'Then don't tell them.'

Bastard, Grogan seethed, but he held his tongue.

Moylan placed an arm of comfort on the man's shoulder. 'Believe me, Danny, the only person who'll be in any danger is Avery – if I don't like what I see.'

Max Avery drove into work the next morning with a thick head.

In celebration of the prospect of starting a new life, he and Maggie had demolished the whisky bottle between them. Last night had been like the days before Josh had been born and before Maggie had been consumed with anger over his continued association with Gerry Fox. Her wanton sensuality, which had been noticeably missing for so many months, returned with a vengeance. Her enthusiasm and inventiveness, the whispered obscenities in his ear, had rekindled the fires of his desire for her like oxygen to flame. They had made love three times before the whisky was finished and they fell asleep, exhausted.

Avery parked on the forecourt and walked to the office with a half-smile on his face, despite the dull throb at the back of his skull. He felt already that a burden had been lifted and even the dismal October morning seemed bright with promise.

A new life.

'Fox just rang,' Floyd said as Avery walked through the door. There was an edge of disapproval in his voice. 'He was bloody angry. Bloody rude, man.'

Avery had just reached his desk when the telephone trilled. Not unexpectedly, it was Fox. 'Where the fucken hell you been, Max? I tried your place last night, but there was an out-of-order tone.'

'I took it off the hook,' Avery retorted. 'And it was you who were out of order, Gerry. What's the idea of worrying Maggie at work?'

Gerry Fox's voice was snappy, irritable. 'Because I didn't want to phone you at home – but you never called back. Everything's changed, Max. New security. I've been told to take a holiday for a couple of weeks – until the dust settles.'

'Listen, Gerry –'

'Be holding your tongue, Max. I'm calling from a public

box and I'm out of coins. Just do what you're told. You've got to drive down to the New Forest.'

'When?'

'Now! You're to be there by lunchtime. Turn off the M27 for Southampton at Junction One. Tuck in on the first left, there's a pub called the Sir John Barleycorn. Buy yourself a drink. You'll be contacted.'

'Look, Gerry . . .'

'Just be there.' The line went dead.

Even with the receiver still in his hand he experienced the unbidden flush of fear. Nausea like toxic bile in his gut. Just as he had when he'd been ordered to the rendezvous in Ireland. The feeling was getting familiar now, but no easier to cope with.

It took several minutes before he could think rationally. Hadn't he passed the Provisionals' test of loyalty? If he hadn't, they'd have disposed of him in the lonely border lanes, a sack over his head and a single bullet in the back of his skull.

No, this call was only to be expected. Everything would be in a state of flux until the Provos could assess the damage caused by O'Flaherty's arrest. He decided to make the trip.

He knew the New Forest quite well; in the early days of their relationship he and Maggie had spent several caravan holidays at sites secreted within the thirty square miles of ancient broadleaf woodland on the south coast. Travelling at a steady speed he reached the Cadnam junction in just over two hours, arriving at the thirteenth-century thatched pub at twelve thirty.

'Hi, Max, how ya doin'?'

He was halfway through his second pint of local Ringwood bitter when the large figure of a man stooped to enter through the low door and paused while his eyes grew accustomed to the dim light of the bar.

Avery stared at Lew Corrigan in surprise.

The American grinned broadly. 'I've just time for a half of stout.'

By the time he'd fetched the order from the bar Avery had recovered from the unexpected arrival of the man he'd left behind in County Monaghan only the day before.

'You're full of surprises,' he said as he sat down.

'Yeah, aren't I just?' Corrigan sipped appreciatively at the black velvet liquid and wiped the traces of froth from his upper lip.

'What's this all about? Why've I been called here?'

'You sound nervous, Max.' Was it Avery's imagination or did the deep-throated chuckle hide a note of contempt? 'Were you followed?'

'I don't think so. I didn't think to look.'

The American drained his glass. 'You're goin' to have to watch yourself, Max. Tighten up on security. We all are. We'll leave your car here and take mine. C'mon.'

Corrigan's car was a rented Nissan Sunny which he drove harshly, turning south onto the A337 towards Lyndhurst. There he swung back north, accelerating hard through the winding forest lanes that threaded their way through the idyllic thatched hamlets of Emery Down, Newtown and Minstead. Twice after passing a tight bend he pulled over in a field-gate lay-by in order to catch any pursuer unawares.

On the second occasion, satisfied that no one was following, he ordered Avery out of the car.

'Are you carrying, Max?'

'Of course not.'

'Let's be sure anyway, eh? And make sure you're not wired for sound. Nothing personal, you understand?'

Avery was quickly frisked. There were no weapons and no microphones.

'Let's get on,' Corrigan said.

He was to double back on himself three more times before he finally returned to Cadnam and picked up the main road to the major port town of Southampton. Not once did he concede to Avery's demands for an explanation as to where they were going or who they were going to see.

Soon stacks of freight containers appeared behind chain-link fences alongside the dual carriageway and the nodding heads of dockside cranes dominated the skyline. They turned into the waterside area, past new hotels built in garish mock-Victorian warehouse style, until they finally reached the Post House.

As they walked through the hotel lobby to the bar, Corrigan indicated a man dressed in a sharp silver-weave business suit. He sat alone at an alcove table reading a copy of the *Financial Times*.

The man looked up as they approached, dropped the paper and rose to his feet.

'This is Con Moylan,' Corrigan announced.

He was a tall man, topping Avery's six feet by several inches. His unusually broad shoulders and large head, with long black hair gelled and swept back until it curled at the nape of his neck, created a powerful presence that also suggested immense physical strength.

'Max, I've heard a lot about you.' The voice was resonant, but deliberately restrained with just a hint of a nasal Ulster drawl.

His hand, too, was large, clutching Avery's in a manner that suggested he was challenging him to a bout of arm wrestling. The dual coloured eyes appraised the Englishman carefully before the grip was slowly relaxed. It was a clear warning that Moylan was not a man to be crossed.

Avery said: 'I'm afraid you have the advantage, Mr Moylan. I know nothing about you.'

The man indicated the two spare seats facing him. 'That's the way I like it, Max.' There was a hint of mirth in the words. 'Do sit. And do call me Con. You'll learn I'm not one to stand on ceremony.'

'Nor am I,' Avery replied. 'So I'd like to know why I'm here?'

Con Moylan leaned back in his chair, elbows on the arm rests and the large fingers of both hands linked together in front of him like a cathedral arch. He regarded Avery unhurriedly before replying. 'You're here, Max, because I told you to be. Because I wanted to see you for myself. I wanted to see what sort of Englishman it was who could vaporise a baker —'

He deliberately allowed the sentence to hang in midair. Anxiously Avery glanced around the room to see if anyone had overheard. But as Moylan could see from his position, the lunchtime crowd at the bar was not within earshot.

Avery turned back to Moylan. 'Not very funny, Con. That sort of thing doesn't impress me. And whoever's idea it was to have me go there, it wasn't a good one.'

The wide chiselled lips opened in a broad, milk-white smile. It was marred only by an overlarge gap between the prominent front teeth. 'On the contrary, Max, it was an excellent idea. I'll remind you that you wouldn't be sitting here now if you'd failed us yesterday.'

'Well, now you've seen me,' Avery replied flatly. 'What do you want?'

Moylan smirked. 'A better attitude to start with, Max, if we're going to have a working relationship. I've some business to put your way.'

'Con runs a big construction company,' Corrigan interrupted. 'He's well known in Southampton. He's got men working on the Channel Tunnel and on the big new Disney park in France. Projects in Germany and the Netherlands. He wants someone who's used to working on the Continent. Someone to look after transport and accommodation for his men.'

'That's not my line of business,' Avery replied tartly.

'But it could be,' Moylan said quickly. 'It's a big contract. You could be a rich man, Max.'

Avery could see the ploy. Moylan was using greed as a weapon, trying to entangle him inextricably with the construction company as a form of insurance. The deeper in he was, the less able he would be to get out again. And the rewards would be an additional and powerful incentive. If ever he chose to try and finger Moylan, he himself would be deeply implicated. Yet he doubted he would learn more about the Provisionals' plans than he had under O'Flaherty.

Moylan might have been reading his thoughts. 'You're a businessman, Max, I appreciate that. Your motivation with us has always been cash, not ideals. Fine, no problem. This deal will put you in the big league.'

Avery could see it all. A massive and profitable work-load, mostly genuine. But just a minute percentage wouldn't be all that it seemed, the truth obscured deep within the complicated business structure of a respectable front organ-isation. And probably he himself would not even be able to detect which was which.

Suddenly he felt weary and for a moment his mind visu-alised the placid atmosphere in the Tate Public Library. A face and hands he didn't know, slipping the coded message from the dust jacket of a book.

Final recall. A new life.

He said: 'I don't think so.' The last thing he wanted to do was open up a new chapter with the Provisionals, just at a time when he was coming in from the cold. It would only incite his controllers at MI5 to apply pressure on him to stay on. 'I couldn't cope,' he added. 'You see, I'd need more staff, bigger premises. And I can't see my bank manager extending my overdraft. I'm mortgaged up to my neck as it is.'

Moylan stared at him as though he were mad. Clearly he hadn't expected Avery to turn him down, to play the innocent game as though he had a real choice in the matter.

'Think on, Max,' Corrigan urged harshly in his ear.

When he spoke Moylan's tone was measured, even amiable, but his eyes betrayed his concealed anger. 'Tell you what, Max, I'll have my lawyers call on you. Set everything out, let you examine the fine print of my proposals. We'll sort something out, I'm sure.'

Avery could hardly reject that out of hand. 'I still think you're wasting your time.'

The Irishman rose to his feet. 'I don't think so, Max. And neither will you when you've thought through the implications.' It was as near to a threat as he could get in a public place. He offered his hand which Avery accepted reluctantly. 'Oh, Max, do remember me to your good lady, will you?'

'Remember you?'

Moylan's upper lip curled back in a smile. 'Yes, Max, I think wee Maggie O'Malley might remember me.'

He turned abruptly on his heel and was gone.

Later, as Corrigan drove Avery back to his car at the Sir John Barleycorn, he became more forthcoming, almost genial.

'I think you quite surprised Moylan back there,' he said. 'He wasn't expecting that reaction. I'm not sure you were wise.'

Avery glanced sideways at him; he saw no reason to hide his contempt of the man. 'And I'm not sure I'm interested in your opinion, Yank. I've done my bit for the boyos. I've got my kid to think of now. There's plenty of young lads across the water full of piss and bravado. Let them have a go.'

Corrigan smiled thinly. 'But they don't have your experience, Max, or your contacts. And they don't have your cover – for a start they're Irish.' Keeping one hand on the wheel, he reached inside his jacket pocket with the other. He extracted the envelope and dropped it in Avery's lap. 'Moylan needs you.'

'What's this?' Avery made no attempt to pick it up.

'A list of requirements. A van, a lock-up, passports . . . you'll see. And a word from the wise. Don't try and cross Moylan on this. It's the big one.'

'What does that mean?'

'Hell, Max, Moylan doesn't let me in on things like that. But I can tell you the Chiefs of Staff in Dublin have taken their time deciding. The whisper is they're going to have another go at your Maggie Thatcher and her Cabinet.'

Avery grunted. 'She's not mine, Yank.' He picked up the envelope and placed it in his pocket, unopened. 'I'll see what I can do.'

Corrigan swung the Nissan into the pub car park. 'Moylan wants a meet in Amsterdam in two weeks for a progress report. Somewhere nice and tucked away. I'll keep in touch.'

'You do that,' Avery replied without enthusiasm as he climbed out.

'Do good on this one, Max, and maybe Moylan will let you retire without a wheelchair.'

The American's laugh was guillotined by the slamming of the door.

# Five

Clarissa Royston-Jones never could sleep on aircraft and the overnight United Airlines flight to Washington proved to be no exception.

She could find no appetite for the food, was irritated by the distorted picture on the in-flight movie, and just couldn't concentrate on the paperback she'd bought at Heathrow.

Instead, contrary to the promise she'd made to herself to cut back, she drank too much. With so few passengers due to fears about Iraqi terrorists planting bombs on airliners, the stewardesses had been unusually attentive with a succession of gin-and-tonics. But still sleep eluded her.

She peeled the wrapper from her second pack of cigarettes in four hours. Her mouth tasted like a cesspit. Christ, she really must cut down. But now was hardly the time.

At least her habit meant she travelled separately from Ralph Lavender whom she had glimpsed snoozing, content with his headset on, in the No Smoking section. The Middle East Desk chief of the Secret Intelligence Service neither smoked nor drank.

Pompous little prick, she decided acidly. All knife-edge

trouser creases, eau de cologne and manicured nails. She even suspected him of plucking his nostrils. It would be typical of the man. And her feelings, she knew, had no bearing on the traditional rivalry between SIS and Britain's Security Service MI5, the Counter-Terrorism Department of which she now headed.

She rubbed along well with many of Lavender's colleagues; it was the man himself for whom she had felt an instinctive dislike. His conceit and arrogance had not mellowed during the years she had known him. In fact she noticed the opposite as the young Turk – ill at ease as a grammar boy amidst his mostly public school peers – had earned his spurs with some cold-blooded and daring intelligence operations. Several were considered spectacular successes despite some unwanted political fallout. He had masterminded a plan to persuade a Star Wars scientist to defect from the former Soviet Union, and it had been his Middle East Desk that claimed responsibility for the death of a leading terrorist called Sabbah, although there were unconfirmed rumours that he was still alive.

Ralph Lavender had earned a grudging respect in the intelligence community, and it was her bad luck that he had liked the idea that had been fielded by Willard Franks of the CIA. Just as it had been her ill fortune that Lavender had in turn sold the concept to the Director General of SIS who had persuaded the Joint Intelligence Committee. The main problem was that it entailed one of *her* 'assets' playing a vital role.

Asset. How she hated that word. It was so heartless, so

without feeling for the human being it represented. Treating someone who was flesh and blood, with ordinary emotions, strengths and weaknesses, like a pawn. But in the case of Willard Franks' Operation Stalking Horse plan, perhaps that was exactly what Max Avery would become. And that was something she found hard to accept.

She remembered him well. A good-looking young man with a strong dimpled jaw and a nose that was a little too large to be perfect, looking as though it might once have been broken. But it had been his eyes that attracted her most, stuck in her memory. Very dark blue, clear and alert. But something else as well. It was a certain sparkle, a hint of mischief, almost as though he saw some joke which she had missed.

That had been six years ago, when they'd sat before the fire in the château in the Ardennes on the night before he began his assignment. She remembered thinking, as they drank their way through half a bottle of single malt, how sad it was that he was some ten years her junior. So sad that she was locked into a long and boring marriage with a man she did not love. Avery would never know how much she had wanted to reach across and hold his face between her hands and kiss him. How close she had come to it. Or what she'd have given to be able to abandon herself to him then.

She sighed wistfully. But, of course, she had let the moment pass. Her role was that of the dispassionate 'controller'. Always correct in her court shoes and business suit with shoulder pads, which on others would have created a glamorous and powerful image, but with Clarissa never quite came off. Always her sensible haircut seemed unflattering, her limbs too gawky and her co-ordination clumsy. But that night, with the former SAS soldier, it could just have been different.

And if it had, she wouldn't have gone on so rapidly to become department head. Wouldn't be in the unenviable position she found herself now. About to surrender the most valuable undercover operator she had. To betray the trust of the man who had aroused her feelings all those years before. About to sacrifice him for expediency.

Typically she fell asleep only an hour before the aircraft landed at Dulles.

Red-eyed, jet-lagged and exhausted, she met Lavender at the luggage carousel. To her irritation he looked bright and even cheerful; she consoled herself that at least she had time to snatch a few precious hours' sleep at her hotel before the afternoon meeting.

As they were escorted through Immigration and Customs, Willard Franks appeared with his chauffeur. 'Hi, how are you guys?' he greeted them. 'Have a good flight?'

'Excellent,' Lavender replied chirpily.

'Bloody lousy,' Clarissa muttered, fumbling desperately in her handbag for her cigarettes.

Franks smiled uncertainly. Lavender caught his eye and raised a quizzical eyebrow. The CIA man took his cue, clearing his throat. 'Er, I hope it won't be too inconvenient, but the meeting's been brought forward.'

'Christ!' Clarissa exploded, her mouth full of smoke. 'When is it?'

'Everyone's waiting now, sorry. But the NSC is anxious for something to tell the President. In fact to save time we won't travel out to Langley.' Franks didn't mention that he had received a call from Lavender before the SIS man left London, suggesting an earlier meeting. Lavender knew he could expect a fight from Clarissa who was reluctant to make her asset available for their purpose. Aware that she was a bad traveller, he advised Franks that depriving her of sleep might blunt her cutting edge. The CIA man saw nothing wrong in that.

As usual the Washington weather was living up to its reputation for unpredictability and the limousine made the tedious thirty-minute journey to the Old Executive Building through sheeting rain more befitting a Malaysian monsoon than an East Coast fall. By the time they reached their destination Clarissa's mood had progressively soured as she determined to remind herself of every thing that she loathed about Washington. There was the city's unmistakable atmosphere of self-importance, the impression given by so many who worked there that it was the centre of the universe. That was manifest in the irksome formality of the place which meant that no executive would dream of going to a bar or restaurant without a jacket and tie, no woman without a smart dress or business suit. She hated the superficial warmth and hospitality because, unlike the rest of America, it was a sham. No help was given, no favour done that wasn't expected to be returned with interest. The green stamp syndrome was rampant, everyone earnestly building up their 'favour banks' for a rainy day.

And, of course, the capital's paranoia about smoking. It was zealously restricted everywhere when it wasn't banned completely. Companies with group-rate medical insurance even insisted on urine samples from employees in case they were having a crafty cigarette at home; secretaries could be seen freezing their little butts off while having a desperate smoke on the windswept pavements outside their offices.

Clarissa ignored the warning sign in the limousine and lit up, earning a disapproving scowl from Franks; she was still smoking when she walked into the secure conference room where a team of grey-suited CIA professionals were waiting.

She and Lavender were introduced to each in turn until finally they came face to face with the bespectacled Dr Melville Mace. A timid-looking man with a white face from ATA at State, he appeared somewhat overawed by the company he kept. Surprisingly it was he, Clarissa learned, who had come up with the concept of Operation Stalking Horse.

Without wasting time, Willard Franks began running through the embryonic plan. 'So you see,' he concluded, 'our only stumbling block is not having a suitable asset in place in a position to influence a European terrorist organ-isation. That's why we were so delighted to hear you Brits were willing to co-operate. That you've actually got someone in there with the Provisional IRA leadership. This Tosca character.'

'I consider Tosca to be an agent rather than a mere asset,' Clarissa corrected testily.

Franks blinked. 'Sure.'

'And he's nowhere near the Provisional leadership.'

The CIA man glanced at Lavender for support, and the Englishman did not disappoint. 'But he does know the Provos' European commander, Clarry. Let's not put ourselves down.'

She allowed the smoke to escape through clenched teeth. 'Correction. He *did* know the European commander. Unfortunately due to a communications cockup, that particular terrorist was recently arrested by Special Branch despite the fact that we at MI5 had allowed him to run. That's the problem you get with the Security Service, Special Branch, Scotland Yard and SIS all with fingers in different parts of the pie. As a result the asset – as you call him – has been placed in considerable jeopardy. So much so that he has advised that we close the whole long-term operation down and pull him out.'

Franks frowned. 'You mean he's got cold feet?'

Clarissa's eyes narrowed behind the veil of smoke. 'That isn't a very charitable way of looking at it. He's a very courageous and extremely experienced operator who's been living a dangerous double life undercover for a number of years. I trust his judgement. And he trusts me to do what is necessary.'

Lavender said: 'But, Clarry, right now we're not in the position to be charitable. There's a war on in all but name. We have to weigh one man's worth against the perils that face our innocent public both back home and here in the States. Airliners blown up, a gas attack, the bombing of politicians – any of these things could happen, and our asset is the only one in a position to reduce that risk.'

'Our asset, Ralph?' Clarissa's voice was hoarse with indignation. 'I think you mean *my* agent.'

An embarrassed smile appeared on Lavender's lips as he glanced at the faces around the table. 'Of course, understood. But both your Director General and the Joint Intelligence Committee have agreed that your – your agent – should come under our joint control for this. Outside the UK he would no longer be strictly under your jurisdiction.'

Clarissa felt fatigue and exasperation combining to defeat her. 'I know that perfectly well. I have no option but to accept this *fait accompli*. But it is my duty to warn you all here that I consider this man to be in extreme peril, and that I want it to go on record that I do not support the use of him in this way.'

Willard Franks nodded sympathetically. 'I understand, Clarissa, believe me I really do. But, as Ralph says, we don't hold any other options right now.'

She stubbed out her cigarette. 'Then you'd better tell me what you want him to do.'

Melville Mace rose to his feet. 'Mr Franks and I have discussed this, and we'd like your man to make contact with the leadership of the Provisional IRA. Tell them he's had this idea that could earn them a lot of funds. I understand it takes some six million dollars to run that organisation each year.'

'That's true,' Lavender confirmed, 'and the RUC in Northern Ireland are having a purge on their income from racketeering and protection. There could well be a short-term cash shortage.'

'My reading too,' Mace agreed. 'But if the Provisionals are going to offer to act for Saddam Hussein it's going to have to be something big to attract him. Something that promises to grab the world headlines.'

Franks chuckled. 'No doubt the bastard will want to see it on the networks.'

Lavender said: 'I was studying Tosca's file on the flight over. He reports a rumour that the Provisionals are considering another attack on the Cabinet.'

'That would sure hit the front pages,' Willard Franks agreed. 'Why don't you look into it, see if your man can find out more details? It could be better and more convincing than starting something from scratch.'

Clarissa wearily tapped a fresh cigarette from the pack. 'And how do you suggest my agent goes about approaching the Iraqis in a convincing way? They're going to suspect that we might already have got wind of any scheme that's put to them.'

'We've thought about that one,' Mace answered eagerly. 'Any approach to the Iraqis will have to be made some-place where security is lax. A Third World country would be best, but there could be communication problems. Most European countries would be out – the Iraqis already realise it's unlikely someone could contact them without being detected. We've got phone taps, mail intercepts and surveillance going on with or without local governments' agreement. The best option for us would be Greece. The Greeks are dragging their feet over the Gulf crisis and there's a strong anti-American feeling since Saddam's seizing of Kuwait has reminded them how we did nothing after Turkey's invasion of Cyprus. Moreover, Athens plays host to numerous terrorist front organisations, so the Greeks hardly consider security against these people to be top priority. No, we think an approach in Athens would be the most feasible.'

'Would we seek co-operation from the Greek Government?' asked one of the other CIA men whose particular concern was one of international legalities.

Willard Franks allowed himself a sly smile. 'Oh, I don't think so. We can't afford for them to turn the idea down and their co-operation could, frankly, be a liability. Apart from which, information leaks like a sieve over there.'

'Even so,' Lavender intervened, 'neither our asset nor the Provisionals can just go knocking on an Iraqi Embassy door and expect to be taken seriously. There'll need to be some sort of introduction, maybe an intermediary . . .'

Clarissa said quietly: 'There may be a way round that. And it could solve another problem that no one's mentioned. To be believed this whole thing's got to be played for real. Even if the Provisionals are taken in by our man – which is by no means certain – there's no guarantee that the Iraqis will be. That means that communications between our man and us will be impossible – or else limited and extremely dangerous. And as it has to be played for real then we, in effect, are creating a threat against ourselves. That's fine whilst our man is in control and we can terminate that threat when it suits us and before it's planned to happen.

'But we have to *guarantee* that our man becomes part of the operation. Otherwise the Provisionals might just say thanks for the idea and run with it themselves. Then we've just created a threat we can do nothing about.'

Although Clarissa's words made sense, Lavender was suspicious; he half-suspected that she was throwing up objections for the sake of it. 'You said using an intermediary could solve the problem?' he pressed.

To his surprise, she said: 'If our man appears to have a contact of his own who can be used as an intermediary, then at least he has an introduction, a foot on the ladder.'

'Splendid idea,' Willard Franks decided.

Clarissa closed her eyes for a moment, desperately fighting the fatigue that dragged at her lids, trying to control the anger she felt at everyone else's total disregard for the man in the field. Their field, her man. 'Although I'm obliged to go along with you all, there is no way I'm going to let my agent go into this without backup. Not only for his own protection – although God knows that's important enough – but also to give him means of secure communication so that we don't lose track of any planned terrorist attack.' She looked pointedly in Lavender's direction. 'Dear Ralph, do remember, if someone *succeeds* in blowing up the Houses of Parliament it'll be my neck — and MI5's — on the block, no one else's.'

Lavender shifted uncomfortably in his seat. 'What sort of backup did you have in mind, Clarry? My people are pretty stretched at the moment checking on possible Iraqi Intelligence movements in every country in our sphere of influence.'

Clarissa took her time lighting the last cigarette in her pack. There was silence all around the table. She held the stage, everyone hanging on her next words, and she rather liked it. Her co-operation in this was going to put a large deposit in her favour bank. And she didn't intend to wait long to collect on it. At last she said: 'My agent-in-place is ex-SAS, so what better than to put together a team of, what shall we say, guardian angels from the Regiment? Throw up an invisible shield around him wherever he goes. They can monitor his movements, watch for trouble, record the conversations he has, take photographs of contacts. That way he doesn't have to put himself at risk trying to use dead-letter drops or send radio signals. He'll be constantly surrounded by a mobile cocoon of surveillance.'

Glances were exchanged. Slow nods of approval. It made a lot of sense.

Lavender said grudgingly: 'I'll put it to the Defence Minister.' He had no great love of the SAS; to his mind they were too cavalier in their general attitude and too given to questioning orders. His orders.

'My asset, Ralph,' she reminded with a demure smile, smoke rising over her face in blue ribbons. 'My terms.'

Willard Franks intervened before the mutual antagonism of the two British officials became counterproductive. 'I'm sure, Clarissa, we're most grateful for your co-operation. It'll be a weight off the President's mind. Needless to say, if there's anything we can do to help –'

In her state of near-exhaustion she almost missed her opportunity. Almost, but not quite. 'Wonderful!' she replied, her eyes suddenly bright and wide. 'How kind, Willard. You see it occurred to me before I left England that it's very risky to place all this responsibility onto one British agent in what is very much an American-orientated mission.'

Lavender was taken aback by her sudden change of tack.

Willard Franks said: 'Er – we're all in this together, Clarry. Saddam could hit London like he could New York. We're allies in this war.'

Her laugh was genuine, almost like tinkling water. For a moment Lavender suspected she had lost her senses. She said: 'You mean it's the old special relationship – our two countries working together? Sharing the risk fairly?'

'Absolutely, ma'am,' Franks agreed. 'It's just that we don't have an asset-in-place to be of any use.'

Clarissa wasn't going to be that easily deterred. She'd done her homework and had no intention of letting Avery sink or swim alone in this hellishly dangerous gamble of an operation. 'Willard, tell me, reports reached London that five men were charged in Chicago last year with attempting to supply the Provisional IRA with small arms and communications equipment.'

He showed his immaculate and expensive dental work. 'I believe that's true.'

'And evidence was given by an American undercover operator,' she continued, 'whose identity was kept secret?'

Franks swallowed. 'I believe that's so and I think I see what you're getting at. But that agent was not on the official CIA payroll.'

The sweetness of her smile didn't falter. 'You mean, Willard, that he is an NOC operator?'

Franks nodded. 'Sure, he's a Non-Official Cover. A dangerous job. No diplomatic immunity, no accountability and no panic button. But we've conducted the Eire operation in co-operation with Ralph's people in London.'

Clarissa's forehead furrowed. 'Then it's a pity that Ralph's people weren't a little more forthcoming with me. Maybe someone, somewhere is empire-building. Anyway, as I've agreed to put my agent at the disposal of the operation, I think you owe me and him a favour, Willard, don't you? Let's you, me and Ralph talk about it over lunch.'

One of the CIA men turned to a bemused Melville Mace and slapped him heartily on the back. 'Mel, I reckon that ol' clown horse of yours could soon be up and running!'

Only Willard Franks seemed subdued. And Clarissa understood why: with such a strong pro-Irish lobby on Capitol Hill, the CIA could only mount its anti-IRA operations with great difficulty and even greater discretion.

All around the table people were congratulating each other on the agreement to co-operate, the meeting breaking up into a series of earnest private conversations.

Clarissa Royston-Jones wondered if the Americans around the table would have been quite so delighted if she had announced that the suggested targets for Saddam Hussein were to be, not the British Cabinet, but President Bush and the White House.

It was three days after his meeting in Southampton with Con Moylan that Avery mentioned it to Maggie.

Normally he said nothing to her about his contacts or his work for the Provisionals. By keeping her at arm's length from his undercover work, it felt less like a betrayal of her trust. He could almost forget how he'd used her in the beginning to make the contacts he needed. For years now he'd tried to keep his home life separate. That way most of his undercover work was conducted in office hours. It helped relieve the endless pressure – and his conscience.

But now he was curious to know how Maggie's and Con Moylan's paths had once crossed. As it was now only a matter of days before he was pulled out by MI5, he decided to find out more.

'I met someone who used to know you,' he said casually as he towelled his hair.

They had just made love. Again it had been like the old days. Ever since he had promised to stop seeing Fox and to plan a new future somewhere else, Maggie had been like a different woman. Her seemingly perpetual fatigue, which he attributed to coping with Josh and holding down her job at the hospital, vanished overnight. Her desire for sex became recharged.

'Who was that?' she asked, water dripping from her body as she followed him from the bath. It had always been her favourite place for love-making.

'An Irish guy who runs a big construction company in Southampton. I was down there the other day. Said he knew you.'

She reached up and kissed him, her breasts cool and damp against his chest. 'Does he have a name?'

'Con Moylan.'

'Con?' She drew back. 'Did you say *Con* Moylan? From Derry?'

Avery smiled, trying to gauge her reaction. 'Well he was from Northern Ireland. I didn't give him the third degree, we were talking contracts.'

Anger flashed in her eyes. 'What sort of contracts, Max? Is he a friend of Gerry Fox?'

He raised his hands in mock surrender. 'No, hardly,' he lied. 'I got to know him through an American I met on that Ireland trip. Moylan's a respectable businessman running several companies.'

Her eyes began to cloud as she stared at him. 'Then if it's the same Con Moylan, he's a changed man.'

'When did you know him?'

'A long time ago.' Her voice was hoarse as she reached for a towel and dabbed at her body with it.

'Tell me,' he coaxed.

She shook her head. 'I'd rather not.'

A thought occurred to Avery. 'Were you in love with him?'

Without answering she took her jade satin robe from behind the door and padded out into the bedroom. When he followed a few minutes later he found her seated before the dressing table staring at her reflection in the mirror as she tugged a brush methodically through her tangled curls. Two dark lines of mascara had trickled down her cheeks.

He stood behind her, resting his hands on her shoulders, his fingers massaging gently into her flesh. His gaze met hers in the mirror.

She said: 'Don't do business with him, Max. I don't want him back in my life.'

'He's not in your life,' Avery replied lightly. 'He's just a business contact.'

'You don't understand.'

'Try me.' This time there was a demanding edge to his voice that he hadn't intended.

She inhaled deeply and closed her eyes; he felt the muscles relax beneath his fingers. At length she said softly: 'If it's the same man, yes, I had an affair with him. It began long before I met you – it must have been in '82 because I remember the Falklands War was on. I was eighteen at the time and I was discussing it with a group of friends in a drinking club one night. Con was with them. He was saying how sending the task force just proved that British imperialism was alive and well. Just as it was in Ulster. I agreed with him, that's how we got talking.' She glanced up at Avery. 'Doesn't sound like the same man, does it?'

He shrugged. 'What did he look like?'

'Very tall. And broad shoulders, I remember that. Heavy

eyebrows and very penetrating eyes. Both blue, but two distinctly different shades. Something about him was rather frightening.' She allowed herself a faint smile as the memory came into sharper focus. 'He had a sort of hungry and mean look about him. Sort of brooding, smouldering almost. He didn't say much.'

'It could be him,' Avery said noncommittally. In fact he was certain it was.

Maggie dropped her hands and the hairbrush to her lap and studied them. 'Only later I learned he was a sniper for the Provies. I suppose he must have been in his late twenties then. I was very in awe of him. He had such a way about him. He could make you do anything he wanted. Bend you to his will . . .' Her voice had trailed to little more than a murmur. 'Con could make you accept things about yourself you didn't want to know . . . He was the one who made me help them, persuaded me.'

'But it didn't last?'

She straightened her back. 'Two years. Believe me that was enough. In the end I broke with him and came to England to get away.'

'You've never mentioned him.'

'No.'

'Was he ever convicted?'

Her laugh was brittle. 'Not our Con. He was never even picked up for questioning. He was much too clever for that. They even called him the Magician.'

'Maybe, like you, he gave it all up?'

'Somehow I wouldn't have thought so, Max.' She

sounded weary, as though examining that period of her life was physically painful.

Avery let the matter drop. He had anyway been to the library on his return from Southampton to leave a message about Moylan and the forthcoming meeting in Amsterdam. He had requested all available information on Con Moylan. Shortly he would know all that there was to know about the man.

He decided not to press the matter further with Maggie, but the next day visited the library and was mildly irritated to find no response to his earlier signals. Give them time, he told himself. His controller would have a lot to arrange. There was nothing to worry about; he had learned to trust the woman he knew only as Clarry quite literally with his life.

At the office he divided his time between the jobsheets, invoices and bills that Floyd had prepared and the list of requirements given him by Lew Corrigan after the meeting with Moylan.

Avery was surprised by the length of the list for any one time. He guessed that it was due to the number of Provo contacts thought to be compromised by O'Flaherty's arrest. Knowing that the organisation never put all its requirements through one quartermaster, it was reasonable to assume that the items were for several of the 'active service units' known to exist on the UK mainland and in Europe. This list would most likely offer more leads to MI5 than anything he had previously handled. It might yet prove to be the one saving grace of O'Flaherty's ill-timed detention.

A lock-up garage; a safe house, short let; a Transit-type van; two cars and a motorcycle, all untraceable, and two 'clean' handguns featured amongst the more familiar requests for passports and credit cards under presumably false names.

There was little here Avery's underworld contacts couldn't supply.

He reached for the telephone. It rang just as his fingers touched it.

'Hallo, Max. It's been a long time.' The accent was guttural, distinctly Dutch. 'It's Henk Vergeer, you remember?'

Avery did not remember; in fact he had numerous contacts in Holland, but was certain Vergeer wasn't one of them. Cautiously he said: 'What can I do for you?'

'Ah, Max, it is what I can do for you, I think. A little gem —' Avery's mouth dropped at the insignificant phrase. The prearranged code. Three little words. A new life. So that was it — 'A Jensen Interceptor, Max, very nice. You do not see many around today. A real collector's item, will fetch a nice price. You should see it.'

His heart had begun to pound as he tried to keep the excitement from his voice. 'I'd like to. Where are you?'

'At my showroom, it is in south Flevoland, not far from Amsterdam.' He gave the address.

Avery said: 'Funnily enough I'm due over in about ten days on business. Would that suit?'

'Of course.' Henk Vergeer didn't sound surprised, but then he wouldn't. Avery's controller knew all about the planned progress meeting with Moylan.

'In fact, Henk, I was thinking of bringing Maggie and the baby with me. We could all do with a break.'

There was a hesitation at the other end of the line. 'Max, my friend, Holland is not very nice this time of year. Very wet, very cold. They would not like it. Springtime would be much better, when the bulbs are in bloom.'

Avery glared at the handset, then chided himself. Of course he was being unreasonable; his controller would want to sort things out properly unless the situation were desperate. Have a preliminary talk with him. Before they were all spirited away, he would want to find out where he and Maggie wanted to live under their new identities.

Avery said: 'I bow to your wisdom, Henk. Of course you're right, spring would be much more pleasant.'

After finalising the arrangements, he hung up in a pensive mood. Something still niggled at the back of his mind; somehow he had never imagined that the end would be like this. It was different, not quite producing the feeling of elation and unburdening that he had expected.

'Max?' Floyd was at the door.

He looked up.

'We've got the Telecom engineers here, Max; someone's reported a fault on our line. I expect it's that new-fangled switchboard.'

Avery followed his manager into the showroom where the engineers waited. Aware that the Provisionals were quite capable of bugging his telephone if they suspected him, he checked that the credentials of the officials were genuine before allowing them access.

Then he turned to Floyd. 'Let's take an early lunch. Fancy a pie and a pint?'

'Something to celebrate?' his manager asked as they walked past the British Telecom van on the forecourt.

'A Jensen Interceptor.'

And a new life. Just ten days away.

# Six

The estate was some twenty miles outside Dublin, set in the world's most renowned bloodstock terrain in County Kildare.

The big house was not visible from the road, its presence marked only by electronic ironwork security gates hung between two ornate and lichen-covered pillars.

Danny Grogan stopped his hired car, climbed out and pressed the intercom. After a brief exchange with the disembodied voice on the other end of the line, he turned to face the video camera perched in a tree. Any visitor would understand the need for security, for this was one of the richest and most successful stud farms and racing stables on The Curragh prairie.

By the time he'd returned to his car, the gates had swung silently open to admit him. He drove cautiously up the winding track for half a mile before he arrived at the stable lines.

'Big Tom' O'Grady was impossible to miss. He was a commanding figure, towering above the group of diminutive trainers and their thoroughbred charges. As usual his tall and bulky frame was clad in heavy country tweeds trimmed at collar and cuffs in brown velvet, the trousers tucked into green Dunlop boots. The waistcoat, green plaid tie and matching pocket handkerchief reinforced the impression of rural gentry created by the iron-grey hair raked severely back from his forehead, and the jutting froth of white beard around his chin.

He was talking on his mobile telephone, no doubt to the security guard at the house, because he turned expectantly as Grogan parked and raised a hand in greeting.

The trainers were dismissed, each mounting his horse and joining the steady line that trooped past Grogan towards the green swathe of the gallops. He stood by his car door, admiring the rippling flanks of the beasts and inhaling the heady smell of dung and animal sweat, and feeling not a little envious.

He had known O'Grady, a member of the Turf Club and racing establishment, since he himself had once been a stable lad here, with high hopes of becoming a jockey until his small adolescent body had decided to put on a late spurt. His life's ambition in tatters, he had returned home to the north, embittered by the hand that fate had dealt him.

'Hallo, Danny, how goes it?' O'Grady's voice was quietly resonant.

Grogan made a deferential and oblique reply before the racehorse owner steered him towards the paddock rail. 'We'll talk over here. See, my latest acquisition.'

The young sable-haired colt pranced friskily across the churned turf, tossing its mane and casting a knowing eye towards the two onlookers as though fully aware of its own unsurpassed bloodline.

'Magnificent,' Grogan murmured, and meant it. Inside he still burned with envy. Envy of Big Tom O'Grady, the lads, the trainers, the jockeys . . .

'Called Harvest Moon,' O'Grady said, not taking his eyes from the creature.

'Harvest Moon. I like that.'

O'Grady leaned easily on the rails. 'And what news from Con Moylan?'

Grogan dragged his eyes away from the vain antics of the horse. 'He's selected the three quartermasters least likely to have been compromised by O'Flaherty.'

'Does that include the Englishman, Avery?'

'Yes. I think he was intrigued that Avery is shacked up with the O'Malley girl.'

'I hope that won't be a problem. He should keep away from her.'

'There's been a lot of water under the bridge. But Moylan always trusted her, so he thinks Avery must be okay. He's used to working with Brits.'

'You told him of your reservations?'

'Sure I did, but Moylan treats me like some bit o' shite he's found on his shoe. Besides, the American thought Avery had passed the test. I'm not so sure.'

'Moylan's his own man, so he is. Always has been. A bit of a wild card, a maverick,' O'Grady reflected. 'Upset a lot of people in the old days. But he was good then, and he's been good since looking after our investments.'

Grogan said nothing, but he'd noticed how far the stud farm had come since his days as stable lad. It had been rundown and near bankrupt then – before O'Grady had access to Moylan's lucrative laundering operation. He guessed it was one of the perks of being a godfather of the Provisional IRA.

'What really niggles you about Avery?' O'Grady asked.

A snort of sarcastic laughter. 'Apart from the fact he's a Brit?'

'Liverpool-Irish,' the other man corrected. 'A subtle difference.'

'It was when he first met the O'Malley girl. She was at some cookery class, then he turned up. I know she said she made all the running, but we can't be sure. She was fresh out of the Six Counties, part of Moylan's unit then. How do we know the Brits weren't onto her and didn't plant Avery?'

'That's a hoary old chestnut, Danny. We went into that deeply before we ever used him in the first place. Gerry Fox did a full investigation at the time. And have any arrests or other incidents happened that could have been linked in any way to Avery – before this business with O'Flaherty?'

The cool autumn air was causing Grogan's nose to run; he cuffed it roughly with the back of his hand. 'That's impossible to tell, Mr O'Grady. Avery's had a small part to play in preparing countless operations. Some have come unstuck, others have been a great success. But then he's never ever been told what's going on. Anyway, the Brits have been masters of the intelligence game since the Middle

Ages – they're not going to let us make an obvious connection.' He stared out at the colt. 'For the next few months, till we get new people in place, Avery's going to do more work for us than ever before. That is setting a dangerous precedent.'

O'Grady nodded his understanding of Grogan's doubts. The man might have an unfortunate personal manner and be ill-educated, but he was nobody's fool. 'We can't just stop mainland and European operations, Danny. What would you have us do?'

'Is there a file on Avery?'

'Of course. The one that Fox compiled way back.'

'Let me go over it, Mr O'Grady, check Avery out again.'

Big Tom O'Grady knew that Grogan didn't rate Gerry Fox very highly. 'I'll put it to the other Council members, how's that?'

'I think that would be a wise precaution. And I'd like to put a tail on Avery, especially when he goes to Amsterdam next week. If he has to make contact with someone we don't know about, that would be the ideal place for him to do it.'

Not for the first time, O'Grady decided that Grogan's looks and manner belied his considerable intelligence. 'But tell me, Danny, is this really a distrust of Max Avery or part of a personal vendetta to prove Con Moylan wrong?'

The gash of thick red lips broke in a smile across Grogan's face, but he did not reply.

O'Grady, pleased that his powers of perception had not diminished with age, nodded in the direction of

Harvest Moon.'Now, Danny, how do you fancy a training gallop?'

For the next hour Grogan was to forget all about Con Moylan and Max Avery as he recaptured just a few of his childhood dreams.

It was with an immense sense of relief that Avery arrived at Heathrow airport for his flight to Amsterdam.

The previous ten days since Henk Vergeer's recall message seemed to have been the longest in his life. He had found it difficult to concentrate on the daily business routine, let alone work on the list of requirements supplied by Lew Corrigan.

On the fifth day someone had called the office from the Moylan Construction Group to inquire about leasing fleet vehicles. It was the Irishman's promised opening gambit and Avery saw no way to avoid playing along. He gave Floyd the job of handling it, much to his manager's delight and puzzlement. Such a large contract would normally be handled by the boss himself.

'You feeling all right, Max?' he had asked.

'You deal with it. I'm a bit tired. Insomnia, that's all.'

It wasn't a complete lie. Most nights sleep had eluded him. He would find himself padding quietly from the bedroom, careful not to wake Maggie or the baby. With a whisky in hand he watched the interminable TV news coverage of distant events in the Gulf.

But it only half registered. His mind was full of what the future held in store, a recurring mental picture of

Maggie and himself walking along some sunlit beach in Australia. In front of them a growing, tanned little boy scampering at the surf's edge, excited and laughing back at them, untainted by the deceit and violence that had become an integral part of his father's life.

At last, without a true identity to conceal, he would be free to marry Maggie and end the long-running bone of contention between them. And free from the omnipresent dread that one careless word or action on his part could lead to the inevitable nightmare: answering a knock at his door to be confronted by a masked Provo and a sawn-off shotgun.

A new life, almost there.

Despite arriving early at the airport he only just had enough time to catch his plane. Blue-uniformed police officers were much in evidence with their flak jackets and Heckler and Koch sub-machine-guns, and long queues had formed as passengers and their baggage were subjected to scrupulous inspection.

On his arrival at Schiphol airport he collected his rented car and took the road east to Flevoland, skirting south of Amsterdam city.

On his first countersurveillance run, turning back on his tracks, he picked up the little green Fiat. Two more manoeuvres and it was still there, the unknown driver a little more circumspect now. Feeling a little unnerved but at least satisfied that he'd identified the tail, Avery continued on his way.

Heer Henk Vergeer's car showroom stood alone beside

the raised dyke road on the outskirts of a village, its white clapboard façade pristine and gleaming under a watery sun. Brightly polished Datsuns competed for attention with Dafs and Citroëns on the windswept forecourt, but all were outshone by the sleek lines of the Jensen Interceptor in metallic shark-blue.

An acne-faced youth with long straggly hair was lovingly waxing the front wing as Avery parked alongside and climbed out.

'So this is it, eh?' he said.

The boy stopped working. 'You must be the Englander Heer Vergeer expects, Heer Avery?' For a moment both stood admiring the machine. 'It is well worth your trip, I think. I prefer only the E-type Jaguar over this model.'

'A little gem,' agreed a voice behind them.

Henk Vergeer was a stout but fit-looking man in his mid-fifties. His tanned features and short-cut silvering hair went perfectly with the hand-tailored goose-grey suit and starched white shirt. He offered a firm dry handshake. 'Good to see you again, Max. You see I do not exaggerate about the Jensen.'

'An excellent specimen,' Avery agreed.

'But you must be tired after your journey. So let's take it for a test drive to my home. My wife has prepared some lunch and we can talk business there.' As he spoke Avery noticed that the man never looked directly at him, all the time his eyes darted from side to side, examining the open polderland and the empty dyke road. Lowering his voice, he said hoarsely: 'Did you know that you were followed?'

'I hoped it was one of yours.'

Vergeer gave a tight, small smile. 'Bring your briefcase and baggage with you. You can leave your car here until we get back.'

When Avery took the driver's seat of the Jensen and coaxed the powerful V6 engine into life the Dutchman said: 'There is a small green car – a Fiat, I think – parked two hundred metres away to the right. I am watching with binoculars when you arrived. That is the beauty of the polder, there are few hiding places. Did you notice it behind you earlier?'

'I'm sure it's the same one.'

'Never mind,' Vergeer said lightly, 'I'll keep an eye on it. If you'd like to turn left, I shall give you directions as we go.'

The car handled beautifully. The massive engine purred and the twin through-exhausts burbled manfully as the Pirelli radials lapped up the tarmac with consummate ease.

'In case you are wondering, Max, I was with the anti-terrorist unit of the *Korps Commandetroepen* until I retired a couple of years ago. Friends of your dear MI5 over here thought my new business might be a useful cover and I am happy to oblige.' He added a self-effacing chuckle. 'With the trouble in the Middle East and the recession I may as well help out. I am certainly not selling any cars!'

'Likewise,' Avery said with feeling. He had taken instantly to the Dutchman. 'And this Jensen?'

'From my private collection. Don't you even make me an offer – it is not for sale!' He glanced over his shoulder.

'Well, well, Max, it seems that the little green car is still with us. Perhaps the driver is lost. Take the next left-hand turn and pull over, will you?'

Avery slowed through the gears so as to give no warning, then, without signalling, turned sharply into the side road and rolled to a halt beside a screen of wild holly bushes.

Seconds later the Fiat appeared, sideslipping across the junction as it took the corner too fast. Avery caught just a blurred glimpse of the driver as he struggled with the wheel, correcting his skid so violently that the vehicle's rear waggled out of control for several seconds. Then it straightened up and sped away out of sight.

'What do you think, Max? Your Irish friends?'

Avery nodded. 'It's possible. I should have guessed that one of yours would have performed better on his home turf.'

'Please, Max, reverse up and continue down the main road. If our friend was following he'll try and pick us up about two miles down the road.'

A few minutes later the Fiat reappeared in the rear-view mirror.

'Don't worry, Max, we anticipated something of the sort. It's been taken care of.' He picked up the car phone and pressed a series of buttons. 'Hallo, this is Henk here. We appear to have picked up a tail. A green Fiat. Yes, it is appropriate. Are you in position?'

They were approaching a cluster of redbrick houses around a crossroad junction and Vergeer told him to slow to fifty kilometres an hour. Ahead of them the narrow road was further restricted by roadworks and a municipal truck. The front grille of the Fiat loomed larger in the rear-view mirror, the driver anxious not to lose his quarry again.

As they passed the roadworks, Avery glimpsed the large red Volvo waiting in the side street. The timing was perfect. Seconds later the Fiat passed through the chicane of road-work cones just as the Volvo nudged out into its path. They heard the squeal of tortured rubber followed by the sharp bright tinkle of shattering glass.

All Avery could see in his mirror was the driver emerging from the Volvo in a yellow rally jacket and a traffic policeman running towards the scene. Then they were lost from view.

Vergeer smiled with quiet satisfaction. 'Now that really has given me an appetite for lunch.'

Twenty minutes later they reached the safe house. It was modern, expensive, and hidden from view behind a high stone wall with wrought-iron gates which led into the well-ordered garden, its ranks of shrubs neatly trimmed back and staked in preparation for the coming winter.

Vergeer led the way up the steps and let himself into the spacious, airy hallway. It was severely decorated with large expanses of plain white walls and teak flooring. The vast lounge was similarly spartan, furnished with a grey hide sofa and armchairs and silver-striped curtains at the panoramic picture window that occupied the entire far wall. Occasional tables held heavy mahogany sculptures of distinctly East Indian origin.

Vergeer left Avery alone to face the three people, two

men and a woman, who waited by the modern marble fireplace, warming the backs of their legs on the heat from the smouldering logs.

John Nash stepped forward first, his hand extended. Wearing a dark suit he was hardly recognisable as the young tough in jeans and leather jacket who had recruited Avery on the ferry six years earlier.

'Good to see you, Max. I've been your controller for the past four years.' He turned to introduce the woman. 'You remember Clarry? She was a hard act to follow. Now she's head of the Anti-Terrorism Department.'

'Max,' she said simply and reached to take both his hands in her own, standing back to look at him carefully, like an aunt surprised how her nephew had grown in her absence.

But she did not like what she saw. The handsome features she remembered were gaunt, the lines on his face more pronounced. His eyes had a haunted look about them, with no sign of the mischievous glint that had once beguiled her in the Ardennes safe house. Had she really done this to him? Was this the inevitable price that had to be paid for the job they did?

Nash was surprised to see her draw close and brush her lips against Avery's cheek. 'Thank you for everything you've done, Max. I can't tell you what you've achieved.'

A light but pointed cough came from behind her. Clarissa's lips tightened perceptively in a brief gesture of irritation. 'Max, you don't know Ralph Lavender from SIS.'

The handshake was unenthusiastic, impatient. 'Heard all about you, Avery. Well done.'

Avery was bemused. 'What's this to do with SIS? I thought my role was strictly with the Security Service?'

'It's the overlap with Provo activities in Europe,' Lavender explained somewhat sharply. 'Our people at Vauxhall Bridge Road have been keeping a watching brief on your case.'

That didn't really answer his query. A watching brief hardly explained the necessity for an SIS man's personal attendance when he was about to be pulled out.

'I'm sorry about that incident with the car on the way here,' Nash said. 'Since the Provisionals might still be a little hesitant about you I've taken precautions. The man in the Fiat was waiting for you at Schiphol airport and Dutch Intelligence have learned from the police at that traffic accident that the driver was a young Irish student at an agricultural college in The Hague. One of the Provos' sleepers, I would guess. So we'll be able to keep an eye on him in future.'

'Well done again, Max,' Clarissa said.

'I thought I'd convinced Moylan I was on the level,' Avery replied. 'It just confirms it's time to get out. The arrest of O'Flaherty has really rattled the cage, I can tell you.'

Nash looked embarrassed. 'I'm sorry about that, Max. It was an absolute cockup. Between the Anti-Terrorist Branch, Special Branch and us the wires managed to get crossed. It was two days before I learned they were holding him at Paddington Green.' He smiled nervously. 'But how are you getting on with this Con Moylan chap? That was a lucky break. Did you know he doesn't show up on any of our computers? If he hadn't broken the Provos' own rules and made contact with you it might have been years before we discovered O'Flaherty's successor.'

Avery shrugged. 'It doesn't matter now, but even if Moylan decides to trust me, I don't think we'd ever have the same relationship I had with O'Flaherty. Bad chemistry, both ways. I just don't think we'd get on.'

'But you could brazen it out for a few more months?' It was Lavender who had spoken, the words sounding more like a statement than a question.

'Months?' Avery stared at the man. 'You must be joking! I nearly got a bullet in the brain in Ireland two weeks ago. The whole thing could go pear-shaped at any moment. And if it does, I've got Maggie and the baby to worry about.' He turned to Nash. 'In fact I thought I'd be bringing them here with me. That was always the arrangement.'

Nash shifted his stance; he did not look comfortable. 'Circumstances change, Max. These things take time.'

Avery's growing suspicions were reinforced. 'A few days, weeks even, I can understand.' He turned and pointed an accusing finger at Lavender. '*He* is talking about months!'

At that point Henk Vergeer reappeared briefly with a tray of coffee and sandwiches before leaving again.

Clarissa used the interruption to take Avery discreetly to one side. 'Max, we are not making a very good job of this. No one wants to come out and say it, but the truth is we are *desperate* for you to stay on. You must realise that there is a war coming in the Gulf and you are in a unique position to help . . .'

He stared at her. 'What on earth has that got to do with me?'

'Let's have some lunch and I'll explain.'

An angry vein pulsed at Avery's temple. 'I'm not interested.'

She placed her hand on his arm. 'Please, Max, just hear us out. A lot of lives might depend on your co-operation. Will you just listen? You owe me that.'

Reluctantly he agreed and listened in silence while the four of them drank coffee and ate. But he found he had little appetite as Lavender explained the scheme with an enthusiasm that Avery did not share.

At last he said: 'Are you seriously asking me to go to Con Moylan and sell him the idea of offering to mount a terrorist attack for Saddam Hussein?'

'In return for funds,' Lavender added. 'And not just any attack. I understand there's a plot under way to assassinate the Prime Minister and senior Cabinet Ministers?'

Avery shook his head in disbelief. 'Possibly, but I don't know any details.'

'We've got an existing contact with the Libyans,' Clarissa reminded. 'You can use it as a route to get to Saddam. Arrange to meet the Iraqis in Athens.' She hesitated, trying to overcome her own instinctive distrust of the whole idea. 'Could you sell that to Moylan?'

'I don't know,' Avery replied grimly, accepting the cigarette she offered. 'The whole thing's a pretty bold plan and I can see how it could work in theory, assuming Moylan buys the idea and trusts me enough to allow my involvement. But I'm just one man, it would be impossible for me to hold the whole thing together by myself.'

'But if you had an ally?' Lavender pressed. 'Someone else you could work with?'

'What do you mean?'

Clarissa said: 'It was a connection I found out by chance. The Americans and SIS have got somebody working under-cover with the Provisionals in Eire. His job is to pinpoint the terrorists' links with Noraid members and other United States citizens. Supplying funds or providing money-laundering services, channelling cocaine and heroin through Dublin, attempting to purchase weapons technology – all that sort of thing. It's a very sensitive area for the Americans, but I gather their man has been fairly successful. It was done with our approval, but I was never privy to his identity. You see he's what the CIA call a non-official cover operator. "Naked" in our parlance. If you can believe it, Max, he's been in an even more dangerous position than you. He's in there with little backup or safeguards. SIS has been co-operating in trying to backdrop him and give him some support where they can. It's been a joint US–UK operation under our "special rela-tionship". Anyway it's time to bring you together for your mutual benefit. His cover name has featured in your most recent reports. Lew Corrigan.'

It was a bombshell. 'That bastard!'

'Maybe not quite the bastard you think,' Clarissa said. 'He'd got a message to us through his controller about that proxy bombing with the baker. *You* didn't set off the explo-sion by design or by accident. There was another radar gun in the vicinity – the operation was run by 14 Int. It was their decision to detonate it prematurely, to save the border-post and hopefully you and Corrigan. Apparently they thought the baker was playing a double game anyway.'

'Obviously you and Corrigan got on well,' Nash observed dryly. 'But that antagonism would strengthen your argument as well as your cover, if you are known to dislike each other, but both recommend the idea to Moylan.'

'Do you think the two of you could make it work?' Lavender urged.

But Avery was adamant. '*Someone* can give it a try, sure. The Provos might take it up. But not me. I've had enough.'

'There is no one else,' Clarissa explained patiently. 'We've got no one else with the reputation you've established with the Provos for pulling things off. Moylan may be suspicious of you, Max, but they can *only* be suspicious. We've made you indispensable to them, otherwise they wouldn't still be involving you. We had you work with the Libyans once before, but Corrigan has had no dealings with them or other Arabs, and he hasn't got your underworld contacts in Britain or Europe, so he couldn't do it alone. But together you can back each other up.'

Avery understood the arguments, the sense of it, but he had waited for this day for too long. 'I'm sorry, Clarry, I'm out.'

A tense silence followed, broken by the sound of Lavender stirring his coffee, the spoon chiming against the china cup. 'That's where you are wrong, Max.'

'Ralph, please –' Clarissa began.

Lavender turned on her sharply. 'No, he's got to be told.' He looked at Avery. 'Your common-law wife, this Margaret O'Malley. We have evidence we've been sitting on for six years. Aiding and abetting specific acts of terrorism between '82 and '84. We've got the dates, the places, witnesses and corroborated statements. If you refuse to co-operate, Max, there's no guarantee it'll all be forgotten. These orders come from the very top and you know what happens if the Security Service is ordered to leave you both out in the cold. It's happened before.'

Avery was furious. This was a clear case of moral black-mail and he did not believe for one moment that Lavender, let alone Clarry, would carry out such a threat. 'Get stuffed.' He rose to his feet. 'If you won't pull us out, then I'll make my own arrangements.' He began walking towards the door.

Lavender's voice was icy: 'Try that and I promise you, you will be put on trial for the murder of that baker in Northern Ireland. We've got full testimony from Corrigan on what happened. It seems you neglected to mention in your report that it was you who held the radar gun . . .'

The door slammed. Avery stood in the hallway, seething. Lavender's words of betrayal spun giddily round his head and he found himself trembling with suppressed rage.

'Max, wait.' It was Clarissa. 'Don't be hasty. Ralph is an arsehole – I'm sorry, not very ladylike, but true. He was terri-fied you were going to turn us down. It was just a stupid bluff and you called it. I told him you wouldn't give in to threats.'

'Are you sure?' Avery glared at her. 'He was right – it's happened to others.'

She looked into his eyes, at last recognising some of the fire she remembered. 'If the Service tried to do that to you they'd have my resignation.'

'And I could be facing life in prison,' he told her bluntly. 'And Maggie, what would she get? Then there's the kid . . .'

Clarissa said soothingly: 'When all this started you told me you weren't sure how you felt about Maggie. You agreed to work for your old army salary with a special bonus and any profits you made from the legitimate business. You've lived well and have some savings, but once the Service pulls its money out and the overdraft and commercial debts are repaid, you won't exactly be worth a fortune.' She smiled gently. 'I remember you said you fancied a sheep farm in Australia. Or was it New Zealand? Well, I doubt you'll have enough for that. But you could have . . .' She left the bait hanging.

Avery's anger flared again, a fire that refused to go out. 'What is this with you and Lavender – the hard man, soft man routine – the threats and the bribes?'

'No bribes, Max,' Clarissa rebuked, herself becoming angry now. 'You'll earn every penny if you go through with this, believe me. I'm all too aware of the risk I'm asking you to take. But the reward will be the sort of treatment that only supergrasses get paid out of public funds. A settlement running to a quarter of a million pounds sterling, re-allocation expenses to wherever you choose and complete new identities for all three of you. That's a pretty secure future for your son.'

He looked at her coldly. 'Forgive me if I don't sound grateful.'

'Oh, be grateful, Max, be grateful. I'll spare you the details of the fight I had to get that for you. The powers that be are delighted with the loyalty and service of people like you. They're just not so keen on paying for it.'

Avery took a deep breath, accepted one of her cigarettes and thought for a moment. 'So it's a case of accepting the Service's generosity or risking its wrath – your personal resignation aside?'

She looked at him reproachfully. 'Your country really does need you, Max. Sorry.'

He shook his head slowly, hardly believing that she had got him to the point of acceptance. Broken him down, demolished his will. Once again the politicians and the face-less mandarins in the corridors of power held all the cards. Had he really forgotten the lessons he'd learned in the Falklands? Was he really willing to be manipulated and used again?

Clarissa saw she had him on the run, saw that his resolve was crumbling. It needed just one final push. 'I've never let you down, Max, and I won't now. I'm taking every precaution to see you accomplish this task in one piece.' She stepped towards the front door. 'There's someone I'd like you to meet.'

Outside another vehicle was parked alongside Vergeer's prized Jensen. It was a red Volvo, the nearside wing and headlight shattered.

'Meet one of your guardian angels,' Clarissa said. 'They've been watching over you for the past week.'

The man was leaning against the driver's door, reading

a British tabloid newspaper. He was of stocky build, probably aged around forty although the tanned face and short
haircut made him look younger.

As he looked up, Avery's eyes narrowed. He knew the
face, had once known it well.

The other man grinned at him. 'It's been a long time,
Max.' He tossed the paper into the open car window and
took a step forward. 'How are you, mate?'

'Christ,' Avery breathed. 'Brian! Brian Hunt! You old
sod!'

Clarissa stepped discreetly back inside the hallway. She
would give the two old comrades time alone. As she walked
slowly towards the lounge she felt oddly moved. For a
second she had glimpsed Avery's face, seen a moment of
absolute pleasure as he set eyes on the man he had served
alongside in the SAS for some eight years. Whatever there
was between the two men she had no part in it. She was
excluded and found herself experiencing a mild sensation
of jealousy. Or was it envy? There was something about the
brotherhood of the battlefield – the death, the maiming,
the stark terror and the black humour of it all – that no
outsider could share or really understand.

In the lounge Lavender was pouring more coffee and
helping himself to the sandwiches Avery had left untouched
on his plate.

'You're a bastard, Ralph,' she said with feeling.

He looked up, a cynical and complacent expression on
his face. 'It worked, didn't it?'

'It worked.'

# Seven

The light was fading when Avery reached Amsterdam.

He had returned his hired car to the airport before taking a train to the centre. The atmosphere in the city was unusually damp and depressing. The narrow alleyways of the red-light district seemed more subdued than usual. The prostitutes, with their peroxide hair and vulgar lingerie, appeared jaded and listless, tapping only half-heartedly on their windows as he passed. Seasoned professionals, they had done and seen it all before; they all knew business wouldn't recover until the war clouds lifted from the Gulf. Even the porn show touts lacked their usual persistence.

The rush hour was starting and he was forced to dodge between the hordes of cyclists racing home from work and the stealthy approach of the city's trams.

He found the *kroeg* on the banks of the Prinsengracht canal, lined with bare-limbed trees and flanked by the neck-and-bell gables of seventeenth-century artisans' dwellings. Apart from its name, the Bruine café was indistinguishable from its numerous rivals, which was presumably why Moylan had chosen it. As Avery opened the door the heat and fug and noisy chatter hit him. A glassy-eyed student brushed unsteadily against him, mumbled an obscenity and meandered away across the cobbled causeway. Avery noted the legend on the back of the youth's sweatshirt: *Good Boys go to Heaven Bad Boys go to Amsterdam*.

Too true, he mused, and went inside.

There was no sign of Moylan or Corrigan amongst the huddled groups of office workers at the tables, so he squeezed into a spare corner chair and ordered a Douwe Egbert's coffee from the fat, balding *patron*.

Idly Avery glanced at the faces around him. If one of Hunt's men was already there, he could not have picked him out. It had been the same as he walked the narrow lanes and crossed the canal bridges: he knew he was under surveillance but, even when routinely checking for shadows he saw nothing unusual. A drunk here, a junkie there, a smart diamond dealer, a secretary or a housewife out shopping. Of course, any one might have been not quite what they seemed.

He allowed himself a ghost of a smile. It was strange to think that he felt better now than he had for weeks, or perhaps even years if he were honest. Meeting Brian Hunt again had been a real tonic.

Now that he had made his decision he felt an immense sense of relief. And that was despite his own misgivings and Ralph Lavender's clumsy attempt to blackmail him.

Things had changed. He was no longer alone, living a lie that he couldn't even share with the closest person in his life. The sense of suffocation and the creeping neurosis had eased, the walls pushed back.

He was part of a real team again. Perversely the prospects of a few more months suddenly didn't seem so bad. They had transformed the game, changed the rules. He had a specific goal to aim for, a definite assignment to achieve.

He looked up at the corner-mounted television, the newscaster ignored by the other customers, the voice-over describing the pictures of warships and lines of American soldiers queuing to enter the gargantuan C-141 Starlifter transport aircraft. No longer surreal images. War was coming, and he was part of it.

The *patron* placed his coffee on the table and pocketed the money in his grease-smeared apron. 'If you want the lavatory it's at the top of the stairs,' he said in English, without being asked.

So that was it. With the comings and goings at the busy café, no one would notice if someone disappeared inside for an hour or two. Avery downed his coffee and stood up. The doorway was behind the cash desk, steep wooden stairs leading directly up to the next floor. Each step creaked as he mounted it, the stair well lit by a single feeble bulb without a shade.

As he reached the landing he caught the pervasive odour of stale urine before he saw the open toilet door.

'Max?' Corrigan was standing on the next flight. 'We're up here.'

Avery followed, wondering yet again how he was going to handle the problem. The American was in deep. According to Clarry, his CIA controller had been unable to make safe contact for some time. It would be up to Avery to make the running, to explain that they were on the same side.

Con Moylan was sitting at a table in the upstairs room. Tobacco smoke filled the confined tent-like space formed by the sloping ceilings.

'I take it you weren't followed?' the Irishman asked.

'Do you mean the green Fiat?' Avery replied tartly as he crossed the bare boards and took a spare seat.

Moylan's thick brows knitted together in a frown. 'What?'

'A green Fiat appeared to follow me from the airport to my appointment at lunchtime.' He looked steadily at the Irishman. 'He lost me, but I can do without that sort of hassle, Con. Either you trust me or you don't. And if you don't, you can go stuff yourself.'

Concern showed in Moylan's eyes. 'It was nothing to do with me, Max, or you wouldn't have known. Are you positive you shook it off?'

'Positive.'

Corrigan leaned back in his chair. 'Not getting jumpy are you, Max?' he goaded.

Avery ignored the provocation, more concerned with Moylan's questions.

'And what *was* this lunchtime appointment of yours?' the Irishman continued casually.

'A car dealer with an old Jensen Interceptor for sale at an exorbitant price,' Avery answered with equal unconcern.

Moylan cut the cat and mouse game short. 'Let's get on. What have you got for me?'

Avery went through the list. He had located a suitable

lock-up garage in Sidcup, Kent. The owner had been happy to accept three months' cash rental in advance, which was paid over by a friend of one of Avery's underworld contacts. The man claimed to be a mechanic who wanted to do some moonlighting on car repairs. There was no official contract, no traceable paperwork. The taxman, it seemed, was the common enemy.

With the housing market in deep recession there was a glut of properties available at knock-down prices. Avery gave details of three, the most suitable being a shabby base-ment flat in Bounds Green, north London, which had been repossessed by the building society.

'I like it,' Moylan said. 'Basements are best. No one ever notices people slipping off the street, no overhead footsteps to tell neighbours when someone's in or out.' He slid a piece of paper across the table with a name and telephone number on it.

'What's this?'

'He's a bus-station manager. Squeaky clean. Hasn't been back to the Province for twelve years. But he pledged alle-giance after his son was killed by the Brits when he was joy-riding in a stolen car. Just say the Magician sends his regards. He'll know who it is. Tell him to make an offer for the flat. He can collect the cash from one of your friendly bookies.'

Avery nodded. 'And short lets on the flat?'

Moylan smiled slyly. 'That works best. Foreign students or labourers. But nothing after January, I'll want it vacant by then.'

They continued through the list, Avery advising on the progress of each item.

At last they were finished and Moylan seemed more relaxed. Avery seized his opportunity. 'D'you reckon there's going to be a war in the Gulf, Con?' he asked conversationally.

The Irishman laughed harshly. 'Frankly I don't give a stuff – unless it gets a few more Brit soldiers off the Ulster streets. And off our backs.'

Avery feigned hurt at the rebuff. 'Perhaps you *should* give more than a stuff. You could make it work to your advantage.'

Moylan appeared suddenly to notice the intense, expression on the other man's face. 'What the hell are you talking about, Max?'

'It just strikes me that the world is holding its breath in case Saddam Hussein decides to launch some kind of preemptive terror campaign in Europe or the States. Maybe he'd pay good money to have the job done for him.'

Moylan stared, clearly surprised by the apparent seriousness of the suggestion. 'Us to do it? You mean the Provies? Are you winding me up?'

'I expect the bastard would pay well. We could probably name our own price.' Avery glanced down at the jottings on his notepad. 'And judging by the amounts you're allocating on this job, you could do with an injection of funds. I guess that legit laundered money suffers in recession like everything else.'

'It's a bloody stupid idea,' Corrigan growled from across the table. 'Everyone will be watching the Iraqis worldwide. You can bet your sweet ass there'll be a CIA guy outside every embassy and satellites will be monitoring all their radio traffic.'

For a moment Avery was surprised by the American's uncharacteristic outburst; usually he was enthusiastic about every act of terrorism they'd discussed. But, of course, he wouldn't have been expecting this. It wasn't why he was in the game. Avery realised now that Corrigan would try to kill at birth any suggestion that put the United States in the firing line. He would get no support from the man until he had the chance to talk to him in private. Meanwhile he would have to argue his case as best he could.

'That's the whole point, Con. Everyone's busy watching the Iraqis and the Arab terror groups. By comparison we can move freely in the West. Saddam would see the advantage of that.'

Corrigan pulled a panatella cigar from his shirt pocket and pointed it accusingly at Avery. 'That is a dangerous move you're suggesting, Max, so drop it. It would mean risking the whole network we've so carefully built up over the years. Dealing with the Arabs at this time would be bloody suicidal. And for what? The benefit of some crackpot dictator who can't be trusted anyway?'

'No, Lew,' Avery retorted. 'For several million dollars that our organisation could sorely do with.' He glanced at Moylan, saw the light of interest in his eyes. 'And no doubt some personal commission for those involved.'

Moylan stroked his chin thoughtfully. 'It's a nice idea, Max, I grant you that. But it would take too long to set up. That UN deadline runs out in the New Year . . .'

Avery went for the jugular. 'Then offer them an off-the-shelf package. This operation we're working on now, for instance. I don't know exactly what you've got in mind, but it all points to an attack on a Cabinet minister. That's something Saddam wouldn't turn down lightly.'

The Irishman frowned reproachfully. 'That's not for you to even speculate.'

'Why are you so goddamn fired up about this, Max?' Corrigan demanded suddenly. 'A few days ago you wanted out.'

A sarcastic smile. 'Maybe I've changed my mind. Maybe I could do with the money. Besides, that visit to Ireland had made me nervous.'

'And maybe your nerves have affected your brains,' Corrigan retorted. He blew a ring of smoke contemptuously in Avery's direction. 'We couldn't get anywhere near the Iraqis without the Americans or the British finding out.'

'We could contact them through a third party,' Avery suggested. 'Like the Libyans.'

Moylan shook his head. 'We're out of touch with them by mutual consent since the mid-80s.'

'I'm not,' Avery said with an air of triumph. 'You probably don't know, but a couple of years ago Gerry Fox asked me to open up a channel with them to get some more anti-aircraft missiles. I don't think it came to anything, but I kept in touch with my Libyan contact.'

It was mostly true. Only it had in fact been a 'sting' operation developed by Clarissa Royce-Jones. Avery had reported Fox bemoaning the need for more weapons to bring down helicopters and she had fed Avery the contact who was a genuine member of the Libyan *Mukhabarat* stationed in Malta. Avery had an initial meeting with the man and they set in motion a series of negotiations for others to follow up in Stockholm, Geneva and Vienna. Avery then distanced himself from the whole business, although he had kept in irregular telephone contact with the Libyan ever since.

The deal had come to nothing because the operation had led to the arrest of two of the Provisional negotiators by the Anti-Terrorist Branch six months later. Libyan diplomats were expelled from several countries and the missiles never even left Tripoli.

'Well I think it stinks,' Corrigan said. 'I'm in this for Ireland, not the bloody Arabs.'

Avery ignored him. 'The Libyans could make the necessary connections with Saddam Hussein. It's at least worth a try.'

Moylan was circumspect, but clearly toying with the idea. 'I could put it to the Army Council, I suppose.'

'You owe it to them,' Avery persisted. 'At least give them the opportunity to reject it. Despite Lew's objections, we can't run this campaign on goodwill, Guinness and rebel songs. It takes money to fight a war, and a lot of it.'

'If we helped Saddam Hussein we'd alienate our entire membership,' Corrigan interjected angrily.

Avery turned on him. 'We just claim any acts as our own.'

Corrigan glared back. 'Saddam Hussein would want the world to know.'

'You don't understand Arab thinking, Lew. I think you'll find that Saddam will be happy enough for just the British Government – and Washington – to know privately he was behind it. And I don't think the allies would see any mileage in going public, do you? If they did, we'd just deny it. I know who our supporters would believe.'

After a considerable pause Con Moylan reached his decision. 'I'll raise the matter at the next meeting of the Army Council.'

Margaret O'Malley had just put Josh to bed when the doorbell rang. She had been expecting the Avon sales representative and so picked up the money for her cosmetics order from the hall table. It occurred to her that it was unusually late for the girl to call: outside it was dark and wet, a strong wind rattling the tree branches in the garden of the flats.

'A filthy night . . .' she began as she threw open the door.

'It is that,' the man agreed.

She gave a small gasp of surprise and immediately began closing the door. 'I was expecting someone else,' she explained nervously.

'Sorry to startle you, Maggie.' The accent was Irish, the tone apologetic.

Her eyes narrowed as she attempted to discern the face that was cast in shadow by the peak of his flat cap. 'Do I know you?'

He chuckled. 'No, but I'm an acquaintance of your husband. My name's Danny.'

She relaxed a little, her initial wariness replaced by irritation that the man should call unannounced. 'Max is away on business in Holland.'

'I know that, missus, it's you I wanted to see.' He tilted his head to one side, and she could see from the hallway light that he was smiling.

A crawling sensation rippled over the tiny hairs at the nape of her neck. 'Me?' Apprehension was clear in her voice. She edged the door further closed; it met with his foot. 'Are you a friend of Gerry Fox?'

The smile persisted, but he didn't answer her question. 'I just want a wee word.'

'I'm not interested!' she snapped suddenly and pushed hard against the door. With her free hand she reached for the security chain. But it was too short, the space too wide.

'Don't worry, lady,' the man said. 'It won't take long.'

'Go away,' she pleaded, pushing the full weight of her shoulder against the door, but inexorably the gap yawned. Her strength was no match for his.

She staggered back, defeated, her hands clutching at the throat of her nurse's tunic. 'What do you want?'

Grogan stepped into the hallway, glancing around with a nod of approval. 'A nice place you have here.'

She said the first thing that came into her head. 'You'll wake the baby.'

'We can talk quietly. No need to disturb the wee lad. Sure, you could make me a nice cup o' tea.'

Unnerved but feeling slightly reassured by his mild

manner, she led him reluctantly to the kitchen. As the water drummed into the kettle she watched him while he removed his sodden raincoat and cap. His face was long, the pale skin the colour of potato flesh and his eyes small and bright like raisins. His black hair was combed straight back across his scalp and curled at the collar of a black polo neck. There was something about him that she found unsavoury, but his manner was not threatening. He appeared quite relaxed.

She plugged in the kettle on the worktop and suddenly the face appeared in her mind again, the duo-coloured eyes boring into her, stripping away her defences. Ever since Max had casually mentioned it, she hadn't been able to get the vision out of her head. It was like a small voice calling out, taunting her. Forgotten memories had chased her, coming vividly and unbeckoned into focus. His face close to hers, his smile fixed with grim satisfaction, his expression one of mild curiosity, watching her reaction as his body pummelled into hers.

'Is this anything to do with Con Moylan?'

He sat astride one of the pine chairs as though it were a horse, his arms folded across its back. 'So you know Max is working for Con?'

'He said they'd met,' she answered cautiously. 'That there might be some business.'

Grogan smiled slyly. 'Some vehicle-leasing contracts, that sort of thing.'

'What's that got to do with me?'

'We feel we don't know enough about your husband –

especially as there's a lot at stake.' He took a pack of cigarettes from his pocket and lit one. 'As you and Max are shacked up, I thought who better to ask?'

They were playing games and they both knew it. Maggie glowered. 'I don't like smoke in the place. It's bad for the baby.'

He ignored her, pointedly exhaling in her direction. 'So tell me when you met Max.'

'I'm sure you know all this.'

'Remind me.'

It was a simple enough request, hardly the third degree. She took a resigned breath and poured boiling water into the teapot. 'It wasn't long after I came over from Derry. My first year in nursing and I went to night school to learn how to cook properly. I was getting sick of fry-ups and beans on toast.'

'Bad for the figure,' he mused, staring blatantly at her breasts, letting his eyes wander down to her hips. 'No problem now though.'

Her eyes hardened. 'I met Max at the class, we got talking and . . .' she hesitated to use the word while under Grogan's cynical gaze '. . . fell in love. That's all.'

'You joined at the same time?'

'No.'

'Who was there first? You or him? It's important.'

'He joined a couple of weeks after me.'

'What did you know about him?'

'Then? Not a lot. Just that he was born in Liverpool. His parents were Irish, we had that in common. But he wasn't very talkative in those days. He's still quiet really, a bit of a loner.'

Grogan studied the smoke spiralling from his cigarette. 'You didn't ask him about his past?'

'Not at first. I didn't want to pry and he wasn't very forthcoming. Besides it wasn't that sort of relationship. A bit of a laugh really, a lot of joking.'

A salacious chuckle. 'You mean he was a horny bastard? You spent all your time screwing?'

Anger coloured her cheeks. She wanted to tell him to go screw himself, then perversely she felt a surge of defiance. 'Yes we did as a matter of fact. We didn't get much time together and – no – when we did, there wasn't much serious talking. The meaning of life and the universe came later. Good enough?'

'So you knew bugger all about his background?'

'Not immediately. But after a while he told me more – gradually, as time went by.'

'You tell me.'

'What exactly?' Irritable.

Grogan refused to be rattled. 'Try at the beginning.'

'Well, as I said, his parents were Irish. County Clare, I think.'

'Avery isn't an Irish name.'

Her eyes flashed angrily. 'I know that. Do you want me to tell you this or not?' To her surprise he smiled as demurely as his thick lips would allow. She poured some tea into a mug and thrust it at him before she continued. 'The family name is O'Reilly. Max's grandfather fought against the

Black and Tans and his father helped the old IRA as a wee boy before he joined the Royal Navy. A stoker, I think, just before the Second World War. He stayed on until '48, according to Max, and tried to set up his own car repair business in his old home town. But it was a depressed time and he couldn't make a go of the business. He went to Liverpool to look for work. That's when he met Max's mother and they got married. Max was born in 1950.'

'And they called him Max?' Grogan raised his eyebrows, watching her reaction carefully.

She glared at the stranger in her kitchen, resentful of his prying into the innocent secrets of her family. 'He was christened Patrick O'Reilly. He changed his name later by deed poll, but you must know that. Ask Gerry Fox, he knows all about Max.'

'Don't you assume what I know or don't know, lady. I'm being nice to you and that's not something I'm known for. So don't push your luck. Now continue.'

Once again she felt the caterpillar of fear on her neck. She swallowed hard, trying to gather her thoughts, praying that the Avon girl might yet call and interrupt this conversation. 'Er – Max's father got a job as a car mechanic in Liverpool. Max had a normal childhood as far as I know. That was until the crash.'

'Crash?' He feigned ignorance, keen to hear her version of events; if Avery were an informer it was possible she was involved in the duplicity. And although he'd heard about the accident he had not yet received the details from the Army Council in Dublin.

'There was a car crash when Max was – I don't know – eleven or twelve, about that age. Both his parents died. There were no surviving relatives so Max was sent to Dr Barnardo's.'

'Where?'

'In Liverpool, or maybe Manchester. It was when he left there that he changed his name. The boys had kept calling him Old Mother Reilly or Potato Paddy, and he hated it.'

'When did he join the British Army?'

'He became a cadet while at Barnardo's, and then just drifted into it. A lot of Barnardo's kids join the forces. He'd have been about seventeen, I suppose.'

'So he was in at the time the Troubles flared in '69?'

Maggie could see the dangerous ground that she was on, but then she was sure Gerry Fox knew. Max had never made a secret of it. 'Yes. In fact he did one or two tours with the Parachute Regiment. But he hated it. As you know the Paras aren't renowned for their manners or social niceties. He got caught up in the Bloody Sunday massacre in January '72. That's what really did it for him. He was deeply cut up, but could hardly let it show to his mates. As far as he was concerned the Paras might just as well have shot his own father or grandfather. That's what it felt like. He was out by the next year. I think he must have been just twenty-three. That brought us quite close together, if you must know, even though he had been on the other side, so to speak.'

'Your uncle? The one killed on Bloody Sunday?'

She was vaguely surprised; Con Moylan must have told him.

'You seem to know everything,' she said tartly.

'You'd better believe it,' Grogan murmured. 'So what did your hero do when he left the army?'

'Got into trouble mostly from what I can gather. I know he worked for a firm of scrap metal dealers, on and off. Then he went to prison after a pub fight. Later he went back to his old job but then got involved with some car thieves and then a robbery. He went down for six years for that. On his release he moved to London to start again with a clean slate. He'd just started importing those cheap little French cars when I first met him. I'm sure you must know the rest.'

Grogan drained his tea. 'I know the rest,' he confirmed and stood up. 'But there are a few gaps. Like which pub did he have the fight in? Where was this scrap metal firm he worked for?'

'I don't know.'

He picked up his raincoat, slipped it over his shoulders. 'Then find out. Try a bit of pillow talk, reminisce after a good fuck. Small details, that's what I need to know.'

She glared. 'Why?'

Grogan retrieved his cap from the table. 'Because my friends want to know.'

'Tell them to go to hell!'

The thick red lips curled into their now familiar smile-cum-sneer. 'Where's the baby sleep? This room here?'

'What?'

Her mouth dropped, his sudden movement catching her off guard. Before she could cross the kitchen floor he

was already into the passageway. The door, with its neat
china plaque bearing the legend Baby's Room, had already
swung open.

'How dare you!'

He turned on her, grabbing her arm fiercely. 'Sssh!' he
hissed. She felt her skin bruising beneath his grip. 'You don't
want to wake the wee chap.'

She trembled as Grogan peered into the darkened room.
It smelled milky, sickly sweet. A soft gurgling sound came
from the Mickey Mouse cot.

Satisfied, Grogan quietly closed the door. 'Handsome wee
lad, lady.' He looked directly at her. 'Now you'd like him to
grow up into a handsome young man like his da, wouldn't
you, eh? Not disfigured with acid or anything like that. Don't
want him to meet with any accidents, do we?'

No words came to her mouth. Her mind was numbed
and her body just wouldn't stop shaking. She stared at
Grogan with a mixture of horror and disbelief.

He said softly: 'So you find out those things I want to
know, there's a good girl. But do it discreetly, eh? And not
a word to Max. We'll keep it just between you, me and the
wee laddie.'

You bastard! she wanted to scream, but she was too terrified to speak.

The doorbell chimed.

Suddenly she broke free of her paralysis and rushed to
the door, expecting the stranger to be at her heels and anticipating the feel of his fingers around her throat at any
moment.

She reached the lock handle and threw the door wide. 'Floyd!' Her gasp was ecstatic.

'Mrs A.' he acknowledged, taken aback by the enthusiasm of her welcome. 'Nice t'know someone's pleased to see me. I've brought over some of the accounts ledgers for Max.'

She dared not look back over her shoulder. 'Come in, come in.'

He stepped onto the mat. 'Oh, sorry, didn't know you had company. I should've phoned.'

Grogan was standing casually in the hallway, arms folded across his chest and an amused expression on his face. Maggie said: 'It's all right, he's just going.'

For a moment the Irishman didn't move, his eyes meeting her glare of defiance. Then he shuffled forward, nodded to Floyd as he passed, then turned. 'I'll be in touch. Thanks for the tea.'

Floyd watched him go, then turned back to Maggie. She was ashen-faced, still trembling. 'Are you all right, Mrs A.?'

She clutched his wrist in an attitude of heartfelt relief. 'Thank you, Floyd, I'm fine.'

The three men left the *kroeg* separately.

Avery went first, Corrigan and Moylan watching from the small window beneath the gable end until the Englishman had crossed the nearest canal bridge without incident and disappeared from view.

Corrigan was next. He left the smoky warmth of the

café and set his face against the raw chill of the wind. His pace was brisk as he set off towards the Amstel canal, scarcely noticing the cold. He had other things on his mind, namely Max Avery.

Until now he had been interested in knowing more about the man in order to provide some evidence of his work for the CIA London Desk chief to hand over to the British. A favour to America's closest ally in the fight against world terrorism. But that had suddenly changed. Avery was more dangerous than even he had realised. Much more dangerous.

The scheme that had been suggested to assist Saddam Hussein had taken him by surprise, as had Moylan's obvious interest in it. Moreover he knew that Avery had a reputation for delivering the goods; he even claimed to have a suitable Libyan go-between. It was bad news. Such an alliance between the Provisionals and the Iraqis could rupture the delicate alliance that had formed in the wake of the Kuwait invasion. If Britain pulled out, the other nations would surely follow and leave an isolated United States facing a humiliating climb-down.

Corrigan's remit was to help London defeat the Provisional IRA, but when push came to shove his over-riding loyalty had to be to his own government.

There was one advantage in being without official cover, he reflected as he reached the sleazy district around Thorbeckplein.

Free of official restraints, he could take whatever action he saw fit. And Lew Corrigan had no doubt that he needed to act fast, to nip dangerous events in the bud while he was in a position to do so. He considered his options, but the need to move fast cancelled almost all of them.

It was not difficult to buy a gun in Amsterdam if you knew where to look, and Corrigan did. Some years before, he had operated in Holland on secondment to the Drug Enforcement Administration and had come to know the violent world of the narcotics dealers well.

He found the tawdry strip joint easily enough. Nothing much had changed except that the prices were higher and the girls, now mostly Indonesian, looked more bored and weary than ever.

The owner remembered him, vaguely, and they had a beer together while Corrigan stated his business.

A new Smith and Wesson automatic would cost around one thousand three hundred guilders. But if he could wait a few days there was some interesting stuff coming in from the old Eastern Bloc at tempting prices.

Corrigan said he wanted immediate delivery. That severely limited the choice and the gun could not be guaranteed as 'clean'. It was always possible he could go down for a crime he didn't commit.

He settled on a heavy Webley .455 revolver that dated back to the Second World War for eight hundred guilders, then a further eight hundred 'rush charge' to include a small plastic sachet of crack. Long ago having learned the benefits of being cash-rich in his line of business, he handed over a wad of notes from the moneybelt secreted around his waist.

With the deal struck he crossed the cobbled street to a late-night bar, ordered a *vieux* brandy and took it to the payphone where he looked up the number of the hotel where Max Avery was staying. As he dialled the number it reminded Corrigan that the Englishman had raised the question of which hotels each was using at the meeting earlier. Moylan had pounced like a cobra, reminding them that they shouldn't be seen together under any circumstances. Bar-crawling was strictly off the agenda.

Avery answered.

'Hi, Max, how'ya doin'?' Corrigan deliberately put a slur on his words.

'I'm glad you called, Lew. I've been trying to ring you for the last hour.'

Corrigan was mildly surprised. 'Haven't been back to my hotel yet. Can't go to Amsterdam and not go a-whorin'!' He forced a chuckle. 'Why you tryin' to get in touch?'

'Sounds like the same problem as you. It's a depressing place to be alone. Wondered if you fancied a drink?'

'My thoughts exactly, pal. That's why I'm callin'!' He added quickly: 'Your hotel will be best, my place is the pits. I'll bring a bottle. Con won't like it, but what the hell. I won't tell him if you don't. So what room number are you?'

Corrigan hung up, ordered another *vieux* and a bottle of whisky, then sat down to wait. Fifteen minutes later a furtive-looking youth arrived to hand over the brown-paper package. He took it to the lavatory and opened it, casting an expert eye over the weapon. It was chipped and worn on the outside, but had been kept clean and oiled. He loaded it and checked that everything functioned satisfactorily.

He holstered it in the rear of his trouser waistband and pocketed the sachet of crack. After the killing he would sprinkle minute quantities in Avery's luggage. Just sufficient for the police forensic experts to conclude that this was just another feud between narcotics dealers.

After a fifteen-minute walk he found the Blauw Zwaan in a back street between the Prinsengracht and Lijnbaansgracht canals. It was a tall, narrow tourist-class hotel that looked as though it were a family-run concern. It was late now and the lobby was empty, so he was able to slip inside unnoticed and take the stairs to Avery's room.

'Good to see you, Lew.'

For a moment Corrigan was thrown by the warmth of the Englishman's welcome; they both knew this was a friendship of convenience in a lonely city. 'Yeah, you too, Max.' He thrust out the bottle of whisky. 'First things first, eh? I'm bushed, you pour.'

Without waiting for a response he walked across the cramped bedroom to one of the two armchairs by the window, removed the scatter cushion, and slumped down. He dropped the cushion back on his lap and exhaled with a sigh. 'These Indonesian broads sure know a trick or two. I'm knackered.' As he spoke he slipped free the Webley with one hand and eased it around his side until it rested, concealed on his lap.

Avery turned from the bedside table, a plastic tumbler

in each hand. 'I was afraid I wouldn't get a chance to talk to you alone . . .'

An offered target. Standing right in front of him. No point in waiting. Get it over.

'Sounds like you're makin' a pass, Max.' Say anything. Thumb easing back the hammer. Muzzle pressed into the cushion to silence the blast.

'I know all about you, Lew.'

Sweet Jesus, another unwelcome surprise from this bastard. Then he was just in time. Had Avery already told Moylan? No matter. Time for that later. It just vindicated his decision. There could be no reprieve now.

Corrigan's finger tightened around the trigger.

# Eight

Avery had no idea how close he had come to death.

'Willard Franks sends his regards, Lew.'

There was an imperceptible narrowing of the eyes as Corrigan registered the use of the familiar name; his trigger finger was tense, poised.

Avery smiled. 'We're on the same side, Lew. It's true – you're with the CIA and I'm with British security.'

Very, very slowly Corrigan lowered the cushion on his lap, his thumb easing on the safety.

Then Avery's jaw had dropped. 'Sweet Jesus,' he had breathed.

He could smile about it now as he drove his BMW back from London's Heathrow airport in warm autumn sunshine. He was buoyed by a renewed sense of purpose, of being part of a team again with his old friend Brian Hunt. That and the promise of an elaborate new identity and financial security for his family's future.

But for a few stark seconds the previous night it had all been very different as he stared into the muzzle of Corrigan's gun.

To begin with the American had been understandably

very reluctant to accept the bizarre situation in which he found himself.

Avery, standing with a whisky glass in each hand, had managed a nervous smile. 'Let's drink this stuff before you shoot me, Lew. It would be a shame to spill it.'

A full half-hour passed, with Avery outlining the joint assignment proposed for them, before Corrigan finally began to accept what the Englishman told him. It was an odd experience – two virtual strangers sitting in the small room of the canalside hotel, revealing the truth about each other as they worked steadily through the whisky bottle.

Avery learned that the reality, if not the substance of Lew Corrigan's background was almost as fake as his own. The man's parents had emigrated to the States when their son was eight years old. His father became a cop on the 75th Police Precinct which, as they also lived in the ghetto tenement area of East New York, did young Lew no favours at all.

Anxious to prove his manhood with the tough Irish street gangs, Corrigan dissociated himself from his father and threw himself enthusiastically into the tribal warfare rituals of the concrete jungle. At the age of fifteen he had virtually abandoned Jefferson High and by eighteen he had already been charged with numerous petty offences. Now the state penitentiary beckoned.

'It was a fair fight,' Corrigan recalled, the whisky mellowing the rough edge of his voice, 'but I'd beat the guy pretty good. My lawyer was a broad in the days you didn't see many female lawyers. Even then she seemed young to me. Good-looking too. But I didn't reckon I stood a chance with a broad defending me. I was wrong. She could see where I'd end up. An institutionalised hoodlum.

'I could have died when my old man turned up in court. Starched shirt and best Sunday suit. All upright and a pillar of respectability. It was her idea, of course. It took some balls for him to stand up and admit I was his son. A cop's son and I had let him down because of the pressures of his job in the toughest neighbourhood in town. When that broad finished there wasn't a dry eye in the house. She pleaded that I deserved a chance, and persuaded the judge to send me into the army rather than to prison. My old man agreed. It was the luckiest break of my life.'

He was just out of bootcamp when the first stirrings of war were heard from a distant land. A place of which young Corrigan had never even heard. Vietnam.

Anxious for excitement he had volunteered for the Green Berets in which he served with distinction behind the lines in North Vietnam, Laos and Cambodia. When the new anti-terrorist Delta Force was formed in 1977 the commander Charlie Beckwith had personally head-hunted Corrigan. Within two years he was to experience the tragedy of the Desert One rescue mission to Iran.

'We did a lot more cross-training with the SAS after that,' he said. 'Maybe our paths even crossed.'

'Maybe. I met quite a few Delta people in the early eighties.'

Corrigan smiled at the memory. 'That's when someone had the bright idea – some SAS vet sergeant, I recall – of putting some Delta guys into Provo country. I'd been on a fishing trip to an old stamping ground in Eire and I mentioned what a fantastic reception I'd gotten from the locals. Told me things after a few pints they'd never tell a Brit tourist. That gave them the idea. Every summer they sent a few Delta guys on fishing or golfing holidays. We picked up a lot of intelligence.

'After '85 I was considered too old at forty for serious active service. I was still a senior training instructor at the Stockade, but I was occasionally seconded to the DEA and Point Four, the backup police unit for American aid. Then I was approached by Willard Franks. Said the CIA wanted to put someone in deep to unearth links with Noraid and the IRA. Someone had recommended me, so I went on another fishing trip, looking up my old Irish pals. One of them was that drunken barber O'Casey. One day I offered the local Provos a little specialist help for which they were very grateful. I was in.'

Avery had watched Corrigan with a certain detachment as they reached the bottom of the bottle. Both men were tired and not a little drunk. The American's personality had changed almost beyond recognition, the hard-faced façade dropped, his defences down. Avery understood the strain he had been under and how this private conversation must be a welcome unburdening. There could not be many people in the world with whom Corrigan could share his dark secrets.

Like the killing of the baker at the Ulster border-post. That had been the only time Avery had ever had to make such a cold-blooded decision about who lived or died. Although the final act had been mercifully taken out of his hands, it did not ease his conscience. He knew he had made that split-second decision: an innocent man was going to die so that he could live.

Just one decision. But how many times had Corrigan, physically assisting Provisional 'active service units', had to make such judgements? And how did he live with himself once he had made them?

He'd been tempted to say something, to express sympathy, but the moment passed when Corrigan said: 'I didn't like you, Max. The moment I saw you and knew what you were doing, I thought how can this sonofabitch do this? Betray his own countrymen?' He chuckled dryly, blew gently on the tip of his cigar until it glowed brightly. 'Little did I know we'd been fooling each other.'

Avery was still turning their conversation over in his mind when he pulled up outside the garden flat. As he opened the front door he heard the irritating whine of the washing-machine. He'd forgotten it was Maggie's day off; he found her hanging the baby's clothes up to dry in the bathroom.

As soon as she turned to face him he knew that something was wrong. Her eyes were red-rimmed and sunken from either too little sleep or too many tears.

'I've missed you, that's all, you darling man,' was her dismissive explanation. 'Silly, isn't it?'

He hadn't believed her for a moment and when he returned from spending the afternoon at the showroom he found her in the same subdued mood.

It wasn't until after supper that he found out what was really on her mind.

'Are you still going to do that work for Con Moylan?' She asked the question casually, too casually.

'It's just some business,' he answered evasively. It was so easy to lie now. Sometimes he wondered if he could still tell the truth, or know the difference.

'I don't understand you, Max. You've stopped seeing Gerry Fox, but now you're getting mixed up with Moylan.'

'This is legit.' Reassuring.

'Don't *lie* to me, Max.' Anger was creeping into her voice now. 'That's bullshit and you know it. So what *is* going on?'

He reached for her hand across the table. 'Listen, sweetheart, legit or not, this is the last thing I'm going to do for Fox or Con Moylan or any of them. I promise. You see, I've looked at the prospects of us selling up and moving away. I've had Floyd go over the books and I've spoken to the accountant. But there's a cash shortfall and trade is bad, really bad. This Gulf business with Kuwait is killing business. The money from Con Moylan will make all the difference.'

She began clearing the plates. 'If anything goes wrong, Max, they'll put you away for a long time. I'll be as good as a widow and Josh . . .'

He came behind her, encircling her waist with his arms. For a moment she resisted, holding herself rigid, then slowly, she melted.

'I'm doing this because I still *believe* it's right,' he murmured into her ear. 'I haven't forgotten Bloody Sunday and I'm sure you haven't forgotten your dead uncle. I want us out of Northern Ireland, it's only right. And until that happens the killing won't stop. Because you no longer approve of the methods, it doesn't mean you're right. I only wish there was some other way – but I have to fight for what I believe.'

Her voice was small. 'I respect you for that, Max. And I envy your certainty.'

'I'm also doing it for us. You and Josh and me. So we can let the likes of Fox and Con Moylan carry on the fight while we start to live again somewhere new. Just one more time, that's all.'

She turned around in his arms and looked up at him, a certain sparkle returning to her eyes. 'What is it that I see in you, Max? Let's go to bed.'

He went with her, satisfied that she was convinced.

In the quiet moments following their energetic love-making, Maggie said: 'Sometimes, Max, I don't think I really know you at all.'

He laughed. 'Perhaps you're better not to know.'

She giggled, snuggling close. 'No, honestly, I really would like to know more about your life before we met. You've never talked much about it. Your time at Barnardo's, what it was like in prison. I don't just want to share your future . . .'

Inwardly he groaned. More lies, more deceit. It pained him more than ever now. But, he reasoned, his cover had stood the test of time. It wouldn't hurt to run through it again, get the story right.

Thank you, Clarry.

'That's Max's home,' Brian Hunt said.

The two men were in the back of a van parked across the street from Avery's ground-floor apartment. A light shone through the drawn bedroom curtains.

'Lucky bastard,' Jim Buckley murmured.

Buckley was a Kentucky boy. At thirty-eight he still retained the upright bearing that had been drilled into him at Parris Island many years before. Although his waist had thickened with the passage of time, regular workouts had maintained his powerful chest and upper body muscles in prime condition. He walked with a slight military swagger that set him apart in a crowd. His hair was black and cropped and receding, the blunt clean-shaven face prone to regular scowling.

He exuded an air of strength and restrained menace despite his short stature; he did not look like the sort of man it was wise to cross. Only a glint of humour in the alert dark eyes gave a clue to the other side of his personality.

'Maggie's his common-law wife,' Hunt said. 'Typical Irish. A real looker and a fiery temper.'

'I've seen the photographs. Lucky bastard,' Buckley repeated.

Hunt smiled at Buckley's apparent envy. 'She's an odd one and no mistake. An ex-Provo turned nurse. Now into good causes in a big way. Max appears genuinely smitten though.'

'Smitten?' Buckley queried. 'What quaint expressions you limeys use. And she's the one that Grogan guy visited?'

Hunt nodded. 'Last night while Max was still in Amsterdam. Luckily we got to bug the place yesterday. Had the meter read by the electricity company.'

Buckley's face was impassive. 'Is there one in the bedroom?'

'No. Just the hallway and the living room.'

'Shame.'

'And the phone's tapped, of course. At the moment we're having to conduct our surveillance from vehicles.' He pointed to a boarded-up shop front across the pavement. Another victim of recession. 'But we move in there tonight. A good view of the front door.'

'Does this guy Grogan spell trouble?'

'I hope not. Max is an old friend of mine. But his cover's good and Box will be keeping tabs on Grogan.'

'Box?'

Hunt laughed. 'Another quaint expression. A nickname for GI5, which everyone still calls MI5. Complicated isn't it?' He glanced at his wristwatch. 'Time we were getting back. Your team should have arrived.'

The seven-man team from the United States' anti-terrorist Delta Force had flown into RAF Lyneham in Wiltshire from Fort Bragg earlier that day.

As Hunt had estimated, the Americans had only just finished unpacking their kit when the van arrived at the Duke of York's barracks in the King's Road, Chelsea. As the headquarters of the territorial reserve 21 SAS Regiment and of the Director of Special Forces himself, it was considered to be the most suitable base. It offered secure communications, ample accommodation space for the Delta and SAS teams assigned to Stalking Horse, and it was a reasonably short journey time from Avery's home and workplace on the far side of Chelsea Bridge.

The members had gathered in one of the smaller briefing rooms. It didn't surprise Hunt to find the British and American teams, all in civilian clothes, adopting an attitude of mutual cautious stand-off at opposite sides of the room.

'Nice to see you guys are all getting to know each other,' Buckley observed dryly as he entered with Hunt.

There were several rows of chairs in the centre which faced a wooden rostrum and large-scale maps of London on the wall behind it. However Hunt was keen to dispense with formality, wanting to encourage a rapid integration of the teams.

'Each of you grab a chair,' he ordered, 'and spread out to form a circle.' He waited for the instant movement and the noise to subside, noticing that there was one woman in the American team, a trim slightly stocky girl with short dark hair. With the ice and the segregation broken, he noted with a smile that the woman now had an SAS soldier on each side of her. 'Right, lady and gentlemen, good afternoon. By way of introduction, I am Sarn't-Major Brian Hunt. Any of you who have cross-trained with us in the SAS will know we are not too fond of ceremony and formality – indeed even less so than you Delta people. From now on I'm just straight Brian, or any other name you dare use to my face.'

The Americans glanced at each other and grinned; the SAS soldiers studied the reactions of the new arrivals without expression.

'Jim Buckley and I are in joint operational command of this rather unusual venture. Primarily we have a role as "babysitters" – street minders and surveillance technicians. You in Delta and the Regiment have all trained in this sort of work, but equally, most of you will be a little rusty. At the moment I have a small group of our best people looking after one of our undercover agents, a man called Max Avery, who is supposedly working for the Provisional IRA, and at the moment we can contain that situation.

'But if everything goes according to plan, our agent will be joined by one of yours, an old friend of Jim here, and the action may shift abroad. That should be to Athens, but there are no guarantees. It could, quite literally, be anywhere – and at a moment's notice. So we'll really have to be on our toes and work together. It is also likely that actual Irish terrorists will be travelling with our people. Obviously they must not be aware of your presence.

'So while things are quiet we've set up an intensive training and rehearsal programme for you all in London. You'll be required to keep up round-the-clock surveillance on two people as they move around the city, bearing in mind they may split up at any moment and you'll have to follow both of them. Any hotel or house they stop at will have to be bugged at short notice and everyone they meet duly photographed and any conversations recorded. In addition, you may be required to intervene discreetly if our agents face any kind of threat. Threat of discovery, threat from the terrorists who believe at the moment our people are genuine, threat from bona fide law officers – any threat to our men or, more importantly, the mission itself. What form such threats might take, when and where, is anybody's guess. We've thrown a few ideas into the training programme just to keep you sharp. But in the end, each and every one of you is going to have to use your initiative on the spot. I won't pretend it's going to be easy.'

The circle of faces remained solemn, but Hunt detected the eye movements, the twitch of a smile here and there. He could feel the undercurrent of suppressed excitement flowing through the group, almost smell the adrenalin. Easy or not, each one was looking forward to the challenge with not a little apprehension. He wondered if they realised just how tough it was likely to be.

'You'll all be tired after your long journey,' Hunt concluded, 'so spend this afternoon just getting to know each other and discuss various ways you're going to handle different situations and scenarios. Open forum with no pulling rank. Here we call it a Chinese Parliament. And no heavy boozing with your new-found chums tonight. The programme starts at 0900 hours tomorrow – including lectures on handling surveillance equipment from our security people. And remember there's no guarantee you'll see a bed again for the next three months.'

He and Jim Buckley left them to it then, each member given a dossier of all the vehicles, weapons and technical gadgetry that would be at their disposal. The two men locked themselves in Hunt's office with three MI5 operatives who the next day would play the roles of Avery, Corrigan and an unknown terrorist companion.

The three stooges would start the day at the Inn on the Park Hotel and move to three different rendezvous points around the city in the morning, where they would meet other volunteer agents drawn from 21 SAS. Sometimes the stooges would be together, sometimes they would separate. They would take elementary precautions to prevent themselves from being followed. There was no point in making everything too complex at this stage, because the first run for the surveillance teams was bound to end in chaos. At midday they would all meet up together for a debriefing and discuss what had gone wrong, how the teams could be improved and what changes should be made. In the afternoon they'd try again.

That evening Hunt and Buckley joined the teams in the sergeants' mess. The transformation had exceeded all expectations. Above the hubbub of earnest conversation and laughter, the clear clash of accents was audible and unmistakable, from hillbilly Kentucky and singsong southern States drawls to near incomprehensible Geordie and broad Scottish.

A fresh-faced American greeted them at the bar. 'Hi, Jim. Hi, Brian, what'll it be? My treat. I haven't enjoyed myself so much in years.'

They settled for beers. 'This is Buzz Berkeley,' Buckley introduced, 'after the film choreographer.'

'Just plain Buzz, sir,' the man said, running a hand through the shaven black hair that stood up like iron filings under a magnet. 'Buzz with the fuzz – you won't forget that.'

Hunt found Buzz's grin infectious. Despite his widely shared anti-American prejudices, which he decided were probably the cultural heritage of two World Wars, Hunt had always been mildly surprised how much he enjoyed the company of his trans-Atlantic cousins. 'How did the parliament go this afternoon? Sorry we couldn't be there.'

'That might have inhibited free thought anyway, sir,' the young man said with a thoughtful and serious expression on his face. 'Well, amongst us Americans anyway. Like you said, the US Army is more formal than you SAS guys, even in Delta.'

'Any new ideas?' Buckley asked.

'We all liked the four-man team idea. It divides neatly into the sixteen total and allows a one-team-on and one-team-off duty approach in quiet periods, given we've basically two guys to watch over. But we don't like the US and Brit divide. It doesn't give us the flexibility we need.'

'That could be a problem,' Buckley said. 'Different working methods, comms and weapons, and almost different languages.'

Hunt smiled. 'How's one of our Glaswegian lads going to communicate effectively with a Montana backwoods boy in a tight corner?'

'We can hack that, Brian, sir,' Buzz replied dismissively.

A very British expression, Hunt noted. 'Especially when you consider the benefits, like if we go to Athens. None of the Brits speak Greek, but four of us do. My mother is from Thessaloniki.'

Buckley indicated the sole female member of the group, currently drawing the biggest and most enthusiastic crowd in the mess. 'That's why we pulled in Gretchen. Fluent Greek speaker, knows Athens like her own backyard. She's actually with the ISA, so she's got more experience of this type of work than the rest of us put together.'

'ISA?' Hunt wasn't familiar with the term.

'Intelligence Support Activity,' Buckley explained. 'The outfit was set up by the Defense Intelligence Agency after the Desert One fiasco. The CIA was found lacking in Humint and experienced in-the-field operators – for years they'd been moving more to satellites and hands-off intelligence stuff. We don't advertise the existence of Activity or what it gets up to. Too many woolly-minded liberals on the Hill would shit themselves if they knew. But the Activity guys don't mind getting their hands dirty.'

'That's why we want to integrate the teams,' Buzz interrupted, anxious to establish his point. 'That way we get a Greek speaker in each team. Likewise, when it comes to the Iraqis, only Jim here speaks Arabic, but all the SAS guys have at least a smattering.'

'I see your point,' Hunt conceded.

It was a mistake. Buzz was in and fighting his corner hard. 'Same as with other skills, sir. Ideally each team must have at least one guy who can ride a motorcycle, one who can handle a camera, and one who has used bugging devices. Every team must be a virtually self-contained unit.'

Hunt was reluctantly convinced. After all, the young American was virtually preaching established Special Forces doctrine. But if they got it wrong on this one, there would be a hell of a price to pay. And it would be Avery and Corrigan who paid it.

Max Avery found the bus-station manager at a pub on the Uxbridge Road. It was the man's regular port of call after work.

He had a sad face, his eyes without sparkle as he sat alone and stared into his pint glass. Avery wondered if he had always been like that, one of life's melancholics. Or had his nightly drink become a ritual mourning for the son who would never grow old? Cut down in his prime because he was joy-riding in a stolen car. An illogical act of juvenile defiance, railing against the madness that was Ulster in the only way he knew how.

Then to be shot dead by a confused and callow youth little older than himself, a rookie soldier acting in the only way that *he* knew how in the madness that was Ulster. Doing his duty, but getting it wrong. The knowledge that the terrorist in the getaway car was in fact an unarmed sixteen-year-old schoolboy would haunt him for the rest of his days.

Avery took the bar stool beside the man and ordered a beer. 'Mr Connolly?'

The sad face turned towards him. 'Yes?'

'The Magician sends his regards.'

There was a long silence in the empty pub. No expression showed on the man's face, no indication of what he might be thinking. He turned back to his drink. 'It's been a long time,' he said, his voice little more than a murmur. 'I thought he'd forgotten me.'

'It's better that way. Safer. For us and for you.'

'How is he?'

'He's fine. He said he'd like a favour.'

'Of course. He was good to me when I needed a friend.'

'He'll be pleased you haven't forgotten.'

Connolly faced him once more, an intenseness in his eyes but still no light, no life. 'You don't forget something like that. Nor his sympathy. I remember what I promised. I am nothing much, but I am a man of honour.'

Avery placed an estate agent's property sheet on the bar. 'There's a basement flat in Bounds Green that we'd like you to buy. Just phone the agents and make an offer.'

The man moistened his lips thoughtfully with his tongue. 'I owe Con, but I don't have that sort of money.'

'There's the address and telephone number of a bookmaker written on those details. He's expecting you. He'll tell you when to bet and how much. He'll juggle the books so you'll be on a winning streak. The flat is vacant, so pay cash and take possession by the end of the month.' He dropped a business card beside the property details. It belonged to a legal wizard who worked for a number of south London villains. 'This solicitor will push things through with the speed of light. It's a repossession so the building society is anxious to sell.'

'What do I do with it?'

'Fill it with second-hand furniture. Let it out very cheaply but short-term. There'll be plenty of takers. Make sure it's vacant by the first of February, then we have someone to move in.'

'Who?'

'I've no idea. You'll be informed.' He finished his beer. 'In due course you'll be asked to sell the flat and lose the money again at the bookies.'

'What about the profit? From the rent?'

'You keep it.'

The man nodded. 'That will be handy. Thank him for me.'

Avery stood, ready to leave. 'And, Mr Connolly, for what it's worth, I'm truly sorry about your son.' He meant it.

Behind the glasses the man's eyes were moist. 'It was a long time ago.'

On the drive back south Avery found his mind dwelling on the man called Connolly. Just another pathetic victim of a savage urban war that had long ceased to have any political validity, if indeed it ever had. Its only purpose now was to keep the terrorist hierachy in business, because without it they had nothing.

But while there were bombings and shootings to perpetuate the hatred, then they would always have a job. They could rely on a steady stream of disaffected young firebrands from the Catholic slums to seize on the cause as the only spiritual straw at which to grasp in their stark and desolate lives. Roused by the rebel songs and sold on the glory of past martyrs they would be willing sacrificial lambs on the altar of Irish history.

And all the while leaders like Con Moylan would feather their nests, using terrorist extortion funds to finance legitimate business like his own construction group. Manipulating and intimidating without conscience, using others like Connolly to do their dirty work.

Not that Connolly was at any great risk; he might later be questioned, but it was unlikely he would ever be arrested. The Security Service would merely watch the flat he was about to buy, watch the succession of occupants, and know where to look the next time a bomb went off on the mainland. Like they'd watch the bookmaker who supplied the money in turn supplied to Con Moylan from Dublin. Such known points of contact were much too rare and important to close down. They might be replaced by others that the Security Service did not know about.

It was eight thirty when Avery pulled up at his forecourt. Lights still burned in the office where he knew Floyd would be waiting. The problem with all the additional work for Moylan was that he was falling behind with the paperwork for his legitimate business. Indeed Floyd had been showing such signs of near apoplexy as the pile of documents requiring his boss's attention grew, that Avery had agreed to work late with his manager to catch up.

As he entered the showroom he noticed the unfamiliar Mercedes parked outside.

Floyd looked up from his desk. 'Someone to see you, Max.' He nodded towards the row of reception chairs in the carpeted oasis of tired and unwatered pot plants.

Con Moylan rose awkwardly from the low chair. 'Sorry I didn't phone for an appointment.'

'This is a surprise,' Avery said, forcing enthusiasm into his voice.

'I was in your neck of the woods and thought I'd drop in.' He patted the side pocket of his cashmere coat. 'Just happen to have that fat contract with me. Thought we could celebrate.'

Avery smiled briefly. 'Sure, why not?'

'Just a few details to iron out. Is there somewhere we can talk?'

'My office out the back.'

Floyd looked up. 'Do you want me to sit in, Max?'

'No thanks, I'll handle this one.'

His general manager frowned, affronted by the exclusion. 'And those papers . . . ?'

Avery raised his hands in a gesture of helplessness. 'Sorry, Floyd, tomorrow perhaps. Best get off home now. I apologise for wasting your time.'

As he took his coat from the stand, Floyd said pointedly: 'I haven't wasted my time, Max. I've been doing the work for *both* of us.' The door slammed.

'Staff problems?' Moylan was amused.

'No, he's right. I've been letting things slip. It's taken a lot of time to organise the things you wanted.' He closed the door to his office. 'I've just seen Connolly. He's agreed.'

'I thought as much.' He sat himself on the edge of Avery's desk. 'But I haven't come here to talk about that. I've been thinking over that idea of yours about contacting the Iraqis.'

Avery's heart tripped, but he managed to suppress the interest in his voice. 'I didn't think you were keen,' he said flatly.

'That was Corrigan, he was dead against it. I thought it was outlandish . . . I mean, we've no dealings with those people, no knowledge of how they work or if they can be trusted. Anyway, I floated the concept to the Army Council.' He smiled. 'And I've been instructed to explore the situation a little further, sound them out.'

He didn't mention that the idea had met with little enthusiasm. Some of the Council members had been full of moral indignation; others, more pragmatic, had seen the dangers of any Provisional IRA link with Saddam Hussein becoming public knowledge. But luckily for Moylan there was no one left on the Council who still bore a grudge from the days when the Magician had tried to tell them how to run their affairs. Today Moylan's star was again in the ascendant, his proven money-making business acumen overshadowing his earlier reputation as a killer. And money was something that always interested the Council. So the vote had gone his way, just.

Avery said: 'We don't have much time. Saddam doesn't have much time.'

'I realise that,' Moylan retorted with a certain irritation. 'You said you had a contact with the Libyans?'

Avery nodded. 'A man called Ali Mahmoud Abdullah. Works in Malta at the Libyan Arab Airlines office at Luqa. He has all the appearances of being a civilian business executive but he's somehow linked in with Gaddafi's intelligence people.'

'Could you talk to him?'

Play it cool, Avery told himself. 'You wouldn't do it yourself, Con?'

Moylan's laugh was harsh. 'You won't find my name on any intelligence computer and I intend to keep it that way. I've no intention of spending the rest of my days in prison. No, if you set it up, I was thinking of sending Fox. He's not the brightest, but at least he can be trusted.'

Avery realised he had to act fast. If Moylan went his own way, he could lose track of events before they'd even started.

'You can't send that idiot, Con, for Christ's sake. If this goes through you'll be talking with the Iraqis, probably military intelligence, not some Mickey Mouse gang of cowboys. Let me go – at least I can speak their language.'

Moylan was surprised. 'Arabic you mean?'

'I did a course at Beaconsfield when I was in the Paras. I was attached to the signals section when it was sent to Kuwait to train Arab technicians.'

Moylan looked thoughtful. 'I see, that could be a bonus I suppose . . .'

Avery pressed it home. 'Ali speaks little English. Besides,

the Arabs need careful handling. You have to know how their minds work, their sensibilities. I've got that experience. Unless, of course, you still don't trust me?'

'I wouldn't say that, Max.' An idea occurred to him. 'I tell you what – you go and I'll send Corrigan with you.'

'Why?' Avery demanded, hiding his sense of satisfaction. 'He doesn't even like me.'

Moylan's eyes glinted with dark humour. 'And you don't like him, right? Excellent. Then you can both keep an eye on each other. That's just the way I like it.'

'If that's what you want.' Grudging. 'When do I go?'

'I don't expect you'd have trouble getting on a flight at short notice. How about tomorrow?'

# Nine

'When?'

'Tomorrow. To Malta.'

'Shit!'

The news transmitted from the bugging device in Avery's office was not welcomed by Sergeant-Major Brian Hunt.

As he had predicted, the first results of the integrated SAS/Delta team's training programme had been little short of diabolical. They had been no match for the MI5 stooges whom they had tried to keep under surveillance; elementary evasive tactics had worked all too well. It was now three days on and the improvements had been vast, but they still had a long way to go to reach the necessary standard. The last thing Hunt wanted to do was divert his best people to Malta.

He turned to Jim Buckley with whom he shared the temporary command-and-control centre in the Duke of York's barracks.

'Which team is shaping up fastest, d'you reckon?'

'B Squad,' Buckley replied without hesitation.

Hunt wasn't surprised. Its leader was Gretchen Adams, the female operator from Intelligence Support Activity, who was the individual with most experience of this type of work. She was backed up by the young Delta man known as Buzz and the two SAS soldiers who comprised the rest of the team. 'Big Joe' Monk and his inseparable oppo Len Pope were veterans of the Regiment; known as the 'Unholy Alliance' they had more undercover experience than most in Ulster with the secretive 14th Intelligence Unit.

Hunt said: 'Then let's call them in and tell them to pack their bags.'

'Just the four?'

'The others aren't ready. They could blow the whole thing.'

'It's a risk, being undermanned.'

Hunt shrugged. 'So is life.'

By the following morning Baker Team had packed civilian suitcases and were ready, dressed in clothes according to their cover roles. Buzz and Gretchen Adams were travelling as husband and wife tourists, armed with a multiplicity of cameras, including one with a powerful telephoto lens. Monk and Pope wore business suits, one taking the briefcase scrambler phone with which to maintain communications with London.

Commercially, it was the worst period in aviation history, with airlines frequently flying less than half-full, so the team had no difficulty in reserving seats on the same Air Malta flight as Avery and Corrigan. Likewise rooms were readily available at the Hilton Hotel on the north shore of the island.

The British Embassy had arranged for two hire cars to be waiting at Luqa airport, so by the time Avery and Corrigan had signed up for their own transport, the members of Baker had already settled in their respective vehicles. They took it in turns to follow their quarry which took a predictably direct route past the suburbs of Valletta and the resort area of Sliema to the more salubrious St Julian's district. There the Hilton was situated in thirty acres of grounds overlooking a grey and uninviting winter sea.

As soon as Avery reached his room he telephoned the Libyan Arab Airline office at the airport. Ali Mahmoud Abdullah sounded guardedly pleased to hear from him, as softly spoken and charmingly polite as always. They agreed to meet in the Hilton's Falcon Bar named after the famous Bogart movie.

It was early evening and most of the lavishly uphol- stered chairs were unoccupied; only a few businessmen sat on stools at the bar talking shop.

Corrigan selected a remote alcove seat while Avery bought two beers. He'd just returned to the table when the Libyan walked in. He was in his thirties, his black hair wind- tousled and his sallow face in need of a closer shave. He wore an expensive charcoal suit but no tie.

Avery waved and the man crossed the floor to join them.

'Good to see you again, Mr Abdullah.'

'And it is a pleasure to meet you after so long, Mr Avery.' They shook hands.

'And this is Lew Corrigan.'

'It's my pleasure,' the American replied. Avery noticed that he had wisely lapsed into a soft Irish brogue.

'A drink?'

'An orange juice would be nice.'

This time Corrigan went to the bar while Avery engaged the Libyan in rhetorical pleasantries, all the time weighing up the man. Despite the gentle smile and quiet voice, something made Avery feel uneasy. It was a few moments before he realised the reason: in contrast to the Arab's apparent composure, his eyes were wary, for ever darting about the room as though expecting trouble. Only occasionally did they meet Avery's gaze directly and even then it was with some reluctance. It served to remind him that Ali Abdullah worked in the same office as the men who had been implicated in the Lockerbie bombing. Perhaps, Avery decided, the Libyan had every reason to watch his back.

When Corrigan rejoined them, Abdullah finally appeared to give both men his full attention. 'What is it I can do for you?'

Avery saw no point in hedging. 'Our people should like to be put in contact with Saddam Hussein.'

The Libyan might just as well have been given an electric shock. He drew back instantly, his eyes wide and the colour draining from his cheeks. But he recovered quickly, his nervous half-smile returning. He made a small clicking noise with his teeth. 'Ah, Saddam, a very bad man, very bad. He is not good. He has set all the world against him.'

'Not quite all,' Corrigan interrupted. 'We believe he still has a few friends left.'

Abdullah's eyes were roaming again, this time watching an American tourist couple who sat nearby: a man with cropped dark hair and a woman in her late twenties whose bare shoulders and arms had the finely toned contours of an athlete.

The Arab regarded her appreciatively for a moment, before murmuring: 'You must understand that Libya does not condone Iraq's annexation of Kuwait by violent means.'

There was a ghost of a smile on Corrigan's face. 'You mean your Colonel Gaddafi is shit-scared the US is going to bomb the hell out of him again if he doesn't toe the line.'

Avery shot the American an angry glance. 'Mr Abdullah, what my friend means is, we understand that whatever is said publicly, despite the rights and wrongs of Saddam's actions, Libya still shares a common enemy with Iraq. And we appreciate that Colonel Gaddafi is not a fair-weather friend. The Iraqis need help against your sworn common enemy. We can provide that help. You can put us in contact with them.'

Abdullah sipped at his orange juice. 'I believe the accepted quiet route is by aircraft to Jordan and then overland to Baghdad.'

Corrigan picked up the line of attack and leaned forward. 'We are not playing games. Your people and us have been good friends in the past. And we are loyal to our friends as you are loyal to yours.'

This time Avery was impressed with the American's intervention.

'I understand this,' Abdullah said softly. 'But you must understand that the United States is watching my country very closely. Every day there is a car parked outside my family's apartment here in Malta and my telephone has a hollow sound to it. You understand what that means? It is a risk even to talk to you, except that we are just casual acquaintances.'

Avery said: 'I understand it is not possible to help us here. We have in mind another place.'

'Yes?'

'Athens. The Greeks have no love for the Americans, and they are friends of the anti-Zionist movements.'

'They are also NATO allies,' Abdullah replied pointedly.

'But reluctant allies in the Gulf,' Corrigan added smoothly. 'The Greeks are asked to support America's stance against Iraq, yet they ask where were the Americans when Turkey invaded Cyprus . . . ?'

Abdullah finished his orange juice. 'And what do the Irish have against the Americans?'

Avery smiled. 'Ask what we have against the British, the sworn enemy of the IRA, Libya and Iraq? The enemy of our friend is our enemy, too. Ask who in the past came within a hair's-breadth of killing the British Prime Minister?' He paused for effect. 'Then ask yourself what has been done that cannot be done again?'

The band of tuxedoed musicians began tuning their instruments on the stage beside the small dance floor; the bar was beginning to fill.

'It is time for me to go,' Abdullah said, unnerved by the influx of new faces.

Avery grasped the Libyan's forearm in earnest. 'Put us in touch with Iraqi intelligence in Athens. As a favour to loyal and trusted friends.'

'The *Estikhbarat?*'

'They would be the people.'

Abdullah hesitated. 'Do you have a business card?'

'Of course.' Avery handed one across.

The Libyan shook his head. 'This is no good. I need somewhere neutral, an address in the Republic of Ireland.'

'Mine,' the American said and, taking a pen from his pocket, scrawled the address and telephone number of Corrigan's Den on a paper napkin.

Abdullah rose to his feet, stuffing the napkin into his pocket. 'It has been my pleasure. Perhaps one day we meet again. If not, give my felicitations to your fellow revolutionaries. *Allah akbar.*'

And he was gone.

Corrigan fell back in his chair, mentally exhausted. 'Well, Max, what do you think?'

'Maybe.'

'Just maybe? Just maybe he hasn't got the right connections.'

'Oh, he's got the right connections all right.' Avery turned towards the door, just in time to see the American couple walk out, hand-in-hand.

'Another drink?' Corrigan asked. 'Your shout.'

Avery grinned. 'Twist my arm.'

He rose to his feet, and froze. At the now crowded bar a man sat on a bar stool staring directly at him. The man smiled, the harelip making the gesture look remarkably like a silent snarl.

Gerry Fox lifted his glass. Cheers.

The surveillance team almost missed Fox. He had disappeared from his known London address, but no one had been expecting him to turn up in Malta.

Gretchen Adams and Buzz had followed Ali Mahmoud Abdullah from the Falcon Bar, intent on getting at least one reasonable photograph of him for the file. A small directional bell-mike concealed in Buzz's hand had already transferred a distorted version of the man's conversation with Avery and Corrigan to the recorder in his sportsbag.

Two of the businessmen at the bar were 'Big Joe' Monk and Len Pope. It was the latter who glimpsed the ginger-haired man raising his glass and whose near-photographic memory was instantly able to put a name to the face.

However much Con Moylan professed to trust Avery and Corrigan, the watchful presence of Gerry Fox suggested that he was not one to take any chances.

Meanwhile back in London, another small but significant event was missed.

Because most members of the SAS/Delta team were still engaged with intensive on-the-street surveillance exercises, no one was available to watch over a low-priority consideration like Staff Nurse O'Malley.

She was on the ward at lunchtime when she received the unwelcome telephone call from Danny Grogan.

'What do you want?' She was aware of the tremor in her voice.

'You know. Have you done what I told you?'

'I haven't had time.'

'You've had plenty of time, lady.' A pause followed, during which she could discern the heavy breathing of his anger. 'How's the wee lad? And the wife of Max's office manager – Floyd's wife Rowena – still looks after your lad while you're at work, does she?'

Bastard! Covering the mouthpiece with her hand, she said in a whisper: 'All right, I *have* talked to Max like you asked. I've got some details, but I don't know if it's what you want, if it's enough . . .' She could hear the fear in her own voice now.

'That's better.'

A few moments later she replaced the receiver. Her hands were shaking as she opened her handbag to look at the sheet of writing paper on which she had made her notes. It felt like an act of betrayal just reading her own handwriting. A tear splashed on the words, spreading the ink in a tiny starburst.

It was dark, wet and windy when she left the sprawling grey hospital building on the south bank of the Thames. As always she walked the longer distance to the Elephant and Castle Underground station to avoid changing trains on her homeward journey to Balham on the Northern Line.

Grogan was waiting for her on the platform, leaning against the grubby white wall tiles as he read a newspaper.

She stood beside him and surreptitiously passed across the folded sheet of lilac paper. He opened it up, hidden from view within the centre spread of the tabloid, and studied it.

'Smells nice.'

To Maggie the scent of the paper had become the stench of treachery. She felt disgusted with herself, ashamed and frightened.

She stared straight ahead at the enormous laughing face on the billboard across the track. 'Is it enough?'

He pocketed the writing paper and the tabloid. 'You've done well. Now you can forget we ever met. Give your wee lad a kiss from me.'

The train screamed out of the tunnel.

Twenty-four hours later Danny Grogan was in Dublin. Although born and brought up in Belfast, for him a visit to the city and the surrounding horse country of the Curragh was like coming home.

No more watching over his shoulder for the RUC or Special Branch shadows; no dread that his quiet drink with the boys would be shattered by a Proddie gunman; no nagging fears that he would be stopped by a British Army spot check.

In Dublin the girls seemed prettier, the beer stronger and the air sweeter.

So he was in good spirits, despite the steady drizzle of rain, as he went to the rendezvous in the public bar of the Burlington Hotel.

He didn't know the messenger from the Army Council: the man wore a nondescript business suit, had the sort of plain face that was difficult to remember, and was generally uncommunicative.

Grogan was pleased when the man left after a few stilted words about the weather, his half of Smethwicks hardly touched.

Opening the envelope he had been given, Grogan extracted the single sheet of computer print-out.

He noted that it was logged for February 1986, the year that Eamonn O'Flaherty, the previous European commander had ordered an inquiry into Max Avery's background before using him for the first small job.

*NAME: (Born) Patrick O'Reilly (Changed by deed poll, 1966) Max Avery*
*BORN: Liverpool 1950*
*PARENTS: Thomas O'Reilly (B. Co. Clare, Eire) Patricia Murray (B. Cork, Eire)*
*HISTORY: Subject's father was born in County Clare, Eire, and served as stoker in Royal Navy until 1948. Settled in Liverpool in '49 where he worked as a motor mechanic, and married Patricia Murray.*
*Subject born in 1950 and raised at parents' home in Emery Street, Goodison Park, and educated at St Francis de Sales Roman Catholic School until 1961 when both parents died in road accident on the A56 en route to a holiday in North Wales.*
*Taken into Dr Barnardo's residential home until 16 (1966).*

In the margin, Grogan was able to add from Maggie O'Malley's note that Avery's first job was at the Tate & Lyle sugar factory in Love Lane, Liverpool.

*At this time subject's name changed by deed poll to Maxwell Avery (See Appendix).*

Grogan took a Biro from his pocket and underscored the paragraph before reading on:

*Subject became involved with petty crime, having several run-ins with the Merseyside Police Task Force of the period. Subsequently in 1968 received 12 months conditional discharge for car theft (joy-riding) following good character reference from Barnardo's. Joined the King's Regiment same year. Transferred to Parachute Regiment in 1970. Returned to civilian life in 1973, working for scrap dealers.*

Again, Grogan was now able to flesh out the detail. The dealer was a Don Merryweather in Bootle.

*Subject then served a 30-month sentence at Liverpool Walton Prison for his part in a pub brawl, followed by a conviction for involvement in a car-ringing organisation. Finally he was arrested for an armed raid on a bookies' shop. Served six years before being paroled in 1982.*

Grogan now knew that the bar fight had been at the Midland public house in Renshaw Street, Avery's time

served at Liverpool Walton Prison. The next three-year
stretch had been spent at Wymot Prison, Preston; his final
term had been at both Wymot and Wakefield Prisons.

*ASSESSMENT: Subject has been known to this organi-
sation for some two and a half years, following a chance
encounter with Margaret O'Malley and subsequently myself.
Has strong Republican family background but claims his
own feelings on the subject remained ambivalent until his
involvement in Bloody Sunday (Jan '72) massacre when
he was serving with the Parachute Regiment. As can be
seen he left the British Army shortly afterwards and then
drifted into crime. Although professing to have reformed, we
know that he has many useful connections with south
London gangland and has had little compunction in
providing acquaintances with illegal goods through his
network of contacts i.e.: quantities of cannabis, contraband
goods, forged banknotes and documentation, pornographic
material and, on at least one known occasion, a handgun.*

*Politically he talks of mild Republican sympathy when
in Irish company, which he appears to genuinely enjoy. His
disgust at Parachute Regiment activities in Northern Ireland
would appear heartfelt.*

*Separate conversations with Margaret O'Malley rein-
forces my view that Avery would not ask questions if asked
to assist in tasks connected with this organisation's logistical
requirements, if the price was right. Indeed his contacts and
cover could prove invaluable, particularly viz European
command. My recommendation is to commence cautiously*

*with this man, setting low-grade and non-attributable tasks,*
*and to assess his trustworthiness again at a later date.*

It was signed GF for Gerry Fox.

So this was the report that had arrived on the desk of
Con Moylan's predecessor. Grogan flipped over the page
to the Appendix to which was attached a number of
documents.

The first was Avery's birth certificate, under the name
of O'Reilly, confirming the home address and names of
both his parents, which Fox had apparently obtained from
the Liverpool University archives. Second was a copy of
the name-change deed procured from Somerset House in
London.

Finally was a copy of Avery's character reference from
the Ministry of Defence, the red book confirming details
of his service career, with comments from his colonel which
were countersigned by Avery himself.

Grogan placed the papers in front of him on the table
and rubbed his chin thoughtfully. It was all very neat, very
pat. He could see why both Fox and O'Flaherty had been
convinced that Avery was probably a safe bet.

As 'Big Tom' O'Grady had pointed out, the idea that
Avery could have been an intelligence plant had long ago
been discounted and Fox's investigation report showed why.
Everything could be checked out; the Englishman's life
was an open book. And no setback to the Provisionals' plans
had ever implicated him in any way.

Nevertheless, it struck Grogan that no one had a way

of knowing whether Avery could have contacted the military after he found himself mixing in the company of Maggie O'Malley's friends, which included others like Gerry Fox who had connections with the Provies. Could he have turned grass out of hidden loyalty, or for money, or both?

Avery's business certainly appeared to have blossomed rapidly in the mid-80s, but then they had been economic boom years. Fox had obtained copies of Avery's company accounts and everything appeared genuine. On another occasion Fox had arranged for the man's telephone to be tapped and for him to be put under surveillance for an entire month – with nothing suspicious to report at the end of it.

There was also Avery's willing participation in the murder of a British soldier in Northern Ireland.

It crossed Grogan's mind that his desire to prove Con Moylan wrong about Avery was getting out of hand.

Once more he scanned the print-out, his eyes again settling on the paragraph he had underscored.

*At this time subject's name changed by deed poll to Maxwell Avery.*

That still seemed a strange thing to do, even for an impressionable teenager. He himself had known a number of O'Reillys and none had felt the need to change his name just because of leg-pulls.

Moreover Maxwell Avery struck him as a strange choice of name, anyway.

It wasn't much to go on, but at least it gave Grogan a

small bone to gnaw on. Just enough to convince himself that this investigation wasn't a complete waste of his time and expertise.

He decided then that he wouldn't make a big thing of it, wouldn't set himself up to be later laughed out of court by Moylan and those on the Army Council. When he had time available he would look into it, no rush, and most probably let the matter quietly drop in time.

Meanwhile he would work on the assumption that there *was* a mystery about Max Avery. But where to begin?

He returned to his hotel and telephoned Directory Inquiries for the number of the Dr Barnardo's orphanage headquarters in London. The woman in the Aftercare Office listened with polite reserve as Grogan explained: 'I'm a solicitor acting on behalf of one of your former charges, a Mr Patrick O'Reilly. He's applying to take up residence in the United States and needs copies of the records you hold. Is that a problem?'

'Of course not, sir. What was the name again?'

'O'Reilly, Patrick.'

'And what period would that have been?'

'Around 1961 to '66.'

'And where was he in residence?'

'Liverpool – would I need to apply there?'

'No, sir. For that period all records will be held on microfilm here in London. If you would care to write your request formally, together with a form of signed consent from your client, we'll be pleased to supply the records.'

Shit! Grogan cursed himself for overlooking the likely

bureaucratic red tape he'd encounter with this approach. 'This is urgent.'

'I appreciate that, sir. We'll act speedily on receipt of your written request.'

'Of course.' A thought occurred to him. 'Incidentally, what's the telephone number of your Liverpool office?'

She gave it to him with a cautionary: 'But they won't be of any help.'

'No, another matter,' he mumbled evasively, thinking that he was due to be in Liverpool in a few weeks' time anyway. 'Thank you so much.'

As the telephone went dead in her hand, the woman stared at the receiver for a moment before replacing it.

*Patrick O'Reilly.* That *was* the name, or was it? She looked up at the cork notice board beside her desk, cluttered with memos, reminders and holiday postcards. It was a long time since she'd last seen it. Hurriedly she unpinned the various items until she unearthed the yellowing paper of the board directive.

#### IMPORTANT

*Re: Inquiries concerning Patrick O'Reilly (1961–66) should be referred to the police without alerting the inquirer. Telephone: 071 408 3000*

It was dated 1984.

Tentatively she dialled the Gower Street number and was mildly surprised when a man answered almost immediately. 'Yes, can I help you?'

'This is Dr Barnardo's in London. I've instructions to ring you if anyone inquires about one of our former charges, a Mr O'Reilly.'

Again she was surprised when the man appeared to know immediately whom she was talking about without any apparent reference to a file or computer. 'Who was it who called, do you know?'

'He didn't give a name, but he had an Irish accent. A solicitor acting for Mr O'Reilly. Needs documents because he's emigrating to America.'

'Is that so?'

'The solicitor will be writing – what do I do?'

'Do what you normally do. But please keep me informed if the letter arrives, if he calls again, or of any other developments. It is important.'

She wondered why this anonymous policeman needed to know; the speculation really was quite exciting. Perhaps their former charge had become an international drug smuggler.

'One more thing,' the man said. 'You might warn your Liverpool office to be on their guard and let us know if anyone there asks about O'Reilly.'

'I'll do that right away.'

At the active operations desk at MI5's headquarters Avery's controller, John Nash, thoughtfully hung up.

So it had begun again. Presumably it was the follow-up to Grogan's visit to Margaret O'Malley. This time the Provisionals would no doubt be even more thorough than Fox had been. And there were two loopholes Nash had yet to close; he could do it now knowing that Avery's cover only needed a short time to run. He jotted two words on his note pad: *Court Records* and *newspaper*, before picking up the internal phone and dialling.

Clarissa Royston-Jones answered.

He said: 'Thought you'd want to know immediately. Someone is sniffing into Max's past.'

It was in the early hours of the morning four days later that the twenty-one-year-old Libyan, who was studying at the Albert Agricultural College in north Dublin, left the city to begin a seventy-mile motorcycle ride north to County Monaghan.

He arrived at first light in the sleepy village street and throttled back so as not to disturb the sleeping residents. It was not difficult to find the peeling signwritten frontage to O'Casey's barbershop; he circled the uneven road once before drawing to a halt. Glancing neither left nor right, he crossed the pavement to the door. There were two letter boxes; one was unmarked and the other bore a small brass plaque which read simply 'Corrigan's Den'.

From his pocket he extracted the large brown envelope which had been given him by a Libyan diplomat in a Dublin café the night before, and squeezed it through the aperture. Remounting his motorcycle, he gunned the engine and rode off back in the direction from which he had come.

Corrigan stirred. The raucous drone of the receding motorcycle pierced his troubled dreams and suddenly he was awake, staring at the fly-encrusted lampshade above his head. Gingerly he swung his feet to the floor, even that small movement triggering the drum beat in his skull. His bleary eyes took in his naked reflection in the cheval mirror, his clothes cast by his feet, and the curving hips and back of the girl on the crumpled sheets by his side.

What was her name? Molly or Madge – he was sure it began with an M. But what did it matter? She'd done her duty for the Provos, and she'd served his purpose. Years ago he'd learned to take his pleasures when and where he could. He never knew when they might be his last. You couldn't fight in dirty wars and remain untouched.

Pulling on trousers and one of his favourite lumberjack shirts, he padded downstairs to the bar. It was still fetid with the smell of malt, stale smoke and congealed vomit. He could still hear the mournful words of the rebel songs echoing around his head; songs that hadn't finished until four in the morning:

> *And it's down in Crossmaglen sure that's where I long to be,*
> *Lying in the dark with a Provie company.*
> *A comrade on my left and another on my right*
> *And a clip of ammunition for my little Armalite.*

The barber O'Casey was asleep on the wooden settle, curled like a baby in his own puke where he had collapsed the previous night. Some night, some celebration. The bomb had killed two RUC constables, blinded one other and maimed a fourth.

No wonder he had needed to drown his misery in drink

and in the girl whose name began with M. He had found out about it all too late; there was nothing he could do.

He opened the door to O'Casey's salon, shielding his eyes against the window light. Then he saw the envelope. Kneeling on the mat, he thumbed it open. A frown creased his forehead. Just a holiday brochure for Greece and a slip of paper. On it, in badly constructed letters, were the words: *From a friend of your friend Abdullah. Allah Akbar.*

He flipped through the brochure twice before he found it. One of the featured hotels had been circled in ball point. He ran his finger across the chart. The Herodian in Athens. Someone had written: Week commencing November 24. One week's time.

A broad grin spread across his face. They'd done it.

He made a pot of coffee, roused O'Casey, then returned upstairs with a mug for the girl called M. She was prettier than he remembered, and much younger. Little more than a schoolgirl. She accepted the drink awkwardly, trying to hold the sheet over her breasts. An embarrassed half-smile. No doubt in the bleak dawn light he was uglier and much older than she remembered.

As soon as she left, he dialled the London number.

'Max, it's Lew. How you doing?'

'Fine. What gives?'

'I was thinking of taking a winter break. Wondered if you might care to come along?'

Avery was cautious. 'Where did you have in mind?'

'A mutual friend recommended Athens. I was thinking of going next Saturday for a week's holiday.'

He heard the sharp intake of breath at the other end of the line. 'Sounds good to me, Lew. I'll tell Con.'

Life had become chaotic from the moment the R-12 bug had been triggered in Avery's home telephone by Lew Corrigan's call from his bar in County Monaghan.

Not only had on-the-street training been stepped up, but preparation was already under way for the entire Delta/SAS team to move to Greece. Communications equipment and a plethora of cameras, microphones, tape-recorders and tracking devices in a multitude of sizes and guises had to be bagged in diplomatic pouches destined for the British Embassy in Athens.

A long shopping list had also been signalled ahead to the SIS station chief for him to organise. It included four motorcycles and six cars, three of which were to be liveried taxis that were indiscernible from the real thing. Sets of alternative numberplates were required; because of the infamous Athens smog, vehicles were banned from the city centre on alternate days, depending on whether the registration ended in an odd or even number.

One motorcycle and one car were allocated to each of the four teams, the remaining two cars held in emergency reserve or for use by Brian Hunt or Jim Buckley who would act as the command-and-control or even make up the numbers when necessary. The key was total flexibility.

Back-street mechanics had to be found to prepare and maintain the covert fleet, day and night, with no questions asked. This necessitated using people who operated on or beyond the fringes of the law.

While one team had been booked into the Herodian Hotel as a party of travel agents inspecting what Athens had to offer as a holiday destination, the rest were to be stationed in a large self-catering apartment in a busy residential suburb where their frequent comings and goings would pass unnoticed.

Vast quantities of grocery provisions as well as compo rations had to be made ready for them. There would be little time for cooking and many meals would have to be eaten in cars or under covert surveillance conditions.

Street maps, bus and train timetables had to be assembled, some of which were forwarded to London to enable the team to familiarise themselves quickly with the streets and city sites. American and British Embassy staff had earlier spent two days with video cameras taping specific routes, the results of which were dispatched to London by air. Others took still photographs of key locations which, when they reached the Duke of York's barracks, were pinned up along side a detailed street map on the wall of the operations room.

After exhausting days tramping through London after their M15 stooges, the team members spent the evenings studying the minutiae of detail about Athens. Tests and more tests were conducted until each member knew the approximate location of every district and its major streets, how to pronounce them and spell the names in Greek. The location of all embassies and larger hotels had to be known along with a variety of popular landmarks.

On the Wednesday evening the entire group was called to an informal meeting which was addressed by Hunt.

Despite the rows of drawn faces, red-eyed with fatigue, he knew that morale was high. The Americans, in particular, managed to appear bright and alert despite the strain they must be experiencing. It amused Hunt to note the comparison with the SAS men who had viewed the whole business with a kind of relaxed disdain, expressed through increasingly irreverent black humour.

The attitude had caused some friction, particularly amongst the younger more thrusting Delta men who felt that the British weren't pulling their weight. Jim Buckley, who had been seconded to the SAS for cross-training on several occasions, had to explain the differences of military culture before the rift became serious. The Americans set about their tasks with a blatant pride and earnestness that the British found amusing – and weren't afraid to say so – whilst the blasé and self-effacing attitude of the SAS troops gave the impression to their trans-Atlantic companions that they weren't taking matters seriously. In fact some had already reached the conclusion that the 'hooligans from Hereford' were downright amateur.

Hunt stood up amid the gathering, some seated, some sprawled on the floor wherever a space could be found. Each had a can of beer in hand.

'I want to thank you all for your supreme effort. I know we've all had our ups and downs and little misunderstandings, but I'm pleased with the way you've shaped up. In fact, when we began the street surveillance training programme two weeks ago, I thought the whole project fatally flawed. Thank you for proving me wrong.' A mild handclapping of applause rippled through the audience, notably from the Delta contingent. 'Tomorrow I fly to Athens with each of the team leaders. As the advance party, we'll be checking all the arrangements and getting to know the city. That'll mean using a lot of shoe leather in pavement pounding . . . '

'All retsina and bouzouki music, more like,' chipped in one of the SAS group.

Hunt smiled. 'Apart from *that*, it'll be hard work. But it means that at least one person in each group will have a thorough knowledge of the city layout and some practical experience of getting about before Avery and Corrigan arrive. Well, that's it. Jim and I have set up a small kitty in the mess. See you in Athens.'

There was an unseemly scramble for the bar.

While the SAS/Delta team celebrated the start of the mission, a hundred miles away in Southampton the usual company of night-time cleaners moved through the deserted offices of the Moylan Construction Group.

Most of the workers came from the poorer or ethnic areas of the city. They did the job to earn extra money or because it was the only work they could get. It was a lonely, miserable drudge under the watchful eye of the supervisor, each person allocated a series of offices each night.

No one thought it strange when two new cleaners joined the force; staff turnover was high. And no one queried the change in work allocation which gave the newcomers the managing director's suite to clean, because it meant nothing to them.

Behind closed doors, over successive nights, the shredded documents in the secretary's wastebin were emptied into a specially marked bag for reconstruction in the laboratories of MI5. Computer discs were duplicated for inspection: it is little known that 'wiped' files can be technologically retrieved from virtually any system. The Fax machine receipt and transmit log was inspected for tracing documents through the stored pages and dialled number recovery facilities. Matching notepads replaced those in use so that impressions of earlier messages could be revealed by forensic tests. Typewriter ribbons were swapped over in order that letters and memos could be reconstructed.

The answering machine on Moylan's direct private line had its tape replaced. With sophisticated verification and enhancement techniques, previously erased messages could be deciphered. Each locked drawer was opened and photographed by Polaroid camera before being examined and the contents replaced exactly as found, using the instant print for reference. Likewise the office safe was examined using electronic keys required to be supplied by all British lock manufacturers to the intelligence services.

A line-powered third wire transmitter was concealed within the telephone junction box which not only relayed calls to the nearby British Telecom-liveried receiving van, but turned the handset into a virtual microphone to pick-up any conversations in the room.

Their work finished, the cleaners locked the office suite doors and carried their black plastic bags down to the waiting truck.

The penetration of the Provisional IRA's new European network had begun.

# Ten

Athens was unusually hot for the time of year.

Humidity was high; a haze of smog pressed down on the sprawling city reducing the sun to an opalescent gleam in the sulphurous sky.

Captain Nico Legakis knew his headache wouldn't go until a stiff Aegean breeze picked up and cleared the polluted air from the most traffic-congested streets in Europe.

As a section head of the Athens Anti-Terrorist Police, it was his function to liaise with the immigration authorities to ensure that the security curtain fell around Greece as it did in every other country in Europe.

But, whereas no country could guarantee a hundred per cent security, Legakis was painfully aware that the gaps in the Greek curtain were embarrassingly wide.

Blue-painted armoured cars belonging to the police might be stationed outside the terminal buildings and armed officers might strut the concourse, but the customs and luggage security checks were as shambolic as ever.

Whilst this laxity offended his sensibilities as a professional policeman, at the back of his mind lurked a grudging pride that no one could conquer the Greeks' natural free spirit which expressed itself in their inbred hatred of rules and regulations.

The Olympic Airways flight from Heathrow had cleared now. Thankfully the only two Arabs on board did not appear on his obsolete wanted list. Yet, had they done so, he seriously wondered whether his boss or the government hierarchy would do anything about it.

Greece had only recently recognised Israel, the previous government having always backed the Arab cause over Palestine in return for Arab support to get the Turks out of Cyprus.

Legakis sighed and walked to the office door from where he could study the stream of arrivals spilling onto the concourse. He was a people policeman. Faces – that was what he liked. You could tell so much from faces, expressions, tone of voice, the choice of words, body language. You could sense if a man was lying, if he felt guilty or afraid.

No one noticed him observing; he was not the sort of man that people noticed. Short and small-framed, he was inconspicuously dressed in a dark suit, unaware that his trouser length didn't quite reach his brightly polished shoes, so that when he walked in his slightly indignant manner the exposed length of ankle gave him a mildly comical appearance. Certainly no woman would give his pale moustached face or his prematurely bald head a second glance. But he was unconcerned; he had won the love of his wife years before and he was content enough with their life together in the shabby suburban apartment with their three cats.

Something odd happened. Someone in the scurrying crowd of new arrivals noticed him. For a couple of seconds their eyes locked, then the man looked away. Strange that. Passengers arriving at their destination either seek out someone waiting for them or else look for the signs to buses and taxis. Few look at airport officials standing on the periphery.

Had he been a customs official, Nico Legakis might have taken an interest in the man. He noted he was tall, broad-shouldered and might have been handsome except that his features were a little too craggy and worn. Clearly a north European, he was dressed for a holiday, but looked too alert and tense to be on vacation. Almost apprehensive.

Legakis's eyes lingered on the man's companion who clutched his arm as he pushed their wayward trolley. A small, pretty woman with a glorious cascade of black ringlets and a bewitching smile. Now *she* looked as though she were on holiday. Instinctively the policeman drew in his stomach, straightened his shoulders; he still had his share of natural Greek machismo and an eye for a handsome woman.

Idly he watched them go.

In truth Legakis, like everyone else in the security service, saw any perceived terrorist threat to his country from Iraq as being greatly overrated. As always it was their indigenous 17 November terrorists he was more concerned about.

A dedicated group of anti-American and anti-Turkish anarchists, they had been the bane of Legakis's fifteen years in the police since they had first struck in '75, assassinating the CIA station chief in Athens.

In all that time the mysterious organisation had never been penetrated and no arrests made.

Rumours abounded as the catalogue of horror mounted. Twenty-seven shootings and bombings against capitalist and authoritarian targets as well as US and Turkish military and diplomatic personnel.

Their impudence and audacity had caught the public imagination. They had tied up policemen and stolen their guns; they had raided ammunition from an army camp in Larissa, and even stolen bazookas from the War Museum – and later used them in anger. The last time had been against the office of the American company of Procter and Gamble in June.

It had been quiet since then. But Legakis sensed that it wouldn't be for much longer.

He walked slowly to the glass doors of the terminal building. The passenger who had looked at him and the woman were climbing into a battered yellow Mercedes taxi.

As it pulled away Legakis lost interest. He did not notice the hired blue Peugeot driven by Jim Buckley draw out of its parking space and begin to follow, leaving a one-car gap between the vehicles.

And he did not notice the girl seated on a motor scooter who had witnessed the arrival of the passengers.

'I can still hardly believe it. On holiday in Athens,' Maggie said, peering out of the smeared taxi window at the traffic streaming past in the opposite direction.

Avery could hardly believe it himself. It had been a snap

decision made after his last visit to the library dead-letter drop. The short coded message had given him an emergency contact telephone number in Athens. It also informed him that Maggie had been visited by a man identified as Danny Grogan; she had been pressured into providing details of Avery's past. Someone, maybe Con Moylan, was checking on him.

He knew now why she had been asking him so many questions lately, going over details of his life before he knew her. At the time he'd been flattered, seeing it as a sign that their relationship was growing stronger.

The truth had hurt, but he didn't hold it against her. As she believed his story herself, she would have seen no harm in co-operating. Protecting their baby son would have been paramount in her mind. Just as protecting Maggie had been paramount to Avery.

That was why he decided not to leave her alone in London again. He feared that Grogan might return, perhaps with more violent threats if she failed to co-operate. And again, she might just accidentally say something that could give him away.

So to hell with Clarry if she disapproved of him taking Maggie with him. And to hell with Moylan, too, if he disapproved.

But that had come as a surprise. The Irishman almost appeared to like the idea. 'Why not, Max? It'll be interesting to see her again.'

As the taxi gathered speed Avery turned to Maggie: 'You need the break as much as I do; more so.'

'I just hope Rowena didn't really mind looking after Josh full-time. We did rather spring it on her.'

'Forget it and enjoy yourself.'

She giggled. 'Who'd have thought – I mean Athens! – just a week ago? You're full of surprises.'

'There's one more,' Avery said. He could see no way to break the news gently. 'And I'm afraid you're not going to like it. This isn't *just* a holiday for me. I'm also doing some business.'

She regarded him curiously. 'Okay, no problem, I can live with that, as long as I see something of you. So, why all the secrecy?'

'It's who I'm doing the business with. When he knew I spoke Arabic, Con Moylan asked me to come here with him and help out.'

Moylan. She felt as though she had just been slugged in the stomach with an iron fist. It might even have been Moylan's own fist; he had done that enough times in the past. Even the transient thought triggered a dull ache in her groin. She felt hot and angry, staring hard at Avery in disbelief. Sometimes she felt she didn't know the man at all.

'How could you, Max? I hate Con Moylan. You just wouldn't believe how much.'

Avery made light of it. 'He seems all right to me. He can't be all that bad.'

'You're not a woman,' she snapped. 'If I'd known he'd be here I wouldn't have come.'

'That's why I didn't tell you – you need a break and we need the money. He's paying well.'

She turned away sharply and glared out of the window, eyes unseeing, her teeth gritted. So Con was paying for all this. It seemed that already he was manipulating her again. Bending her to his will. After a few moments she said: 'What's he up to, Max?'

'He's not *up* to anything, sweetheart. This is genuine business. He wants to build a timeshare complex on the coast and he's mixed up with some Arab consortium who are putting up the finance. He has some problems with them. You know what crafty buggers they can be.'

She looked back at him fiercely. 'No, I don't know. But I can tell you Con Moylan would be more than a match for any of them.'

Avery smiled sympathetically. 'Not when he can't speak the language.'

Her tart reply was interrupted by a sudden jolting as the taxi driver hit the brakes. He had been racing down the Kalirois carriageway as though it were a Formula One circuit and now took great exception to the car which pulled out in front of him, unaware of his meteoric approach. He thumped the horn and lifted both hands off the wheel in an appeal to the Almighty for justice.

Tut-tutting heavily, he swung off into a shady side street and proceeded to menace any and every pedestrian who dared to cross his path. It was to his passengers' profound relief that he finally stopped in the narrow Rovertou Galli outside the smoked glass frontage of the Herodian Hotel.

Avery paid him off and turned to Maggie. 'Look, I'm sorry this thing with Moylan has upset you. But let's forget about it, for tonight at least. Let's just celebrate you and me being together for once without Josh bawling, you going off on nightshift or Floyd coming round with some accounts query.'

She looked at him and smiled. How could she not forgive him? How was he to know the depth of her fear and hatred of Con Moylan? How could anyone be expected to understand?

'I forgive you, Max. I'm being a silly cow.' She snuggled up to his arm as they climbed the steps to the sunless interior of the building. 'There's no time to go out before dinner – let's go to bed.'

She was ravishing.

The porter had only just closed the door when she sprang at Avery, planting his face with kisses, nipping playfully at his skin with her small sharp teeth. Then she found his lips and began exploring his mouth with her tongue, sucking hungrily while she ground the centre of her body against his thigh.

They didn't get undressed, there was no time as her frantic sense of need fanned his desire like a flame. It was an animal thing with no need for preamble as she sought the zipper of his trousers while he pushed her back onto the bed, her dress around her hips, the satin material of her loose-cut knickers pulled aside. A gasp escaped her lips as he drove himself home, feeling the involuntary contraction before she relaxed her muscles to draw him in deeper. He slowed, prolonging the moment, ignoring the impatient tattoo of her small fists beating on his back.

Faster suddenly, then slowing again, teasing, feeling the warmth of her labia enclosing him, her inner constrictions deliberate now, coaxing, sucking at him with delicious urgency.

It was a battle of wills, she demanding, he withholding. He found himself staring into her bright green eyes just inches from his own. Her teeth glistened as she half-smiled, half-snarled, manoeuvring her body beneath him, forcing herself onto him, impaling deep and hard, then pulling back, soaking in the soft rippling sensations that ebbed through her. Like surf, she thought, sweeping on a beach, each successive wave faster and more powerful than the last. Her eyes closed and a small gurgle of sound escaped her throat. Her stomach convulsed suddenly, violently, her breasts tossed from side to side.

He lost the battle as the lips between her legs drew on him again in deliberate muscular spasm. He exploded in her then, but still she didn't stop. On and on until she'd milked him dry and he fell against her, their skin sodden with sweat, their breathing hard, forces spent.

Her hand ruffled through his hair. 'I love you, Max.' He could scarcely hear her whispered words above the pumping of her heart against his ear. 'Don't let that ever change.'

It was well into the evening before they were ready to go out, walking the short distance to the labyrinth of alleyways that made up the Plaka quarter. The ancient winding streets huddled on the northern slope of the Acropolis, cafés, bars and souvenir shops packed together, vying for attention. There were few tourists but still the atmosphere was cheerful, the air filled with the strains of bouzouki music and the smell of barbecued meats.

They found a courtyard table in a quiet taverna and lingered over their meal beneath the stars. The entire evening had taken on a soft and magical air long before they began their leisurely stroll back to the hotel.

'Let's have a nightcap,' Maggie suggested, noticing a number of residents clustered around the bar. 'Fortify me for a night of torrid passion.'

'God, you're insatiable,' Avery laughed.

'Sure I think Athens must agree with me.' She lowered her voice as they approached the bar. 'I'm as randy as hell, Max Avery.'

He ordered two beers and joined Maggie on one of the sofas. He didn't recognise the young American couple who had followed them in: the woman wore a long wig and the man had dyed his fuzz of cropped hair since he had been in Malta.

'Do you really think Australia is a possibility?' Maggie asked. 'I've always fancied there.'

'I can't see why not. Or New Zealand.'

'Too quiet. Too sober.' She giggled. 'We Irish lassies like a bit of life. Talking of which, how many bottles did we have at that taverna?'

'Two.'

'Mmm.' She looked down at her glass. 'When will you put the business on the market?'

'No point before Christmas. In the new year, once the

threat of war with Iraq is out of the way. Trade won't pick up until then. We wouldn't get a good price.'

'So you still need Con Moylan's money?' Immediately she cursed herself for bringing up his name.

'Good evening, folks.'

That voice. It was as though her words had released the genie from the lamp. She looked up and her night of dreams was shattered.

Moylan stood, loose-limbed and casual in an expensive silk-shot suit worn with a lemon sports shirt and kid leather loafers. Of course he looked a little different to how she remembered, but not much. Whereas over six years she had seen worries of business take their toll on Max, time had hardly added a line to Moylan's face. The hair was different, still long but gelled back in the modern style, not wild and black and free, blowing in the Ulster wind as she remembered it.

'Hello, Con,' Avery was saying but she hardly heard, aware only of the small thrill of apprehension in her chest.

'And how's our little colleen? It's been a long time.'

As he spoke she realised she had been avoiding looking directly at his eyes. As if some small voice inside her head was telling her that if she didn't actually look into them, then somehow everything would be all right. She found herself peering almost sideways at his mouth as it moved to say the words. Seemingly focused in close-up, the only features she was able to see were his strong white teeth and the chiselled lips which had curled into the familiar gentle smile. To her consternation she felt the sudden rush of heat between her legs, the brief unbidden ache of longing. How often had she seen that deceptive smile hovering above her while her own mouth was contorted with pain as a cry of ecstasy escaped her lips? The words of the man who had taught her everything she knew about sex and life and herself. The dark side of herself she would rather not have known.

He took her hand; his skin felt cool against the warmth of her own. 'Con,' she said simply and at last she looked directly into his eyes. One sapphire dark, the other wintry pale, both cold and distant, the hard pinpoint pupils seeming to bore into her head, into her mind. There was something mesmeric about them, just as there always had been. She knew then with a sinking spirit that nothing had changed at all.

'And this is Lew Corrigan,' Avery was saying.

Despite his size, she had been too preoccupied to notice the American standing to one side of Moylan.

'You must be Maggie.' His hand was enormous, his grip fierce and warm. He had an engaging smile that crinkled the leathery tanned skin around his eyes, which she noticed remained shrewd and appraising.

'Pleased to meet you,' she murmured.

Moylan beckoned to the barman. 'I need a drink. Why don't you two join Lew and me . . . ?'

Maggie made her move. 'You stay, Max, I've got a headache coming on. I'll see you later.' She took the key from the table and moved away quickly, careful to avoid Moylan's knowing look.

'You've got one fine lady there, Max,' Corrigan observed, watching the movement of the tight miniskirt as she headed for the elevator.

'Thanks,' Avery responded absently as he sat back on the sofa. But his mind was elsewhere, puzzling over Maggie's reaction to meeting Moylan again. He had sensed her body freeze, almost smelled the fear on her skin. It was strangely disturbing to witness. Never had he seen her cowed before.

For his part Con Moylan seemed totally unaffected. He dropped down into the chair, ordered beer from the barman and leaned forward eagerly over the coffee table. 'Lousy flight was delayed. Nothing more exhausting than going nowhere.' He shrugged. 'Any contact with our friends yet?'

Avery shook his head.

'So what happens next?'

'They know where we are, Con, and what we want. So I guess all we can do is wait.'

When the three men left the bar ten minutes later they almost caught the surveillance team off guard.

Joe Monk was on the top floor in a position from which he could observe the elevator doors and the stairhead, while Len Pope was fitting the listening device in the room shared by Moylan and Corrigan. They had only had a few minutes in which to act since knowing which room the hotel would allocate to them.

The induction bug was no bigger than a grain of rice, drawing its power from the nearest mains cable in the building. It was affixed to the curtains; according to Pope's lore, while someone suspicious might inspect the top pleats of curtains, lower folds were never examined. Unfortunately, as it was considered too risky to bug the receiver itself, the transmitter would only give them one side of any telephone conversation, at least for the moment. By using the standard SAS lock-picking tools they had been able to check both adjoining rooms and found one to be unoccupied; later Pope would complain about his ground floor room being too dark and ask to change it. A joke to the effect that 403 was his lucky room number should get him what he wanted.

Both Monk and Pope picked up the signal from Buzz who was still in the bar. Using his concealed chest mike, he warned that Moylan was heading for the elevators with Avery and Corrigan. Pope had just slipped from the room when Monk reported that the men had reached their floor. Just as Moylan rounded the corner in the corridor, Pope disappeared into his adjoining room. He moved swiftly to the ordinary looking briefcase which housed the radio receiver, then remotely activated the bug in Moylan's room, put on his headset, and adjusted the sound level.

'What do you want to do tomorrow if we haven't heard?' It was Avery's voice.

'You and Maggie can play at tourists,' Moylan replied. 'Go and enjoy the sights. Lew and I had better stay here in case they try and contact us . . . '

'Con, what the hell are you doing?'

Pope frowned; Avery sounded anxious.

'I don't trust the Iraqis, Max. A portable radio on FM is the simplest bug-sweeper there is.'

Pope froze, his eyes widening. Christ! He reached out and flipped the deactivate switch.

He just caught Avery saying, 'Who the hell's going to want to wire your room –?' when it cut out.

Pope punched his fist into his open palm in frustration. That was one thing they hadn't anticipated. That Con Moylan suspected that a wary Iraqi *Estikhbarat* might have bugged their room.

Shit, shit, shit!

Within minutes, news of the near disaster reached the operational base in the apartment block in the essentially residential district of Pangrati to the east of the city.

Jim Buckley replaced the receiver and recounted the event to Brian Hunt. He added: 'Max and Lew were quick to cotton on – took over the room search themselves. One of them even dismantled the phone before Moylan thought of it.'

'We'll have to tread really carefully if Moylan's going to be this hyped up,' Hunt reflected.

'You goin' ahead with the direct tap?'

Hunt nodded. 'It's essential to know what's going on. Lew reckons he and Monk will patch into the wire in the corridor tonight when it's quiet.'

'Good. I'll be twitchy until we can plug into any calls. It's vital to give us warning of where they're going – as it is, we need to get two teams into position for first light. Let's hope they've all managed to get some sleep.'

However, although the rest of the teams were crashed out on camp beds in the three bedrooms, sleep was not yet a luxury that Hunt and Buckley could afford.

Eyelids heavy with fatigue, they kept vigil in the kitchen over a couple of whiskies, waiting for one more vital delivery.

The previous two days had been thoroughly shattering for both them and the team leaders. Not only had all the vehicles, equipment and supplies to be checked, but a crash programme of orientation had also been essential.

Armed with maps they had quartered the streets, at first on foot and then by vehicle to familiarise themselves with one-way traffic systems and dead ends. After a couple of days it was amazing how much geographical information could be absorbed – even of a complex sprawl like Athens. Once studied, each district began to take on a personality and broad category of its own: Evangelosmos and Ilissia were the areas for embassies and big international hotels, like the Hilton and the Caravel; the suburban sprawl of the south-east; the fashion boutiques and café-life around Kolonaki Square; the tourist mecca of Plaka; the illegal immigrants and down-and-outs around Omonia, and the student stronghold of Moussio. All districts radiated out from the vast National Garden park, a tranquil eye in the middle of the maelstrom that was the traffic of Athens.

It was past midnight when Stafford Philpot arrived.

Now in his late seventies, his tall thin body stooped with age, the quintessential Englishman was the ideal choice as general organiser and go-between with the British and American Embassies. The staff of both were desperately anxious to keep their necessary involvement secret, fearing the disastrous diplomatic fallout if the Greeks discovered what was going on.

Philpot had parachuted into Greece for the SOE during the Second World War to help organise resistance against the occupying Nazis. He fell in love with the place and later married a beautiful Athenian girl. Despite a later career in the Foreign Service and in intelligence work, he would always return to his beloved Greece and the family home between postings.

Since his retirement twelve years earlier he had divided his time between writing features on Balkan politics for newspapers around the world and keeping in touch with old friends from his resistance days, many of whom were now members of the Greek Establishment.

Certainly no one would suspect the old man in his loosely knotted club tie and threadbare suit marked with soup stains.

'Sorry to have put you to all this trouble,' Buckley apologised as Hunt made some tea; Philpot reluctantly declined the whisky on medical grounds. 'You must be finding it a strain.'

There was a bright light in the faded blue eyes that defied senility. His voice was still resonant, the public school vowels pronounced with precision. 'Nonsense, dear boy, haven't enjoyed myself so much since my wife was alive. You've saved me from terminal boredom! Since Percy called me from the embassy two weeks ago, I haven't touched a drop. That'll please my doctor, the miserable old fart.' He glanced around the kitchen. 'I just hope I haven't let you down.'

Their safe house, the carefully selected provisions and all their transport – Philpot's achievements verged on the miraculous.

'You've done wonders,' Hunt assured.

The old man's face lit up with pride and he dumped the heavy plastic bag on the table as though it contained mere groceries. 'These are what you've been waiting for. Some are a bit ancient, I'm afraid.'

Hunt opened the first bag: an old Luger, a Beretta and a Walther. They completed an arsenal of locally acquired firearms which would throw no suspicions on either the American or British Embassies if things went wrong.

'I think most are from Turkish and Serbian sources,' Philpot said after sampling his tea. 'A bit rusty, but nothing that can't be cleaned up. Can't promise they don't have a history, of course.'

Buckley smiled. 'You must know some damn dubious people, Stafford, to have assembled this lot at short notice.'

The old man laughed. 'You really should not ask questions, dear boy. Let's just say I looked up a few trusted friends from my wartime days. Sadly not all became successful politicians and businessmen.'

Philpot's delivery completed the teams' inventory and Hunt noticed his reluctance to leave for the small apartment he rented in a back street behind the National Library.

Both Hunt and Buckley were sad to see him go, but their desperate need for sleep meant that they were blissfully thankful when he eventually did.

★    ★    ★

Storm clouds could be seen gathering as the first dawn light filtered over the eastern Athens skyline.

Len Pope stirred on the bed where he lay, fully clothed. Cranking open one eye, he saw Joe Monk seated on the end of the twin bed next to him. He was listening intently on the headphones.

'What is it? A phone call?' They had wired into the line two hours earlier.

'Sssh!'

Suddenly Pope was wide awake; he slid from the bed to crouch on the floor by the other man's side. Monk lifted one earphone from his head and cocked his ear towards their door.

Pope heard it, too. Soft footsteps in the corridor outside.

'I knew it,' Monk breathed. 'Something's been pushed under the door.'

'A newspaper?'

'Not unless Moylan can read Greek.'

'Want me to see who it was?'

Monk nodded. 'Don't go far. I might need you back in a hurry. Keep in touch.'

Len Pope slipped on his jacket which was fitted with a short-range Clansman PRC 349 radio system, including a lapel mike and flesh-coloured earpiece. Silently he opened the door, peered into the corridor, then stepped outside.

Monk was aware of someone grunting in the next bedroom, the sound of disturbed sleep.

'Jesus,' a voice mumbled. Monk thought it was Moylan. Then a bed creaked as the man stood, the sound enhancer picking up the pad of bare feet on the carpet. Again a rustle of paper as the man stooped to the floor.

'Con?' This time it was unmistakably Corrigan speaking. 'What the hell are you doing?'

Moylan cleared his throat. 'Someone's pushed this note under the door.'

'What's it say?'

'Oh, shit, it's in Arabic or something.'

'Let's see.' Another rustle. 'Our Libyan friends – it must be.'

'Stupid buggers. How the hell do they expect me to read this?'

'Call Max, he knows the lingo.'

Monk heard the telephone being dialled and, five minutes later, Avery had joined them.

'Peace be upon you, et cetera,' he read aloud, aware that the surveillance team should be listening in. 'We are friends of Mr Abdullah in Malta. We wish to meet you at the National Gardens. There is a map enclosed, the place marked X. You will be contacted at ten o'clock this morning.'

'Where is that?' Moylan asked.

'Just up the road from here,' Corrigan answered. 'According to the map the place is a bloody maze.'

'That'll be why they chose it,' Avery observed.

Moylan said: 'I wonder why they didn't phone us?'

'Like Abdullah said in Malta, they think the CIA are watching their every move,' Corrigan replied.

Avery continued reading: 'The letter concludes with the usual Arab rhetoric, *Inshalla*, et cetera. Signed Ahmad.'

'And may the fleas of a thousand camels infest Ahmad's armpits,' Corrigan muttered.

Still listening, Monk reached for the telephone and rang through to control. When Hunt answered, he said: 'Brian, they've made contact. There's an RV arranged for 1000 hours.'

'Where?'

'The National Gardens.'

'We're on our way.'

# Eleven

Events were to move fast that day.

Monk eavesdropped on a furious row between Avery and Maggie as he explained that he had to go on an urgent appointment with Moylan and Corrigan, giving her no option but to visit the city's sights by herself.

Leaving her in a sullen silence, he joined the two men at reception.

Outside there was an unaccustomed chill in the air, the sky overcast with threatening cloud. Yet the change in the weather had done nothing to dampen the spirits of the Athens motorists. Traffic continued to thunder through the streets in an endless, reckless torrent. Shoals of motor-cyclists, invariably carrying their helmets hooked on their elbows in defiance of the law, weaved at high speed between hurtling cars, hooting taxis and lumbering single-deck Ikaras buses.

Junction by junction as the lights changed, the three men made their way towards the National Gardens, crossing warily as vehicles shrieked to a grudging halt.

Just a short distance into the park, the strident noise of the traffic became transmuted to a background hum. They had stepped into another world, dense and green. A forest of trees towered above them, the evergreens absorbing the city sounds. A path meandered through a tranquil glade between untended shrubs where birds trilled in celebration of their haven of sanity amidst the chaos of Athens.

'Cats,' Corrigan observed. 'There are bloody cats everywhere.'

He was right. Cats walked stiff-legged across their path, watching their intrusion with disapproval; cats stalked the undergrowth for rodents and unsuspecting birds; others sat hunched enigmatically on branches; still more waited, as though listening, by the groups of old men gathered on the seats beneath the trees to exchange the day's gossip. Everywhere, pairs of eyes could be seen in the shadows, ever watchful and all-seeing.

A final twist in the path brought them to a secluded circular fish pond, the area cordoned by rustic fencing.

'No one here,' Moylan observed. 'Is this it?'

Avery turned the map upside down. 'I think so.'

'I can see why they chose it,' Corrigan said, peering at the fleeting flashes of gold beneath the surface of the pond. 'Far from prying eyes.'

They waited until ten minutes past the hour before the contact appeared. He was in his early twenties, walking along the path with an air of studied nonchalance, hands thrust in the trouser pockets of the beige suit he wore with a shirt but no tie. His complexion was sallow, Middle Eastern, his hair black and unruly.

Every few paces he stopped and looked around, up into

the trees as though trying to identify the source of bird-song.

As he drew level with the three men he suddenly turned and said something in a language that only Avery understood.

'Yes, we are the friends of Ali Abdullah,' Avery answered. 'And you?'

The young man spoke nervously from the side of his mouth. 'I am Ahmad.'

Avery noticed that another Arab-looking individual had appeared on the far side of the pond; he carried what looked like a Polaroid camera. 'What's going on, Ahmad? Do you know that man?'

'Listen,' the Libyan hissed. 'You are to go to the restaurant at the top of Mount Likavittós. If you use the path, it is just below the summit. Do not take the railway. Be there at one o'clock lunchtime. Do you understand?'

'I understand.'

Ahmad suddenly stepped aside and the Arab across the pond raised the viewfinder of the Polaroid to his eye. There was a click and a whirr.

Moylan was suddenly alarmed. 'What's he saying, Max? What's he up to?'

Avery turned back to Ahmad, but the man was already sauntering away, moving a little faster now. On the far side of the pond, the other Arab had melted into the shadows.

Moylan was agitated. 'What's going on, Max?'

'It looks like we've got a lunch date.'

Above his head a mangy tabby watched from its precarious perch in the fork of a tree, eyes staring, its ears pointed and alert.

Gretchen Adams captured the scene on an 800 mm lens Olympus with an X2 converter, shot from dense under-growth on the far side of the fish pond.

When the three men began their return walk to the hotel, she and Buzz followed with their arms lovingly linked. As they neared the Herodian, an inconspicuous Volkswagen Passatt pulled into the kerbside ahead of them; Jim Buckley was driving and Brian Hunt reached back to open the rear passenger door.

The couple climbed in.

'Well?' Buckley demanded.

'They met an Arab-looking guy,' Buzz replied. 'They exchanged a few words, then another guy took a photo-graph of them.'

Gretchen released the cassette from her camera and handed it to her chief. 'We were all taking pictures of each other,' she said with disgust. 'Well, not quite true. They didn't see me, but then I couldn't get an angle on the Arab with the camera.'

'It was a bloody farce,' Buzz agreed. 'They'd chosen a place where they couldn't be overlooked. Gretch and I had to crawl through the undergrowth on all fours. There were people about – got some weird looks when we came out afterwards covered in mud and dead leaves . . . '

'But not a complete disaster?' Buckley pressed.

'I'm not so sure,' Buzz replied. 'I used the directional

mike, but the quality was piss-poor – too much background noise.'

'What did they say?'

'They talked Arabic,' Buzz explained, rewinding the cassette secreted in his sportsbag. He pressed the play button, the burble of voices almost indistinguishable from the background clutter of rustling leaves and birdsong.

Hunt strained to hear. 'Something about Mount Likavittós . . . A restaurant?'

Gretchen nodded. 'There are two places up there. A smart restaurant and a self-service place.'

Buzz regarded his commander with defiance. 'Hell, chief, can't we put a bug on Avery or on Lew? Otherwise it'll be a disaster just looking for somewhere to happen.'

'And what sort of shit are those two going to be in if they're found to be wired?' Buckley retorted.

Gretchen interrupted. 'What about those fountain-pen transmitters? They're pretty neat. They actually write as well.'

Buckley turned to Hunt. 'What y' think, Brian?'

'I don't think we have much choice, Jim. Let's do it.'

In the meantime Monk and Pope were able to confirm the lunchtime rendezvous by tuning into the conversations between Moylan, Avery and Corrigan back at the hotel.

Maggie had still not returned from her sightseeing by the time the three men left for their meeting.

As they hailed a passing yellow Cortina taxi, a second Toyota Corolla cab pulled out farther down the street.

It was manned by three members of Charlie Squad. Luther Dicks, a black Delta trooper from Rock Creek in

Washington, was at the wheel. His unlikely oppo was Brad Carver, a blond redneck from Mississippi who, to the surprise of anyone who didn't know them, was Luther Dicks's closest friend.

In the rear sat Villiers, a veteran sergeant who was very much SAS old school. Coming near to the end of his active service life at forty-four, the rangy Glaswegian was as proud of his missing front teeth – knocked out in a Malaysian bar brawl – as he was of the gallantry medals that languished in his bottom drawer back home.

By contrast the second SAS man, riding a motorcycle behind the Corolla, was a new-wave recruit to the Regiment. A non-smoking keep-fit fanatic, his only vice was given away by his apt nickname. Grammar school educated and now in his late twenties, 'Randy' Reid made the most of his almost embarrassingly good looks.

It was Ran Reid's job to take over and catch up with Moylan's taxi if the tailing Corolla lost it at lights or in heavy traffic. But then Luther Dicks was grimly determined that this was not going to happen. No crazy Greek taxi driver was going to prove himself a match for a Rock Creek boy. Besides, his oppo Brad Carver would never let him hear the last of it.

In the event the journey to Likavittós, the highest point in Athens, passed without incident. The taxi dropped its fares on the perimeter road that encircled the huge hump of a mountain. To Charlie Team's surprise their quarry did not take the funicular railway, but took the laborious zigzag pathway to the top.

After a heated radio exchange with Bravo Team, who were about to take the mountain train, it was decided not to follow on foot. It became clear that Moylan, Avery and Corrigan were following instructions – any tail would be easily spotted trudging in pursuit up the open mountainside.

By the time the three men completed their exhausting ascent, spits of rain in the air had developed into a downpour, driving diners from the marble-paved terrace to seek refuge inside the restaurant.

Moylan was first through the door, angry and exhausted after the prolonged climb, and was met by the obsequious head waiter. 'Please, I take your jacket to dry. Your friend waits for you.'

The customer rose, smiling, to greet the approach of three men. Portly and in his fifties, he had an olive complexion and short curly hair once black but now turning to silver. Dressed casually in a cashmere sweater and slacks, his expensive dental work glistened white and gold beneath a generous moustache.

'Mr Moylan, it is my pleasure.' His platinum bracelet rattled against a Rolex Oyster Perpetual watch as he shook hands. 'Join me please, all of you. The food here is wonderful.'

'You have me at a disadvantage,' Moylan said, noticing that the Polaroid print, taken at the National Gardens that morning, was propped against the condiment set.

The man introduced himself as Nassir al-Arif, his words picked up by the microphone concealed in the sportsbag carried by one of the American tourist couple seated at the nearby window.

Al-Arif explained that he was a Lebanese of Iraqi parentage. A trader in many different commodities, he based himself in Athens, which he considered to be at the crossroads of Europe and the Middle East.

Over the next hour he ate and talked with equal enthusiasm. Always effusive and polite, his string of questions were nevertheless probing and relentless. Yet never once did he touch on their real identities or the true purpose of their visit, asking instead about Moylan's construction business, his relationship with Avery and Corrigan, and their supposed reason for being in Athens. Feigning forgetfulness, he would double back on some minor point or other, until it became clear that they were being carefully vetted. Despite Al-Arif's smiles it was obvious that the question of the American's nationality was troubling him.

In hushed exasperation, Moylan said: 'Look, if we were trying to deceive you, we'd have got Lew a false passport and you'd be none the wiser. He's as Irish as I am.'

Finally Al-Arif appeared satisfied. 'I think, Mr Moylan, I may be able to help you.' He produced a crocodile wallet from his trouser pocket and plucked a business card from one of the folds. 'If you are to trade you will want a trustworthy shipping agent. This man has an office in Piraeus. Go there tomorrow morning. Let's say eight o'clock. I will tell him to expect you.

'Now, please allow me to pay for your lunches, it has been such a pleasure.'

\*          \*          \*

In the late afternoon Brian Hunt and Jim Buckley called by at Stafford Philpot's tiny apartment.

Despite having obviously interrupted his nap, the old man was overjoyed to see them, insisting they joined him for a pot of Earl Grey. He led the way into a dimly lit living room filled with dark antique furniture and decorated with faded photographs and memorabilia of his war years and subsequent postings around the world.

Two bright eyes stared unnervingly from the gloomy recesses of a Welsh dresser.

'Don't mind Aristotle, he's a very inquisitive cat. I sometimes think he must know more than is good for him.'

Buckley placed a fan of blown-up photographic prints on the table as Philpot poured tea into unmatching Dresden china cups. 'Good, then perhaps Aristotle will be able to put a name to this character? Apparently Libyan, calls himself Ahmad.'

The American explained about the morning meeting by the fish pond while Philpot reached for his half-moon reading glasses.

'Can't help you there,' the Englishman said at length. 'My guess is Ahmad is just one of Gaddafi's humble foot soldiers. You'll probably find he's registered as a mature student at some college here.' He poured tea into a saucer for the cat before looking at the second selection of prints taken at the restaurant. 'Ah, Nassir al-Arif if his passport's to be believed.'

Relief showed on Buckley's face. 'You know him?'

'He's an old hand here. Operates as a merchant in all sorts of shady business including exporting ancient arte- facts. But apart from that he has a lot of connections in Cyprus and Lebanon. Considers himself to be something of an honest broker between rival Arab factions. The National Information Service – that's the Greek secret service, of course – have Al-Arif marked down for connec- tions with Iraqi intelligence. But whether official, unoffi- cial or freelance, well, who knows?'

Hunt accepted one of Philpot's offered gingernut biscuits. 'You're very well-informed, Stafford.'

The old man placed his elbows on the table and laced his matchstick fingers together. 'Old habits die hard. Besides our head of station here helps me keep my hand in, asking advice about this and that. I suspect largely because some of my old friends from my SOE days are now high-ranking officials in Greek Intelligence, and we still keep in touch.' Philpot reached out and stroked his cat; Aristotle purred contentedly and blinked at the photographs. 'Tell me, what did Al-Arif have to say for himself?'

Hunt shrugged. 'Mostly asked a lot of general questions. I've listened to the tape transcript. It's not very clear quality, but it sounded as though he was just establishing that they were who they claimed to be. In the end Al-Arif offered to put them in touch with a shipping agent in Piraeus. Unfortunately we didn't get a name.'

'Ah,' Philpot exclaimed. 'That all fits, I see it now. The Iraqis have obviously asked Al-Arif to vet Moylan and your people before passing them down the line. And I think I can help you there. It's a pound to a penny that the shipping agent is Khaled Fadel.'

'How d'you know that?' Buckley asked. 'If it's not an improper question.'

Philpot regarded him with watery blue eyes. 'Dear boy, you may know that both you Americans and ourselves made the embarrassing mistake of bolstering Saddam Hussein's war machine during the Iran–Iraq conflict to ensure the Islamic Fundamentalists didn't gain ground . . . Well, many of the secret arms shipments went through Khaled Fadel. A well-established and, may I say, respected pillar of society – a charming chap to boot.' He smiled, revealing age-stained teeth and receding gums. 'Only I believe you will find he is also the *Estikhbarat's* main agent in Athens.'

Buckley's grin was wide. 'Bingo! Stafford, you're a genius.'

Aristotle looked around curiously at the three smiling faces.

The next morning the surveillance teams were already in place when Moylan, Avery and Corrigan left the hotel to take the train to the port of Piraeus.

In the adjoining carriage the rangy Glaswegian Villiers and young Ran Reid were benefiting from the improved communications; the night before Buzz had surreptitiously passed a fountain-pen transmitter to Corrigan in the hotel bar.

As the microtape revolved silently in Reid's TWA bag, he was simultaneously able to listen to the conversation via a fine, flesh-coloured lead that ran up the sleeve of his jacket to the transparent plastic earpiece. He learned how, despite the fact that Avery had taken Maggie out alone to eat the previous night, she remained irritated at the prospect of being left for another day's lonely sightseeing by herself.

When Moylan's trio finally emerged from the forecourt of Piraeus station, Luther Dicks and Brad Carver climbed out of a parked car and took over the tail on foot. Villiers and Reid went to the car, started the engine and drove ahead to position themselves outside the office of the shipping agent Khaled Fadel.

Dicks and Carver shadowed on opposite sides of the street, one behind and the other considerably ahead as their quarry walked along the palm-dotted waterfront of the third largest port in the Mediterranean. Here cruise liners and inter-island ferries sat stolidly and businesslike at their berths, the very heart of Greece's thriving maritime trade.

Moylan and the others turned off then, down Gheorghiou, a wide street lined with shops, to cut across the peninsula to reach the marina in Limin Zeas bay. In marked contrast to the main port, the harbour was surrounded predominantly by residential apartments. Hundreds of private yachts of every shape and size nuzzled the quayside, their lanyards chiming a discordant symphony in the stiff winter wind blowing off the steely Mirtoan Sea.

Ahead of Moylan's arrival, Villiers and Reid parked beneath the trees with a clear view of Fadel's office. They had no cause to think anything of the blue Mercedes van in the blue and white-striped livery of the state OTE telecommunications organisation situated some thirty metres away. They had no reason to suspect that the van was tapped into the roadside telephone junction box, or that it was fitted with a powerful telescopic camera.

Likewise the three occupants of the OTE van had no reason to suspect the two Englishmen who had parked nearby.

Indeed Lieutenant Andreas Groutas of the Anti-Terrorist Police was not of a mind to pay any great attention to the harbourside scene he had under surveillance. The young policeman's apathy was a symptom of the malaise that had for so long dogged his department. Years of failure to penetrate his country's biggest terrorist threat – 17 November – had led to a deep-rooted sense of frustration and failure. Sometimes, he thought, he would rather admit to being a traffic cop than a supposed hunter of terrorist killers.

And now, due to pressure from the Americans, he had been assigned to a respected Iraqi businessman who might or might not have some vague connections with Saddam Hussein's intelligence service which presented no threat to his country whatsoever.

For Groutas it had been hardly worth leaving the generous warmth of his girlfriend's thighs earlier that winter's morning. Only loyalty to his boss, Nico Legakis, made him abandon the idea of phoning in sick.

He liked and respected Nico. A policeman's policeman. Despite his little bald head and white weasel face with its twitching moustache, Nico was the true professional, even down to his half-mast trousers. Sometimes Groutas thought

Nico Legakis was the only man in the department to take his job seriously.

Three men stopped outside the office of Khaled Fadel, checking the street number against a scrap of notepaper.

Dutifully Groutas hunched over the tripod, adjusted the camera lens focus, and pressed the cable release. Three clicks. That was enough. He doubted that anyone would give them more than a cursory glance back at the department.

'This must be the place,' Moylan decided.

The glass-fronted door was sandwiched between a café and a shop selling designer yachtwear. Steps rose sharply to an office suite on the first floor. There a matronly Greek receptionist with henna-rinsed hair and gigantic gold earrings was watering pot plants.

'Con Moylan for Mr Fadel.'

She smiled sweetly. 'Oh, yes, he is expecting you. This way please.'

The picture window in Khaled Fadel's office offered a panoramic view of the windswept harbour. Underfoot the carpet was deep-pile cream, complementing the beige-painted walls with their adornment of maritime prints. Everything else in the office was a combination of soft charcoal leather, chrome and smoked glass.

Fadel himself was sprinkling a packet of granulated food into an enormous tropical fish tank beside his desk.

He looked genuinely pleased to see them as his secretary announced their arrival.

'Please, please, please,' he said, indicating a long plush sofa. He was small and slender, dressed in a closely tailored dark suit. Aged in his early fifties, his manner was nervous and apologetic, as though for ever fussing that everything was not quite right. The short black hair glistened with brilliantine and his face bore a small Saddam Hussein looka-like moustache.

'My friend Nassir thinks maybe I can help you,' he said, plumping an armchair cushion as he sat.

Moylan eyed him steadily, waiting for him to settle down. 'I think it is we who can help you. We sent a message.'

'Ah, yes.' At last the fidgeting stopped. The small dark eyes became intense. 'And how was Malta?'

The Irishman ignored the question. 'Then you understand why I am here?'

Fadel smiled and tugged meaningfully at his earlobe. 'I make a point of always talking confidential business over coffee. Somewhere quiet. There is a nice place by the harbour. But first, I believe I understand the nature of your trade. A very rare commodity these days.'

Moylan frowned, trying to read between the lines. 'Not so rare I'd have thought.'

Fadel smiled politely. 'Ah, many may *trade* in such commodities, Mr Moylan, but in recent months I find that few are in the position to *deliver*.'

'I am in the position to deliver,' Moylan asserted.

'How soon?'

'Soon enough.'

'And the price?'

'To be negotiated.' Moylan allowed a sly smile to cross his face. 'But it won't come cheap.'

'Of course not.'

Fadel rose. 'Let us talk over coffee.'

He led the three men back down the stairs and along the windswept avenue for two blocks until he reached an expensive restaurant. At that time in the morning no one else sat at the rows of tables. The only sign of life was an old marmalade tom stalking through the forest of chair legs.

Fadel remained silent until the waiter had finished serving. When he spoke, he was a changed man, his words clipped and decisive. 'Forgive all this subterfuge, Mr Moylan, but I cannot be too careful. These are desperate days for my country. Every morning my office is electronically swept, you understand? Although nothing is found so far, I cannot take a chance. I am trusted and respected here with many Greek friends. But the Americanos – huh! They bully their NATO allies into co-operation. Whatever you have been told, Mr Moylan, I am not a spy. Just a true patriot and loyal Ba'athist member. The party has been good to me. The party is always good to its trusted servants. It is therefore my duty to do all I can to help my country and the party in its time of need.'

Bullshit, thought Avery, although he had to admit he might have been taken in had Stafford Philpot not marked Fadel's card.

'For that reason,' the Iraqi was saying, 'this will be our first and last meeting. There are few enough of us left on the outside who can help our leader in his hour of need. So tell me exactly what the exalted Irish Republican Army can offer Iraq?'

It was strange, eerie, hearing those words spoken in a deserted restaurant in Piraeus on a dismal winter morning. With a chill, crawling sensation running down his spine, Avery suddenly realised he and Corrigan had done it. The stalking horse was over its second hurdle.

Moylan hesitated, glancing first at Avery, then at Corrigan, who was looking on with studied nonchalance. This really was not for their ears. He took a deep breath. 'Our plan is to take out the British Prime Minister and the entire British Cabinet.'

# Twelve

Sophie Papavas watched naked from the bed as her boyfriend of twelve months walked from the shower cubicle across the shabby flatlet to where he had discarded his clothes the previous night. Her black cat watched him too, curled up against her thigh for warmth.

The policeman had a good body, she had to admit. Lean and hard-muscled with a thick mat of black hair on his chest and legs. Andreas Groutas wasn't ashamed to show it either, never happier than standing before the shaving mirror without the modesty of a towel, fully aware that she was looking at him. Certainly he did not lack in Greek come-and-get-me machismo.

She didn't mind that, she had been brought up on it. But what she did not find so endearing was his arrogant policeman's swagger when he walked. It looked so ridiculous when he was bare-arsed, she mused, as though he thought his prick were a truncheon.

He noticed her movement as he pulled on his trousers. 'You're awake then.'

'I've been awake for ages.' The cat uncurled as Groutas

approached the bed, its upper lip drawing back to expose tiny sharp teeth.

He grunted. 'You should have told me.' He glanced at his watch. 'I still have time to fuck you before I go.'

'Not this morning, it's too soon.' She grimaced to indicate that she was still sore.

He looked down at her and grinned, taking it as a compliment. She wore little make-up, really didn't have to with those long black lashes and sensuous dark features. Her hair was as black and silky as her mother's had been, worn in an untamed muddle that tumbled over her shoulders, almost reaching her breasts. His eyes lingered on them, appreciating their ripe fullness, the dark tantalising stubs of her nipples, and the youthful swell of her belly below. And the tufts of coarse hair peeking from between her thighs, matched by the shaggy armpits as she reached to pull up the tangled sheet.

Something began to stir in him. Bloody waste. 'It's probably best. Nico wants to see me. Nine o'clock prompt.'

'The captain calls and the baby lieutenant goes arunning,' she teased.

'Nico's all right,' he responded, buttoning his shirt. 'At least I don't have to go back to that idiotic surveillance until after lunch.'

'What surveillance is that?'

'You know you shouldn't ask – and I shouldn't tell.'

She feigned hurt. 'You are getting just like your boss. A typical policeman who trusts nobody but other policemen. Not even your devoted lover.'

He relented. 'If you must know, it's some Iraqi shipping agent down at Piraeus.'

For a split second she forgot herself. Her mouth dropped. It must be. It couldn't be anyone else. Then she recovered, forcing a girlish giggle and hoping he hadn't noticed the rush of blood to her cheeks. 'I don't want to know!' she said snootily, raising her chin in a gesture of indifference.

But Andreas Groutas had hardly heard. Returning to the bathroom to gel his hair, he was saying: 'I've a whole stack of photographs of people visiting the premises. Nico will want to go through them all with a magnifying glass.'

She glanced at the large buff envelope he had left on the chair beside the bed. Three minutes, she told herself, he never spent less than three minutes ensuring each hair on his head was exactly placed, checking his eyes and baring his teeth at the mirror, generally preening and admiring himself.

Hurriedly she tipped the contents of the envelope onto the bed. A few strips of negative and two dozen prints. She froze, her eyes widening. That was one of them. She thumbed through two more. All three. Moylan, Avery and Corrigan. Sweet Mother of Jesus!

From the bathroom she heard him rinsing his hands. Quickly she stuffed the three prints under the bedclothes, then as an afterthought removed the strips of negatives.

The envelope had just been returned to the chair when Groutas re-entered the room, pulling on his jacket. 'I could get back here at lunchtime, if you want? You know?'

Her white teeth glistened. 'I'll live without it until tonight. I've tutorials all day, so I need to revise over lunch.'

He laughed. 'You'll end up being a nuclear scientist or something one day.'

There was a wicked gleam in her eye. 'I thought I might join the police force.'

He liked her style; for a typical Leftie student, she had a nice sense of humour. They kissed and he left.

As the door closed and his footsteps receded she hissed: 'Bastard!' through clenched teeth. 'Strutting bourgeois bastard. Fascist pig!'

After a quick shower she pulled tight Levis up over her naked, touch-damp body and plucked a floral blouse from her meagre wardrobe. Hurriedly she put out the cat's food. Today was going to be very important; from now on things could get dangerous. She felt a small thrill of anticipation glowing in her lower belly.

It really had been too much to endure, even for the movement. To be screwed nightly by a policeman whose avowed intention was to bring it to the so-called justice of the Establishment.

But today the 17 November was to begin its campaign of vengeance.

Stopping only to gather the photographs and negatives from the bed, she hurried out of the flat. It was only a short ride by scooter to the shabby, sprawling Technical University in Moussio district. The old paint-peeled walls were disfigured by Go Home Yank slogans and covered with fly-posters for rock groups and avant-garde plays, like sticking plasters attempting to hold together the rotting fabric of the building.

Sophie parked and locked her scooter in Exarchaia Square as she always did and waved as she crossed to the pavement café where they always met for a breakfast of cigarettes and strong coffee. Some of her friends waved back. Today she detected an air of excitement in the heated conversation of her fellow students.

'What's going on?' she asked, dumping on the table the helmet that she never wore.

'Didn't you hear on the radio?' one of the boys asked.

'No.' Damn Andreas! 'What?'

'There's been a rocket attack on that industrialist tycoon Vardis Vardinoyannis!'

'No!' So it had happened. 'Was he killed?'

The boy shook his head. 'His Mercedes was armour-plated.'

'Typical,' said another youth. 'The bourgeoisie can afford anything.'

One of Sophie's girlfriends added: 'They say it's 17 November. Do you think it was one of those bazooka things they stole from the War Museum?'

The boy laughed. 'You've got to hand it to them. The cheek of it! Mind you, I prefer it when they direct their attacks against the Americans – God, if I wasn't studying I'd love to join them. Think of the excitement of it all – running rings around the police.'

They wouldn't have you, Sophie thought, not with that self-opinionated mouth of yours. She said: 'We'll have more than the Americans or the police to worry about if we're late for this morning's lecture.'

They broke up then, joining the stream of students gravitating towards the polytechnic, walking down Stournari Street with its shops full of computers, drawing materials and technical textbooks.

A youth was handing out leaflets by the rusting green gates. Recognising her, he slipped out the bottom leaflet from the pile and gave it to her. She barely glanced at the cheaply printed invitation to a student dance. Careful that no one else could see her, she flipped it over and read the handwritten note on the back. *Today. Time and place as discussed. Be careful. The Professor.*

Her heart skipped. She knew then that not a word of that morning's tutorial would sink in. The time would drag until the lunchtime break.

She was one of the few who knew the Professor. Not his identity, of course, no one knew that. But she knew him by sight, although not his name nor what he did when he was not running one of the most long-lasting, undetected terrorist cell networks in Europe. She did know that he was most certainly *not* a professor. That *nom de guerre* had been jokingly assumed after press speculation that the terror gang's leader was some Left-wing academic. It was a reasonable assumption to make, Sophie supposed, as the movement took its name from the date of an abortive student uprising in 1973 against the then ruling junta of generals.

The message meant only one thing. The Irishman had

passed the test; the Iraqis' test, not hers. She was to make contact with a group of members from the Provisional IRA.

She knew that the Professor was not altogether happy about it. After all it had been he who had contacted the Iraqi intelligence agent Khaled Fadel and offered to fight on Saddam Hussein's behalf against their shared enemy, the Americans. It had been his idea, his crusade for the greater glory of Greece and the proletariat, and with no financial reward. As a matter of principle he had rejected Fadel's generous offer out of hand. To have accepted would have implied subservience, and she knew too well that the Professor was subservient to no man.

Now the Irish were on the scene. Offering heavy muscle, a vast organisation and resources that 17 November could only dream about. She resented that, and she suspected that the Professor did too. But by working with the Provisionals they could strike far beyond their usual capabilities – even to the very heart of the world's imperialists. It would be a marriage of convenience.

When the lunch bell sounded she sought her tutor and informed him she felt unwell and would therefore be taking the rest of the day off. Returning to where she had parked her scooter, she rode off south. For once she wore her crash helmet; it would not do for anyone to recognise her now.

Ten minutes later she arrived in the run-down neigh-bourhood of Monastiraki. In the shadow of the Acropolis, beside the railway line, the huddled alleys of the flea market were home to the Athens underclass, where lowly street traders in every conceivable commodity rubbed shoulders with black marketeers, smugglers, pimps, prostitutes and drug pedlars.

Sophie Paravas nosed her scooter through the throng, hooting to clear a passage as she wobbled her way deep into the market, finally dismounting at one of the shabby stalls under a weathered khaki awning.

The man she knew only as Michalis was rearranging his motley collection of militaria. Like most men she knew, she considered that he had never grown up. His face remained chubby and boyish, despite the massive clump of unruly hair and a beard of equal proportions. And the thin, wire-framed spectacles added to the impression of the introverted, eternal student.

Only his height and his huge shoulders, emphasised by his usual olive anorak, ran counter to the image. The combined effect of his size and all that hair reminded Sophie of some enormous cuddly toy, big and harmless. Yet she knew that nothing could be further from the truth.

He looked up as she wheeled her scooter in. To her mild irritation he hardly seemed to notice her, not even a lingering glance at the tight cut of her jeans.

As though talking to no one in particular, he said solemnly: 'Come through the back.'

He led the way into the dingy recesses of the concrete building, between avenues of storage boxes and books bundled with string. The place smelled of damp and mildew.

'Is the van ready?' she asked.

He stared at her for a moment, his eyes unblinking

behind the spectacles. 'What do you think?' he replied quietly.

The shoebox was hidden beneath some hessian sacking. He prised off the lid and offered her the box. They were wrapped in oilskin. Ancient they might be, but they were beautifully preserved: a Turkish-made MKE Kirikkale automatic, modelled on the Walther PP, and a pre-war German Luger.

She smiled. 'I don't have to ask which one you want.'

For once he responded: a twitch of a smile as he reached lovingly for the Luger. Without a second's hesitation she took the MKE, checked the safety, the magazine and the breech and pocketed the spare 7.65 mm ammunition from the box.

Satisfied, she said: 'Let's go.'

The three men returned from Piraeus to find Maggie in the hotel reception area contemplating an afternoon of more solo sightseeing.

'So the wanderers return,' she observed icily. 'Where are you off to next?'

At the end of their meeting with Khaled Fadel, he had told them merely that they would be contacted 'in due course'. None of them could have guessed how soon that would be.

Moylan said: 'You can have your husband back for the afternoon. Tell you what. Let's make it up to you – I'll treat us all to a good lunch. Someone told me the Krikelas is good, near the Caravel Hotel.'

Although she wanted nothing to do with Moylan, it seemed churlish to refuse to go; both Avery and Corrigan clearly relished the idea of something more than standard taverna fare.

There were no taxis outside in Robertou Galli and they began walking towards the busy main street, Moylan and Corrigan in front, Avery and Maggie behind, discussing the Greek dishes they had cooked at evening classes years before.

No one noticed the rusting blue minibus with its painted-over windows parked under the trees beside the narrow pavement.

As they drew level, the rear door was thrown open and a young woman in tight jeans stepped out, blocking their path.

Tossing her mane of black hair, she announced simply: 'I am Sophie. Please, you will all get in.'

They were suitably stunned, it taking a moment for the men to realise that this was an elaborate security precaution, to pluck them unexpectedly from the streets of Athens. She could also tell that they were surprised by her youth and, judging by the expression on the men's faces, her striking good looks. Males, she thought scornfully, were so predictable. Even taken off guard at a moment like this, they couldn't separate their brains from what they kept in their underpants.

'I wasn't expecting this,' Moylan said guardedly.

'That's the idea,' Sophie retorted, nodding to the open doors. 'Now quickly, please.'

As the Irishman and Corrigan climbed in, Maggie held back, turning to Avery: 'Max, I don't understand what's going on. Who is this girl?'

He ushered her forward. 'Get in, I'll explain.'

Sophie followed them in. Before the doors slammed shut, the driver, hidden by a curtain, was pulling away. It was dark in the back of the minibus, lit only by a shaft of daylight from a spyhole in the painted rear window.

Maggie was bewildered and alarmed as she bounced on the hard bench seat, clinging to Avery's arm as the vehicle hurtled round a series of corners. 'Please, Max, stop the lies,' she pleaded. 'Tell me the truth!'

Sitting opposite, Sophie watched her with mounting concern. 'Doesn't she know? I thought she was one of you?'

'She is,' Moylan retorted irritably. 'She's with Max here, but she doesn't know what's happening. We didn't know you were going to pull a stunt like this.'

Corrigan added: 'You'll have to tell her now, Max.'

Maggie's eyes widened. 'Tell me what?' She fixed Moylan with a contemptuous stare. 'This *is* something to do with the Provies, isn't it, Con? Dammit, I knew you'd never change.'

'There's more to it than that,' Avery said quietly.

A slow smile spread across Moylan's face. 'Put her in the picture, Max. She's in it again now up to her pretty little neck with the rest of us. There's nothing she can do about it.' A dry chuckle. 'Quite like old times.'

Suddenly she felt quite nauseous in the rattling confines of the minibus. Nauseous with the sickening sense of fear

in the pit of her stomach. That and the feeling of humili-
ation at allowing herself to be so obviously deceived. And
by Max of all people. He had lied, lied, lied. How could
he? All the time he had known. He had betrayed her trust,
risked the future of their own baby son.

Avery was saying: 'The Provisionals – we – are giving
the Iraqis a helping hand.'

For a moment she thought she'd misheard. She stared at
him. Of all the things she expected to be told, it certainly
wasn't that.

'The Iraqis?' she asked incredulously, glancing at Sophie.
'The Iraqis? What! You mean Saddam Hussein?' It was too
weird a concept for her to grasp.

'The Iraqis need specialist assistance,' Moylan added,
showing some amusement at her reaction. 'And we're going
to give it – for a very high price.'

'You're mad!' she shouted suddenly. 'All of you!' She
made a lunge for the rear doors. 'Will you stop the van? I
want to get out!'

Avery grabbed her arm and wrestled her back into her
seat. 'Shut up, Maggie! There's nothing you can do about
it.'

Her nostrils flared. 'You bastard!' She spat the words,
flailing at him with her fists until he was obliged to restrain
her wrists.

Sophie had observed the exchange with growing apprehension, aware that she had made a dangerous mistake. She
had assumed that all four, whom she had watched arriving
separately at the airport, were members of one of the world's

most feared and respected terrorist organisations. How was she to have known that Avery's wife was an innocent and ignorant party?

Maggie was glaring at Avery with contempt. 'You just used me. What was the idea, to use me to improve your cover? Make us look more like a bunch of tourists?'

He shrugged. 'It seemed like a good idea at the time.'

Suddenly she snapped, and her lungs emptied in a bellowing roar. 'BASTARD!'

Moylan reached quickly forward, his long fingers clasping her chin like a dog's muzzle, stifling her cry. He pinched the jaw hard, twisting her face askew at an angle that contorted her mouth.

'She'll have to learn to co-operate,' Sophie warned darkly.

Moylan's grip intensified. 'Oh, she'll co-operate all right.'

It was all Avery could do to contain himself. Inside he was seething. Cursing himself for having brought her to Athens and now finding it impossible to come to her rescue without blowing the entire operation apart.

'Leave it out, Con,' he demanded, his tone barely restrained. What he really wanted to do was to smash the man's head against the side of the van. To shatter his skull into a hundred pieces.

Moylan must have picked up the vibes, noted the under-tone in Avery's words. He pulled an uncertain half-smile and released his grip, leaving Maggie to nurse the red weals on her skin. 'I think there's a lot you don't know about that girl, Max.' The idea seemed to amuse him.

'I'm not interested,' Avery retorted, his voice firm and level. 'She's told me about her past and about you.'

'Not everything, I bet,' Moylan goaded.

'As much as I want to hear, Con, thank you. And if you so much as touch her again, I'll break your fuckin' arms for you. Right?'

Maggie had regained some composure, and began to put her thoughts into more rational order. She regarded Sophie with suspicion. 'You are not an Iraqi.'

The girl smiled thinly, relieved that Maggie had calmed down. 'That is very perceptive of you,' she said sarcastically, then glanced at Moylan. 'Khaled Fadel did not tell you about my organisation?'

Moylan frowned. 'Organisation? Aren't you with Iraqi intelligence?'

'No, Mr Moylan, and please never make that mistake. Iraqi intelligence can hardly breathe, let alone walk freely, without the Americans knowing about it. That is why you are dealing with us. Our organisation is unpenetrated and is the avowed enemy of the United States. That is why we are acting as surrogates for the Iraqis at this time. It is in our mutual interest.'

Moylan was bemused. 'Then just what the hell *is* your organisation?'

A hint of pride crept into her voice. 'We are the 17 November.'

Outside the Herodian Hotel, Brad Carver had left Luther Dicks in their parked car while he positioned himself ready to follow on foot when Moylan's group left the hotel to go to lunch.

Farther along the street he noticed that the Glaswegian Villiers was also in position. In a nearby side street Ran Reid waited on his motorcycle.

Moylan and Corrigan stepped out of the foyer; Avery and Maggie were close behind. They all appeared to be engrossed in conversation. In the car Luther Dicks picked up the American's voice through the fountain-pen transmitter. 'No taxis, we'll find one at the cross roads . . .' They all moved on. Farther up the street Villiers started his motorcycle; Brad Carver closed up the rear.

It was difficult to see what happened next. Parked vehicles obscured the view and the pavement was in shade. Suddenly a girl was standing in front of them, talking to Moylan. No one had seen where she came from. It was as though she had materialised from thin air.

There was an abrupt rush of movement. People were clambering into a parked minibus. The doors slammed. A cloud of exhaust burst over the street and then the minibus was on the move.

'Charlie One to all units,' Dicks called out. 'What the hell is going on?'

Villiers came on first; he'd been in the best position to witness events. '*Charlie Three to One – it appears our friends have been abducted in the van. They were approached by a girl on the pavement and they seemed surprised. Suggest Charlie Four goes in pursuit.*'

'Roger to that,' Dicks snapped. 'Did you read that, Charlie Four?'

Ran Reid had picked it up, revved his motorcycle. '*I'm on my way, One. Out*'.

He roared out of the side street, slowing momentarily to allow Villiers to throw himself onto the pillion before he accelerated hard after the minibus.

In his stalk mirror Reid saw Luther Dicks's car pull in to collect Brad Carver before joining the pursuit.

Meanwhile the minibus had swung north and now waited to join the relentless torrent of traffic coursing along the Dionissio Areopagitou that flanked the southern side of the massive ten-acre rock on which the Acropolis stood. Reid held back, noting that the registration plate of the minibus had been obscured, no doubt deliberately. Then he resumed the chase, leaving a one-car gap as the minibus swept northwards around the outskirts of the tree-filled Areios Pagos park before reaching the busy Thissio neighbourhood. There it crossed the railway line and headed west into the sprawling industrial wasteland of the city's suburbs.

He was settling in for a long ride when, after a few miles, the minibus turned off abruptly into the yard of a derelict factory. Reid crossed the mouth of the turning, then pulled in. Villiers dismounted from the pillion and sauntered back to the corner for a clearer view. He was just in time to see a bearded man pushing open the corrugated iron gates of what appeared to be a dilapidated warehouse. The man returned to the vehicle before driving it into the gloomy interior. Moments later the gates closed again and the scene returned to its former dereliction, tumbleweed, old newspapers and discarded food cartons scurrying in the breeze between the hulks of rusting trailers.

Villiers returned to the motorcycle where he found that Reid had been joined by Luther Dicks and Brad Carver, who were consulting a large-scale map in the back of their car.

'There's no way to approach without being seen,' Villiers reported.

Dicks jabbed his finger at the map. 'It's a sort of cul-de-sac,' he agreed. 'But maybe we can approach around the back. Wanna try, Ran?'

While Reid and Villiers rode around the back streets to find an unobserved route through to the warehouse, Carver attempted to tune in to the signals from the fountain-pen transmitter carried by Lew Corrigan. It was dead.

It was cold and dark in the cavernous void of the old warehouse. Somewhere in the blackness water dripped from a broken pipe; nervous scurryings could be heard in the surrounding debris.

Sophie Papavas lit a paraffin lantern to illuminate a small area in which old tea chests had been arranged to serve as makeshift tables and chairs.

In anticipation that they'd be searched, Corrigan had surreptitiously dropped his fountain pen on the floor and kicked it into the shadows. He had guessed right, and the searches found nothing.

The girl appeared less anxious. 'It is not very comfortable here, but it is safe to talk. That is what matters.' She looked directly at Moylan. 'Our mutual Libyan friends say that you are to be trusted, that you are responsible for the actions of the IRA in Britain and in Europe. Is that so?'

The Irishman shifted uneasily. It wasn't something he was accustomed to discussing with close colleagues, let alone strangers. 'Yes.'

'And these two men?'

He was beginning to resent her interrogation, already unnerved at finding himself in the company of what he regarded as a bunch of crackpot loony anarchists. 'Max Avery is what we call a quartermaster. He organises some of our logistics in Europe – safe houses, vehicles, documents, that sort of thing. He also speaks fluent Arabic for when we deal with the Iraqis.'

Maggie listened, dumbfounded; she had no idea he had been quite so deeply involved.

'But he is English?' Sophie queried.

Moylan smiled thinly. 'You can't have everything. He's English by birth, but his parents and family were Irish. He's been with us for six years now.'

Her dark eyes settled on Corrigan. 'And this man is American.'

'Adopted. He was born and brought up as a child in Eire. His parents emigrated to New York, but now he's come home to work with us.'

She took in the American's hard, weathered face and the flinty blue eyes that met and held her gaze. Something about them, she thought, something fathomless. Impenetrable. He could be thinking that he wanted to make love to her or that he wanted to kill her, and she would never know the difference.

'He has a speciality?'

'Lew is an explosives expert.'

Corrigan said: 'If we are indeed in the company of the 17 November movement, then I guess congratulations are in order.'

She glanced at him, surprise registering on her face.

'I heard about your attack on the radio this morning,' he explained. 'The industrialist in the Mercedes?'

Her eyebrows rose. 'You understand Greek?'

'Enough. My ex-wife's family were Greek immigrants in New York. I picked some up.'

She regarded him with new respect. 'Perhaps congratulations are premature, Mr Corrigan. We failed to kill our target.'

He unravelled the Cellophane from one of his cigars and lit it. 'Then clearly you would do better with our expertise.'

Still she felt unnerved by those eyes. Was he mocking her or was he serious? She said sharply: 'That is for us to decide.'

Moylan was becoming increasingly irritated at her offhand manner. 'We've specific plans of our own to offer the Iraqis. Khaled Fadel was keen enough.'

'In principle the decision has been taken,' she confirmed, 'but it now depends whether the Professor agrees to work with you.'

'Who?' Moylan asked, baffled.

'Our leader. We are not Iraqi puppets; it is for *us* to agree.' She had the Greek habit of using exaggerated hand movements to emphasise her words. Slim hands with bitten carmine nails. 'We must be satisfied not only that you are who you claim to be, but also that you are willing and able to carry out what is agreed.'

Moylan had taken enough. He sprang to his feet. 'What in God's name do you expect us to do?'

The driver of the minibus, who had been watching warily from the shadows, stepped quickly forward. Moylan found himself looking into the muzzle of a Luger.

Maggie gasped with surprise.

Sophie remained calmly detached. Raising her hand, she said: 'It's all right, Michalis, I can handle this. Put that thing away.' Guns were not toys and she had no time for the way men used them to threaten or as playthings. Like a penis extension. She waited for Moylan to resume his seat. 'We have a quite simple task for you to perform. As an act of good faith – both ways – we want you to assassinate a member of the Greek police force.'

The words were picked up on Villiers' hand-held directional mike in his precarious position high up in the rafters of the warehouse. He had entered stealthily through a rear fire escape and had inched along a rusting gantry before he was able to point the pistol-mike towards the pool of light fifty feet below him.

'That's bloody madness!' Moylan was storming. 'I haven't come all this way to be ordered around by some bunch of student revolutionaries . . . '

'Very efficient revolutionaries,' Corrigan interjected. He could see they were in danger of blowing everything without Moylan's co-operation. If they chose, Sophie and her driver would just vanish into thin air and that would be an end of it. 'A fifteen-year campaign and not one arrest. On that score they run a tighter ship than we do.'

Avery read the American's tack and decided to back him up. 'For the sort of money we can demand, it's worth a little madness.'

'Max!' Maggie protested.

Moylan glared at the young terrorist. 'I'm still a free man today because I distance myself from people like you. I've had my share of hands-on killing. Now I leave that to the kids who still have to prove something to themselves.'

'Don't insult the girl,' Corrigan warned. 'Don't want her mate waving his gun about again.'

Sophie Papavas regarded Moylan thoughtfully. 'I can appreciate your position. Perhaps it is unfair to ask you as leader of these people. We would not expect the Professor to place himself in any personal danger. It is a leader's job to lead.' She paused, looking at the two other men. 'What about the others? Because, I am afraid, if they too are unwilling, then you have nothing to offer us.'

This was it. Break point – when the entire match could go either way.

Corrigan drew heavily on his cigar. 'This assassination – when is it to be?'

'It can be tonight. Everything is set up and in place.'

The American looked sideways at Moylan. The man's face

was a mask, resolute. Avery made no move, gave no indication that he was about to volunteer. Corrigan understood that. Had known from the start that Avery was beginning to crack, had been in the front line too long. For him the stakes were too personal now. He would have felt the same if his own ex-wife had been part of the equation; in real life, love and duty rarely mixed. So it would be down to him, again.

'I'll do it,' he said.

Moylan glanced at him, his lips twitching almost imperceptibly in the immobile face.

Sophie nodded slowly. 'So the American shows himself in his true light. Willing to kill someone he doesn't even know for personal gain.'

Moylan reacted angrily. 'That's what you wanted, that's what you've got. What sort of game do you think you're playing?'

The Greek girl's eyes narrowed. 'Oh, it is not a game, I assure you. The American runs true to form. His origins may be Irish, but he has been infected by his adopted country – infected by greed and commercial imperialism.'

'Bullshit,' Corrigan growled.

'So I know exactly where I stand with him,' Sophie continued, turning to Maggie. She leaned forward until her face was just inches from the Irish girl's. 'But I have to be sure of *all* of you. The American has offered to do the job. Fine, so he no longer concerns me. You are my greatest worry now, Mrs Avery.'

Maggie swallowed hard. 'What do you mean?' Her voice was a whisper.

Avery, too, could scarcely believe he'd understood correctly. This was something he hadn't remotely expected. He said angrily: 'It's your fault my wife's got involved in this. It was you who snatched us off the street.'

'On the contrary,' Sophie replied evenly. 'I would say it was you who took the risk of bringing her to Athens while she knew nothing of your plans. But now your stupidity has become my problem to solve. You seem certain she will co-operate and that she will keep her mouth shut. Fine for you, but my people want insurance if we are to work with you. So – your wife will do the killing. That way we are assured of her commitment.'

Maggie opened her mouth in protest, but no sound came out.

Avery rose to his feet. 'Right, that's it. I've had enough. I'll do what you want – or Lew Corrigan will. But not Maggie. She's a nurse and a mother, for Christ's sake. She's never done anything like this.'

'Then we have nothing more to discuss.' Adamant.

It was an impasse. The chips were down and the bluff was called. A brittle silence fell over the small group, the tension hanging in the air like static electricity. The two Greeks were armed, they were not. Everyone was suddenly very aware of the turn that events might take.

'She'll do it.'

It was Moylan who spoke.

'The hell she will –' Avery began.

But Moylan was on his feet. He positioned himself in front of Maggie and looked down, locking his gaze on hers.

'We both know you'll do it, Maggie, don't we? And we both know why.' The lantern light caught the curl of his lips as he smiled. 'Our little secret, eh?'

She stared up at him, mesmerised. She felt herself begin to tremble, her courage shrink. Her mouth moved to form the word. Bastard. But there was only silence until she said hoarsely: 'I'll do it.'

'Christ, Brian,' Jim Buckley complained, 'can't you go any faster!'

Hunt carved up yet another of the single-decker buses and received a deafening blast on its air horns for his pains. Rain was sluicing across the carriageway, the array of head-lamps dazzling on the water that spilled from the over-loaded drains. He jumped another set of lights, hooting a warning that sent pedestrians leaping aside as wings of spray exploded from his wheels.

They slithered out of the junction, tyres spinning on the uneven road.

'I'm doing my best to kill us,' Hunt said through clenched teeth. 'What more do you want?'

Buckley grimaced, realising suddenly that he was demanding the impossible. 'Sorry, Brian. I'm a nice guy really. I'm just having a bad day.'

Hunt slewed the car around another tight corner into a narrow side street. 'You can say that again,' he agreed with feeling.

'Sod this rain,' the American said as the wipers struggled against the torrent.

And sod everything else too, Hunt thought savagely.

They'd been caught off balance ever since the minibus had abducted Moylan's party outside the hotel, and they hadn't got back on level footing yet.

Villiers had almost killed himself on the rafters of the warehouse in his desperate effort to find a way in and then the tape recorder attached to his directional microphone had malfunctioned. Afterwards there was no way to analyse the conversation with 17 November, instead having to rely on Villiers' memory of the snatched words in his earpiece.

As night fell a motorcycle had been uncovered from a tarpaulin in the warehouse and, using a wooden plank, had been rolled up into the minibus. Moylan's party then climbed aboard with the two Greek terrorists before they drove off for an unknown destination. Luther Dicks and Brad Carver were in close pursuit.

It was only then that they had been able to reach Villiers. The Glaswegian was sheepish about what he'd heard. 'I can't swear I've got this right, Brian, but it seemed they want Moylan's lot to kill a Greek cop. Corrigan offered to do it, but the Greek girl insisted that Avery's wife carry it out.'

'Jesus,' Buckley breathed. 'That's not on the agenda.'

Hunt understood though; he'd seen the ploy used enough times by terrorists on both sides in Northern Ireland. 'They want to convince themselves Moylan's people are genuine and get insurance that no one will talk. Being party to a murder is a good incentive to keep your lips buttoned.'

'What the hell do we do now?' Buckley had asked. 'Intervene or let it run?'

It was a question to which there was no easy answer. And there had been no time to consult with London or Washington before they received the call from Dicks and Carver. The blue minibus had parked in one of the maze of back streets off Omonia Square.

They located the Americans' surveillance car and pulled in behind it. Dousing the lights, Hunt and Buckley splashed through the pavement puddles to the other vehicle.

'What's happening?' Buckley demanded as they climbed in.

Luther Dicks jabbed a forefinger at the rain-streaked wind-screen. 'That's the minibus up ahead – on the left about a hundred metres away.'

'Got it,' Buckley confirmed.

'We think they're watching that apartment building behind us. Tatty sort of place, d'you see?'

'I see it, but how can you be sure?'

'One of them – a guy with a beard – walked down there a few minutes ago and took a look around, then went back to the minibus . . . '

'Hold up!' Carver interrupted. 'Something's happening . . . '

As he spoke the lights of the minibus came on and the vehicle pulled out, driving steadily towards them.

The four watchers were stunned into silence. Had they been spotted? Was the minibus driver coming to investigate?

When the minibus drew level, it turned suddenly into a narrow alleyway on the opposite side of the street. It drove in for a few metres, then stopped. Again the lights went off.

The four watchers scarcely dared breathe as the rear doors opened. Someone climbed out into the shadows: a slim figure dressed in black leathers and a bulbous crash helmet. Presumably the girl called Sophie. She was joined by the driver, the man with the beard. Together they extracted a wooden plank and ran out the motorcycle.

Then a second figure emerged. The snug jeans emphasised the distinctive feminine flare of Maggie's hips. She too wore a helmet with its visor down and stood disconsolately with her hands thrust into the pockets of a dark jacket.

Once the doors were shut and the driver had returned to his seat, Sophie mounted the motorcycle and gunned it into life. She waited for Maggie to mount the pillion, then rode slowly past the watchers' car, finally stopping in the shadows a short distance from the apartment block entrance.

The tension in the surveillance car became unbearable. Even when Baker Team's backup taxi arrived, parking near to the apartment block, the sense of remoteness and isolation remained. The windows began to fog with condensation as the rain continued its remorseless drumming on the roof.

'This isn't right,' Buckley said suddenly. 'We can't just sit here and witness a cold-blooded murder.'

His words echoed the thoughts of each man in the car. The feeling of helplessness and guilt was absolute.

'Unfortunately,' Hunt murmured, 'there's not a damn thing we can do about it.'

# Thirteen

'It's a filthy night,' Andreas Groutas said as they approached the back streets off Omonia Square. 'I'm grateful for the lift.'

Nico Legakis was as cautious with his driving as he was with every other aspect of his life. To the irritation of the drivers behind him, he slowed in anticipation of the traffic lights changing. 'It's been a filthy day,' he replied sourly. The 17 November movement had struck again – albeit unsuccessfully – and now his boss and the politicians were baying for results.

'Maybe we'll get a lucky break soon,' Groutas said, but there was little conviction in his voice.

'Maybe. Which is your street?'

'Two more on the left. You must come in for a coffee. I'll find those missing prints and the negatives. They've probably fallen behind the bed.'

Legakis had already reprimanded the young officer for his carelessness; it wouldn't do to labour the point. Perhaps it was the reference to the word 'bed' that triggered the thought: 'How is young Sophie?'

'The same wild and free spirit,' Groutas replied; he enjoyed making the older man envious.

'You should marry her.' It was Legakis's inevitable advice to the bachelors on his staff. 'She'll calm down then – make a good wife.'

'I will, soon.' Noncommittal. 'Ah, turn here, Nico. That's it. Our apartment's on the right.'

The policeman parked fastidiously, edging back and forth until he was tucked neatly against the kerb. Groutas stood impatiently on the pavement, hunched against the driving rain, while his boss fiddled with the key in the lock.

He didn't hear the motorcycle start up, the engine noise muted by the hiss of rain and the rattle of the wind in the streetside trees.

'C'mon, Nico, it's pissing down,' he grumbled.

The sudden pulse of light dazzled him. A single blinding headlamp. Instinctively he raised his arm to shield his eyes. A sudden roaring sound filled his ears, the orb of light engulfing him.

Wheels screeched on the wet tarmac as the motorcycle slewed. Nico Legakis froze in terror at the driver's door, believing momentarily that he was about to be run down.

His mouth dropped as the motorcyclist braked, swinging the bike out to give the pillion passenger a clear field of fire.

Two-handed grip. Slim, white hands, wet with the rain. They seemed too small for the heavy weight of the gun that pointed unwaveringly at Andreas Groutas.

The man stood rooted to the spot. The rounds spat like fireflies, the noise sharp and painful to the ears. Legakis ducked, lost his footing on the slippery road, and fell against the side of his car. One, two, three. He lost count of the rounds, his head now filled with the terrified scream and the noise of the revving machine as it surged past him.

He recovered from his initial shock, staggered to his feet, and splashed around the car to the rain-slicked pavement. The force of the bullets had thrown Groutas up against the entrance steps of the apartment block. He lay with his legs splayed, his hands clasped at his stomach in a vain attempt to stop the sticky red liquid from bubbling up between his fingers, livid against the stark white of his sodden shirt.

Legakis cradled the man's head in his arms and muttered meaningless words of comfort as he looked around in desperation for help.

In the surveillance car, Buckley grabbed the microphone. 'X-ray, this is X-ray. Tell Gretchen to grab a medical kit and give a hand. Pronto!'

Hunt glanced at him sideways.

Buckley shrugged. 'Hell, Brian, we gotta do something.'

On the steps to the apartment Legakis was dimly aware of a car door slamming, the clatter of a woman's shoes on the pavement. He glanced up as she approached.

'It's all right,' she said in Greek, 'I'm a doctor.'

Legakis could not believe his luck. He felt the relief flood through him. 'Thank God! But I think it may be too late . . . '

He stepped aside to let the woman tend the injured man, suddenly becoming aware of the single headlamp returning down the street. The entire event can have taken little more than sixty seconds and it occurred to him that he had witnessed the motorcycle turn from the corner of his eye. In the panic and confusion it hadn't fully registered. Now he realised. The killer was coming back. To check that the victim was dead? Or to kill him too?

In his heart he *knew* it was the 17 November. And he understood just what a coup his death would be for them – a captain in the Anti-Terrorist Department. Well, he'd damn well take one of them with him.

His hand reached inside his raincoat until his fingers found the handgrip of the Sturm Ruger Speed-six revolver. He flicked off the safety with his thumb and leapt to the pavement, half stumbling in front of his parked car. Using the engine block for cover, he raised both hands, levelling the pip sight on the snub barrel at the advancing circle of light.

He held his breath. Aware of the blinding whiteness expanding to swallow him, the pitch of the accelerating engine rising to a maniacal shriek of protest. Back on the hammer. Wait, wait, wait . . . he told himself.

Fire! Once, twice. The recoil and double blast momentarily disorientated him, the brilliance of the light searing into the back of his eyes. He felt the cold wind of the slipstream on his face as the motorcycle thundered past.

Then he was up, legs wide apart in the middle of the road, raising both arms, elbows locked, the barrel rock-steady despite the black spots floating before his eyes. The pip sight lined on the receding pillion. He squeezed the trigger.

To his surprise he hit his mark. For a moment the motorcycle wobbled uncertainly, then reared like a startled horse. The pillion passenger's body detached itself from the rear saddle, crashing heavily to the ground. The sudden imbalance of weight caught the rider off guard and the machine veered out of control, crunching into a parked car. Glass shattered and metal complained noisily as it crumpled under the impact.

Nico Legakis stared in amazement, hardly believing the result of his own action. After all the activity there was a sudden and shocking stillness. The rain still lashed remorselessly, pounding at the two bodies, motionless where they had fallen in the street. The distorted front wheel of the motorcycle still spun, light catching the gleaming rim.

Slowly the rider of the machine began to stir, crawling onto all fours. Legakis hesitated, unsure what to do. The wreckage was some fifty metres away, blocking the narrow street. He began running towards it, determined to make an arrest.

He wasn't anticipating the sudden emergence of the blue minibus from a side alley. It swung into the street beyond the stricken rider and stopped. The rear doors were thrown open and two men leapt out, both rushing towards the injured pillion passenger. A third man, the driver, joined them. Legakis was aware of just two things about him, wild hair and beard, and a gun in his hand.

The policeman's feet skidded on the greasy road. Christ, he was a dead man!

Two shots were fired as he leapt for the cover of a parked truck. Sparks ricocheted off the wing beside his head. He fell to his knees, gasping for breath. With his heart pounding, he edged forward, head low, to peer around the wheel.

The rider was on his feet now. His? Even as he watched, Legakis corrected himself. As the driver helped the limping figure, the slender build and manner of the walk told him it was a woman.

Legakis raised the Sturm Ruger at the bearded man. This time he would finish the job.

Shit!

He didn't see exactly where it came from. Suddenly a car had driven out of its parking place to block the narrow street and shield the killers from his view.

How many more of them were there? This was lunacy! He needed backup and fast, or he'd lose them all and get himself killed into the bargain. He aimed his revolver and fired calmly into the tyres of the blocking car. He grimaced with satisfaction as he heard the hiss of air and watched the vehicle slump sideways.

Then he was on his feet, running madly back towards his own car.

As he approached, he saw that the woman doctor was still tending the wounded officer on the steps. Suddenly he felt bad. 'How is he?' he called as he reached into the window for the radio mike.

'He needs an ambulance,' she shouted back. 'Fast!'

Legakis spoke rapidly over the radio, irritable that the duty officer failed to understand his garbled explanation of events.

'Anti-terrorist marksmen needed now! An ambulance! An all-cars alert to seal off the district!'

With a sinking heart he began to repeat his instructions, rain streaming down his pinched white face, dripping off the ends of his moustache. Farther down the street, beyond the blocking car, there was no sign of the blue minibus, the rider or the pillion. Just the wreckage of a motorcycle remained.

It was five more minutes before the first police squad car arrived, siren wailing. The ambulance followed closely, then the armed Anti-Terrorist police.

The rain had eased and now a crowd gathered behind the cordon across the street. Nico Legakis felt depressed. He'd been so near, yet so far. At least the medics reported that Groutas was stable. In the gyrating blue light of the ambulance he watched the stretcher with its attached drips being lifted aboard.

'He owes his life to that doctor,' observed the senior medic.

Legakis looked towards the steps. Only a cat sat in the doorway, swishing its tail. 'Where is she?'

'Said she was late for an appointment.'

'I suppose you didn't get her name?'

The medic shook his head and left with the ambulance.

Legakis crouched down beside the cat and ran his hands through the damp fur. 'Sometimes I think it is only you cats who know all the secrets of Athens. You see it all, but you're not telling, are you?'

*        *        *

The hotel receptionist smiled demurely. 'They telephoned fifteen minutes ago, you just missed them. Apparently a business acquaintance has invited them to stay at his villa for a few days.'

'They didn't say where?'

'I'm afraid not.'

'Did they take any luggage with them?' Brian Hunt asked.

'I really didn't notice. They're keeping their rooms on here, so perhaps they just took a few things.'

'Thanks.'

Thanks but no thanks, Hunt thought angrily and rejoined Jim Buckley in the foyer with the news.

'Another bad day,' the American said bitterly.

That was putting it mildly. It was a totally unmitigated disaster. Their action in driving the surveillance car between the terrorists and the shooting policeman had led to unwelcome consequences. Not only had they been forced to abandon the shot-up surveillance car but, in their efforts to save Margaret O'Malley's life, the blocking vehicle had prevented Bravo team from giving chase to the blue minibus. It had disappeared without trace into the drizzling Athens streets.

'Any news from that warehouse they used?' Hunt asked.

Buckley shook his head. 'I've put Monk and Pope on watch, but no one's returned there. Doesn't look like they will now.'

It was then that the taxi pulled up outside and Stafford Philpot climbed out. He was breathless and the spiky wisps of white hair suggested he had come straight from his bed; the striped pyjama top beneath his suit jacket confirmed it.

'I got here as soon as I could, dear boy.' The eyes were bright and alert. 'So sorry to hear about your problems.'

Hunt went over the evening's events.

'And you're sure the young gel was injured?' Philpot asked finally.

'No doubt. Maggie appeared to be hit in the thigh. We've got Gretchen phoning around all the hospitals now.'

The old man grimaced. 'I doubt they'll take her to one of them, even if it's serious. If it's a case of life and death, my guess is they'd take matters into their own hands.' Hunt and Buckley exchanged glances; it did not bear thinking about. 'On the other hand, they've possibly got access to a sympathetic doctor.'

'We're going to have to split up the teams,' Buckley decided. 'Watch the airports and the port at Piraeus in case they try to leave the country, but . . . ' He looked despondent.

'It's like looking for the proverbial needle?' Philpot suggested. 'I'm afraid you're right. In geographical terms Greece and its islands have one of the longest coastlines in Europe. So if our friends of the 17 November are determined to disappear, dear boy, I fear they will do just that.'

Buckley turned to Hunt. 'Time to bite the bullet, Brian. Who's going to tell our masters we've lost them? You or me?'

'I'll toss you for it.'

★        ★        ★

Avery had no idea where they were or where they were going.

But after the shooting he had no time even to think about it. His priority was to stop Maggie from bleeding to death. They had stretched her out on the floor of the minibus and cut away her jeans to reveal the ugly red wound in her upper thigh. The high velocity round had scraped the femur but had thankfully passed straight through, leaving a gaping exit hole. Avery had dressed it to staunch the blood using the cleanest materials they had available.

She was on the edge of consciousness by the time the bus trundled down the deserted market streets of Monastiraki and into the garage adjoining Michalis's stall.

'How are you going to get us out of this bloody mess?' Moylan demanded as the gates were closed behind them.

But Sophie was unmoved. 'Mrs Avery will be attended to. We are not amateurs. Just be thankful that idiot motorist got caught in the crossfire – it may have saved all our lives. Meanwhile you are to be congratulated on killing a fascist pig. You have passed our test.'

Moylan couldn't believe what he was hearing. 'Don't think I'm interested in working with you after this! Sweet Jesus, you just said yourself – you nearly got us all killed.'

Avery was in no mood for arguments. 'Maggie needs a hospital and fast.'

Sophie placed a reassuring hand on his arm. 'Don't be concerned. Michalis has telephoned for transport, a taxi driver who does what he is told without question. We have medical facilities. Don't forget the police will be watching the hospitals to find her. Murder is a serious offence.'

Corrigan patted his shoulder. 'Sophie's got a point, Max. Let's see what she has to offer.'

'Trust me,' Sophie said. 'Your wife will be in safe hands.'

'I want out,' Moylan said.

Sophie turned on him and he took a double-take as he found himself staring at the business end of her MKE automatic. 'You wanted in, Mr Moylan, and now you've got what you wanted. But you follow our rules now. Understand?'

He understood.

Minutes later the taxi arrived outside. As they left the building, Avery and Corrigan lifting Maggie into the rear seat, Michalis was already changing the registration plates of the minibus. By the morning it would be resprayed a different colour.

It was a slow and steady drive that took them the seven miles to the marina at Limin Zeas harbour. The taxi was driven onto the lower quay level and past the long succession of expensive moored yachts until it reached the area where local fishing boats were moored.

A small motor launch, crewed by one man in a black seaman's sweater, waited at the bottom of the stone steps. The sailor was clearly impatient as they lifted Maggie down into the craft.

Moylan realised suddenly that Sophie was making no attempt to join them on board. 'You're not coming with us?'

She shook her head, but offered no explanation. Before he could say more, the outboard burbled into life and Sophie cast down the rope. Then she was swallowed up by the night, the launch slapping purposefully into the run of short, choppy waves as they headed out to sea under a brooding, moonless sky. The necklace of harbour lights slowly sank below the horizon.

Avery began to doubt that Hunt's men had been able to follow them; they were as isolated and alone in the utter blackness as astronauts adrift in space; the only comfort was the reassuring chug of the outboard.

Corrigan saw the lights first, a multicoloured string of them running the full length of the yacht that bucked gently at its sea anchor.

The vessel loomed large out of the misty sea: some seventy feet of pristine white hull that must have cost the owner millions. Strains of Vivaldi wafted from above as they approached beneath the davits on the aft sundeck where two white-uniformed crewmen waited to help them aboard.

'What language are they speaking?' Moylan asked as they lowered Maggie carefully onto the waiting stretcher trolley.

'Arabic,' Avery replied tersely.

'That is correct,' said a voice from the open saloon doors. 'You speak the language?'

Avery squinted to get a better view of the man, but the light was behind him, creating a silhouette. 'I speak some.'

A light chuckle. 'Then we must be careful what we say.'

'My wife –' Avery began.

'Your wife is in safe hands. There is a qualified surgeon on board and a mini operating theatre.'

'Your boat?' Corrigan asked.

'Alas, no. This boat is owned by a senior member of the Iraqi Ba'athist party. It is registered in Panama and is, fortunately, one of the few of the country's assets to have been overlooked amid the flood of sanctions and reprisals.'

'I'd like to be with my wife,' Avery said as the crewmen wheeled the stretcher through the saloon to the main corridor.

The stranger ushered them inside and closed the doors. 'As soon as the operation is complete – yes, of course, you may be with her. Rest assured the surgeon is one of Iraq's best, trained at Guy's in London. He is all prepared – we received a telephone message from our friends in Athens.'

'Are you the Professor?' Moylan asked.

Under the chandelier lights of the sumptuously appointed saloon they could see the stranger clearly for the first time. He stood at several inches under six feet, his stout body dressed in a white linen suit which he wore with a burgundy polo shirt and Gucci loafers. The tanned, heavily lined face with its beetle eyebrows and his straight silvered hair suggested that he was in his mid-fifties. A gold wristlet chimed musically as he raised a finger and tapped the side of his bulbous nose. 'That is for you to guess and for me to know. But you may call me – let us see – Giorgós. Yes, that is always a name I have liked.'

Corrigan eyed the man cautiously. 'Well, Giorgós, I think I speak for all of us when I say we're getting a little bit sick of playing silly buggers. Who the hell are we dealing with here? 17 November or the Iraqis, or what?'

The man gestured towards the two zebra-skin sofas that formed an L-shape around the mock-coal fireplace. 'Make yourselves comfortable.' As the three men took their seats he said: 'In case you cannot tell by my accent, yes, I am Greek. You are indeed dealing with 17 November. I am in regular secure contact with the *Estikhbarat*. When dealing with me you are in effect talking to God.' A faint smile. 'I refer, of course, to President Saddam Hussein. I have use of this yacht until the owner is again able to leave his own country. The crew are Iraqi, drawn from members of Saddam's praetorian guard, so that their loyalty is assured. Nevertheless it is wiser not to discuss anything in front of them.' He crossed to the stained antique globe and opened the shell to reveal a concealed drinks cabinet. 'Now I expect you could all do with something fortifying after your traumatic evening.'

After pouring three whiskies and an ouzo for himself, Giorgós raised his glass. 'To a deadly new alliance – the great Provisional IRA, the 17 November and the Republic of Iraq – drawn together by our common enemies, those two bourgeois imperialist nations, Britain and the United States.'

Moylan felt as uncomfortable as Avery and Corrigan with such rhetoric. 'Let's get down to basics,' he said. 'We have a plan to offer Saddam Hussein. To mount an attack to kill the British Prime Minister and the entire Cabinet. Is Iraq interested or not?'

Giorgós's thick lips parted in a smile. 'Of course. Otherwise we would not be talking. Tell me, how soon could this operation be put into effect?'

Moylan studied his glass. 'Realistically – to get it right, surveillance, dry runs and so forth – probably mid- to late January.'

'That may be too late. The UN deadline expires on the fifteenth of January, and land war can be expected to begin at any point after that. Probably on the seventeenth.'

'What makes you think that?' Moylan asked.

'Iraqi military intelligence say that there is a window of four days – from the seventeenth to the twentieth – when there is no moon and there are high tides to assist amphibious landings. The Americans will no doubt want to make a flank attack with their famous Marines.'

Corrigan shook his head. 'That's too soon. Old Georgie Bush isn't going to risk American lives without a helluva softening up first. The Pentagon will be terrified of getting bogged down in another Vietnam scenario.'

Giorgós raised one heavy eyebrow. 'You seem very certain.'

'I am. I was with the Green Berets for years. I know the military's thinking. You can expect days or even weeks for artillery and aerial bombardment before any land attack.'

'The next window of high tide and moonless nights is in mid-February,' Giorgós said.

'Then there's nothing wrong with our timing,' Moylan added quickly.

'Perhaps not,' Giorgós conceded. 'In any event Saddam

is not anxious to precipitate the start of hostilities. Only if it comes to war will he strike. He still believes the Americans will not have the stomach for it.' He sipped at his drink. 'But first we must talk of funding. I understand that it is primarily why you are here. It is a sad fact of life, but our two organisations clearly have different motivations on this business.'

Moylan said: 'Giorgós, this is a matter between you and me.' He spared a glance in the direction of Avery and Corrigan. 'I'm sure this is understood.'

The Greek was gracious. 'Of course, gentlemen, I'll have you shown to your quarters. And, Mr Avery, I shall have you called as soon as your wife is out of surgery.'

It was with some reluctance that the two men left the saloon when the steward was summoned.

Giorgós poured more drinks for Moylan and himself. 'Your caution is very wise. Secrecy is our ultimate defence in this business. It is how 17 November has survived so long. If you don't want people to know, then don't tell them.' A ghost of a smile crossed his face. 'We Greeks are known for our philosophy and there is one truth that people in our line of work should recognise – women are far better at keeping secrets. A man finds the burden intolerable if he cannot tell one other soul. His priest, his best friend, his lover.'

Moylan found himself drawn to the quietly spoken Greek. Found himself wondering about the man's true identity. He appeared both cultured and wealthy – he could imagine him as a lawyer or a politician – hardly the popular image of an anarchist. Amused, he said: 'And who do *you* tell your secrets to, Giorgós?'

A gentle laugh. 'Only my cat, Mr Moylan, only my cat.'

It was a moment shared. 'I think the Provies should try that back home.'

'You trust the two men you have with you?'

'Of course.'

'But not too far, I hope? On the subject of money, I am authorised to offer you one million dollars. One third on agreement, one third when everything is in place, and the final third after the satisfactory conclusion of events.'

Moylan smiled. It was a fat profit for a job they planned to do anyway. 'And expenses? There are vehicles and safe houses needed. They do not come cheap.'

Giorgós nodded. He knew well the euphemisms for backhanders. 'That, too, will be covered.'

'Then I think we have a deal.'

The Greek regarded the other man for a long and pensive moment. At last he said: 'Of course, we could have a much, much bigger deal.'

The words threw Moylan. 'I'm sorry, I don't understand.'

'I think that you do not realise just *how* welcome your offer is to the Iraqis. But not just for an attack on your government, useful though that would be. You see, Saddam has his back to the wall. Although he is not convinced there will be war, if it happens he is determined that he will not lose. Yet he knows he cannot win by conventional means, despite speculation to the contrary in the media. But his top military advisers and the *Estikhbarat* have come up with a formula to guarantee Iraqi victory in the event of war.'

Moylan was sceptical. 'Personally, I don't see it.'

'No, few in the West know how Saddam thinks. They do not realise just what he is capable of. He has spent millions of his country's meagre resources on chemical and biological weapons – that cannot have escaped your attention.'

'The Americans, French and British are well-equipped to deal with that. The Soviets have always been expected to use that stuff.'

Another smile. 'On the battlefield, yes. But at home – in their own backyard?'

'I don't see . . . ' Moylan began, but even as he spoke the words, he realised that he did. He felt a momentary mild tremor in his heart; for a second the glass shook in his hand.

'Deadly weapons designed to destroy Israel,' Giorgós explained, 'will be turned on Saddam's old friends, Britain and the United States. Typically the Americans have betrayed him and, as a result, he will show them no mercy.'

Moylan shook his head. 'Even if he could pull off such a stunt, the Americans wouldn't back down. They've got too much to lose.'

'Oh, they'll back down all right, you need have no doubt about that.' Giorgós stood and walked to the double doors that gave onto the aft sundeck and stared out into the night. 'To the south of here is the island of Crete, famous for its invasion by German paratroopers during the war. On it is the US naval facility and airfield at Soúda Bay. Normally it is a backwater, a refuelling and replenishment base for the Sixth Fleet. But today it is a hive of activity, a major staging post for Desert Shield. Just imagine the impact of an unannounced attack using a deadly combination of anthrax and clostridium botulinum vapour.'

'What?'

'Of course, you do not appreciate the devastation that such chemical and biological systems can wreak. Anthrax is highly virulent and will cause death within twenty-four hours if inhaled or ingested. Usually it is pneumonia, septi-caemia and the subsequent failure of vital organs that kills. Within a day there would not be one survivor amongst the Americans who man the base. The shock effect in Washington would be colossal.'

Moylan was stunned. 'The Iraqis would do that?' He regarded Giorgós closely. '*You* would do that?'

When the Greek answered his voice was low, scarcely more than a hoarse whisper. 'The question is, my friend, will *you* do that? Will the Provisional IRA extend its hand of friendship to helping us attack Crete – and other targets?'

'What other targets?' Moylan was starting to feel out of his depth, unable to grasp the magnitude of what was being suggested.

Giorgós stared at the chandelier as he spoke. 'In the same way that the United States concluded World War Two with the unannounced delivery of an atomic bomb, so Saddam Hussein is prepared to destroy the Crete base. A small demonstration of what is to come. It will be followed by

a warning of similar attacks on Washington and London
and other cities of the Gulf allies. Having demonstrated his
ability and willingness to go through with such an attack,
Bush and his allies will be obliged to seek a face-saving
climb-down. If they do not, the threat of similar attacks on
Paris, Cairo and Damascus will soon crack the alliance wide
open.'

Moylan swallowed hard. 'But after Crete it will all be
bluff, you mean?'

'Oh, no, Mr Moylan, that wouldn't do at all. If it proves
necessary, then it must be done. The United States must be
seen to make a humiliating climb-down and to give up all
pretence at being the world's policeman. The Crete attack
will be carefully staged for maximum effect, but already
plans are well advanced for attacks on Washington and
London.'

'You're joking?'

Giorgós appeared not to hear. 'Cylinders of respirable
anthrax spores have already been smuggled into Britain by
agents of *Estikhbarat*. It is intended that they be invisibly
dispersed by a tug passing on the Thames through London.
Anything up to a half-million casualties might be expected
and large areas of the capital evacuated.'

Moylan felt suddenly a chill, as though a draught were
passing through the saloon, but Giorgós had already closed
the doors. 'And Washington?'

'Simultaneously with any London attack, a mere ten
milligrams of botulinus toxin will be injected into food
supplied to the Senate kitchens in Washington. Hitting the

Americans where it hurts most. Iraqi experts predict some five thousand victims of whom half would die. No one will ever laugh again at the 17 November.'

'You really are serious, aren't you?'

'More importantly, Mr Moylan, the Iraqis are serious. Serious enough for them to offer nothing less than two billion dollars to your organisation for helping to plan and carry out these attacks. Is that something that would find favour in Dublin?'

Moylan grimaced. 'I really don't know.' He meant it. He could imagine the consternation and controversy it would cause in the Army Council. Even the diehard hawks like himself had their own set of ethical values, no matter what the rest of the world might think of them. Two billion dollars was an enticement beyond belief, but these were strong moral dilemmas. Firstly the Provisionals would be acting purely as mercenaries – in it for the cash. But then that was nothing new. Anyway, weren't they already offering to attack the British Cabinet on the same grounds? And they'd assisted other 'brothers' in their struggle against oppression, like ETA, the Basque separatists, and the ANC in South Africa, as well as most other European terror groups.

But this was different. Chemical, biological and bac-teriological weapons had a universally bad press. The user would win no friends, would win no propaganda victory outside of the Arab world, he was sure of that. Bush might back down and allow Iraq to remain in Kuwait, but it would be only a matter of time before the Americans sought their revenge on Saddam Hussein. And for the Provisionals to be involved would alienate every supporter they had ever had, if it became known. And even two billion dollars wasn't worth that risk. Innocent Irishmen would die in London, and the strong pro-IRA lobby in Washington, whose support had proved so beneficial over the years, would be wiped out at a stroke.

No, he could not see the Army Council giving its approval to such lunacy.

Giorgós had been watching him in silence. He appeared relaxed and untroubled as though they had just been discussing the price of vegetables. Now he took a seat opposite the Irishman.

'Of course, our own helpers and contacts are mostly Greek. None would be told the purpose of their part in the overall operation either here or abroad, but in the final analysis we lack the expertise and the manpower to carry out the final acts beyond our shores. For that we would deal with *any* skilled terrorist faction with the necessary ability. Do I make myself clear, Mr Moylan?' The brown eyes had assumed a new intensity, unblinking, uncompromising.

Then suddenly Moylan understood. Understood exactly what Giorgós was proposing. He had been one step ahead all the time.

Giorgós stood up then and rang the service bell. 'We will talk again in the morning. Meanwhile I'll have you shown to your cabin.' He moved across to one of the built-in inlaid cupboards and produced a large manila envelope. 'But make no mistake that any of this will be easy. As you will see, already you have almost been compromised.'

Moylan took the envelope. 'What do you mean?'

'Taken by the Anti-Terrorist Police outside the office of Khaled Fadel, Iraq's agent in Athens.'

The Irishman stared at the photographs in horror. Grainy blow-ups taken on a fast film. Avery, Corrigan, himself.

'Luckily,' Giorgós said, 'we were able to intercept them, before they fell into the wrong hands.'

Moylan was doubly flabbergasted. 'How on earth . . . ?'

'Do not ask. Just let it be a lesson. Not least of which is that our organisation is not to be underestimated.'

At that moment the white-coated steward arrived.

'Good night, Mr Moylan. And think over everything I have said this evening.'

'I will,' Moylan promised quietly.

He was still in a subdued and thoughtful mood when they arrived at the small, oak-panelled cabin. The crisp linen sheet had been turned down on the bunk and a small collection of toiletries had been laid out by the marble washbasin, together with a bottle of Johnnie Walker Black Label and a lead crystal tumbler. In the compact wardrobe hung a tracksuit and a thick terry-towelling robe. Giorgós, it seemed, had thought of everything to make his stay comfortable.

His mind, though, was racing and he knew he would not sleep. Not yet. He poured a stiff measure of whisky and stretched out on the bunk, propped against the pillow and staring at the beads of spray glistening on the glass of the scuttle.

So this was it. He was at the crossroads, there was no doubt about it.

Ever since he had been a boy in Derry, it was as though life had been preparing him for this moment. This destiny. He had been brought up in a Catholic family steeped in tradition, stories of British injustice and occupation handed down through generations. He had listened to parents, grandparents and uncles, sometimes out of polite- ness, but often with a sense of awe and the first stirrings of anger and indignation. But like any other small boy, his interests had been in keeping rabbits in the backyard of their terraced house, building with his Meccano set, and playing football against the walls of the narrow streets. With adolescence came a grudging interest in girls, a mystifying and aloof species which he studied from afar. He found himself interested in a detached, curious sort of way – the same way that he was interested in the fighting stag beetles and the hawk moths he kept in the jars in his bedroom.

Academically bright, he had gone to technical college and along with others in the class of '67 had developed a social conscience, steeping himself in the history of the people's fight worldwide against oppression as espoused by the likes of Marx, Trotsky and Mao Tse Tung.

Then, when he was aged just twenty-two, the first British troops were drafted into Ulster to protect the minority Catholics from their Protestant neighbours in the flaring sectarian violence. And within months the truth dawned: the army of occupation had arrived. With this realisation the subliminal inner hatred which had permeated him during his formative years, began to ferment and boil.

Like many others of his age he rallied to the tricolour, volunteering for the local PIRA battalions. But there was a difference. He soon saw where the leadership was going wrong. He had studied the experts; the Provie chiefs, evidently, had not. Soon he began to distance himself, even moving to England for several years to avoid being intimidated into ill-conceived action. Until, that was, the time was right.

And time was to prove the wisdom of his decision. By the mid-70s British Army Intelligence had riddled the Provisionals' ranks with informers and spies until the PIRA godfathers had been forced to rethink and introduce a secure-cell system for its organisation. Only then had Moylan returned to the province, now convinced that it was his mind and intellect that the movement desperately needed – a thinker and planner with a clear vision of how a terror campaign could be fought and, more importantly, won. There were plenty of illiterate louts from the rural backwaters and the urban ghettos ready to put their lives on the line. Not for Con Moylan years of rotting in the Maze prison or shot down in some midnight ambush.

He rose swiftly through the ranks, only ever taking part in actions that he himself had planned in meticulous detail, certain of their success and his escape from the security net. He became known as the Magician, earning a grudging respect from his peers. But he was also detested for his arrogance by his rivals who resented the way he outthought and outmanoeuvred them at every turn. And was always proved right.

Now he drained his glass and poured another generous measure.

Always right, he repeated grimly to himself. It had got him to the very top layer of the organisation. Hated perhaps, but also trusted and respected. So much so that he had been entrusted with Provisional funds to invest in a legit- imate – well almost, he smiled to himself – construction business. Again he had delivered – this time laundering money and providing fat dividends to boot.

Yet despite his achievements one thing still eluded him. The most important thing of all. Power, power to do things his way.

Because, despite the fact that he had always been proved right, still the Army Council would not listen. Still they ran operations their way – not his. Terror was a weapon like any other. To be effective, it had to be used to its full extent. Otherwise it was as impotent as a sword in its scabbard or a gun with the safety on. He didn't hold with telephone warnings or with neatly defining military and government targets. That never swayed public opinion.

What swayed the mindless masses on the mainland was when you bombed your way into the headlines. When the ordinary men and women felt the deadly touch of terror in their daily lives.

Clearly Giorgós – or whoever he was – understood that.

What were his words? 'We would deal with *any* skilled terrorist faction with the necessary ability.'

Faction? The Greek had chosen the word carefully, very carefully. Had he deliberately sown the seed? Faction — splinter group. Giorgós had cast the bait, and he understood exactly the nature of the fish he wanted to land.

Moylan saw it then. All along the Greek had realised the Provisional Army Council might well reject his proposals. Had known that he needed a fearless and ambitious maverick with the will and determination to go along with such an audacious plan.

Had that been the reason for the test, for murdering a total stranger on the streets of Athens?

Two billion dollars.

For two billion dollars Giorgós could land his fish and Saddam Hussein could win his war.

Moylan sat up suddenly and stared at his own reflection in the dressing-table mirror.

And for two billion dollars the Magician could wash his hands of the Provie old guard and go it alone — the leader of a new and powerful splinter group with untold wealth to conduct the terror war against Britain as he had always wanted. Absolute power in his hands.

He raised his glass to the shadowy image of himself in the mirror. 'Giorgós — I think you've got yourself a deal.'

# Fourteen

'So you're writing a book on the history of Liverpool?'

David Sinclair was fascinated. He'd always had a hankering to write himself, yet somehow had drifted into the social services and eventually the Dr Barnardo's organisation. 'But I wouldn't have thought there's room on the market for another one. A lot have been written.'

Danny Grogan sipped the welcome cup of coffee as he sat in the modern office in Childwall. Inside, it was warm and cosy with Christmas streamers on the wall; outside, it was cold and wet, rain lashing relentlessly at the window. 'This one's about the *people*, not the city. Had to include Barnardo's, didn't I?'

'Well it's all very different now. We've only a few kids in residence. Mainly teenagers with behavioural problems or physical or mental disabilities,' Sinclair explained. 'Modern times, you see. There's no stigma attached to being a single mum any more and the social services are far more effective nowadays.'

'But in the past?' Grogan asked.

'We had several branch homes, each looking after forty to fifty kids. Had them in Liverpool, Southport, Lytham St

Anne's and the Wirral. You should visit Alexander Drive or Aigburth Road. They're both nursing homes now, but it'll give you a flavour.'

'I might do that. In fact I've got a mate who was in one of your homes.'

'Oh yes?'

'His parents died in a car crash back in '61. Horrible business. Nice Irish family by all accounts.'

'Catholic?'

'Sure.'

Sinclair appeared mildly surprised. 'That's unusual.'

'Why's that?'

'Well, Irish kids with a Catholic upbringing more usually go to the Nugent Society – used to be called the Liverpool Catholic Social Services.' He thought for a moment. 'But then if it was a road accident, the police may have referred him directly to us. That sort of thing wasn't unknown.'

'Suppose you don't have any record of my mate here? He'd be tickled to know.'

'I'm afraid he'd have to try London.' As an afterthought he said: 'What was his name? Don't tell me another of our lads has become a famous writer like Leslie Thomas?'

Grogan smiled. 'I'm afraid Patrick O'Reilly is no writer.'

The name struck Sinclair like a thunderbolt. Only a few weeks earlier he'd received the strange call from London, warning him that the police were interested in anyone inquiring about a former charge called O'Reilly. 'Well I'd like to be of more help,' he said, mopping up his spilt coffee with a tissue, 'but this really is a busy time for me – what with Christmas coming, you know.'

The Irishman could hardly miss the abrupt change in tone. 'Of course, I understand. But you might know of someone who might have known my friend. A retired matron or whatever? You know, for a bit of colour and background for the book.'

Sinclair was on his feet. 'For '61? Afraid not. They'd all be long gone by now. I think I really must refer you to our head office in London. So sorry.'

Grogan took the hint and followed the man to the door. He drove back to central Liverpool deep in thought. Just why the hell had the man from Barnardo's been so suddenly put on edge, almost as though mention of Avery's original name had spooked him? Or was it just his own imagination?

He parked at the back of the Feathers Hotel and returned to his poky little room on the top floor. Taking a bottle of Bushmills from his overnight bag, he poured a slug into the plastic tooth mug, sat on the bed and stared at the telephone.

What next? he thought.

What else was there that he could check out? Realisation slowly dawned that there was not a lot. It occurred to him that since his parents died in 1961, Avery had spent most of his life in one institution or another. Barnardo's, then the army, then in prison for the best part of ten years. Very little could be verified outside of official records.

Prison. Now that was a thought.

He consulted his pocket book then dialled a number in St Helens. A man answered, his voice slurred by drink although it was not yet noon.

'Michael, you old lag, this is Danny Grogan. I need a favour.'

There was a light belch at the other end of the line. 'Nice to hear you, Danny. It'll be a pleasure, but you'll have to be quick. I'm due to appear in court in the new year – after that I might not be around for some time.'

'Can we meet tonight then? At the Big House, say six o'clock?'

'I'll see you then. We'll make a night of it.'

He hung up with a smile in anticipation of a good night on the town. Knowing full well he would be in no state to do much work the following day, he resolved to attend to the next item on his list.

Glancing at the information supplied by Margaret O'Malley, he made a note of the name: Don Merryweather, scrap dealers in Bootle, where Avery had worked after leaving the army.

He found the yard in a derelict back street near Gladstone Dock. That week's persistent rain had reduced it to a water-logged morass of mud over which towered a depressing hill of rusting wreckage. The owner had taken refuge in an ancient Portakabin that was long overdue for replacement.

As Grogan entered, Merryweather looked up from the girlie magazine spread out on his desk. He was a big man, solidly built with heavy muscle running to fat, a beer belly straining the grease-smeared old sweater he wore.

'Yes?' he asked in a less-than-charming tone. The grey eyes in the blunt, florid face wore an expression of habitual suspicion.

'I wonder if you can help?' Grogan began politely. 'I'm thinking of employing a man who used to work for you. Trouble is, he's got some form.'

Merryweather grunted. 'Who hasn't in this city of thieves?'

'I thought you could give him a reference.'

'You should have phoned first, saved yourself a trip. I don't give references.'

'Then just an opinion,' Grogan pressed. 'It's important to him and important to me.'

The scrap dealer eyed him in stony silence for several seconds before saying gruffly: 'I don't give references, because I don't employ people. Just the odd casual.'

Grogan understood. 'I'm not from the Inland Revenue or Social Security. Just an opinion, that's all I want.'

Resignedly Merryweather closed the magazine in front of him. 'What's the name?'

'Max Avery.'

Merryweather didn't even blink; if the name meant anything to him, it only showed in the imperceptible tightening of his thin lips. 'Oh, him.'

'Worked for you – sorry, *with* you – when he left the army in 1973, he says.'

The scrap dealer almost laughed, but not quite. 'I didn't see much of the beggar. He worked here on and off over, what, ten years. Spent most of the time at Her Majesty's pleasure until he went south to London.' He thought for a moment. 'That was in '83, I think. Swore he'd go straight. Some chance.'

'What was he like?'

Merryweather shrugged. 'Kept himself to himself mostly. Few friends that I knew of. I just took him on when he came out the glasshouse. It's not easy for an ex-con. He never tried to cheat me, but then he wouldn't.'

'No?'

The man nodded towards the little painted shield mounted on the wall beside the current price list for metal scrap. Parachute Regiment. 'I was in from before Suez up to 1960. There's a code of honour amongst ex-Paras. He wouldn't cheat me, not like some of the little oiks I've had in here.'

'I see.'

'Doesn't mean he wouldn't rob *you* blind, of course.'

Grogan smiled awkwardly. 'Nothing else you can tell me, I suppose?'

Merryweather shook his head. 'But leave a card and I'll contact you if I think of anything.'

But Grogan was already backing towards the door. Just being in the presence of an ex-paratrooper made him feel hot under the collar. Para rash, he called it. Mumbling that he'd left his business cards in his other jacket, the Irishman retreated into the raw north-westerly that was blowing in across the docks.

Merryweather watched him through the misty window as he climbed into his car. He returned to his desk and jotted down the registration number before putting a call through to the anonymous office in Gower Street. The man called Max Avery had never worked for him; he had never even met the man. But there is a code of honour amongst Paras and the ex-Para sergeant who had seen action in Suez would never refuse a request put to him through his former CO.

Meanwhile Danny Grogan returned to Liverpool and made his way to the Vines, a splendidly ornate Edwardian pub in Lime Street where Michael was waiting. He had already begun drinking in earnest.

'I thought we could go down to Flanagan's and pick up a couple of tarts,' Michael enthused in a thick Dublin drawl. He didn't make mention of his wife or their five children in his council house in St Helens. 'And if we don't get lucky, we could try and grab a granny at the Grafton later.'

'Sure, sure,' Grogan said. He actually quite fancied picking up one of the older women who liked to make the most of their freedom while their husbands were serving time. Older women knew what they wanted, and were only too pleased to get it. 'But business first. I want you to put out the word. Did anyone know a man called Max Avery? He was inside for long stretches between '73 and '83.'

Michael showed only a mild interest; he had no involvement with the Provisionals and had no idea that Grogan was one of them. 'Which clinks, pal?'

'Walton, Wymot and then Wakefield.' He handed over the list.

'It'll take a few days.'

'It's important, Michael.'

'I know that. And it's going to cost you a few bevvies.'

It was after midnight when Clarissa Royston-Jones received the first inkling of bad news.

'Then you'd best come over.'

She replaced the receiver on the cradle of the bedside telephone and lowered her feet to the floor.

Christ, two in the morning. What the hell did Ralph Lavender want at two in the frigging morning? He'd refused to give any clue, but his agitated manner suggested that it was serious.

She was alone in the terraced house in Pimlico, so it would be convenient to talk; her husband, an orchestral conductor, was frequently away. She couldn't remember where; was it Birmingham tonight? But wherever he was she knew he'd be shacked up with that thirty-seven-year-old cellist from Macclesfield.

Pulling an unbecoming plaid dressing gown over her silk pyjamas, Clarissa wondered unkindly if there was ever a moment, day or night, when the cellist managed to keep her knees together.

She fished in her handbag for her cigarettes and peered blearily into the mirror as she lit one. Before she'd gone to bed after one gin too many she'd neglected to remove her mascara; now she looked like a hollow-eyed junkie, her hair hanging in disarray.

Sod Ralph Lavender. She was buggered if she was going

to dress up for his benefit. Let him know it was inconvenient and he was a bloody nuisance.

Compromising with a quick face wash and the run of a comb through her hair, she went downstairs to the kitchen and put the kettle on. It had only just boiled when the doorbell rang.

To her surprise the familiar figure of Willard Franks stood alongside Lavender on the steps.

'We've lost them,' the American CIA officer announced as she poured the coffee in her front room. 'They vanished into thin air after the shooting.'

She distributed the fine china cups. 'And you say it was Maggie O'Malley who shot the policeman?'

Lavender nodded. 'I don't know what Max was thinking of, allowing her to do it.'

Clarissa regarded him through the rising cloud of steam and tobacco smoke. 'From what you say, he didn't have much option. It was clearly the big test to get them into the 17 November network. If he'd tried to prevent it, he'd have blown your whole operation. Presumably Maggie agreed to do it under pressure – this Sophie person, you said, was armed. What else was Max supposed to do? You wanted him to get into bed with the Iraqis and that's exactly what he's done.'

Willard Franks said: 'Regardless of your asset's actions – or lack of them – it still places us in an uncomfortable position. Party to the attempted murder of a Greek police officer, the damage to our relations with Athens could be catastrophic if it became known.'

She had not missed the innuendo. 'Suddenly Max has become my asset again, has he?'

'Willard didn't mean anything by it,' Lavender rushed to the American's defence. 'But it is a fact that your people in MI5 know Max better than we in SIS do, and both Willard and I are getting tied in more closely with Desert Shield events in theatre. Although it really is just a sideshow, this Stalking Horse thing is proving a bit of a distraction when there's so much else to concentrate on.'

'I see,' she said, cigarette smoke hissing through clenched teeth.

'I wondered if your people would care to go over to Athens – sort things out?' He made his best attempt at a smile. 'See what you make of it.'

Clarissa said: 'But as you pointed out at the start of all this, Ralph, Europe is outside my jurisdiction.'

'But when all is said and done,' Lavender replied, 'Max *is* one of yours. You understand how he works. Besides there is – or soon will be – a war going on. We can't afford to be inflexible. And I suppose it can be considered to be part of your remit in counter-terrorism. I've cleared it with the Director General and he's happy for your people to take over.'

I bet he is, Clarissa seethed. Both Lavender and SIS were happy to take the credit when it was all a new and bright idea, but at the first sign of trouble it was to be dumped back in her lap.

She looked at Franks. 'And how do you feel about this, Willard? After all, Lew Corrigan is *your* man.'

The American looked abashed. 'Hell, Clarry, the truth is since it's British politicians who appear to be the potential target of this operation, we consider this to be more directly a decision for London. Now our people have made contact with the Iraqis, I don't think the President will be too concerned; at least that part of it is going to plan.' He opened his palms expansively. 'We're happy for you to pick-up the reins — and, of course, we wouldn't dream of pulling Corrigan out now.'

'I should hope not,' Clarissa murmured sourly.

Lavender rose to his feet. 'Well, thanks again for your co-operation — and I'm sorry to bring bad news at such an ungodly hour. Do keep me posted. Hope you don't mind.'

She did, of course, but at least she felt a mild sense of satisfaction at being called back in when the going was getting tough. Despite having misgivings about using Max in the venture, she had to admit that she would enjoy rising to the challenge.

As soon as Lavender and Franks had gone, she put a call through to John Nash's home number to explain the situation.

'I'd like you to get on to the office and arrange a ticket for me on a morning flight to Athens,' she concluded.

Nash sounded put out. 'I'm Max's controller, ma'am. Are you sure this is a job for the department head?'

'Probably not.' She blew a perfect smoke ring and watched it spin towards the ceiling. 'But I'm going anyway.'

\*    \*    \*

For the next three days, as the yacht steamed back and forth through the Aegean Sea, Con Moylan spent his time locked in private conversation with the man they knew only as Giorgós.

It was a frustrating time for Avery and Corrigan, not knowing what was being discussed and not being able to talk about it between themselves as it seemed highly likely that the cabins were wired.

The consolation for Avery was that Maggie had recovered well from her operation, being able to sit up in her bunk. He had met the surgeon only briefly, a pleasant and self-effacing Iraqi, who blushed deeply when Avery praised the neat job he had made of stitching the messy wound.

'Of course, your good lady will need to convalesce for several weeks and will need to use a walking stick. The muscles are torn and will take time to heal.'

Most of the time Maggie's mood had been subdued, almost morose. That was only to be expected after what she had been through. Avery reasoned that it had been the shooting of the policeman that had shocked her more than her own injury, but she refused to talk about it.

'Just leave me alone, Max,' she had said each time he attempted to comfort her.

In the early evening of the third day he had chanced to find Corrigan alone on the aft deck. The American was hunched over the rail, smoking a cigar and watching the westering sun as it finally broke through the persistent rain clouds. A blood-red light bathed the sky and sea alike.

For once there were no Iraqi crewmen within earshot.

'How's Maggie taking it?' Corrigan asked.

'Badly,' Avery replied, joining him at the rail. 'I think she holds me responsible for what happened.'

'Can't blame her for that. It was you who brought her to Athens.'

'I know that,' Avery replied tartly, then checked himself. It was hardly Corrigan's fault. 'Anyway, thanks for offering to do the shooting – that can't have been easy.'

Corrigan made light of it, and his eyes gave nothing away. 'I've got used to it over the years. Killing people I don't know. Trusting that my people know the truth. Knowing damn well that half the time they don't. Just put my mind in neutral.'

'If Con hadn't interfered, Sophie might have let you do it.'

Corrigan turned to him. 'What is it with that guy and Maggie? It was like he had some sort of hold over her, playing mind games.'

'I don't know, Lew, and I'm not sure I want to. All she's told me is they had an affair years ago. She won't say more.'

'Looked to me like he enjoyed that business. She's shit-scared of the guy.'

Avery stared at the horizon. 'And I'm beginning to think not without good reason.'

At that moment the doors to the saloon swung open and Moylan emerged, looking pleased with himself. 'It's nice to get some fresh air for a change. Don't you just love the smell of the sea?'

Corrigan said: 'What have you and Giorgós been

hatching? We haven't seen either of you all day again.'

Moylan stared out at the sunset. 'We've had a lot to discuss,' he replied absently.

'I thought it was just a question of price? Our side of things is well under way.'

The Irishman turned on him. 'So that's what you thought, was it, Lew? Well, now, isn't that interesting? But you might just remember that I'm running this show, not you.'

Corrigan raised his hands. 'Okay, Con, okay! I was curious, that's all.'

'Well, don't be. It's not good for your health. As it happens, the Iraqis are interested in our help in more ways than I realised.'

'What do they have in mind?' Avery asked.

Moylan regarded him coldly. 'The same applies to you, Max. Giorgós insists we run this on a purely need-to-know basis, and I agree. His outfit's record at remaining unde-tected speaks for itself.'

'Where do we fit in?' Corrigan asked. He added cyni-cally: 'If *that*'s not being too inquisitive?'

Moylan afforded a smile. 'That's better. And yes, there's work for you both to do. Max, I want you to get back to the UK and continue with the project you were working on. But there are some additional requirements.' He was talking rapidly, the enthusiasm clear in his voice. 'Lew, Maggie and I have other work to do here. We are going to disappear until all this is over. Giorgós and the Iraqis have it all planned. You'd be impressed.'

'Maggie's going back with me,' Avery said.

'Don't be a fool, Max,' Moylan retorted. 'She won't be able to walk for a week and then she'll be hobbling around on crutches. What chance do you think you'll have at the airport with the Greek cops looking out for a murderer who fits her description?'

Avery regarded him darkly. Both he and Maggie were trapped on this yacht and they all knew it. 'You're a right fucking bastard, Con – you're responsible for that –' He stopped himself in time; it was not a wise moment to antagonise him, to reveal how he really felt. 'You should have backed Lew when he offered.'

'This whole thing was your idea, Max,' Moylan retorted, 'and if we hadn't gone along with them we'd have blown it. Or worse, been found in that warehouse with bullets in the back of our heads. So no more whinging, right? We're going to have you put ashore on the Greek mainland. You can tie up the loose ends at our hotel, give some reasonable explanation for our absence, then get back to London. The launch will take you as soon as it's dark. So why don't you go and say your goodbyes to Maggie?'

'If she's not coming, then I'll stay here with her.'

'Are you trying to get us all killed? We all know too much. Giorgós has made it quite clear what will happen if we back down now. Those armed Iraqi guards will feed us to the fucken fishes.'

There appeared to be no way out. 'How long will you be away?'

'For as long as it takes.'

'I'll want to be in touch with Maggie – and she'll want to know how the baby is.'

'Forget it, Max. I'll be in contact with you. I'm working out a secure channel of communications with Giorgós. Don't worry, she'll be in safe hands.'

Avery opened his mouth to protest, then thought better of it. He was tempted to make one last bid to take her with him, but he realised it would be fruitless. Moylan held all the cards and was clearly in no mood to compromise. He certainly wasn't going to risk Maggie running foul of the Greek law.

He felt Corrigan's hand on his shoulder. 'Don't worry, Max, I'll look after her, see she comes to no harm. You just get on as best you can.'

For a moment their eyes met, the unspoken words passing between them, the bond established.

Down in the cabin Avery found Maggie in the same black mood. It wasn't improved when he told her of Moylan's plan for him to return to London.

'And you're going, of course.' She gave a brittle laugh. 'It's funny how everyone does what Con says. What is that power he has over people?'

'You tell me.'

There was a sorrowful look in her eyes. 'Why didn't you listen to me, Max? Why did you have to get involved with him?'

'I love you.'

She turned her head away quickly. Her voice was husky when she spoke. 'You'd better go.'

*    *    *

At first light Avery was put ashore at the coastal village of Varkiza, some fifteen kilometres south of Athens.

The inhabitants were already stirring in the quiet streets and by the waterfront he conveniently found a yawning local taxi driver watching the mini-TV mounted on his dashboard.

Relaxing on the drive north to the city, Avery was able to marshal his thoughts and consider what he should do next. Although no one appeared to be following, he knew that was no guarantee. While he had known virtually nothing about the 17 November until his arrival in Greece, he had learned fast that it was a very slick, professional and ruthless operation with contacts in high places. The man called Giorgós had impressed him, not least with his strict attitude to security. The man clearly took nothing for granted and trusted nobody. And that would include him.

There was a second consideration, which had been brought home with a jolt when Moylan told him that Giorgós had produced the surveillance photographs taken by the Anti-Terrorist Police. He had no way of gauging how much the Greeks knew, and throwing the murdered policeman into the equation simply emphasised the danger he was running. On arrival at his hotel or at the airport, he would not be surprised to find a reception committee of detectives waiting for him.

That, he decided, should be avoided at all costs. The overriding priority must be to get a message to his controller. He had taken enough, the situation was getting out of hand and Maggie was at risk in more ways than one.

It was vital to get the entire operation closed down. While everyone was aboard the Iraqi yacht, it was an ideal time. Moylan could be netted with the mysterious Giorgós and their plans, whatever they were, stopped dead in their tracks, and Maggie and Lew Corrigan could be rescued.

As the taxi approached the outskirts of Athens he made his decision and told the driver to pull over at a wayside telephone kiosk.

He rang the emergency number that he had committed to memory. A woman answered, speaking in Greek. 'Hallo, who is it?'

'Tosca.'

'Could you repeat, please?' This time in English, the accent distinctly American.

'This is Tosca, it's urgent.'

'Hold the line please.' The background sound of voices was muffled as her hand was placed over the receiver.

Moments later a man came on the line. 'Tosca? God, am I pleased to hear from you.'

He recognised Brian Hunt; just hearing the familiar voice made him feel better. 'Brian, I've got to talk to someone quickly.'

'This line isn't secure, Tosca. Do you need a face-to-face?'

'Yes.'

'Your hotel?'

'No, it's possible the Greek AT are on to us and our other friends know I'm going there.'

'Then it'll have to be a park-bench job.' A rustle of paper;

Avery guessed that the team had prepared a list of suitable rendezvous points. 'Konaki Square. There are a number of open-air cafés on the north side. Take a seat in Le Quartter away from other people. Someone will sit at the table next to you.'

'I'll be there in half-an-hour.'

He hung up and returned to the taxi, telling the driver to take him to Konaki Square. The man appeared not to understand and became quite angry, repeating a word that Avery didn't understand. At last the Greek gave in with a shrug and sank into a sullen silence. Shortly after, the taxi was caught up in the lunatic chaos of rush-hour traffic tearing back and forth across the city.

The vehicle dropped him on the south of Konaki and he walked across the leafy sloping gardens to the upper level where glitzy fashion boutiques faced the café awnings across the narrow street. Athenians were starting their day with breakfasts of honey and yoghurt and thick strong coffee.

He sat at one of the brass-topped tables in Le Quartter, ordered coffee and lit a cigarette. No one appeared to notice him.

Five minutes passed before a woman wearing a pink trouser suit and dark glasses hovered by the entrance, peering at the menu board. She looked to be in her fifties, tall with an unflattering pageboy hairstyle, and was loaded down with the usual tourist trappings of camera, guidebook and map. There was something familiar about her slightly clumsy movements as she negotiated the scattered chairs and selected the table next to his.

After ordering lemon tea she turned to him and said: 'Excuse me, do you speak English?'

He was stunned. Clarissa. 'Yes.'

She smiled broadly. 'Oh, what luck! I'm hopelessly lost. Perhaps you can look at my map and show me where I am.'

'A pleasure.'

She spread it out on his table, using the ashtray and a bottle of olive oil to hold down the edges against the light breeze. Under her breath she said: 'I always feel rather foolish with these charades, Max. Do just prod your finger at different places on the map as if you're explaining things.'

Clarissa Royston-Jones might have felt foolish, but she was an accomplished actress, interspersing their conversation with sudden peals of laughter and throwing in occasional comments about Athens in a slightly louder voice. To all the world she was a gregarious tourist thankful for meeting a fellow countryman.

'Where the hell did you get to, Max?'

'After the shooting they took us to a garage in Monastiraki, then by taxi to Piraeus. A launch was waiting to take us to a yacht anchored outside the harbour.'

'No wonder we lost all trace.'

'Lew had to ditch the pen mike at the warehouse. Just as well as we were thoroughly searched.'

'Where are the others?'

'Still on the yacht.'

'How is Maggie?'

'Recovering. They even had a surgeon and operating theatre on board.'

'Some yacht. Tell me about it.'

'The *Sun King*. It's registered in Panama, but the owner is some high-ranking Iraqi. The crew are all armed and loyal to Saddam Hussein.'

'Who was on board? Someone from Iraqi intelligence?'

'No, a Greek. Just gave his name as Giorgós. Claimed to be from the 17 November.'

'Do you believe him?'

'I think so. The Iraqis seem to be using them as legmen. They've got an unpenetrated cell network and, of course, Greeks are free to wander anywhere in the world.'

'So the Iraqis want to take up the IRA's offer?'

'It would seem so, but I can't be certain. Lew and I have been effectively cut out. Moylan and Giorgós have been huddled together for days. No one's saying anything.'

'I was afraid that might happen. But, tell me, what's your role in the plans?'

'I'm on my way back to London to continue preparing for the attack. Moylan will be in touch with me.'

'Where are they going in this yacht?'

'No idea. But look, if it can be intercepted then all your problems are solved – you nip everything in the bud, and we get Maggie and Lew out safely.'

'Yes, I'm sorry about what happened to Maggie.'

'Not as sorry as I am. How is the Greek cop?'

'He died.'

'Christ.'

'I can't say I approved of you bringing Maggie here, but then I suppose I'm just being wise after the event.'

'So what do you think?'

'To intercept the yacht? It wouldn't be my decision.'

'But you could influence those who make it.'

'Perhaps. But I don't see London or Washington being too happy about closing down. Iraq still has plenty of time to make other arrangements before the UN deadline in mid-January.'

'You don't understand, Clarry. I want Maggie back. I want us both out – now. If you don't act, Moylan will go into hiding until everything is in place. And then it'll be too late for you to know what's going on or to do anything about it. Your only chance is to get them on the yacht.'

'I see.'

'I hope you do. I've had a glimpse of 17 November's organisation and it's pretty impressive. If they go to ground, you'll have the devil's own job to dig them out.'

She nodded her understanding and began to fold up the map; they had been talking for long enough. 'What are you going to do now?'

'Collect my things from the hotel and get the first flight for London – if I get through security.'

'What do you mean, Max?'

'The Greek police had photographs of Con, Lew and me. They had Khaled Fadel under surveillance. Somehow the 17 November got hold of them.'

She pursed her lips in a silent whistle of surprise.

'You see what I mean about their professionalism.'

'I do. Well, good luck, anyway. At least you're back where we can see you. If you *do* run into any problems with the Greek authorities, we'll see what we can do.' In truth she knew that would not be very much, and wondered if Avery realised that too.

He did, and he watched her go with mixed feelings. Still nothing was resolved, yet it was a comfort to know that Clarissa still had a personal hand in his control.

'Hallo, Max.'

The sudden sound of the voice from behind made him jump, his coffee spilling in its saucer.

Gerry Fox pulled out one of the chairs and sat down. 'I thought I'd better wait till the lady went – not your type, I'd have thought.'

Avery was still trying to overcome the shock, trying to stop the uncontrollable trembling in his hands. 'A tourist – lost her way.'

'Women and maps!'

'But for God's sake, Gerry, what are you doing here?'

'Orders from Moylan. I got a call from him in London the day before yesterday. Luckily all the flights are half-empty due to the Gulf scare.'

'But how . . . ?'

'How did I find you?' He chuckled, pleased to see he had the upper hand. 'Your taxi driver's with those 5th of November people. He was supposed to bring you to me, but you didn't understand what he was saying and he spoke little English.'

'I wondered what he was getting so irate about.'

'Anyway, he followed you after he dropped you here, then used his radio.'

Avery closed his eyes. What a fool he'd been! His mind had been so preoccupied that it hadn't even occurred to him how convenient it had been for the taxi to be waiting where he came ashore. 'I needed a coffee and time to think,' he said, then added: 'Actually it's the 17 November.'

Fox was flippant. 'Same difference. The point is Con wants me to work with you on the plans, help out. Says that way we can keep an eye on each other. Suspicious bastard! But my orders are to stay close. Real close. If you go for a shit, I wipe your arse. That close.' He chuckled. 'And vice versa, of course.'

Inwardly Avery groaned.

They travelled back to the Herodian Hotel together. Fox checked the place for a police presence before Avery went in. He explained to the receptionist that his wife and companions had decided to stay on with friends in Greece and that he was collecting their luggage and settling the bill. If the receptionist thought that strange, she gave no indication. Between them, he and Fox cleared the belongings from the two rooms into four suitcases and took a taxi to the airport.

No detectives were waiting; by two in the afternoon they were on the flight to London.


'It was a good funeral,' Nico Legakis said, 'if there can be such a thing. The entire department turned out to see him off. There were a lot of flowers.'

Sophie Papavas sipped her coffee and stared at the stampede of traffic thundering past the café in Alexandre Avenue, just a short distance from the ugly marble monolith of police headquarters. 'I'm sorry, I didn't have the stomach for it.' She lit a cigarette. He noticed that her hands were trembling and his heart went out to her. 'I suppose you still don't know who did it, Nico – may I call you Nico?'

He felt flattered. 'Of course.'

'I feel I know you so well – through Andreas.'

Legakis nodded his understanding. 'It was a strange business. Two women on a motorcycle, a minibus and another car which was left abandoned. It had been stolen, of course, some months ago. False number plates.'

Her shoulders lifted in a gesture of hopelessness. 'Do you think it was gangsters?'

'Gangsters are not in the habit of shooting policemen in the Anti-Terrorism Department. So if it was not a personal motive, then I fear the worst.'

'The 17 November?'

He nodded.

'I read the newspaper report. It said nothing about them.'

Legakis took a swallow of his beer. 'That is because they have not claimed responsibility.'

'The paper said it was you who actually wounded the killer?'

He exhaled thoughtfully, puffing up his cheeks. 'A lucky shot. It should have made the woman easier to trace, but not yet. Perhaps a doctor has been paid to treat her privately.'

'I hope you didn't mind me calling you. It helps to talk.'

He was beginning to understand what Andreas had seen in her. 'I am pleased. It helps me too. I was fond of Andreas, you know. I have had a bad few days, Sophie. It is good to relax for a few minutes with someone who isn't a policeman.'

She toyed with her coffee. 'I find your company comforting.' She struggled for the words: 'You're so calm and wise. It's like talking to my father – only not my father. I cannot talk to him. Perhaps it's because you are a policeman.'

'I didn't think you liked policemen.'

Sophie looked up. 'I lived with Andreas for a year.'

Legakis regarded her carefully. 'That was because he was young and handsome, not because he was a policeman. He told me you were a rebel at heart, a bit of an anarchist. Like most students I see.'

'Maybe I'm growing up,' she teased.

He said suddenly: 'Who is Giorgós?'

She stared at him and for a moment he thought he noticed a flush of colour in her cheeks. But he could not see her eyes behind the sunglasses.

He added: 'We have talked to your friends at the university – to make sure there wasn't a student there who was jealous of your affair with Andreas.'

'How dare you!' she blustered.

He smiled a thin, sympathetic smile. 'I am afraid that we must check these things – most murders are domestic.'

'I would not cheat on Andreas.'

'Of course not. But it could have been unrequited love.

Jealousy from someone you don't even know who is obsessed with you. You are a very pretty woman.'

She was about to retort when she realised what he had said. There was no reason why she should blow this in a fit of anger. As Giorgós had said, it was time to move up the ladder. The lieutenant was dead, and now a captain in the Anti-Terrorism Department was within her grasp – if she played it cool.

Demurely she said: 'Thank you, Nico, that's sweet. But it is Andreas's relationships you should be looking at. He was the one for affairs, despite what he told me.'

'And Giorgós? Your fellow students say you have mentioned this man from time to time.'

'He's just a friend.'

'What is his full name?'

She said the first thing that came into her head. 'Molfetas, I think, but I only call him Giorgós.'

'Where does he work?'

'I don't know. He's a businessman. Usually he's travelling abroad. Sometimes he phones me when he's in town.'

'So you have no number for him?'

'No, I'm sorry. It really is just casual.'

'Of course. But ask him to contact me next time he calls. Just to eliminate him from the inquiry, to tidy up the paperwork.'

She made a sudden movement, reaching for her shoulder bag. 'Look, Nico, I must go now or I'll be late for my tutorial. Perhaps we could meet again and talk soon. Go for a walk at the weekend perhaps, a stroll in the National Gardens.'

'Ah, a nice thought, but . . . '

She did not miss the flicker of interest in his eyes and the sudden expression of regret for something that could never be.

'I'm sorry, Nico, I forgot. Your wife.' Was that too obvious? She laughed, mischievous. 'And your cat. Andreas said you love cats.'

'Very much. Sometimes I think I prefer them to humans. They know so much, don't they? But they never tell.'

'Pardon?'

'If cats could speak, then many of my problems as a policeman would be over.' He read the uneasy smile on her face. 'A private joke of mine. Look, about that walk. One lunchtime would be all right, during the week when I am on duty. That would be a pleasure.'

'Monday?'

'Monday.'

'Dear Nico.' She rose and leaned across the table to brush her lips briefly across his cheek. And as she did so her breast touched his arm. Just fleetingly, but it was enough. In that split second his mind *knew* the weight and feel of her breast, the texture of its skin, knew how she would look naked.

'Take care.'

'One more thing, Sophie. I'd forgotten with the chaos of these last few days. Have you found any photographs or negatives in your flat? Fallen behind the bed perhaps? Andreas thought he might have dropped them there by accident – we were coming to look for them at the time he died.'

She looked puzzled. 'No, I've found nothing, and I had a good clean-up this morning.'

'Well, let me know if you find them.'

'Of course. Till Monday.'

And she was gone, astride her scooter and inching out into the traffic flow.

He paid the bill and headed back to the office, his half-mast trousers flapping around his white ankle socks.

If he didn't know himself better, he might have thought he was falling in love.

# Fifteen

It felt strange returning to the gloom and depression of a London in the grip of recession and bracing itself for a war that was now generally regarded as inevitable.

Strange, too, without Maggie. Although Christmas lights had already made their appearance, none of the restrained air of festivity seemed normal to Avery.

Normality was Maggie fussing over presents and card lists, worrying about finding time to bake the mince pies, panicking over her lines for the hospital panto, and fretting about which holiday shifts she had been allocated.

Having Gerry Fox like a second shadow was not normality either.

'And how's Mrs A.?' was the first question Floyd asked when Avery arrived at the showroom.

'She's staying on in Greece for a while – we met an English couple with a villa.' He made light of it. 'She needed the break.'

The manager's mouth then opened with surprise as he saw Fox wandering around the display of cars.

'Is he with you, Max?'

'Gerry? Yes, he's going to work with us for a while.'

Floyd was incredulous. 'Him? What does he know about motors? We should be cutting back on staff, man, not increasing.'

Avery forced a smile. 'Acting unpaid, Floyd. Just a little business venture we're looking at.'

'Are you going to let me in on it?'

A tap to the side of the nose. 'Bit confidential, Floyd, sorry. I'll fill you in when we know where we're going.' Quickly he changed the subject. 'How's Josh been? No trouble I hope?'

'No, he's a great kid. Rowena's getting quite attached to him.'

'So she wouldn't mind looking after him for a while longer?'

'How long?'

'Not sure, Floyd. A few days, maybe weeks.'

His manager frowned. 'What's going on, Max? Is everything all right?'

'Never better.'

That night he went back to Floyd's house to see the baby, with Gerry Fox in tow. To Avery's irritation the child seemed more interested in the sandy-haired Irishman. It was strange that, to see a terrorist on his hands and knees amidst the colourful rubble of playbricks, blowing silly sounds and making faces which had Josh burbling contentedly with mirth.

'I've always liked kids,' he confided later back at Avery's flat where he was quick to make himself at home. 'Never had any, of course.'

'Perhaps getting married would have been a start.'

'Who'd have had me?'

'True.'

From the start it was hell living in close proximity to Fox. Over the years Avery had learned to endure the one-sided friendship, but now it really irked. The man was uncouth, virtually every sentence he spoke laced with filthy sexual innuendo. Within a couple of days the living room was littered with beer cans and takeaway cartons; he seemed to fill the place faster than Avery could empty it. Ashtrays overflowed and everywhere he looked the plastic smiles of teenage nudes seemed to be smiling up at him from the pages of the girlie magazines that Fox left scattered around.

There was no escape for Avery; the atmosphere had become claustrophobic. Fox was following Moylan's instructions with unnerving obedience, never leaving his side for a moment, either at the showroom or when they went on some errand together to fulfil some requirement for the Provisionals' 'shopping list'.

The man's presence even made some of Avery's under-world contacts seem uneasy. But Fox appeared not to care. Moylan had elevated him to a position of trust. Now it was he who knew the secrets, and he was clearly revelling in his new-found status.

But worst of all for Avery was not knowing whether Clarissa had taken his advice; whether the British and American Governments could be persuaded to seize the Sun King.

If only he could contact her, get an update on what

London and Washington had decided. But with Fox's unwanted and limpet-like companionship, there was nothing he could do. He had not been left alone for long enough to extract his code books concealed in the office cupboard door. And when he had said he was going to the public library, Fox had insisted on going with him. Even his dead-letter drop was out of reach.

The only consolation was knowing that Brian Hunt and his team were lurking nearby, somewhere, that both his home and offices were bugged. Yet it was only a small consolation, because he knew that they no more dared risk contacting him than he dared contact them.

On his third night back, something profoundly disturbed Avery as he lay on the double bed, alone with his thoughts. However hard he tried, he could not conjure a mental picture of Maggie. Until then it had been so easy; now he found himself searching for the family album in the wardrobe. It was almost with relief that he turned the page to find the pert urchin face grinning out at him amid the mass of black ringlets. *Morecambe. Summer '88.* The caravan holiday when she had told him her news. News about Josh. She had never been happier, never looked prettier.

He fell into a troubled and dream-filled sleep.

The dull thud of the helicopter rotors was like a distant heartbeat. Heavy, remorseless and closing.

'*If* Sun King *maintains her present course, ETA will be ten minutes,*' Jim Buckley's words fed into Brian Hunt's earpiece above the deafening thunder of the engines.

It was just a courtesy, but a welcome one. He was only along for the ride; this was a Delta show, and Buckley and his men were in their element. Hunt had never seen them exude such confidence. Ever since the operation had begun, he had only ever witnessed them struggling in the less familiar role of covert surveillance under difficult conditions. This was different, this was what they were trained and practised at, honed to the knife-edge of perfection. The surgical strike.

The three Sikorsky MH-53J 'Pave Low IIIs' came in line astern, their furious downdraught breaking up the choppy wavetops just feet below. Into the twenty-five-mile range now, when at any moment *Sun King's* radar might pick-up the telltale radar blips on her surface radar amid the sea clutter. Might have, but wouldn't, because somewhere out there in the black night a carrier-borne Grumman A-6 Prowler aircraft from the Sixth Fleet would be jamming the yacht's radar and communications facilities.

And in the few minutes while the yacht's crew puzzled over the source of the atmospheric interference and debated the likelihood of an unforecast electric storm nearby, the two Aeroscout Bell OH-58D tiny helicopter gunships escorting the Sikorskys closed the gap, each bristling with 2.75 inch rockets and a 12.7 mm machine gun.

The formation moved in with practised precision, the aircraft and crew members drawn from Task Force 160, the elite 75-helicopter unit from Fort Campbell in Kentucky, which specialised in covert night flying, and who were the blood brothers of the troops of Delta Force.

When the signal had been passed from Washington, following a hastily called SIGS group meeting to discuss the request by Clarissa Royston-Jones, elements of TF160 force had been diverted en route to Desert Shield. The cavernous C5 Galaxy transports had unloaded the heli-copters at NSA Sigonella in Sicily where the rotors were reassembled.

The NSA maritime surveillance satellite that had been tracking *Sun King* showed that it was in international waters, some hundred and fifty miles off the western coast of Greece. To the chagrin of the British SAS men, who were to return to London, Jim Buckley's team flew out of Athens to join the assembling helicopter task force at Sigonella.

Hunt, wearing US desert-pattern fatigues and a sand-coloured SAS beret with the winged dagger, shared the mounting excitement of the Americans in the first Sikorsky. In the ruby glow of the hold light, the colour chosen to preserve night vision, he glanced at the row of familiar faces of those who had become close friends over the past weeks.

Luther Dicks at the hatch, first to go, sat with a fixed white grin set in a glistening black face, his buddy Brad Carver inevitably by his side. Next in line was the ever cheerful Buzz, seemingly unperturbed by any thought that things could go wrong. These would be the first three down of the eleven-man stick, with Hunt coming last. Individually they appeared to have put on considerable weight in the previous few days, until it was realised that each now wore body armour beneath his fatigues, the Stars and Stripes recognition patches blacked out. Every bellows pocket bulged with extra ammunition, supplies, medical and marine survival equipment over which the paraphernalia of abseil harnesses had been fitted. Blacked-up faces and knitted US Navy watchkeeper's caps completed their awesome appearance.

Up in the cockpit, the copilot resembled a creature from a distant planet with his image-intensifying night-vision goggles which amplified the meagre ambient light from the stars in the Mediterranean sky. The pilot meanwhile was flying 'at the edge', skimming the sea surface with only metres to spare, relying on his instruments, which relayed the forward-looking infra-red input to the flight-deck screen, while the rolling-map display pinpointed their position from the central navigation system.

Only they were in a position to witness the sudden and brilliant arc of fire that burst like a meteor across their vision. A searing light split the sky in two, burning into the retina of the naked eye as the rockets thundered from the pods of the first Bell gunships across the bow of the unsuspecting yacht.

A second dazzling display of noise and pyrotechnics lit the darkness as the second Bell launched its rockets across the Sun King's stern.

Even before the flux of light had faded, the crew of the first Sikorsky could hear the nasal voice over the radio, operating on international frequency – 'Sun King, *do you read? Repeat* Sun King *do you read? This is the United States Sixth Fleet operating in accordance with United Nations Resolutions 660 and 661. Repeat* Sun King *do you read, over?'*

The message was repeated before the yacht came on air. A timorous voice said: '*This is* Sun King, *this is* Sun King. *What do you want of us?'*

The expressionless American voice came back on the air. '*Heave-to immediately. Repeat heave-to immediately and prepare to receive a boarding party.*'

Seconds later the para flare was fired from the opened hatch of the leading Sikorsky. It spun skyward like a shooting star, then burst into a blinding, wavering source of incandescence as the chute deployed. It lit up the silken shrug of the waves and the glistening white outline of the yacht, her creaming wake subsiding as the vessel slowed.

Then Luther Dicks was at the hatch on one side, Brad Carver at the other, clipping karabiners to abseil ropes and cross-checking as the helicopter hovered. The yacht deck gyrated giddily below.

'GO DELTA!' the jump master screamed.

They were gone, feeding the rope unchecked and one-handed through the descent lever, leaving the second hand free to fire their short-barrelled Colt Commando assault rifles. The deck loomed, late brakes were applied. Dicks saw the yacht rise up to meet him on the swell. He landed heavily, cursed, and stumbled to his feet, arcing his body around, the Colt jutting defiantly in search of resistance.

Carver was at his side, covering his back, Buzz already

landing with the others close behind. It was a bewildering spectacle, the deck illuminated like a movie set from the flares, the air filled with deafening noise and salty spume kicked up by the phenomenal downblast of the rotors.

They were on the upper deck, precision dropped afore the small stack, but aft of the varnished timber wheelhouse. As Buzz and the fourth Delta trooper headed for the steps and the accommodation cabins, Dicks and Carver advanced on the wheelhouse.

Suddenly the door flew open and a diminutive Filipino crew-man in white jacket appeared, visibly trembling with his hands stretched high above his head.

'Down! Down!' Dicks yelled.

The man threw himself obediently to the deck, clearly expecting his head to be blown off at any second. Carver kicked the prone legs apart, checked for concealed weapons, then left him for the follow-up team.

They found two other Filipinos in the wheelhouse, the yacht's master and another crewman both of whom raised their hands instantly.

Dicks relaxed, relief ebbing through him. 'Shit, man, where's all those goddamn armed I-raqis?'

'Ask them,' Carver suggested.

'You heard!' Dicks thundered. 'You got I-raqis on board?'

The two Filipinos looked at each other nervously, then edged backwards as they were confronted by the menacing bulk of Luther Dicks. 'No Iraqis, sir. They go.'

'Go where?' Carver demanded, beginning to feel deprived of the action he'd been expecting.

'They go away yesterday.'

'Holy cow.'

Jim Buckley strode into the wheelhouse with Hunt just a few paces behind. 'Okay, you guys, what gives?'

'These jokers say the Iraqis left yesterday,' Carver said.

The yacht master's head nodded vigorously, his grin fixed tight with fear. 'Yes, it is true what I say, sir.'

Buzz appeared at the door. 'All mid-decks cleared, chief. No resistance.'

Buckley frowned. 'No Iraqis, no guns?'

A shrug. ''Fraid not, chief.'

'And no sign of Corrigan, Moylan or other passengers?'

'None at all, sir.'

Buckley turned back to the master. 'Right, you, who did you put ashore and where?'

'I do not understand?'

The Delta commander's Colt .45 automatic was out in the blink of an eye, its snub muzzle jammed against the Filipino's ear. 'You understand.'

He understood. 'We put passengers ashore yesterday, sir.'

'Including the Irishman and the Greek?'

The Filipino nodded frantically. 'Mr Giorgós, yes, but I do not know the other nationalities.'

'Two men and a woman?'

'Yes, with injured leg.'

'Where did you put them ashore?'

'A village in the bay of Lakonikós Kólpos.'

Buckley grimaced. The southern tip of the Greek mainland. 'And the Iraqi soldiers?'

'They are transferred to another ship.'

'What ship?'

'I do not see. It is dark.'

The American resheathed his Colt and turned to Buzz. 'Get hold of Gretchen in Athens and send her down south. See if she can't get a lead at that village. Get the name of the place from this jerk.'

'Please, we go now?'

'Goddammit no!' He seethed. 'I'm a nice guy but you really are pushin' your luck. This is an Iraqi vessel and I'm confiscating it on behalf of the United Nations.'

The Filipino showed his teeth. 'Please, this is a Panamanian vessel, sir. It is owned by a Jordanian.'

In exasperation Buckley turned to Hunt. 'Jeez, aren't they goin' to just love this in DC?'

Avery heard the bad news a few days later when the telephone rang in his office. Fox looked up from his newspaper as he answered it.

'Villiers here – I'm a friend of Brian Hunt. He said he thought you might have a vacancy for a mechanic.'

Thank God, thought Avery, but checked himself before speaking. 'Might have a job if you've the right qualifications. When would you be free for an interview?'

'As soon as poss. At your office?'

Avery glanced across at Fox who was watching him with idle curiosity. 'Let's keep it informal – over a beer at lunchtime.'

Even then, Fox insisted on going too. Villiers looked the

part down to the oil under his fingernails, greasy jeans and a generally unkempt appearance. He gave his job-hunting spiel and list of qualifications so convincingly that Fox was clearly taken in. When the Irishman went to the lavatory after drinking three pints in quick succession, Villiers grabbed his chance.

First came the news that the *Sun King* had been found, but with no trace of Maggie, Corrigan or Con Moylan. Charlie Team had returned to Greece to search for them with Stafford Philpot's help, but he didn't hold out much hope.

Meanwhile it was Clarry's suggestion that Villiers, a qualified SAS driver-mechanic, started work in Avery's repair garage to make two-way communication easier given Gerry Fox's omnipresence.

By the time the man returned from the lavatory, Villiers had the job.

Meanwhile Christmas was approaching with even more than its customary speed and Fox's virtually constant presence was even getting to the equable Floyd. 'Sometimes, Max, I think you and Fox have become Siamese twins. D'you always have to drag him along when you visit Josh? Sorry, I'm out of order. It's just that Rowena doesn't care for him too much. To be honest she's been pretty ratty lately.'

Avery caught the nuance. 'Is Josh getting too much?'

Floyd looked uncomfortable. 'Well, it's been nearly a month now, Max, and the strain is beginning to tell. I mean, when is Maggie coming home? It all seems very strange.'

'Can I confide in you, Floyd?' He decided he'd have to make it sound convincing. 'What I told you about Maggie staying with some new friends we met was perfectly true, but I didn't give you the real reason. We had one hell of a row – I mean the relationship nearly broke up then and there. We both decided she needed some space – time to think things out. That's why.'

'I'm sorry, man, I didn't realise. And have you heard from her?'

'A postcard or two,' he lied. In fact the only messages he had received had been relayed by Fox. Moylan had established communication with him, sealed letters arriving by motorcycle courier. Avery had tried to ascertain a pattern, but it appeared that a different firm was used each time. Fox would read over the letters in private, then update him on Maggie's recuperation. Apparently she was already able to walk with a stick and she 'sent her love'. That was it. No amount of insistence could persuade Fox to tell him where they were; in fact, Avery soon realised that the Irishman didn't know himself.

In the meantime his own preparations for the big attack had been progressing steadily. He had located a wrecked white Transit van at a breaker's yard in north London, and had purchased the number plates and documents. He had then bought an identical brand new vehicle which he parked on the forecourt.

Floyd had been furious, claiming that it was a ridiculous time to spend money on new stock when even second-hand vehicles weren't moving. To his surprise a buyer turned up the very next day, a man with an Irish accent whom Avery had never seen before. Cash was handed over and, just before the man drove away, Avery handed him a canvas bag containing the number plates and documents of the wreck.

Avery couldn't be certain, but he guessed the vehicle would be taken to the lockup he'd arranged to be rented in Sidcup.

Six off-the-shelf new identity packages had been obtained from an underworld specialist. The man regularly paid overlanding students from Australia and New Zealand to request the National Health cards to which they were entitled during their stay. Once issued, these were used as a basis to apply for British passports, driving licences, banking facilities and credit cards.

Avery made a mental note of the six names, before handing them over to Fox.

It struck him that he had never been asked for such a concentration of requirements before; he had never been in a position to know so much in such a short period of time. He could almost believe that Moylan was avoiding the use of other regular quartermasters and suppliers. It was odd, but he wasn't complaining; it would make it all the easier for MI5 to piece together the intelligence jigsaw.

'It's going well, Max,' the Irishman had confided in their local pub a few days before Christmas. 'Your part in this will soon be over. Just one more request I've had from Con.' Avery recalled the motorcycle courier who had arrived at the showroom that morning. 'We need half-a-dozen six-inch Guinness gas cylinders – you must know a few publicans.'

'Gas cylinders? What the hell does Con want those for?'

Fox laughed. 'Why d'you think?'

'I've no idea.'

'Good.'

It was a lie, of course. The Transit plus the cylinders meant only one thing. A mobile mortar launcher. A home-made version of the Mark 10.

He felt an involuntary tensing of the muscles in his stomach. It was getting close now. But by prudent security measures Moylan had virtually succeeded in squeezing him out, using Fox to liaise between him and other quartermaster suppliers and the Provisional active service unit who would actually carry out the attack.

Mortars. So that was how they were going to execute their 'spectacular'. From where? And when?

His thoughts were interrupted as Fox reached into his pocket. 'And Con has a present for you.' He dumped a brown paper package on the table. 'Don't open it here. But there's ten thousand on account. And there's plenty more where that came from, he says.'

Avery forced a grin to his face. 'Then I guess it's my round.' Almost as an afterthought he said: 'The Iraqis want us to do some other work for them, Gerry. Has Con said anything to you about that?'

' 'Course not,' Fox replied tartly. 'His messages just tell me what to get or do, and how to reply to him. It changes each time. Keepin' it all to himself, he is.' He allowed himself a smile. 'Bloody galling to be honest.'

Avery let it rest there. If he pushed the matter further, it might just raise suspicions. Like it or not, he'd just have to be patient.

It took just two days to locate and purchase the spent Guinness gas cylinders through a contact of a contact; they were delivered to the lockup garage in Sidcup.

Danny Grogan was not a man who was good with words.

It took him three drafts and half-a-bottle of Bushmills before he was reasonably satisfied with his report to the Army Council on his investigation into Max Avery.

That morning he had visited the small St Francis de Sales Roman Catholic church and school complex in Hale Road. It was just a short distance from Goodison Park, the home ground of Everton Football Club. Claiming to be a researcher for the *This Is Your Life* television programme, he persuaded the bemused and harassed secretary to allow him to search the archives to trace old classmates of a famous local footballer. Naturally he was sworn to secrecy about the identity of the intended victim celebrity.

It took him twenty minutes to locate the yellowing file of Patrick O'Reilly. The final entry read:

*Patrick is a bright and willing pupil. He is very self-disciplined and applies himself to his studies, although Maths and History continue to require a more determined effort. Likewise sport, for which he shows little interest. Next term we expect to see a marked improvement in these subjects.*

That would have been just before the road accident which killed his parents, after which the child was taken into care by Dr Barnardo's.

Momentarily Grogan shared the shock and numbing horror that the young O'Reilly must have felt, the sense of loss. He imagined how the tragedy must have stunned the family's friends and neighbours. He even felt a lump forming in his throat.

Then, as suddenly as it had begun to gather, the moisture in his eyes dried. In his mind's eye he could see Max Avery. Try as he might, Grogan could feel no sympathy for the adult man. Somehow, as he scanned the teachers' handwritten assessments of the child, he could not believe he was reading about the same person.

Yet he knew it was. The previous day Grogan had at last received the requested documentation of Avery's time with Dr Barnardo's from the organisation's headquarters via the firm of Dublin solicitors to which he had given the task.

He had checked the records to confirm that the boy's parents had been buried in the vast Anfield Cemetery, just a short distance from Goodison Park.

Avery's army record was hardly in doubt, backed by the Ministry of Defence red book, and Don Merryweather had confirmed that the man had worked for him between prison sentences. That brought him up to the moment of his apparently chance encounter with Margaret O'Malley at the cookery class in London.

Almost reluctantly, Grogan completed his third draft, conceding in his final paragraph that he agreed with Gerry Fox's earlier findings.

Max Avery was certainly no intelligence plant. That was not to say he couldn't have turned informer once he found himself in Provisional IRA company. But there was absolutely no evidence whatsoever to support this.

No doubt his conclusion would come as a great relief to the Army Council, not to mention Moylan, who had apparently disappeared to Europe to mastermind some operation or other.

Just after the motorcycle courier collected the envelope, the telephone rang. It was the ex-con Michael. 'Can you meet me tonight, Danny? At the Philly?'

When Grogan arrived at the Philharmonic public house in Hope Street, his friend was making the most of his expected last few days of freedom, several empty beer glasses already spread before him.

'This friend of yours, Danny. I'm afraid I've got zilch. No one has ever heard of him. I've spoken to blokes from all three prisons who served time during the same periods. Your Mr Avery must be the original Invisible Man.'

Grogan smiled irritably; this was not what he wanted to hear now. 'Perhaps he kept himself to himself.'

Michael gave him a pained look. 'Haven't you ever been inside?'

'No,' Grogan answered truthfully. His role as go-between to the Army Council demanded that he had no record for either criminal or terrorist activities.

'Well let me tell you, inside everybody knows everybody else's business. Gossip is a way of life. If Max Avery had been there, *someone* would remember him. Perhaps you got the prisons wrong, or the dates.'

'The details are correct.'

'Who gave you the info?'

'Avery's wife.'

Michael shrugged. 'Well, I'd be a bit wary of this character – unless you can check things out independently. I'd offer to break into the Probation Office at Walton, get hold of his Summary of Information sheet from the file but they don't hold files longer than five years . . . '

'Is there another way?'

'You could try the Court Register. That'll give you the trial dates and the adjudication details, sentence and so forth. Apply to the chief clerk – say you're a solicitor researching a client's defence.'

Grogan did not enjoy the rest of the evening. Although Michael had been adamant, he didn't want to share the man's belief that Max Avery couldn't have passed through the prison system unremembered. There were always exceptions to every rule. Yet the nagging doubt lingered, growing in size with each passing hour.

Tip O'Hare was a keen gardener.

It was just as well, because he had found little in the way

of gainful employment since moving to the outskirts of the remote Limerick village six years earlier.

For three mornings a week he would help out in the local grocery store; the rest of the time he spent tending the crops in his garden or pottering in the greenhouse beside the ramshackle bungalow with its leaking tin roof. He'd improved the soil and its yield, allowing him to sell the small surplus to the grocer; it provided a welcome supplement to the modest retainer paid by the Provisional IRA.

He did not object to the quiet life. There had been a time when he didn't think he'd live long enough to get married and have a child. Now he'd had six years to watch his wife grow fat and middle-aged and his daughter start to become the young beauty that his wife had once been.

Sometimes he was nostalgic for the old days. That adrenalin buzz, the dark wet nights and the sudden flash of explosive, the whiff of cordite . . . He still watched television news programmes about events in the north, read the newspaper reports avidly. But now it seemed a million miles away. Sometimes he could scarcely believe it had ever happened. And even less could he believe that the call would ever come.

But it came the same morning that the muck truck came. The freshly delivered mound of manure was still steaming between the overwintering leeks and sprouts when the car drew up alongside the broken picket fence.

O'Hare leaned on his fork. He knew all the vehicles from the village and thereabouts; he didn't recognise this one. It was an old Ford Cortina, its orange-peel paintwork patched with filler.

The driver wound down his window. 'Tip O'Hare, isn't it?'

O'Hare stiffened. Was this trouble? He wasn't dressed for trouble, not in his tweed fishing hat, old jumper and corduroy jacket. If ever he was going to die, he had always imagined it would be in black denims and a balaclava. 'Might be.'

'Don't you remember me?'

The face was familiar, more lined, more grey in the thick black hair. 'Sullivan. It *is* Sullivan?'

'Have I changed that much?'

'It's been a long time.'

'Listen, I've a message for you. The Magician is back.'

Just like that. The Magician.

To hear that *nom de guerre* again. It was strange, uncanny. Chilling and thrilling at the same time.

Six years since he'd served with Sullivan in the Magician's active service unit. No one of O'Hare's lowly rank knew his true identity. But even now he could still picture him: tall and thin, with abnormally broad shoulders, the hair dark and wild. And those eyes. Startling eyes, one electric blue, the other pale, eyes that could bore into your very soul.

The Magician was one of the first unit leaders to intro-duce a secure cell system, impregnable security. Nobody else in the whole of Londonderry knew the identity of them or their leader at that time. That was how they had survived. That was why he had a wife and could enjoy seeing his daughter grow up. That was the measure of what he owed the Magician.

But those were the days before the hatred and the petty jealousies boiled over. Resentment at the Magician's notoriety and success, his arrogance – and perhaps envy of the beautiful black-haired girl who always stood silently by his side. Oh, yes, her too, especially her. If his enemies had known that . . . But they had known enough anyway.

O'Hare had heard no mention of him since. Had imagined he'd been imprisoned or killed. No one appeared to know what had become of him. Now this.

Sullivan said: 'Are you available to go on a trip? You'll be gone some time.'

'That's no problem.' He indicated the mountain of manure. 'That will have to wait. Tell me, have you seen himself?'

A shake of the head. 'Just a call from Fox to meet him in London. You remember Gerry? He gave me six parcels. This is yours.'

A brown package was handed over. Tip O'Hare waited until Sullivan had gone before he retreated to his greenhouse, sat down, and opened the seal. Inside was a typewritten note of instructions, a British passport, an airline ticket for Athens and – a thick wad of dollar bills.

The Magician always had been generous, with everything. Including the black-haired girl.

From beneath a stack of plastic seed trays he drew out the old red Oxo tin. Inside, the handgun was perfectly preserved in its oilskin wrap, but he would not be needing that. The balaclava, though, might come in useful.

*　　*　　*

He would never have thought it possible, but he had done it. He of all people – Nico Legakis – had made love to Sophie Papavas.

From the bed in the flatlet he watched the plump fullness of her bottom as she tottered to the bathroom, closed the door and ran the water.

His reflection stared back at him from the cheval swing mirror by the wall. Skinny white legs protruding from striped boxer shorts, a singlet hanging on his bony shoulders and that familiar weasel face with its moustache and the pale bald crown.

You, Nico Legakis, have done it. How many times had Andreas made love on this bed, looked at himself in this mirror as you are doing?

Was he going mad? In five short weeks he had become beguiled and besotted by this child-woman. Had betrayed the wife to whom he had been faithful since she had become his teenage bride. Yes, this was a kind of madness, an insanity. But he was helpless to resist. Able to think of nothing but her during every waking moment of the day; only sleep brought relief and even then she haunted his dreams. No, he had never been in love like this, yet it was hardly a pleasure.

Because the pain of the hopelessness of it all was almost too hard to bear. For despite everything, he knew he would never, ever leave his wife.

Sophie came out of the bathroom in a rush. 'God, look at the time! I'll be late for the afternoon lecture!'

He watched, fascinated, as she pulled up her denim jeans

and the lush thatch of pubic hair, that had opened to admit him just an hour before, disappeared from view. Strange that, he thought. A girl who doesn't wear knickers. Or perhaps none of the youngsters do today. How could he be sure it wasn't the fashion? Still he found the knowledge strangely exciting.

He slid on his shirt and began to do up the buttons.

'Oh, look, Nico, I forgot to mention it. I have to go away for a few weeks.'

His heart sank. 'Away?'

'It's a project with the college. I've been asked to help out.'

'Where?'

'On Crete.'

He felt suddenly irrationally and insanely jealous. She would be going away with students, some of them handsome young bucks of her own age. He'd seen them hanging around the Technical University in their skin-tight jeans and cutaway vests. Then another thought occurred to him. 'You're not going to see Giorgós?'

She gave a small derisive gasp. 'Of course not! I haven't heard from him in ages. Look, Nico, darling, you're all I care about. Now, I must fly.'

Her shirt and jacket were on, her earrings in place. She kissed him swiftly on the cheek. Grabbing her shoulder bag, she raced for the door. 'Lock up when you leave. Same time tomorrow?'

'When do you go to Crete?'

'Just after Christmas. In the new year,' she called out as she closed the door. 'Bye!'

He finished dressing in a depressed silence, black thoughts crowding in on his mind. His imagination working overtime as he thought about Sophie in Crete with young male students, with the elusive Giorgós, doing with them what she had done with him. What a girl will do with one man, he knew, she would do with another.

Just a few days before she went. And in between, Christmas.

A bleak Christmas that he would be obliged to spend at home in his apartment. With his wife and their cat.

Was he willing, he wondered, to pay the price of love?

# Sixteen

The ANEC Line ferry emerged from the dismal morning mist like a gigantic, slab-sided white whale. A bitter north-easterly wind followed, blowing down from Turkey and the frozen Siberian wastes far beyond. It agitated the placid waters of Soúda Bay, whipping the wavelets into irritable explosions of foam that ran with the ship like a shoal of pilot fish.

Maggie peered from the lounge window at the greyish purple hump of headland that separated the murky waters from the bruised and sullen cloud.

'It's out there somewhere, in the mist.'

The sound of Con Moylan's voice startled her. She had not been aware of him waking from his resting place on the upholstered seats.

Her head didn't turn; she was suddenly all too aware of his presence as he stared out through the drizzle-specked glass, his face just inches from hers. That once familiar smell of him was in her nostrils again, disturbing the long-buried memories. The smell more pungent now, faintly rancid from the soiled vest and old denims that he wore.

Then she realised what he had said. 'Out there?'

'The United States Navy – Naval Support Activity,' he murmured. 'Refuelling jetties for the Sixth Fleet on the northern side of the bay. And above it on the hillside is their airstrip and staff base, officially the 115th Hellenic Air Force.'

'Americans?' she puzzled. 'That's why we're here? I don't understand.'

'You don't have to.'

There was something about his tone that frightened her and yet excited some obscure emotion deep inside her. A feeling that reminded her of the old days.

She looked at him then, closely, but he seemed unaware of her searching gaze. It was uncanny, like stepping back in time. In the month since Avery had gone, Moylan had begun a gradual metamorphosis. During that period they had been secreted away at a secluded villa in a remote part of southern Greece; no one had told her the exact location. She had been confined to the house and its grounds with a growing sense of isolation and mind-numbing boredom despite the stock of English magazines and pirate videos that someone had thoughtfully supplied.

Once a week groceries would be delivered from the local village store and she was expected to prepare the meals each day. Mostly Corrigan and Moylan were absent and she began to long for the prospect of company in the evening. Invariably the American would appear and attempt to cheer her up with improbable anecdotes about his past life. His efforts were appreciated and she came to like him, enjoying the cynical wit beneath the hard-bitten exterior he showed to the world.

Con Moylan, on the other hand, she rarely saw.
Irrationally she found herself angered each time the dinner
she had cooked went to waste. And when he did turn up
and she vented her frustration, he just smiled. 'You always
were beautiful when you were angry, sweet little mouse,'
he said softly, and left her furious with herself for having
let her feelings show.

Sweet little mouse. That was what he always used to
call her. Standing before her like some all-seeing, all-
knowing and all-forgiving antichrist figure and she the
wretched whore washing his feet with her hair. He had
not lost the art of humiliating her, of reinforcing her sense
of worthlessness, destroying her confidence. It made her
boil to think of it, and it irked her even more to realise
that he could do it again now and still she couldn't prevent
him.

In fact, each time she saw him he seemed to revert more
to the mental picture she had of him on the day they had
first met. The gel was gone and his hair was again wild,
thick and black, scarcely traced with silver. It accentuated
the full dark eyebrows and the tiny hairs that linked them
above the mesmeric blue eyes. His stubble was left unshaven,
too; looking at him she could imagine that hardly a day
had passed since their time in Ulster.

Corrigan, too, had begun a transformation. His grey-
blond crop grew longer, defining more clearly his receding
hairline and thinning crown; at a nearby town he had an
ear pierced and a gold ring inserted.

And a week before the ferry trip to Crete Moylan had

told her: 'Stop washing your hair, Maggie, and yourself for that matter. You're going to be an orange-picker, not a tart on the game. I don't want all the men getting the hots for you.'

'Oranges?' She didn't understand.

'Lew will explain to you. I'm sure you can get to love yourself as you really are.'

Another expression he had used all those years before. Calculated to lower her self-esteem and increase his control over her mind. Words that made her flesh creep, yet brought an unexpected flood of warmth to her loins.

She turned away from the view and observed the mass of pathetic humanity that had transformed the elegant lounge into a temporary refugee camp. Dishevelled figures lay outstretched on the chairs, curled on the deck, using rucksacks as pillows, or hunched over tables and studying their first cigarettes of the day with bloodshot eyes.

These were the orange-pickers. The dross, the flotsam and jetsam of Europe who made their way to the Crete island in winter where back-breaking work in the harsh mountains could earn them the pittance they couldn't even make in their own countries. Mostly they were Slavs from Albania, Yugoslavia and Bulgaria, but there was a fair sprinkling of dropouts and those fallen hard on their luck from most places. There was a middle-aged American hippy with long hair and a bald pate who mumbled incoherently about the Tet offensive to anyone who would listen; two buxom girls from the former East Germany who had been informed by some wag that this would be easy money; a

Czech gypsy with wanderlust, and a Scotsman emotionally and financially destroyed by divorce.

In the cold light of day they all began to stir, cough and blearily regret the several drinks too many of the night before.

'I've been away too long,' Moylan said.

She turned her head. She was doing it again. Whenever he talked, she listened. Like a slavish pet.

'From Crete?'

'From the front line, Maggie. I hadn't realised how much I missed it, how much I needed it. The planning, the tension, the rush of adrenalin and blood to the head. I've been away from it all too long. Maybe from you, too.'

'That was *my* decision,' she said hoarsely.

He appraised her for a moment and then said quietly: 'The biggest decision you ever made, and it was the wrong one. I think you realise that now.'

You conceited bastard, she wanted to say, why do you always undermine me? But somehow the words stuck in her throat, and she didn't know why.

The ship's foghorn reverberated eerily around Soúda Bay as the vessel edged past the Hellenic Navy moorings on the south side and began a series of manoeuvres to bring the stern ramp in touch with the bleak quayside area.

She saw Corrigan then, talking to the girl. He and Sophie had feigned their first meeting in the bar the night before. He had made some lewd remark and she had slapped his face in front of everyone. Not the most promising start to the supposed affair they were about to engineer, but it served to convince their fellow orange-pickers that it was genuine. Because, such is life, by the end of the evening they were laughing and joking together, he with his hand resting contentedly in the back waistband of her faded jeans, she without a murmur of complaint.

Maggie had not been pleased to see Sophie again. She had taken a dislike to her from the start and sensed that the feeling was mutual. Every time they met, they would face each other like two hostile cats, eyeing each other with suspicion, claws ready.

Maggie wondered why there had been such an instant and instinctive antipathy to each other, until it occurred to her that there was little difference between them. Sophie could have been her just a few short years ago. The realisation was unnerving.

Most of the orange-pickers joined the queue for buses; a few approached the line of taxis. As though by chance, she and Moylan found themselves beside Corrigan and Sophie and decided to share the cab.

It soon became evident that this was a far cry from the Crete recognisable to the thousands of summer tourists. The fountain in Soúda town would not play again until spring, and most restaurants and tavernas would remain shuttered while their owners returned to their farms or back to winter jobs in Athens. Only a few squalid bars stayed open for the locals, offering prices that the Cretans could afford.

With customary disregard to life and limb, the driver raced towards the large fishing port of Hania, then along

the corniche lined with forlorn and empty hotels and apartment blocks.

After twenty minutes they reached the resort village of
Platanius. It comprised no more than a row of boarded-up
gift shops and tavernas on each side of the narrow coast
road. While the beach strip had been surrendered to the
holiday industry, the locals had taken to the old village, a
collection of stone cottages perched high on the inland
hills.

The taxi dropped them at the square where the woman
in the newspaper kiosk directed them to a small hotel above
a patisserie. It was the only accommodation available and
the last of the rooms had already been taken by the orange-
pickers who had arrived the previous day.

They took refuge in the Café Neon, where those pickers
who had not found work that day gathered to drown their
sorrows in strong coffee and cheap Metaxa. Within half-
an-hour Sophie had persuaded one of the local property
owners to open up two of his summer beach apartments
at an exorbitant rate.

The desolate two-storey stucco block, with its orange-
tiled roof, was one of many small developments squeezed
into the scrubland between the main street and the beach.
It was difficult to imagine how different it would seem in
summer, set amongst mimosas and bamboo clumps in the
scrubby backlots by a grey and uninviting sea.

Corrigan and Sophie took one apartment. Moylan
opened the door to the second and suddenly Maggie
realised that they were alone together. The room was

sparsely furnished in pine, the walls bare plaster and the rough stone floor cold to walk on.

Maggie shivered. 'Isn't there any heating?'

Moylan was unconcerned. 'There's a small cooker by the sink.' He handed her a sheaf of drachma notes. 'Go up the grocery stores and get some provisions. It'll be your job to keep us fed, if you can manage that. Don't spend too much, we're supposed to be near destitute.'

She felt cold, hungry and miserable. 'This is ridiculous. Why can't we just behave like tourists? Stay at a decent hotel?'

Moylan found it amusing. 'In case you hadn't noticed, there are no winter tourists here. Nobody gives a sod about the orange-pickers.'

'And do you seriously expect me to spend all day picking bloody oranges, Con?'

He regarded her coldly. 'I expect you to do what you're told – that is if you want to see Max and your son again.'

Anger flashed in her eyes. 'Why do you have to involve Max and me?'

'It was Max's idea to work with the Iraqis – or has he neglected to mention the fact?'

She studied him for a long moment. Looking at him now she was inclined to believe him. Already she had begun to think that she didn't know Max at all. She was confused by his inexplicable actions, and hurt by the succession of lies he had told her. Confused and betrayed, utterly devastated.

She slumped on the edge of the bed in a final act of defiance. 'Well, I want no further part of it.'

An easy grin spread across Moylan's face as he towered above her. His expression gave no hint that he was about to strike. She merely caught the blur of movement as his hand came down, then felt the strong fingers digging into her hair. A squeal of agony escaped her lips as the roots lifted the skin of her scalp and she was obliged to stand again to prevent her hair coming out in bloody clumps.

Then his fist twisted so that her head was bent back and her breasts thrust forward. Her watering eyes were just inches from his and she could feel the warm escape of his breath on her face. Momentarily their eyes locked in a battle of wills. Long, long seconds passed as he slowly tightened his grip on the knot of hair; two tears began to trickle down her cheeks.

His mouth descended on her offered throat. The kiss was harsh, angry and devouring, sucking in her thin white flesh. He heard her gasp in his ear as he allowed her skin to escape along the sharp edge of his teeth like a cheese-grater.

He felt her resistance go, the struggle end, and lowered her back down to the bed by her hair. She looked up with dark, resentful eyes. Tentatively she put her hand to her neck. Specks of blood came away on her fingertips. He saw then that she was trembling. Nothing had changed.

Later that day, when she served the stew for the four of them, Maggie caught Corrigan staring at her. Was it her imagination or was there a questioning look in those impenetrable eyes? Guiltily she glanced at the two single beds, each made up and untouched. Was that what he was thinking? That she was going to sleep with Moylan, or perhaps already had?

.

Well, sod the American. Let him think what he liked. She was determined that Moylan would never have a hold over her again. Not now, not ever.

In the late afternoon they returned to the Café Neon and joined the other orange-pickers. They asked around about work, as any newcomers would. What was the pay like? Rotten, four and a half thousand drachs a day and you were expected to fill fifty boxes. What was the work like? Back-breaking, especially on the steeper mountain slopes. What was the chance of getting work? Good if you accepted a lower rate; this year there were too many workers from the disintegrating provinces of Yugoslavia who were willing to take whatever was offered.

But the questions were academic. Moylan *knew* they would get work. The next morning there would be a red Toyota truck arriving which belonged to a farmer who worked farther along the coast. His guilty secret was a hidden crop of marijuana in the hills. Co-operation with 17 November was the price he had to pay to keep it that way.

In the fading twilight, when the mud-splattered labour trucks began rumbling into the village square, they returned to the apartment block. A rusting Renault saloon had been left in the muddy parking lot, the car key passed under Moylan's door.

'Our transport,' he announced. It appeared that Giorgós had thought of everything. 'And time to get things moving.'

Corrigan welcomed that at least; ever since they had left the *Sun King*, he had been kept in the dark; he had been used as a virtual errand boy while Moylan and Giorgós schemed together. Maybe at last he'd learn the nature of their plans.

First they drove back along the coast road to the old fishing port of Hania. They found their contact in one of the seedy bars amid the narrow streets of the red-light district.

Captain Vranas, a man of few words, was in his late forties with crinkly shoulder-length hair and a heavy Groucho moustache. By summer he was a fisherman, and by winter a smuggler of narcotics. This time he was also a gunrunner and happily exchanged a workman's toolbag for an envelope of drachma notes from Moylan. He promised the second main delivery for the coming Sunday when there would be only a token customs presence in the harbour.

The deal done, they returned to the car.

Sophie then took the airport road out of Hania. It was dark and blustery now on the peninsula, with rain squalls riding in on a bitter north-easterly wind.

They swung off the road close to the airport terminal building, following the signs for Mouzourás, a village situated in the centre of the knuckle of land which formed the north coast of Soúda Bay. This was remote farmland and rough pasture with few house lights to be seen through the slanting rain.

Shortly after passing through Mouzourás, Sophie pulled over to the side of the narrow road and switched off the lights.

'The track you want starts here,' she announced.

Moylan placed Vranas's toolbag on his lap and opened it. Each of the four Czech-made Vzor pistols was individually wrapped in oilskin; a separate parcel contained several magazines of ammunition. Another package contained woollen balaclavas.

He turned to Corrigan. 'Time you and I did a little reconnaissance. We'll leave the girls in the car and go on foot.' He handed the American one of the weapons. 'Just in case.'

With pistols loaded and balaclavas on, the two men stepped out into the wild, wet night. Moylan led the way up the rough cart track which veered to the left and into a line of rolling hills.

After twenty minutes they had a commanding view of the road below. Beyond the strip of tarmac, bright arc lights could now be seen, throwing the huge aircraft hangar into sharp relief against an angry sky.

Seconds later Corrigan's suspicions were confirmed.

The air began to fill with the thunderous roar of huge General Electric turbo fan engines and then the flashing strobe light of a massive C5 Galaxy strategic transporter blinked its way out of the cloud layer. The great bat-like silhouette dropped rapidly towards the outstretched lines of runway lights.

'This is an American facility, Con.' It was a statement, not a question. And Corrigan could scarcely keep the note of indignation from his voice.

'Of course it is, Lew. What else would Saddam pay the sort of money we want for? C'mon, there's a derelict building along here – this rain's bloody freezing.'

They found the old farm cottage, roofless and overgrown with creepers, some fifteen minutes later. Moylan settled into a sheltered corner and drew a pair of Zeiss binoculars from his jacket pocket.

Half-a-mile distant, behind a high security fence, was the administrative heart of Naval Support Activity, the entire place lit up like a picture palace. One giant hangar and a cluster of low buildings no doubt housed offices, the chow hall, clinic and clubroom that every US base had. Even from that distance Corrigan could smell the whiff of avgas on the wind as the Galaxy was refuelled in readiness for the onward flight to Saudi Arabia.

'Take a look,' Moylan invited, handing over the binoculars. 'A juicy soft target. Giorgós reckons there's around a thousand personnel. And we're going to take out every goddamn one.'

Corrigan focused on a group of people talking on the steps of the admin block. Suddenly they were very real, so close that he felt he could reach out and touch them. Tired, laughing faces sharing a joke. Eyes and teeth. Each an individual.

He said the only discouraging thing he could think of. 'Don't be ridiculous, Con, you'd need a squadron of Phants to take out a place this size . . . '

There was a mirthless chuckle in the darkness beside him. 'You obviously haven't seen what anthrax spores can do.'

It had all become too much for Nico Legakis. Life without Sophie Papavas was hell.

Once he had welcomed the peace and tranquillity of his home – a refuge from the hurly-burly of police work and tiresome office politics.

But now his quiet and unassuming wife had been getting on his nerves. He began to hate the way she sat in her armchair every evening, reading or knitting, with hardly a word to say. Even the domestic routine was getting to him. He wished that, just for once, his supper wouldn't be ready the moment he opened the front door. That, just for once, there wasn't a crisply ironed shirt laid out on his bed each morning.

It began to occur to him that he was deliberately creating mental discontentment to justify his infatuation with Sophie.

He had promised her that each day he would visit the flat and feed her cat, and he welcomed the opportunity to spend a few minutes in the squalid room with its precious memories. To be surrounded by her presence, the pop-star and Che Guevara posters on the walls, the bed that smelled of her, the lingerie drawer in the dresser. For minutes he would sit there, some intimate item pressed against his cheek, and imagine how it would feel against her skin.

But as each day passed since her departure for Crete, he became more morose. Five days now and still no letter; she had promised she would write to her own address so that there was no risk of correspondence falling into the wrong hands.

Had she forgotten?

Was she too preoccupied with some acne-faced student of her own age? Or with the mysterious Giorgós?

Her cat was sitting on top of the wardrobe. It showed no inclination to come down for its food. Wearily Legakis found a chair and stood on it, reaching for the animal.

Then he saw it. A small handbag, covered in a fine layer of dust.

Curiosity got the better of him; that and the maggot of suspicion and jealousy eating away at his imagination. He retrieved the bag and tipped the contents onto the bed.

A few drachma notes in a gold clasp and some loose change; a few condoms in garish colours she had never used with him; some till receipts. A small black diary.

A reference to Giorgós? Some clue as to her other lovers? He flicked through the pages, the most recent first.

'*The pig has fallen for it. God, he makes my flesh creep.*'

With a sinking heart he looked at the date. It was the first day they'd met at the café near police headquarters. The day she'd suggested a walk in the gardens.

The anti-terrorist policeman and the anarchist student. First Andreas and now him. What did it mean? Suddenly all thoughts of Giorgós were forgotten. For the first time in a month he loved his wife again.

He shook out the last contents of the bag. A little strip of negative film fluttered out. Holding it to the light he could see the reversed image of the faces. He recognised the entrance of Khaled Fadel's office in the background.

The cat curled itself lovingly around his feet.

'I always said you knew,' he murmured.

# Seventeen

On their return from the reconnaissance drive to the Soúda Bay airbase, Con Moylan laid down his security rules for the team.

At all times they were to work in twos so that they could keep an eye on each other. No one was to attempt to phone home: Maggie for news of Max or her child or anyone else to speak to family or friends.

Likewise, by operating in pairs, if anyone forgot to act in keeping with his or her cover, there was always someone to pull them into line.

'It's vital we maintain our cover before and after this operation,' Moylan concluded. 'Later, the police will be swarming everywhere like chickens without heads. A bunch of harmless down-and-outs picking oranges with good alibis will raise no suspicions. Our lives depend on keeping it that way.'

Satisfied that no one had any doubts about the fate that would befall them if they disobeyed his instructions, he handed the girls a few grubby drachma notes and told them to make themselves scarce at the Café Neon.

When they had gone, he turned to Corrigan. 'I'd rather

keep the fine details of all this between the two of us, Lew.
The women could get spooked, do something unpredictable.'

'You mean this anthrax business?'

'Start talking germ warfare, stuff they don't understand . . .'

'I thought you were joking.'

Moylan's smile became fixed. 'It's no joke, Lew. I just
hope you can handle it – fellow Americans and all that
crap. High explosives kill a man just as dead as anthrax. It
all depends on the political message you want to give.'

Corrigan's face was as deadpan as a poker player's. 'What
political message?'

'The one thing the US and the Brits fear from Iraq is
the use of chemical or bacterial weapons. Just some ordinary bomb attack is hardly likely to stop the Desert Storm
build-up. This is a big boys' war – think of the impact,
though, when they realise they've been hit by anthrax.
Something that barbed wire and concrete can't stop. They'll
be helpless and they won't know where and when it's going
to happen next. That's why the Iraqis are willing to pay
megabucks. So, can you handle the idea or are you going
to get cold feet?'

'No problem.' The words tripped lightly off his tongue,
but inside his head was reeling with the implications and
the problems he faced. Now it was down to him and him
alone to stop it. He reasoned that he still had a few days
left. At the very least he had to be sure of the location of
the anthrax and get a better knowledge of Giorgós's
organisation on Crete. He would have to judge his moment

carefully, be sure that everyone and everything was picked up in one fell swoop. He said: 'How exactly do you plan to pull off this stunt, Con?'

Moylan took a bottle of Metaxas from the kitchen shelf and two tumblers. 'Ampoules of anthrax delivered by the good old Provie workhorse – the Mark 10 mortar. Fired from that old farm building, an airburst over the base. Can you deal with that?'

'Me?' Taken aback.

'You're the explosives expert, Lew.' He formed the fingers of one hand into the shape of a gun. 'Sniping was always my forte.'

Moylan handed him a tumbler.

Corrigan accepted the drink, felt he needed it. 'Getting all the kit might be a problem.'

Moylan shook his head. 'I've told Giorgós everything we need. It'll be coming with the next consignment from that Greek Vranas. Together with the stuff for the second project.'

'Second?'

Moylan's eyes were sparkling like a child's. 'The Iraqis also want a visual spectacular for the benefit of the world media.'

'Christ, Con, isn't wiping out an entire US base with anthrax impressive enough?'

Moylan frowned. 'C'mon, Lew, think it through. The anthrax is for governments. They'll try and hush it all up anyway, but it'll serve its purpose, get them running shit scared. However, NBC isn't going to get very excited over hundreds of sleeping bodies; besides, Saddam doesn't want to alienate what allies he has left. Publicly he'll deny any knowledge of the anthrax attack, although both sides will know the truth. For his world media image he wants a nice macho strike against the United States – something *no one* can deny.'

'What does he have in mind?'

'Taking out a few US warships in Soúda Bay. All video-recorded by us and distributed to the networks worldwide within twenty-four hours.'

Corrigan shook his head. 'Con, I don't think you understand. That sort of double operation is going to require more people than the four of us . . . '

Moylan jabbed a finger at the American. 'No, Lew, it's you who doesn't understand. I haven't told you the half of it. For a start, I've mobilised six of my lads from the old days – experienced people with no known record who the Army Council have pensioned off.'

'You mean they're coming here?'

'Two of them, yes. Another couple are setting up a similar anthrax attack on London using an old Thames tug. And the other two are headed for Washington. You're going to love this – a mass poisoning of the Senate by getting at the kitchen food supply. The Iraqi *Estikhbarat* have got it all worked out. We're going to help Saddam take the war right into Bush's backyard.'

You're mad! Corrigan bit his tongue just in time. Mad? No, Moylan was no more mad than Saddam Hussein. They were both just shrewd and calculating, and with a ruthless determination to win that ordinary mortals couldn't begin to comprehend.

Moylan was saying: 'Giorgós tells me that the United States has hired some fifteen Greek merchant ships to meet the logistical overload of Desert Storm, and 17 November has got cells on those ships and inside one of the shipping agents in Athens. Two ships are scheduled to put into Soúda Bay for refuelling on their way to the Gulf – and they're loaded to the gunwales with ammunition.' He paused for the words to sink in. 'I'm sure you know what happens when an ammo ship goes up? It'll vaporise the ship, ignite the refuelling terminal and take out most other ships at the anchorage.'

Corrigan swilled the drink thoughtfully round his glass.

The following day came all too quickly.

Corrigan's alarm sounded and he turned in his disturbed sleep, momentarily disorientated. He felt the hand on his chest, nails rasping across his flesh. In a split second he was wide awake, the Vietcong assassin in black pyjamas dissolving before his eyes.

Sophie was smiling at him. 'You have a bad dream I think, Americano.'

He lowered his hand and focused on the naked body seated on the edge of his bed as she reached across him to kill the noise. 'What time is it?'

'Six thirty. There is one hour before the orange trucks come.'

'Christ.' He swung his legs off the bed and turned on

her. 'Don't touch me again like that when I'm asleep. It's not a good idea.'

She showed her teeth in a provocative smile. 'Why, we are supposed to be lovers?'

He sat upright, stretching his back. 'You don't like Americans, remember?'

'I like to think of you as an Irishman.'

'Your privilege,' he grunted. 'But my bad dreams can be real bad. So next time be careful.'

She took in the American's hard, weathered face and remembered how those inscrutable flinty eyes had first intrigued her. Did he want to kill her or make love to her? She would never know.

She said: 'I'll make some coffee.' And walked across to the small cooker, not bothering to dress.

'Put some clothes on,' he ordered.

She pouted her disapproval at him. 'Haven't you ever been married, Mr Corrigan? Or seen a naked woman before?'

'Plenty,' he said, pulling old denims over his boxer shorts. 'And I've been married. But I prefer to have women when I want them. Pay money and you don't have to listen to any garbage. No romantic crap, no candlelit suppers. It's cheaper that way.'

'So sex is like food and drink to you?' she provoked, taking her time to pull on an old cotton dressing gown. 'Nothing to do with love?'

He shouldered on a checkered lumberjack shirt and peered out of the window at the first hint of daylight.

'Maybe something to do with treachery,' he murmured.

She was curious; his rejection excited her in some in-explicable way. 'You sound like a man who has been hurt in love.'

He turned sharply on her. 'I've done my share of hurting, believe me.'

'I think I do.' She paused, careful to choose her words. 'And I wonder if someone hurt you so much that now you hate all women. There are many men like that.'

'And you'd know, would you?' he challenged. 'What would you know about it? The rich bitch daughter of some wealthy middle-class Greek — a girl who's had a cosy life with everything done for her.'

Involuntarily she took a backward step, the full lips parting as her chin dropped. 'What do you know about me?'

He saw her expression and grinned suddenly. Taking a cigar from his shirt pocket, he said: 'I'm guessing, but I've been around.' He flicked his thumb on the old Zippo lighter and exhaled a cloud of smoke. 'That's usually your type. Poor little rich girls who can afford the luxury of getting their rocks off with anarchists. Fighting some imagined battle for the real victims of society who are too busy scratching an honest living to do anything about it them-selves. Is that how you see it?'

She didn't answer him. Feeling as though this relative stranger had violated some secret inner part of her being, she attended to the coffee.

When she handed him one of the mugs, she said: 'You do not like me.'

'I don't like you or dislike you. I'm just doing a job.'

'And has your job always been to kill people?'

He regarded her for a moment, the warmth of the hot mug welcome against the chill of the unheated room. 'Mostly.'

'And you enjoy what you do?'

'I have done, on occasions. But usually it's been a matter of survival. Me or the other guy.'

'And here in Greece, why are you doing this? Is it something you believe?'

'I'm doing it for the money.'

'To pay for the cause that you do believe in? Your fight in Ireland?'

He was tempted at that very moment to slap her. To shout at her and tell her what a stupid spoiled bitch she was. That he had seen hundreds of men and women killed and maimed for causes that someone else believed in. That what she was doing was purging her own guilt for being born with the proverbial silver spoon, for never having had to struggle to survive as others did. But there was no point, because fanatics like Sophie Papavas could never recognise the truth, even when it was staring them in the face.

Instead he just said: 'We all have to believe in something.'

Her eyes widened with intensity as she misinterpreted his meaning, certain that she had detected a chink in his steely reserve. 'I will not be a burden to you.' Then she smiled. 'And unlike other women in your life, I promise I will not betray you.'

The sky behind the hills was beginning to lighten, throwing them into bold relief. 'I'm pleased to hear that, Sophie. Very pleased.'

By seven thirty Corrigan and Sophie had joined Moylan and Maggie with the rest of the roughly dressed orange-pickers who gathered in the village square.

They stood stamping their feet against the dank dawn air, condensation rising like a forest mist as mouths blew warm air on white pinched fingers. Then the first of a line of rickety trucks bumped their way down the main street, landowners standing arrogantly in the cargo holds surveying the rows of dejected hopefuls like old-time slavers.

'Three thousand drachs for fifty boxes,' called one farmer. A group of hollow-faced Slavs raced forward, eager for work at any price.

Others held back, waiting for the offers to improve.

'Four thousand,' called another. 'And a hundred drachs bonus for every box over fifty.'

Another appealed to the older, more reliable workers. 'Lower slopes only. Save your backs.'

Moylan's group had waited to one side as Giorgós had instructed. The farmer in the red Toyota pick-up soon iden-tified them. 'I want some supervisors. People who can drive. Four and a half thousand each for a day.' He ignored the mass of waving hands and beckoned to Moylan. 'You four will do. Get aboard.'

They were joined in the back of the truck by a work gang of mixed nationalities before the farmer set off for the cloud-hidden mountains.

Eventually the bone-shaker ground to a halt in one of the remote high passes where irrigation pipes ran like black snakes through the lower branches of the endless rows of orange trees. The farmer waited until the workers had taken their plastic crates and trudged across the mud to their allotted lines. He exchanged a few words in Greek with Sophie before setting off to supervise new arrivals.

'What did he say?' Moylan asked.

'He says he doesn't know what we're doing here and he doesn't want to. He says if we pick oranges, he pays us, otherwise he doesn't.' Sophie appeared to find that amusing. 'We have use of this truck during the day, but you must be back here by three o'clock to load the crates. He says make sure you keep the truck full of diesel.'

Moylan surveyed the dismal orange grove; the pickers all seemed too busy to notice them. 'Let's make it look good. You girls grab a couple of crates and muck in with the others. Lew and I got things to do.'

They glared at him with open hostility, then reluctantly took their crates from the tailgate and joined the rest of the workers. It was beginning to rain.

The pattern was set. Each day Moylan and Corrigan would leave the girls in the groves while they took the truck – ostensibly to supervise other work gangs or deliver loaded crates to the farm. In fact they spent their time in reconnaissance and planning for the two-pronged attack on the Soúda Bay base.

Two days were spent travelling to the distant city of Iráklion, where they staked out a suitable lorry for carrying the launcher which would fire the anthrax bomblets. The following night they stole it from the builder's yard and took it to a remote barn in the hills which Giorgós had arranged for them.

Every afternoon as the light began to fade, the two men would return to the orange groves in the farmer's pick-up. There they would find the sodden and mud-splattered workers lined up like refugees, their painfully gathered harvest before them for the count and meagre pay-out.

'You bastard,' Maggie had mouthed at Moylan on the first day. Her face was drawn with fatigue, the skin scratched by branches and her hair matted with earth. Angrily she held up her hand; the fingernails were filthy, split and bleeding. 'You knew it would be like this, didn't you?'

But he had just smirked and turned away.

Certainly neither of the girls had the strength to argue. Like the majority of the orange-pickers, they barely had the energy to eat their meal at the end of the day before crashing out to sleep like the living dead.

Saturday came as a blessed relief.

Having spent most of the day in bed, the two women were clearly looking forward to getting cleaned up for an evening of civilised recreation in Hania town.

Moylan watched Maggie as she emerged from the shower in her dressing gown. He said nothing as she selected her clothes and prepared to take them into the bathroom.

'Get dressed in here.'

The sudden sound of his voice made her jump. 'What?'

'You heard. I want to see you.'

'For Christ's sake, Con. It's all over between us, it has been for years. Don't you understand that?'

A muscle pulsed at the side of his mouth. 'And you still don't understand yourself, do you?'

Her laugh was brittle. God, how she hated him, hated the way he could make her stomach churn with fear. Hated that brooding sense of power he exuded. The stare of those eyes that could rip the clothes from her back like a razor blade, the cruel twist of a mouth that might or might not be smiling, daring her to disobey.

This time she was determined to stand her ground. 'I understand myself, Con. And you. As soon as you knew I'd been abused as a child it began, didn't it? You exploited that, played on my guilt. You used me for some little psychological experiment. Playing power games, mind control.' She added with contempt: 'Your little pet mouse.'

This time the smile was distinct, his teeth as strong and white as she remembered them. 'Pet mouse – that's right. But the simple truth is Maggie, you enjoy being abused. That's why you felt guilty. I taught you to accept yourself as you really are, that's all.'

'BASTARD!'

Her scream of pent-up anger took him off guard, and he raised his eyebrows in mild surprise as she snatched her clothes from the bed, and stormed towards the bathroom.

At the door she turned to face him. 'When I first met you, Con, I was no more than a child myself. I felt guilty and confused about my past. You preyed on that. On my sense of shame and lack of self-esteem. I felt a shit and you just reinforced it. You knew how I worshipped you, believed everything you said. I haven't forgotten the day you gave me to the members of your unit. Do you remember what you said to them?'

He stared at her in silence.

'You said, "Do what you like with her – she'll not complain." And they bloody well did.' She glared at the ceiling in frustration, needing inspiration for the words she sought. But the memory of her kneeling within the circle of naked men distracted her. She was close to tears when her words finally came out in a half-choked sob. 'Well, I've grown up since then. I met Max and he's shown me there's another way. A way that's kind and considerate. He respects me like you never could.'

Moylan regarded her with an amused, cynical expression. 'Is that so, Maggie?'

She glared back in defiance. 'And for your information, Con, I've had counselling. Apparently it is quite usual for abused kids to feel guilty for a number of reasons, not least because they feel partly responsible – and ashamed at their own natural bodily responses to what happened. It doesn't mean that they – or I – ever enjoyed it. EVER!'

She disappeared and slammed the door, falling back against it, her chest heaving as the tears trickled down her cheeks.

Holding up her hands she found that they were trembling. She had meant every word that she had said. Yet, even as she had spoken them, she was aware of a small voice at the back of her head calling for him to come to her and bend her will to his.

Her teeth sank into her clenched knuckles.

Max, for God's sake, help me.

That night the four of them ate at one of the few quayside restaurants still open before returning to the red-light district to seek out Captain Vranas. As taciturn as before, he confirmed that their second consignment would be coming ashore the following night. They should be there to meet it with the necessary transport.

On Sunday night Moylan and Corrigan drove to the barn in the hills, picked up the stolen truck and went on to the rendezvous spot. It was a remote cove on the seaward side of the Soúda peninsula and when they arrived, Vranas's small gang was already carrying the weatherproofed items up the precipitous cliff path. With the deal complete and money exchanged, Moylan drove the truck back into the hills to the barn where everything was unloaded. It had been thoroughly planned; nothing was overlooked. Empty gas cylinders for the launchers; industrial steel tubing to make the bomblets; propellant and warhead explosive; a camrecorder, and a custom-made case for the anthrax spores.

Corrigan's work began in earnest the next day. An emergency generator provided lighting and power in the ramshackle building of rotten slatted timber patched with large expanses of polythene.

Moylan opened the small black case with its three glass

ampoules of anthrax inset into separate cushioned compart-ments. The American noticed that he was sweating heavily as he placed them on the old trestle table.

'For Christ's sake don't drop them, Lew.'

Corrigan gave him a pained look. 'I don't intend to.'

'How are you going to trigger them for air-burst? A time-fuse?'

The American shook his head. 'Too tricky – we're talking mere seconds here. I suggest a straight burn-through of propellant to the initiator. That way it'll explode at the point the missile reaches its maximum height – over the base. No room for error.'

Moylan smiled nervously. 'Then the sooner we get the bombs safely packed up the happier I'll be.'

Corrigan set to work with the wet-welding gear to cut the industrial tubing into twelve equal lengths, pinching in the top of each cylinder with a heavy-duty vice and soldering the seams. Three of these improvised bomblets would carry the anthrax ampoules; nine others would be used as test or explosive rounds.

Using a razor-bladed craft knife, he cut a block of poly-styrene for each of the three ampoules in order to prevent them from shattering accidentally. One was placed in each cylinder nose cone and packed with approximately fifteen pounds of good quality gunpowder, together with the initiator which would trigger the warhead explosive and disperse the anthrax. Then a steel funnel was inverted and wet-welded to seal off the warhead. When fired, the propel-lant would burn through from the base of the bomblet and into the tube of the funnel until it ignited the initiator.

'Christ, Con, I'm starving.' It was cold and draughty in the barn and they hadn't eaten since dawn.

Moylan laughed, clearly not unhappy for a reason to leave the close proximity of such a lethal cocktail of explosives and anthrax. 'I'll get the sandwiches from the truck.'

As Moylan left the barn, Corrigan softened the plumber's lead he had purchased locally and poured a plug of the molten substance into the funnel tube of the three warheads. He was packing the propellant charges when Moylan returned. 'What d'you want?' Moylan asked. 'Cheese and pickle or pickle and cheese?'

'Just a minute. Let's get these bastards sealed.'

Five minutes' soldering had the bases of the bomblets fixed into position, together with the electric detonators which would fire each device. 'You can rest easy now, Con. Just don't get these bastards mixed up with the others.'

Moylan pulled three cans of spray paint from another of the Iraqi packages. 'Red might be appropriate, I think.' He chuckled. 'Then yellow for explosive rounds and white for testing.'

After lunch they weighed the three anthrax rounds and packed three more with conventional explosive Semtex warheads, using different fuses and initiators to the equivalent poundage – Moylan had decided on a mixed six-barrel barrage to add to the confusion and to create some visible damage. The warheads of the remaining six test bombs were filled to the equivalent weight with sand.

'When do you want to start testing?' Corrigan asked as he watched Moylan bury the last of the bomblets in the pit of soft earth in one corner of the barn.

'That can wait until the new boys arrive from Ireland. They're experts with mortars.'

'When do they get here?'

'Just a few days. Giorgós wants to keep them in Athens until he's sure no one from Brit intelligence has followed them. I've assured him they're clean, but you know how paranoid he is.'

'Better safe than sorry,' Corrigan said.

Just a few days, he thought. When he could identify the rest of Moylan's team and would know where they were – that's when he'd make his move. Go for a wrap and a clean sweep.

When Danny Grogan put down the telephone, his hand was trembling.

He didn't want to believe what he had just heard. The chief clerk of the court had been most apologetic. Of course, as a solicitor Grogan would be welcome to inspect the Court Register on behalf of a client. But there had been an accident, a minor fire in which the imitation leather bindings had been damaged. The volumes he wanted were being rebound and wouldn't be available for several more weeks.

Christ, was this pure coincidence or some kind of conspiracy?

The ex-con Michael had told him that Register sheets

were numbered consecutively and that the adjudication was entered by the hand of the clerk of the court. They were virtually impossible to tamper with – even by experts.

Of course, experts such as Special Branch or MI5 would have access to everything. Birth and death certificates, Ministry of Defence references – even records of an institution like Dr Barnardo's.

And Max Avery had spent almost his entire adult life in one government or private institution or another, where information about him could be controlled or forged. Except for Don Merryweather. And he was an ex-Para.

But even experts couldn't tamper with a Court Register.

No, not tamper, he corrected himself – just temporarily withdraw them – or was that just fantasy?

His head reeled and he slumped down on the hard hotel bed.

The school reports at the St Francis de Sales school. He was convinced they were genuine: the paper had aged and included a dozen different teachers' handwriting. Not impossible, but a hell of a big forging job to undertake. And who would have anticipated anyone looking at them? After all, Gerry Fox had never thought of that.

Then Barnardo's. What had that man said? It was unusual for a Catholic kid to be referred to them. Had someone slipped up somewhere?

He suddenly grabbed his notebook from the bedside table and began writing in a hasty scrawl:

*Early education — confirmed by school records.*
*Dr Barnardo's — NIV — no independent verification.*
*First job at Tate & Lyle — NIV. The factory had closed down*
*in the early '80s.*
*Military service — NIV.*
*Civilian life — only Merryweather's word — NIV.*
*Criminal record — NIV.*

God, he thought, virtually nothing was verifiable since Barnardo's. And then O'Reilly's name had been immediately changed by deed poll to Avery.

But that was '66, three years before the Ulster troubles had begun. No one in intelligence could have foreseen they would need an agent-in-place, and no one would recruit a sixteen-year-old. It was crazy. He was going mad, becoming obsessed.

Again he came back to the fact that Maggie O'Malley was convinced her first meeting with Max Avery had been pure happenstance.

Then a thought occurred to him. The O'Malley girl had been active in the Provisionals until just before coming to England. What if she'd been under surveillance when she'd met Avery? And what if *only then* the security forces had recruited him? If so, did they have to build up a false background based on a real person? Possible?

Possible.

Then where was the real Patrick O'Reilly?

He raced out of the hotel and hailed a passing taxi to take him to the offices of the *Liverpool Echo* in Old Hall Street.

His impatience was mounting as he was shown to the basement archives.

'Those old issues are all held on microfilm rolls,' the librarian explained helpfully. 'And there's a photocopying device you can use when you find what you want. Now, what year was the car crash?'

'1961. July.'

The librarian's finger ran along the rack, then hovered at the empty slot. 'Oh dear, that particular roll appears to be missing.' He smiled apologetically. 'I do believe that's the one. Someone was researching in here a couple of weeks ago. Spilt coffee over it. Completely ruined. I'm so sorry.'

Bastards, bastards, bastards!

Grogan rushed out into the grey daylight of the street, his lungs heaving and his heart pounding. He had to know. *Had* to!

Surely someone must remember the accident if an entire family perished? A taxi cab pulled up to deliver a passenger and he almost pushed the woman to the ground in his anxiety to get in.

'Where to, pal?' the driver asked sardonically. 'Casualty Department, is it?'

Grogan gave a dry snort of a laugh. 'Could be right there – No, Goodison Park. Emery Street.'

Fifteen minutes later he paid off the taxi which left him standing alone in the street where the young Max Avery had lived until the accident.

It was narrow, immaculately kept, the two-up two-down terraced houses opening straight onto the pavements. Even the few monstrous attempts at mock stone cladding and aluminium picture windows underlined the overwhelming sense of civic pride, despite the obvious poverty of the owners. Even so, he noticed, almost every house had a burglar alarm box fitted outside.

He found the number. As with all its neighbours, the front window boasted clean ruffled net curtains and a small display of china ornaments. The doorstep and surrounds glistened with fresh red paint.

The distant sound of the bell chimed from inside and a child began to bawl. A mother shouted irritably. Moments later the fat young woman opened up, a cigarette in one hand and by the other a toddler with a rubber dummy in its mouth.

'Yes?'

'Sorry to trouble you, madam. I'm from the *Echo*. I'm doing a feature on great tragedies in Liverpool's history.'

The woman looked confused. 'Why ask me?'

'Some people used to live in this house. A family called O'Reilly – the parents and a wee lad – his mother and father died in a car crash back in 1961 . . . '

She became suddenly suspicious and started to back away. 'I wouldn't know, only moved in ten year back.'

'Please, is there anyone who might have known them?'

The door began closing, but he edged his foot into the gap. She said: 'Aren't many old 'uns left here, 'cept Mrs Davis over the road. She's a right busy.'

'Sorry?'

'Busy Lizzie. Likes knowing other people's business. Now if yer'd get yer foot out me door, I got nappies to change.'

Grogan crossed the street, aware of the afternoon darkness closing in and drizzle in the air. He was not hopeful as he tapped the old lion's head knocker.

However, old Mrs Davis welcomed any visitor for whatever reason. Anything for an excuse to talk to someone and to share a pot of tea.

'A lovely family,' she murmured, the cups rattling in her rheumatic hands as she placed them on the table. 'The street was so shocked when they heard the news. I remember the funeral – everyone turned out. Three hearses.'

'Three?'

'So sad. Wee Paddy's little coffin – adorned with flowers. They were buried together in Anfield Cemetery.'

Grogan's head was spinning. He felt a sensation like a hot clammy hand on the back of his neck. 'I know, I've been there, Mrs Davis. But there are just two stones for the parents.'

She smiled sadly: 'This is a city full of vandals today. Young Paddy's headstone was broken or stolen some time ago. I stopped visiting after that.'

'Can you remember when that was?'

'I do believe it was 1982, just after the Falklands War.'

The year that Max Avery met Margaret O'Malley.

And now Avery was back in London. At the heart of a secret Provisional operation to attack Downing Street.

Danny Grogan left his tea untouched.

# Eighteen

Christmas had come and gone.

It had been the most depressing period of his life that Max Avery could remember.

He went through the motions of decorating the artificial tree; although the baby was too young to appreciate it, he knew it was what Maggie would have wanted. At least having the child home again for the holiday break had helped to take the edge off his loneliness and had distracted him from worries about Maggie's safety. Being plunged into the domestic mayhem of feeding, playing and washing baby clothes left little time for self-pity.

The change was almost therapeutic, but not so much as the welcome absence of Gerry Fox.

He had taken himself off to Dublin on Christmas Eve to visit friends and relatives and it was seven days into the new year before he returned. The down side to the Irishman's departure was that Avery received no more news of Maggie.

But all that changed when Fox turned up one evening in early January. He had just arrived back on the Dublin–Heathrow shuttle and had clearly been drinking.

'Thought you'd be pleased of my company after being stuck here with the laddie all this time. Let's go out for a pint!'

Anxious for word of Maggie, Avery called a neighbour's daughter to babysit and went with Fox to a nearby pub. Despite the Irishman's apparent drink-induced euphoria, Avery sensed that something was wrong. As the evening progressed it occurred to him that it was Fox who wanted the company and comfort of a friendly face.

When the barman switched on the television for the late evening news, Fox muttered abuse as the recently appointed Prime Minister, John Major, appeared to give dark hints of what was to befall Saddam Hussein and Iraq if they didn't pull out of Kuwait.

'Bloody android!' Fox sneered, his words now almost incoherent. 'The plastic Prime Minister talking war like he's the fucken Duke of Wellington. We'll see how tough he is when the Provies blow him out of Downing Street.'

Avery urged him to keep his voice down, but picked up on the slurred words. 'You must be kidding, Gerry. They wouldn't get close enough now – not when the police are on war alert.'

Fox grunted. 'Con could do it, believe me.'

'The mortars, you mean?'

The Irishman regarded him with watery eyes. 'You must have guessed, surely.'

'Is there a date fixed?'

'I've said too much. Shit.' He hiccupped and stared morosely at his beer. 'Still, maybe it won't happen now.'

Avery frowned, now sure that something was wrong. 'What happened in Ireland, Gerry?'

Fox seemed uncertain how much to say. 'Hell, I guess it doesn't hurt to tell you. A couple of days ago I got a visit from Danny Grogan and a delegation from the Army Council. A very unpleasant experience, Max, I can tell you. Nearly shit myself when they started waving a gun at my kneecaps.'

'Why should they do that?'

'They're getting cold feet about this linkup with Iraq, and they're worried about Con's disappearance. To put it bluntly they think they're losing control of him — some of them even think he might be setting up his own splinter group. You know, like those ILNA crazies.'

'What gives them that idea?'

Fox shrugged. 'Con got me to activate some cells of his own — but apparently he didn't have proper authority. Six people the Army Council have been keeping clean for the future.'

'Where have they gone?'

'How the hell should I know? I just delivered sealed orders, although the rumour was that two of them had gone to the States. And that's what I told those bastards from the Army Council — dammit, after all my years of loyal service.'

Avery made sympathetic noises and went to buy another round of drinks. This was an astonishing revelation if it were true. It also meant that he was in dire risk of losing track of whatever else Moylan might be planning.

When he returned with the beers he asked: 'So the Army

Council is still going ahead with this Downing Street attack?'

'I don't know, Max, everything's up in the air. Grogan made me tell him how to get a message to Con – each time he sends me something by courier he gives me a new telephone number abroad. The people who answer always have the same accent – Greek, I think. I talk open, but use agreed code words for certain things. My guess is the contact tape records what I say and then plays it back down the line to Con.'

'Still no idea where he is?'

'I think he must be in Greece somewhere, but who knows?'

'What message did Grogan have for Con?'

Fox gave a bitter smile. 'Didn't let me listen, did he? My guess is he's given Con an ultimatum – report back to them in person or else he'll face a Provie court martial.'

'And how do you think he'll react to that?'

'Frankly, Max, I just don't know any more. The way I feel, I just hope he tells them to shove it. Con's paying more than they ever did, that's for sure.'

Avery could understand now why Fox was such a troubled soul. After a lifetime on the Provisionals' payroll he found himself facing a conflict of loyalties. He was between the devil and the deep blue. Whichever way he jumped, he would make a deadly and unforgiving enemy.

He said: 'I suppose there's been no news of Maggie?'

Fox shook his head. 'Sorry, Max, Con's stopped mentioning her in his reports. Must have slipped his mind.'

The conversation lapsed as the alcohol took its effect on Fox and Avery had to support him on the way back to the flat.

When he returned from paying off the babysitter and checking that Josh was asleep, he found the Irishman snoring on the sofa.

Avery retreated stealthily to the hallway. Fox's overnight bag lay where he'd left it by the front door. The temptation was too much – he had to find out what was going on, and quickly.

He examined the padlock. It was a flimsy affair and he slipped back into the bedroom to search for the collection of spare luggage keys he and Maggie had accumulated over the years. The second one he tried fitted.

It took only a few moments to find what he was looking for – a slim red memo book secreted between the covers of a girlie magazine. There were five pages of entries in Fox's handwriting, each one dated. Each entry appeared to be a note made after one of Moylan's messages. Many of the jottings were abbreviations of logistical items that Avery had been asked to procure. Others were presumably requests to other quartermaster sources he did not know. There were dates – for rendezvous or deliveries? – and prices. Some references looked as though they could be for weapons, others probably for vehicles or properties. Only Fox himself would be able to make certain sense of them.

Avery frowned. The last two entries read:

*Tug? How much? Advise.*

*Aerosol generator – inquire indust or agricult suppliers.*

Tug? Did Fox literally mean a Thames river tug or was it an abbreviation for something else? Certainly it might be a novel means to escape after an attack on Downing Street when the police were sealing off roads.

And an aerosol generator. What the hell was that?

Then he saw the date. *January 31. Hit on 10.*

His heart began to thud. He checked back in the living room; Fox had curled into a foetal ball, sleeping contentedly with his mouth agape. Avery closed the door silently and returned to the bedroom. He placed the notebook on the dressing table and switched on the fluorescent strip light. He located the pair of old trainers in the bottom of his wardrobe and extracted the Minox document camera that he had rarely had cause to use. He snapped the five pages of the notebook, removed the cassette spool to his pocket, then replaced the miniature camera in his trainers. He returned the notebook to Fox's case and relocked it.

Tomorrow he would deliver the cassette to Villiers in the workshop and pass on the vital information. Downing Street was the priority target. Thursday, January 31st.


It was another pre-dawn start at the beachside apartments in Platanias.

Corrigan and Sophie were awoken by a knock on their door.

It was Maggie. 'Con hasn't been back all night – some emergency meeting with Giorgós. I couldn't sleep, so I thought I'd do a proper cooked breakfast if you fancy it.'

Sophie scowled at the interruption, but Corrigan liked

the idea. 'Give us five minutes Mags. If Sophie doesn't want hers, I'll have it.'

A watery sun was rising out of a grey and lacklustre Mediterranean as Maggie served the bacon, eggs and sausage.

'What was the emergency?' Corrigan asked, taking an eager mouthful.

'I've no idea. But Michalis – you remember Sophie's bearded friend – he called around midnight with a car. I don't know what it was all about.'

The Greek girl had been nursing a mug of black coffee by the window. 'You can ask him yourself. Michalis has just dropped him back.'

All faces turned expectantly as Moylan entered. He seemed unexpectedly cheerful. 'That smells good,' he said, looking at Maggie. 'Get some for me, little mouse.'

'Problems?' Corrigan asked.

'Not really. Giorgós just wanted me to go over our plans. Talking of which, Lew, I've got a job for you. Giorgós says the Iraqis need a full briefing, a complete update before they come up with our next stage of payment. I want you to go and meet up with Max.'

Corrigan's mouth dropped. 'Where?'

'They want a meeting in Jordan.'

This was the answer to his prayers. The chance to meet again with Avery and set in motion a plan to take out the entire Crete, London and Washington operations. To snatch Maggie and seize the anthrax rounds – to ensure the Stalking Horse ploy cleared the last and fateful hurdle.

'When?'

'My two men arrive on a flight into Iráklion today at lunchtime. You can take the same aircraft out. You'll travel via Athens.'

'Who are these guys of yours?'

Moylan smiled. 'No need for you to know the names, Lew.' He looked at Maggie. 'But you'll remember them, little mouse. They'll certainly remember you.'

She knew exactly what he meant and the blood drained from her face.

For once Moylan decided that they could give orange-picking a miss; he'd have much to discuss with the newcomers and the girls would have to buy in extra provisions. And when his taxi arrived at noon Corrigan was ready, his small handgrip packed.

Maggie rushed to his side and kissed him quickly on the cheek. 'Take care, Lew. Tell Max I love him and want to be with him soon.'

'I will.' He only wished he could tell her just how soon he intended it would be.

'And ask after Josh, will you?'

'No problem. Everything will be all right.' As the car door slammed and the taxi splashed its way through the muddy puddles of the parking lot, Moylan watched on impassively.

Maggie said: 'I don't understand, Con. I thought there was a major problem when you rushed off to that meeting last night?'

He stared after the taxi. 'There could have been, sweet

mouse. But it's all under control. The Iraqis have their own way of dealing with these things.'

Avery awoke to the harsh sound of knocking on the front door. Blearily he looked at the bedside clock – 7 a.m.

By the time he'd found his dressing gown and made his way to the door, Fox was taking the package from the motorcycle messenger.

'Another note from Con?' he asked.

Fox nodded. He wasn't a great conversationalist first thing in the morning, and particularly not this morning. His hair was unkempt and his eyes puffed from too much alcohol the night before. He trudged into the living room, slumped on the sofa and prised open the package.

'Airline tickets,' he muttered, puzzled. 'London–Paris, Paris–Malta, Malta–Cairo and . . . Cairo–Jordan.'

'Jordan?'

Fox opened the typewritten note and scanned it briefly. 'Christ, Con wants us in Jordan!'

Avery's spirits lifted instantly. At last something had happened. At last he might have a chance to do something positive.

'Why, Gerry? Why Jordan?'

Fox was still bemused. 'I'll tell you what it says: 'Business going well – deal all set up. Want you and Max to join me and Lew in Amman, Jordan, for finalisation meeting. Tell Max that Maggie's looking forward to seeing him' – ah, isn't that sweet?'

'Of course,' Avery said thoughtfully. 'You've seen the

news, Jordan is now the only route into and out of Iraq. I expect it'll be a meeting with Iraqi intelligence officers. That's also the reason for the roundabout route. Anyone flying to Jordan from London will be under suspicion.'

Fox looked pleased. 'Could be quite exciting.'

'When does he want us to go?'

He glanced again over the note. 'Oh, shit! The flight for Paris leaves Heathrow at eleven – two hours checking in – we'd better leave within the hour.'

Avery's first thought was the film cassette; he had to get it to Villiers and tell him about Downing Street. His second thought was Josh. 'I can't do it, Gerry. I've got the baby to think about.'

'You'll have to cope – come up with something.'

He did – Floyd. That was his only chance. He reached for the telephone and called his manager's number.

Rowena answered, her own children bawling in the background.

'Just the lady,' Avery said. 'Rowena, sweetheart, I have a big, big favour to ask. Something important's just cropped up. A great business opportunity. But it means I have to catch this morning's flight to Paris. Is there any chance you could take Josh for me?'

Her resistance was token. 'Well, yes, Max, I guess I can manage. He's a sweet kid.'

'I have to leave by eight – could Floyd come round and collect him before then?'

'I'm sure he can.'

Avery felt immediate relief. He always travelled light

and it didn't take him long to pack a flight bag. He had just fed and changed the baby when Floyd arrived. His manager did not look happy. With no more than a cursory 'Good morning', he dutifully carried the bag of clothes and toys out through the driving rain to the car. Avery followed with the baby in his carrycot. As Floyd scrambled into the shelter of the driver's seat, his boss opened the rear door to put the baby inside.

Rain was running down Avery's face. 'Floyd, listen to me, I'm in trouble . . . '

Floyd's reaction was instantaneous: 'You can say that again, man, I've had the bank manager on . . . '

'Shut up and listen!' Avery snapped. 'I mean real trouble, and I need your help.'

'Is this to do with Fox?'

Avery nodded impatiently. 'You'll find a miniature film cassette in one of Josh's bootees. I want you to give it to Villiers with a message . . . '

'Villiers? That new Scots mechanic? Is he in on this?'

'Call him into the office. Speak to him alone.'

Floyd shook his head. 'No, Max, don't get me involved in any of this. Don't ask, a refusal might offend.'

'It's not what you think. Villiers is undercover.'

'You mean police?'

'Something like that.'

Realisation dawned suddenly on the manager's face. '*That* explains why you hired him. What is this, Max? Drugs?'

'No, Fox is with the IRA.'

Floyd's mouth dropped. 'Oh, Sweet Jesus . . . ' he breathed. 'You're winding me up . . . '

'Just trust me. I don't have time to explain. Tell Villiers that the target is Downing Street. January the 31st. A mortar attack.'

The manager's eyes widened until they were in danger of dropping out of their sockets.

Avery pummelled his fist on the roof. 'Now get the hell outa here!'

Willard Franks and Dr Melville Mace had just passed through security at Heathrow on their way to catch the Washington flight when they received the call.

Officials hustled them through the red tape and organised the police car to return them to MI5 headquarters in Gower Street. They arrived at the same time as Ralph Lavender who had hurried across London from the Secret Intelligence Service offices in Westminster Bridge Road on the south side of the Thames.

There was a welcome smell of coffee in the air as they entered the Director General's panelled office. He interrupted his conversation with Clarissa Royston-Jones to greet them. 'Sorry to interrupt your journey, gentlemen, but suddenly things have started to move. I've ordered in some sandwiches, but while we're waiting I'll let Clarry bring us up to date.'

She had a rapt audience as she reviewed the latest developments. She concluded: 'So it looks as though at last we know where your men Lew Corrigan and Con Moylan are – or at least where they will be tomorrow. Jordan. When you were at Heathrow this morning so were Avery and Gerry Fox. They're flying out to join them. We picked this up from a sound-tap in Avery's flat.'

'What do you read into this?' Lavender asked.

'I think this is the last big planning meeting with the Iraqis. That's why all of them are wanted there. It'll also be our last chance to pull the net. Through Max we've already got the full run-down on the major London attack — as it happens a mortar bombing of Downing Street itself. At least we can stop that dead in its tracks.

'So in order to find out what else might be planned, I recommend we dispatch our guardian angel team to Jordan and get everyone in one fell swoop. In fact I've already taken the liberty of placing two of our surveillance people on Max's flight. The rest of the team are on standby to fly direct to Amman.'

Lavender glowered. 'I think you're being a bit previous there, Clarry.'

'Do you really?' she sneered. 'Well I would remind you that you handed this unwanted baby back to me. It's my opinion this operation should have been strangled at birth and this is the ideal moment to close it down.'

The SIS man fumed. 'The Jordanians aren't going to take kindly to a bunch of our heavies turning up — it's a delicate political situation there. What exactly do you intend them to do?'

Clarissa lit a cigarette before answering. 'To interrupt the meeting with minimal necessary force and release Max, his wife and Corrigan for a full debriefing.'

'And Con Moylan?'

She watched her smoke gyrate towards the ceiling. 'Well, if we catch him with the others, we can't expect co-operation from the Jordanians at this time. So we either take him to a safe house for interrogation *in situ* or . . . '

'Or?' Lavender pressed.

'He might have to be negotiated.'

'Pardon me? Negotiated?' Franks was not familiar with that particular British expression.

Lavender helped out. 'Meet with an accident.'

'Jesus Christ.' The CIA man blew out his cheeks in disapproval. 'I've gotta agree with Ralph – that's a high-risk option at this moment. Word is the opening phase of the war is just days away – hardly the time to rock the boat. I'd want to be mighty sure Con Moylan is hatching something real serious before I ask the National Security Council to agree to that.'

Clarissa said: 'There's a rumour that Moylan has sent two of his men to the States, but it can't be confirmed. Only Corrigan – or Moylan – can answer that one.'

'Rumours. Don't we have *any* other indications?' Franks asked in frustration.

It was the Director General's turn to intercede. 'Avery's managed to get us film copies of Fox's notebook. It's being analysed at present, but it appears to be a shopping list. Maybe there's something there that affects you. Believe it or not, it appears to include a Thames tugboat and an aerosol generator, whatever that is.'

Melville Mace spoke reluctantly for the first time. 'Using

a tugboat with an aerosol generator to attack London would be in line with our simulation findings.'

'So we could have *much* more than a mortar attack on Downing Street to contend with?' the Director General mused.

'We've got to anticipate the worst – including rumours about a cell sent to the States – unless we can get to Corrigan,' Clarissa pressed.

The Director General reached a decision. 'I must agree with Clarry. She has my support.'

Willard Franks nodded in grim and reluctant confirmation. 'I'd best cancel my return trip to Washington.'

Clarissa reached for the telephone. 'Then I'll press the button.'


Lew Corrigan touched down at the Queen Alia International airport with an immense feeling of relief that he was away from Moylan and that his part in the mission would soon be over.

He could sense that he'd flown to the edge of a war zone the moment he set foot in the terminal building. It was overflowing with refugees who had escaped overland from Iraq, now reduced to camping out in desperation to get any available flight out of the city.

Mothers attempted to hush crying children and men talked furtively in small groups. And amongst the uniformed Jordanian police trying to maintain some semblance of order, businessmen in sharp suits were everywhere, the predictable opportunist vultures who gathered whenever there was a buck to be made from the misfortunes of others. But in addition to the influx of wheeler-dealers, diplomatic reinforcements and media news teams, he knew there would be a generous sprinkling of agents from both allied and rival Arab intelligence organisations. No doubt the CIA, the British SIS and Mossad would all be busy trying to identify Iraqi spies or Palestinian activists passing through the choke-point with the outside world.

It would be more prudent, he reasoned, to meet Avery before risking contact with the American Embassy. At least the Englishman, returning from London, would undoubtedly be under close scrutiny from the combined SAS and Delta team.

He took a forty-minute taxi ride to Amman and the Date Palm Hotel. The fly-blown one-star hostelry was situated in the back streets behind the Abdali bus station. He checked in, showered, then lay on the creaking bed until the call came at six o'clock.

A taxi was waiting to take him to the rendezvous. The driver doubled back and checked several times for anyone following before he finally stopped in one of the poorer quarters of the city. As Corrigan stepped out onto the crumbling sunlit pavement a man emerged from the doorway of a dusty laundry shopfront. He was short and stocky with a heavy moustache and ferret-like eyes which glanced nervously up and down the street before he beckoned.

'Psst! This way, please.'

Corrigan followed him into the shop and past a wooden counter to the indifference of the Palestinian laundryman who was serving a woman in the traditional black chador. Through another opening, along the workshop of humming washing machines and the pervasive smell of starch and detergent, and up a flight of wooden steps to a room.

After the intense brightness of the street it was like a coal cellar, stuffy and just hairlines of white discernible through the closed shutters.

His guide sensed Corrigan's unease. 'It is to keep the room cool,' he explained.

'Mr Corrigan.' Another voice. It came from the far dark corner. 'We meet again.'

He squinted into the gloom. 'Again?' The voice did sound vaguely familiar.

'Take a seat.'

'I would if I could see.'

The sudden influx of light was blinding as the lamp behind the desk was switched on and shone directly in his face. 'Is that better?'

Corrigan fumbled for the chair, certain now that things were not right, wondering who else was in the room? The man of mystery leaned forward and the light illuminated his face in profile, the perspiration glistening on his skin. Khaled Fadel, Iraq's fussy and apologetic agent from Athens with the Saddam-lookalike moustache.

Corrigan caught a whiff of the cologne and relaxed a little. The man was a pussycat, hardly the killer type. 'Mr Fadel, you had me worried for a moment.'

'I'm so sorry. But surely you have no reason to fear us?'

The American forced an uneasy smile. 'Oh, you know, these troubled times . . . Talking of which, you seem to have no trouble getting about.'

A self-effacing laugh. 'Dear me, no. We Iraqis are not as stupid as the Western press would have people believe. As you might imagine I have several identities and passports – not to mention good friends in Athens. It is not so difficult. Besides, it was imperative that I come here. It was I who began this and President Saddam Hussein is most insistent that I see it through personally.'

Corrigan's eyesight was beginning to adjust; he sensed the presence of others in the room. 'Is Max Avery here?' he asked.

'Alas, not yet. As he comes from London, he must take a more devious route to allay suspicions. He is due to arrive tomorrow.'

The American cursed inwardly. It was important he spoke to Avery; he couldn't allow the Iraqis to keep them apart. He said: 'I could give you a full briefing now, but I think it best I wait until Max arrives. There are some overlapping points we'll need to sort out. You understand such operations are complex.'

Fadel appeared relaxed, resting his elbows on his desk and interlacing his fingers. 'Indeed I understand, Mr Corrigan. But in fact, I will not be requiring a briefing from you or from Mr Avery.'

'Pardon me?'

'I am fully up-to-date with events via Mr Moylan and the man we know as Giorgós from the 17 November.'

'Then . . . ?'

A gentle smile. 'Why are you here? I will tell you. You are here because President Saddam Hussein orders it. He does not like to be made a fool of.'

Corrigan frowned, desperately trying to quell the sudden drumbeat of his heart. 'I don't understand.'

'But I think you do – one-time Sergeant Lew Corrigan of Delta Force, now attached to the CIA, probably as an NOC operator.' A steely glint had come into Fadel's eyes. 'No, please don't insult me by denying it. You see, despite the best efforts of Western counterspies, elements of our international intelligence operation still work quite well. One such is an agent in Washington who runs under a 'false flag', as we call it. Although he is a freelance on the Israeli Mossad payroll, he is actually one of ours. You see Mossad does not have copyright to inventive intelligence; they are frequently blinded by their own brilliance. In times of crisis like this, Capitol Hill is very co-operative with Tel-Aviv. Besides, the questions he asked concerned Libya and Northern Ireland – not connected with the current crisis. He simply said that Mossad suspected that you were a go-between for the IRA and the Libyans and that they sought advice about assassinating you.' Fadel smiled; he clearly thought it all rather clever. 'Imagine the surprise when Langley, Virginia, warned him off most strongly, hinting broadly at the role you were playing on their behalf . . . '

Corrigan's head felt as though it were about to explode – no longer capable of taking in the words. His only thought now was how to get out of the room alive.

'Mr Moylan might be sitting where you are now,' Fadel was saying, 'but he discovered that your friend Max Avery was similarly working for British Intelligence. He had the good sense to come clean and tell us. We then decided to investigate your credentials as a matter of priority. Now, with you and Avery removed, Mr Moylan believes that the operations can still go ahead without prejudice.' He was starting to sound absurdly like a lawyer, and paused for dramatic effect to light a cheroot. 'What I want to know, Mr Corrigan, is what is the full purpose and extent of your mission?'

Corrigan grunted. 'You're mistaken.' What else could he say?

'Please.' The voice was unnervingly soft.

'I have nothing else to say.' Final.

Fadel sniffed airily and studied the tip of his cheroot. 'That is what I thought. So we will see if you think the same way once you are in Baghdad. There they have ways of setting tongues wagging.' He nodded to someone behind Corrigan.

The American had been ready for it, coiling his muscles like restrained springs. As he heard the sudden movement behind him, he thrust the chair backwards with all the power he could muster. He felt the resistance and heard the crack of wood against someone's shin.

At the same time he pitched himself towards Fadel's desk, hands outstretched to heave it up and over on top of the man. But he never made it. More hands grabbed at his biceps and he felt a stunning pain explode in the back of his neck. The expert blow winded him, toppling him like an oak, so that he found himself on all fours. Someone was pressing down on his back, a forearm around his throat like a steel band. His vision began to mist, bright lights bursting like a firework display before his eyes.

He hardly felt the Teflon-coated hypodermic as it was stabbed into his backside to deliver the knockout dose of diazepam. To the relief of the half-dozen Arab heavies, the big man's resistance began to flag almost immediately, enabling them to secure his arms and legs with plasticuffs. When he lost consciousness, his body was rolled inside a Persian rug and manhandled into the boot of the waiting Mercedes taxi.

It would be a long journey over the Jordanian border and across the three hundred miles of desert to Baghdad.

# Nineteen

As the Egyptair passenger jet touched down at Amman, Max Avery felt a sense of relief similar to that experienced by Lew Corrigan twenty-four hours earlier. But the reasons were quite different.

When he and Gerry Fox had departed from Heathrow the previous day, he had been astounded to find that the aisle seat opposite his was occupied by none other than Brian Hunt.

The SAS sergeant major was dressed in a business suit and made no attempt to communicate with him until they were halfway through the flight to Paris; then Avery found Hunt behind him in the short queue for the toilets.

'We're going to finish it in Jordan,' his friend said conversationally, smiling as he spoke for the benefit of Fox. 'Do you know where the meeting place is?'

'No. We're to be contacted on arrival.'

'The lads are taking a direct flight, so they'll be there before you tomorrow. Priority will be to get you, Maggie and Lew out, then negotiate Moylan and Fox if they resist – plus any Iraqi spooks, of course. Just be sure you three keep your heads down when the shit hits the fan.'

'Roger,' Avery acknowledged. 'Any independent news from Lew?'

'Zilch.' Hunt shrugged. 'Sorry, mate. Tell me, you got duty-frees in that Heathrow bag?'

The queue was shortening, with just one woman waiting for a door to open.

'Yes, why?'

'What's inside?'

'A bottle of Johnnie Walker and two hundred Stuyvesant.'

A man emerged from one of the doors and the woman disappeared.

'Be prepared for a switch in Amman.'

The second door opened; another passenger came out. It was Avery's turn. 'Good luck.'

Hunt left the plane at Paris. While Avery flew on with Fox to Malta, then changed for a stopover in Cairo, the SAS sergeant major took a taxi to the splendid British Embassy building in the rue du Faubourg St Honoré. There the SIS station chief signalled London for certain coded items to be sent via diplomatic pouch to Jordan on the next available flight, together with a Heathrow duty-free bag, Johnnie Walker whisky and Peter Stuyvesant cigarettes. Hunt then made his own way direct to Amman, arriving late that evening. He was picked up by the British military attaché and driven to a safe house owned by one of the expatriate community in Jordan. There he was reunited with the entire Delta/SAS team who had flown in from London earlier that day, their specialist weapons and communications equipment delivered by diplomatic pouch through the British and American Embassies.

When Avery arrived the next day, he pushed his way ahead of Gerry Fox in order to clear immigration first. It gained him a few vital minutes during which the Delta man called Buzz deliberately collided with him in the melée of passengers, pointedly dropping a Heathrow bag at his feet. Avery took the cue, dropping his own bag beside the other.

The exchange took only a split second and was completed before Fox cleared the barrier.

'Just taking a leak,' Avery explained casually, walking off in search of the lavatories. Once inside, he located a vacant cubicle and sat down to open the duty-free bag. In addition to the whisky and cigarettes were two packages. One contained a very small Beretta 84 and magazine holding thirteen short 9 mm rounds, just about the optimum combination for concealment and hitting power. In the other was a black plastic box no bigger than a cigarette packet with a short rigid aerial and two powerful magnets attached, plus a fountain-pen transmitter similar to that which had been passed to Corrigan back in Athens.

The type-written note read: *Use hardware at your discretion. Use pen-bug to converse with us. If possible fit homing device to any vehicle taking you to RV. Brian.*

Avery considered the risk of carrying the gun. He reasoned that no one was likely to suspect a weapon on someone who had just come off an aircraft; besides which, carrying it hardly proved his intent to use it against his supposed Iraqi allies. The hardest part would be explaining how he'd smuggled it into the country. In bits, he decided, and a lot of luck with lax security! On the other hand having the advantage of the Beretta might make all the difference in getting Maggie out alive.

Using the elasticated holster-grip provided, he strapped the weapon to his ankle, and pocketed both the homing device and the pen-transmitter. Outside he found Fox waiting impatiently.

'You got the trots, Max?'

'Something like that.'

'Well, let's get on. I feel as conspicuous as a spare prick.'

'Where to?'

'Date Palm Hotel.'

Like Corrigan the day before they discovered that the only remotely exotic thing about the sleazy hotel was its name. Yet Avery felt cheered when he noticed the American's signature on the hotel register.

In response to his question the receptionist just said: 'No, he is not here. He goes out yesterday and does not come back.'

Two hours later a telephone call from reception advised them that their taxi had arrived. When they approached the vehicle, Avery allowed Fox to board first, then deliberately dropped his cigarette lighter into the gutter. Cursing, he stooped to retrieve it. While momentarily out of sight, he palmed the small homing device and held it beneath the chassis until the magnets gripped. He then climbed in beside Fox and slammed the door.

A hundred metres away in a battered Nissan Sunny, the local CIA driver tuned the Doppler shift of the receiver unit which picked up the signal pulses emitted from the homer.

'Let's hope the mother don't drop off,' he muttered laconically to Hunt and Buckley who sat in the back.

As he slipped into gear and drove after the taxi, the separate voice transmission came over the radio when Avery asked about their destination. Not surprisingly the driver declined to understand.

Four local CIA cars took it in turns to follow within visual distance as the taxi backtracked on itself numerous times. It nearly lost them by executing a sudden U-turn in a crowded street. The immediate pursuit car was too close to follow suit without giving the game away. But the driver of Hunt and Buckley's Nissan, now travelling backup, was alerted to the evasive manoeuvre by a sudden negative reading on the Doppler unit. Just in time they were able to negotiate a frantic three-point turn and be waiting, facing the right way, before the taxi came into view. After it had passed, the CIA driver took up the discreet chase again.

'C'mon, you mother,' the man groaned after a further ten minutes of obvious time-wasting.

No sooner had the words left his mouth than the tracking unit, which had been switched to 'null', began a bleep-tone indicating that the taxi had made a left-hand turn.

He accelerated rapidly to bring them into viewing range, glimpsed the narrow side street, and steered blindly into the dust thrown up by the taxi's wheels.

'*What's this, a laundry?*' Avery's voice suddenly filled the vehicle, crackling with static, for the benefit of the eavesdroppers.

'Something's happening,' the driver warned.

In the back Jim Buckley jabbed a finger. 'There's the taxi, look! And the laundry.'

'Keep going!' Hunt hissed.

The driver grinned in his rearview mirror. 'Keep yer socks on, man, I know my business.'

The Nissan tucked into a row of parked cars fifty metres along the street; farther back, Avery and Fox were stepping out onto the pavement.

'Best wait,' the driver decided. 'They might just be switching cars. I'll get another of ours around the back in the next street.' He spoke rapidly into his throat mike, giving their location to the other three cars in order to surround the laundry on all sides.

'*Are we going upstairs?*' Again Avery deliberately asked the question for the benefit of the eavesdroppers. Then: '*Is Lew Corrigan here?*'

A stranger's voice answered. '*I know no names, Englishman.*'

Avery persisted. '*He's American, a big guy.*'

Then Fox broke in, sounding irritable. '*For Christ's sake, Max, we'll find out in a second.*'

'*And a woman with long black hair?*' Avery continued.

'*Please – do not ask,*' came the politely evasive reply.

Buckley exploded with frustration. 'Dammit, he *must* know if there's a woman there! I don't like the sound of this.' He leaned over the seat to the driver. 'Call into HQ and get the full backup team down pronto.'

'Whatever you say, chief.'

While the CIA man radioed to bring in the unmarked van with the eight-man support unit and specialist equipment, Buckley called on the members of the four surrounding cars to gather in a nearby waste plot.

As the Nissan bounced over the rubble, the first members of the team came running towards him.

Big Joe Monk and Pope arrived first, heavy 9 mm Brownings worn to the rear beneath their jacket flaps and radio earpieces and throat mikes invisible to any onlookers.

Hunt wasted no time. 'Max and Fox have gone up to the first floor of that laundry. Find a way onto the roof next door and see if there's a route across.'

The two men set off at a brisk pace just as Gretchen Adams and Buzz arrived, running. 'You two, into the laundry.' Hunt had already removed his jacket. 'Take this in. Talk about the stains – anything to stall – stay in there for as long as it takes.'

'Hey, Brian!' Buckley called from the back of the Nissan. 'Max is in there now.'

As with Corrigan the previous day, Avery and Fox were shown into a dimly lit room, unaware that the surveillance team was taking up assault positions outside.

This time, however, Fadel switched on the desk light immediately. Fox glanced around at the six shadowy figures standing with arms folded. He'd witnessed enough kangaroo courts in Ulster to recognise the intimidating setup.

'Where the hell is Con?' he demanded, feeling the warm collar of fear tightening around his neck.

Fadel smiled graciously. 'Mr Moylan sends his respects, and regrets that he cannot join us.'

Avery's heart sank. 'And my wife, where is she?'

'With Mr Moylan, I believe.'

'And where is that?' Avery demanded, his anger rising fast.

'I am not at liberty to say.'

Fox, too, was now certain that something was seriously wrong. 'Lew Corrigan is supposed to be here – or is he still with Con, too?'

Fadel toyed with one of his cheroots. 'By now, I expect, Mr Corrigan is in Baghdad.' The smile transformed him, the corners of his mouth curling like a dog's snarl. 'That is where we best deal with spies and traitors.'

Fox's mouth dropped open, feeling the distinct miss of a heartbeat in his chest. 'I don't understand.'

But Avery did, instantly. Con Moylan had somehow found out about both him and Corrigan and was handing them to the Iraqis on a plate.

For the benefit of the eavesdroppers, he said: 'Is that the reason you're waiting for us here with six armed men?'

Outside, his words were picked up by Jim Buckley in the car. Immediately he passed on the information to Hunt who had just sent two Americans, Brad Carver and Luther Dicks, and the SAS team of Villiers and Ran Reid scurrying towards the rear entrance of the laundry workshop.

'Six armed hostiles,' Hunt repeated. 'And it sounds like

Max has been tumbled. If we wait for the backup to arrive we could be listening in on his execution.'

'Christ,' Buckley breathed, 'don't you just love it when this sort of thing happens?'

'We'll have to go in,' Hunt decided.

Buckley nodded, listening intently as each group in turn radioed in to confirm that they were in position.

The last to report were Monk and Pope: '*Listen, Brian, we've got down onto an outbuilding roof. It's just below a first-floor window. Shutters are closed, but I can hear the mumble of voices. Speaking English. I think this must be the room. Over.*'

'Roger, Joe. We'll follow your lead. Inform when ready. Sunray to all units – standby, standby.' He repeated the command, then turned to Buckley: 'What news on the backup?'

The Delta commander shook his head. 'Ten minutes and stuck in traffic.'

Hunt grimaced. The van with the second half of the team had all the specialist assault equipment, including respirators, flak jackets, gas grenades, and abseil gear – in fact everything to ensure the safety and success of the assault. But it was still ten minutes away. Ten minutes versus a man's life. An old friend. It was one hell of a decision.

Monk's voice came over the net. '*Joe to Sunray, Joe to Sunray. Confirm ready, confirm ready.*'

Hunt exchanged an anxious glance with Buckley as he listened intently to the transmission from Avery's pen-mike. The American nodded glumly.

The SAS sergeant major said: 'Calling all units. GO, GO, GO!'

On the flat roof of the outbuilding, Monk and Pope heard the order intoning in their earpieces. Both men had donned balaclavas to preserve their anonymity and now rose in menacing unison, swinging open the shutters. As the butt of Pope's Browning pistol shattered the fly-blown pane, Monk pitched in the stun grenade.

Despite the wax plugs they wore, the succession of earsplitting detonations were mind-blowing as the dark room lit up with the searing dazzle of three million candelas. Pope swung his Browning automatic through the stalactites of glass that still clung to the frame.

'MAX, DOWN!'

Immediately inside the window was a desk, Fadel cowering beneath it. The chair on which Max Avery had been sitting now lay on its back, after he had rolled himself clear when the grenade went off. Still groggy, he was staggering to his feet, half-leaning against the far wall.

In the middle of the floor stood Fox, his eyes wide with shock and his hands clasped to his ears to protect himself from the excruciating pain.

But it was one of the six Arab henchmen that Pope took out first. An almost instinctive shot, no time available for lining sights. Two rounds so close together that they registered as one continuous note, tearing through the offered body to kick chunks of plaster from the wall behind. A short swing of the Browning to the right. Second target, some firearm lifting into view. Again the pistol recoiled in Pope's double-handed grip, spitting flame.

Now Monk's weapon was drawn, taking out the third man, the force spinning him round in grotesque mimicry of a ballerina before depositing him face down on the floor.

Fox overcame his paralysis and dived for the door. Monk's aim followed, squeezing the trigger as the pip sight covered the man's back. But fear had given the man extra speed and the rounds scorched through the material of his jacket to kick splinters uselessly from the door surround. Monk cursed, hearing the sudden commotion beyond the door and the solid sound of heavy-calibre handguns. The noise was followed by a squeal from Fox and he toppled back into the room, clutching at his chest. He hit the floor with a thud, just as Gretchen and Buzz burst into the room, their firearms blazing, carving into the three henchmen who still stood. Their bodies were thrown in different directions by the hail of bullets, their own weapons falling away before they could be fired.

Monk swung through the window, landing amid the choking swathes of cordite. While the two Americans stood warily at the door checking for signs of movement, he moved across to Avery.

'You okay, mate?'

Avery nodded numbly, then forced an uneasy grin. He held up the small Beretta in his hand. 'You bastards didn't give me the chance to use it.'

Monk's tombstone teeth grinned through the hole in the balaclava. 'Use it for what? Shootin' rabbits?'

Avery's eyes widened. Behind Monk he glimpsed Fadel's arm outstretching from beneath the table, his hand scrabbling like a white spider for the dropped Iraqi gun.

'Behind you!' Even as the words escaped his lips, he pushed Monk aside and aimed the Beretta. But Gretchen had the target first, blasting out three rounds from her heavy .45 Colt auto, so powerful that they shifted Fadel's body a couple of feet across the floor.

'STOP!' Avery yelled.

'For Christ's sake, Max,' Monk said, following him across the room. 'She had to be sure he was dead.'

Avery's hand came away, dripping blood. 'She made sure all right.'

Gretchen approached, a bemused expression on her face. 'What's the problem?'

'He's the only one who knows where Maggie and Con Moylan are. And what the bastard's got planned.'

'The only one?' she echoed.

Avery rose wearily to his feet. 'Unless you count Lew Corrigan.'

'And where's he?' Monk asked in genuine innocence.

'In Baghdad.'

Corrigan awoke with a thunderous headache, immediately aware of the jolting of the vehicle.

Light flooded into his vision, momentarily blinding him. He blinked and squeezed his eyes, slowly focusing on the man whose face was just a few inches from his own.

Where was he? He could remember nothing. Arriving

in Jordan. A taxi ride. The laundry. The darkened room. Oh, Jesus Christ, it wasn't just a bad dream.

'Hallo, hallo, Americano, wake up. Welcome to Baghdad.'

The young soldier wore green fatigues and leaned forward, smiling to reveal slightly crooked teeth. He looked due for his weekly shave, the lengthy stubble making it difficult to distinguish his adolescent moustache.

Corrigan found a water canteen thrust into his face. 'You thirsty, Americano? You drink, yes?'

His hands were bound and he was obliged to swallow from the offered spout. He took in his surroundings as he drank: there were two other soldiers in the battered van, both armed, watching him with idle curiosity. Grubby curtains covered the side windows, but the material was thin and he could see it was daylight outside.

The soldier restoppered his canteen. 'You come to Baghdad before?'

Corrigan regarded him closely; it appeared to be a serious question. 'No. I haven't been to Baghdad before.'

One of the curtains was brushed briefly aside. He glimpsed the tarmac carriageway and the grass and trees of some parkland, all flatly lit by diluted morning sunlight.

'Qadisiya Expressway,' the soldier explained proudly.

'Very good, very fast. Like in America.' The curtain fell back into place. 'You come from New York?'

Corrigan's first instinct was to say nothing, to follow the rules. But this man was clearly naive, probably from a country village or a city tenement. It seemed churlish to ignore him. 'Sure, New York.'

The man grinned again. 'New York, yes. The Big Apple. One day I want to go New York. See the Statue of Liberty, the White House, Disneyland.'

'Sure you do.'

'But not now, I think. I am not welcome. No Iraqi is welcome by Mr Bush.' He grinned widely. 'But you are welcome here. My name is Nizar.'

Despite his situation, Corrigan felt himself almost liking the man. 'Lew. Sorry, can't shake your hand.'

Nizar shrugged. 'Soon you go home. No war. I trust Mr Perez de Cuellar of United Nations. He will find peace. I do not think Mr Bush will bomb me. We will be friends. I come and visit you in New York.'

Corrigan grunted. 'It would be a pleasure.'

They had taken a couple of turns and now the vehicle slowed. Nizar fingered aside the curtain again and Corrigan could just see that they were passing through gates in a high wire fence. A moment later the rear doors of the van were thrown open. Waiting outside was an army captain and an immaculately dressed civilian in a sharply cut blue suit, the effect completed by gold cufflinks, calfskin loafers and a silk Hermès tie. His hair was silvered and swept back from his forehead and he had a small toothbrush moustache. Behind the pebble-lenses of his tortoiseshell spectacles his eyes were grotesquely magnified.

'Ah, you have arrived at last, Mr Corrigan.' His English was as oily smooth as his dress sense. 'It is a long journey from Jordan, not too uncomfortable I trust?'

Corrigan scowled; he could smell trouble. 'Better than a Greyhound coach,' he murmured.

'You are a very honoured guest, Mr Corrigan. I look forward to making your acquaintance personally.' He nodded towards Nizar. 'Now I regret you must be blindfolded.'

Despite the cloth around his eyes, Corrigan was able to discern the rough ground underfoot, suggesting a patch of derelict land. Then the odour of damp concrete and mildew as they entered a building. Across a large room, through a security door, and down steps. A lot of steps. Down and down again until he became aware of the distinct drop in temperature.

When the blindfold was removed, he found himself in a room with plain limewashed walls and utilitarian office furniture. It was uncannily quiet apart from the hum of air conditioning.

The man in the Hermès tie now sat at his desk on which there were no papers; behind him hung a portrait of President Saddam Hussein.

'We have a lot of talking to do, Mr Corrigan.'

He did not respond.

'My name is Dr Hassan. That is what you will call me. And your name, your *real* name?'

'You already know it. Lew Corrigan. You've got what you see.'

'And you work for the CIA.'

He had already decided to keep to his cover story, because it was so near to the truth. 'I work for Con Moylan, the Irishman.'

'He thinks you are an American spy.'

'Then he's a fool. You should have *him* here too.'

The eyes blinked behind the pebble-lenses. 'He might very well have been here too, Mr Corrigan. Only he came to us as soon as he discovered the truth about your friend. In other circumstances we might have killed him for his stupidity. Believe me, our beloved President considered it long and hard. Fortunately for Mr Moylan our agent in Athens believed he spoke the truth, and Fadel has the ear of the President.' He relaxed back in his chair. 'Besides which, the work on which you people are engaged is pivotal to the entire war that could be about to break upon us.'

'I know that,' Corrigan replied testily. 'I've been working on the weapons Moylan intends to use. Ask yourself, does that sound like the action of a spy, for Christ's sake?'

Dr Hassan toyed with the gold pen on his desk. 'I imagine the intention of both you and Mr Avery from England was to have the CIA intervene before the operation was complete.'

'I don't know anything about Avery – I never did trust the bastard.' He was fighting for his life now.

'But we *know* that you were a member of the American Delta Force and we *know* you are what the CIA coyly calls one of its desirable assets.'

Corrigan saw the opening and went for broke. 'But had it occurred to you that I might put my loyalty to Ireland before that of the United States?'

'What exactly do you mean?'

'That I was kinda freelancing for the CIA, sure – I'd

been pensioned off and needed the cash. Those mothers don't give shit for years of service. When I got back to Ireland I found I liked it there. Liked the people and realised I could help their cause. Could help people like Con Moylan win their war. It's what I know best.' He paused and, as calmly as he could, took the last crumpled cigar from his shirt pocket. As Dr Hassan leaned forward to offer a light, it was all Corrigan could do to stop his hand from trembling. 'You see, I could hardly tell Moylan I was with the Agency or that I was ex-Delta, could I?'

'You are suggesting that my people and Mr Moylan are mistaken?'

'You couldn't be more so. Just ask yourself who the hell in the CIA would approve of the way I've assisted you and the IRA?' He watched the Iraqi's face closely, sure that he had succeeded in sowing the first seeds of doubt. 'And I'm willing to continue assisting your people now, despite what's happened. You're about to face one helluva catastrophe and I'll help in any way I can. But the best thing you can do is tell Con Moylan he was wrong and get me back on his team. You *need* me.'

Dr Hassan nodded sagely. 'We certainly need you, Mr Corrigan. But here in Baghdad – secure where you can do no more damage. Instead you will be held as a hostage to the truth. When the time comes you can tell the world how you acted with the CIA to discredit Iraq by using bacteriological warfare in the name of Saddam Hussein.' His smile was slow and mean. 'Because I do not believe a word

you have told me. From now on you will tell the truth —
that I promise you.'

Maggie sat beneath the orange tree to shelter from the
rain. It had been falling with growing persistence all
morning from the leaden sky. Now her jeans and jacket
were sodden, her long black hair plastered to her scalp, the
wet ends dripping into the plastic sandwich box on her lap.
Her tears mixed unnoticed with the raindrops running
down her face.

Since Corrigan's abrupt departure for Jordan she had felt
desperately, achingly alone. His mere presence had somehow
created a protective barrier between herself and Con
Moylan. Now she was exposed and vulnerable. Vulnerable
to the way he stared at her, a mocking half-smile on his
face, just waiting for the moment when she would break.

Each day she was driven with Moylan and Sophie to
the groves; the only difference was that now they were
joined by O'Hare and Sullivan. Neither man spoke much,
but she could read their thoughts. She knew they remembered her as certainly as she remembered them. And in her
mind she unwillingly saw herself looking down on her
white and naked body crucified on the floor of the remote
barn in Ulster. Giving herself not to the cause and not
even to Moylan, but to Moylan's will. Looking down at
herself as though she were the departed spirit of her own
corpse.

And, perhaps, that was exactly what it had been then.
As Moylan told her, he had put her in touch with the darker,

forbidden side of herself, the subliminal need to have all rights and decisions taken from her. To submit to someone else's power. Moylan's power.

'You are like Séverine in Buñuel's *Belle de Jour*,' he had once told her.

And, only three years earlier, she had felt compelled to see the movie at a little arts theatre in London. Catherine Deneuve's performance had left her profoundly unnerved; she left before the end.

Through the sheeting rain she saw the jeep approaching, driven by an East German girl she had met at the Café Neon.

All the other workers were sheltering, too engrossed in their flasks of hot coffee to notice her.

Neither Moylan nor the others were there; as usual only she was left to work. Moylan was doing it deliberately, she realised that. Working at breaking her spirit, moulding her to his will again. Each evening he would smile when he saw her exhausted state, would even laugh when he interrupted her in the shower, saw her weight loss and the bruised flesh that now showed her ribs. But he didn't touch her. Not Con Moylan. He would wait until she came to him.

Sod him! She sprang to her feet and ran, slipping and sliding down the mud slope, almost falling in front of the jeep as it braked.

'Maggie!' the East German called. 'What are you doing?'

'I'm not well, Erika. Are you going back into town?'

'I must deliver these crates. You want a lift?'

The farmer watched them go. He had his instructions from the Irishman and had too much to lose by ignoring them. He reached for the CB radio in his truck.

Half an hour later the jeep was splashing through the puddles of the village square in Platanius. Maggie thanked her friend and sprinted through the rain to the white Telephone Exchange building. There she paused, water dripping on the tiled floor beside the row of cubicles.

Suddenly she realised she had no money. No doubt that was why Moylan never gave her more than enough to cover provisions.

She approached the attendant's desk. 'I want to call London.'

He nodded boredly. 'Use Number Four. You pay me after.'

Her heart leapt. At least she could make the call and worry about the consequences later. There was no point in calling home. No doubt Max was still in Jordan with Lew Corrigan. But she could phone Floyd. Find out how Baby Josh was, see if there was any other news . . .

In her excitement she misdialled twice. Then tried again. It rang, that familiar tone. Almost as though she were reaching over the miles to touch reality again. Still it rang. No one answered.

Come on, come on!

A click. The tone stopped. She heard the muted sound of a baby's cry. Then: 'Hallo?'

'Rowena, it's Maggie.'

'Maggie?' Incredulous.

'Yes, yes. How's Josh?'

'He – he's fine.' Flustered. 'Listen, there are *people* here. They want to know where you are . . . '

Con Moylan's hand closed on the cradle and the line went dead.

'You stupid bitch!'

She drew back, startled, and let the receiver fall.

'Who were you phoning?'

A hard swallow. 'Max's manager, that's all. To find out how the baby is.'

'Stupid bitch,' he repeated, and replaced the receiver. 'Do you want them to find out where we are?'

'I wouldn't have told them, Con, believe me.'

'They could have traced the call.'

She frowned. 'Floyd?' A look of bewilderment on her face. 'I don't understand.'

'Not Floyd,' Moylan hissed. 'The intelligence people.'

'I still don't understand; why should they?'

He glanced around the Exchange. 'Never mind. Come back to the apartment now. Don't argue and don't make a fuss.'

He paid the attendant and led her back to the building on the seashore. Opening the door, he pushed her roughly inside; she stumbled against the bed, sitting awkwardly on the edge.

'Con, for God's sake,' she pleaded, 'don't hit me.'

He slammed the door behind him and looked down at her. 'That's what you'd like, isn't it?'

'Don't be ridiculous. I'm worried about my child.'

'Well, don't be. He's all right. I know what's going on back there. If you want to know, ask me. I told you all not to phone anyone for *any* reason.'

She stared miserably at the hands in her lap. 'When are you going to let Max and me go?' she murmured.

He drew himself to his full height. 'I've already let Max go. And that American bastard.'

'Lew? What do you mean, let them go? Where?'

'I've sent them to Baghdad.'

'Baghdad?' she echoed stupidly, not sure she had heard correctly. 'You mean they're in Iraq?'

'Delivered into the hands of their enemy. When they went to Jordan, they walked into a trap – into the hands of Iraqi intelligence.'

'But you're working for them.'

'I am, sweet mouse, but Max and Lew weren't.'

'What are you talking about?'

He lunged at her then, grabbing a fistful of her wet hair, twisting it into a tight clump behind her head until she yelped. 'You, you stupid fucken bitch, have been living with a bloody Brit spy for the past six years. Sleeping with the enemy. Screwing a bloody informer.'

'Don't be ridiculous,' she gasped, squirming with pain.

'Your lover boy was a plant. God knows how the Brits pulled it off, but they had you targeted. Wanted to get to others through you. So they dangled the bait and you swallowed it. Hook, line and sodding sinker.'

She finally wriggled free and stared up at him in

defiance, her eyes welling with tears of pain. 'I don't believe you.'

'Since when do I care what you believe? If you want to believe that bastard loved you, then that's your funeral. I'm just telling you the truth.'

Suddenly his words cut through the fog of confusion in her head. It was as though an electrode had touched a point in her brain, sparking like a short circuit. Realisation coming through that Con Moylan was telling her the truth.

He watched her in silence as her mouth went slack and her eyes widened to stare blankly in shocked disbelief. Then slowly, very slowly, she crawled back across the bed and curled against the pillow for comfort. On the bare wall she saw the past six years parading by like a motion picture on a screen.

It had all been a lie. Right from the very start. From the moment of their very first meeting. And she had made it so easy for him. Him?

Moisture hung like dewdrops on her lashes as she looked up at Moylan. He stood there, huge shoulders slightly hunched and his dark hair as wild as it had been in the old days, watching her dispassionately. Her voice was very small: 'Who is he, Con?'

'I can't tell you that. I don't know if Max Avery is his real name or not. I just know that he never was Patrick O'Reilly – that was the identity they used. A dead child.'

Child. The use of the word hit a chord. Josh. Their baby. Another lie. He had said he didn't want children and now she knew why. She had enjoyed referring to Josh as their love-child. Hell, what a joke! How shocked he must have been when she fell pregnant. Or was that all part of his cover too?

Moylan said: 'We might find out more from the Iraqis. They have their methods.'

She looked up at him. To her own surprise not a word of protest escaped her lips. Yet she could imagine what they would do to the man who had lied to her all these years. Used her and her body. Just as Con Moylan had done, and her own father before him. Just like everyone had always done. She no longer cared what happened to Max. Or to herself.

All she could feel was the utter emptiness of betrayal. Loneliness and fear. She buried her face in the pillow, unable to stop the sobs that wracked her body, overwhelmed by the despair of it all.

For a long time he just stood, watching her in silence. Watching the smooth arch of her back, the abandoned thrust of her legs. Waiting for all the love and warmth to flood out of her. Waiting until she was drained, devoid of all emotion. Waiting for his moment.

She had almost forgotten he was there when she felt his hand on her hair. Rough, but not vicious like before, curling strands tightly around his fingers.

His hand moved down over the nape of her neck, and his forefinger traced a line along the curve of her spine until his palm came to rest in the small of her back. She felt the heat, radiating out like the power of a faith healer.

'You should never have left me, little mouse.'

# Twenty

Lights burned all night long in the offices of the Metropolitan Police Anti-Terrorist Branch in New Scotland Yard as officers prepared for an elaborate series of dawn raids to thwart a planned attack on 10 Downing Street.

During the afternoon Max Avery had flown out of Amman on a direct British Airways flight to London. A Security Service car drove him straight to MI5 headquarters in Gower Street for an initial debriefing with his controller John Nash and Clarissa Royston-Jones. Willard Franks and Melville Mace were invited to sit in on the meeting.

For the first time Avery was able to confirm the minutiae of detail he had accumulated.

Clarissa could not hide her sense of relief. 'I cannot tell you how grateful I am for what you've done, Max.'

'I'll second that,' Franks intoned.

'Everybody appreciates your efforts,' Clarissa confirmed. 'Not least John Major. He's been most concerned about your personal safety. Didn't know the details, of course, but enough to appreciate the risks you've been running.'

Avery lit a cigarette, but even now he couldn't properly relax. For him it was far from over. At last he was in from the cold. But alone. It wasn't meant to have been like this. He said: 'Maggie's still out there, Clarry. What are you going to do about it?'

Her eyes met briefly with Nash's troubled gaze. 'We're doing all we can, Max. Every country in the alliance has got descriptions of both Maggie and Con Moylan.'

'Lew must know where they are,' Avery said.

'But, Max — he's been taken to Baghdad.'

He stubbed out his half-smoked cigarette. 'So what are you going to do — just forget about him?'

'He's the Americans' problem now,' Nash interjected.

'The matter will be taken up in Washington,' Franks confirmed. 'But quite honestly I don't see there's any obvious solution.'

'How about trying to locate him and get him out?' Avery suggested testily. 'You must have people in Iraq.' It wasn't just Maggie who was on his mind; he'd come to regard the American as a personal friend.

Franks smiled unconvincingly. 'I hardly think Generals Powell and Schwarzkopf are going to be impressed with that idea. Any harebrained scheme to send in some rescue mission could jeopardise the entire Desert Storm plan.'

Avery was disgusted. 'Is that a measure of exactly how grateful you are to me and Lew? To let him rot in some Iraqi jail, to be subjected to interrogation by their people?'

The CIA man leaned forward earnestly. 'Listen, bud, that's exactly why we used an NOC on this caper. Non-Official

Cover – got it? Lew knows the score. He's on his own.'

'When the war's over, it'll be a different can of worms. No doubt Saddam will be dead or toppled and the new people will release him. That'll be Washington's thinking. It might be otherwise if we were aware of a serious threat to us. But you've nailed this Downing Street attack and there's no evidence of anything else.'

'Con and Giorgós had other things planned,' Avery retorted. 'Besides, Gerry Fox told me Moylan had sent some people to the States.'

'But that's all speculation,' Franks countered. 'To be honest, Max, the latest reading at Langley is that we've got Saddam so boxed in he doesn't have the capability to strike back – with or without the IRA's help. Especially now they realise you and Lew were plants. If I were them I'd abort any plans I had.'

Avery looked towards Melville Mace for some support, but as usual the man remained tight-lipped. Maybe he had a sense of guilt, realising that indirectly he had been responsible for Corrigan's predicament.

When the meeting came to a close, Avery was driven to an MI5 'safe' apartment in Chelsea Cloisters where he immediately called Floyd to check on his son's well-being. It cheered him to hear the youngster's gurgling conversation when Rowena brought him to the telephone and to learn of Maggie's brief, interrupted call. At least he knew she was still alive. After fencing off Rowena's questions, he hung up and dropped back on the bed. Still dressed, he fell immediately into an exhausted sleep.

It was nine in the morning when the telephone woke him.

Clarissa Royston-Jones sounded weary and dejected. 'Hope I haven't disturbed you, Max, but I want you to come in. I'll send a car around in fifteen minutes, okay?'

'What's happened?'

'Not over the phone, Max. Let's just say the police raids this morning were not entirely successful.'

He just had time to wash and shave before the chauffeur called and he was thankful when he arrived to find Clarissa pouring coffee for the gathering around the table: the Director General, Nash and Ralph Lavender from SIS.

To his surprise Willard Franks and Melville Mace were also there again. 'Clarry here is making a habit of calling us back each time we get to Heathrow,' the CIA man explained with a humourless smile.

Clarissa handed Avery a cup. 'I'm afraid when the Anti-Terrorist Branch swooped this morning, the birds had flown. The flat in Bounds Green was being rented by an innocent German couple on holiday, although someone had hidden two handguns under the floorboards.

'And when the police arrived at that lockup garage in Sidcup, they found that the local Fire Brigade had beaten them to it. The place had been torched – no doubt to destroy any evidence.'

Avery nodded wearily. 'I suppose Moylan had a few days to sort things out. He must have known about me before he told Fox to take me to Jordan.'

Clarissa toyed with her cigarette packet, fighting her

overwhelming urge to light up. 'I'm not sure it was anything to do with Con. Something surprising has happened. He's been fired in his absence from the board of the Moylan Construction Group. The chairman, an Irish horse-breeder called Tom O'Grady, cited gross dereliction of duty. They've got a new managing director.'

'Yes?'

'One Daniel Grogan.'

'Christ!'

Nash said: 'We think Con Moylan's gone rogue, Max. And the Army Council has either closed down the Downing Street operation or taken it back under their control.'

Avery recalled the incident of the baker at the border-post bombing. 'What will you do about Danny Grogan?'

Clarissa smiled apologetically. 'Nothing just yet – yours is the only concrete evidence against him.'

Nash said: 'The police also raided all known associates of Gerry Fox. He had a sort of girlfriend, a hooker in Kilburn. She said he'd brought parcels to her flat and repacked them for posting on. She assumed it was porn material – he was into that. But detectives found brown-parcel wrappings in the dustbin with Greek postmarks and a number of polystyrene cartons – the sort of stuff used to send fragile items through the post. These had Arabic mark-ings on them – and, thank God, the officers on the scene called in a lecturer from London University to translate.'

'And?' Franks pressed.

Nash consulted the paper in front of him. 'One carton

translated as Botulinus Toxin Type A – 10 milligrams.'

'Sweet Jesus,' Mace murmured.

'What is that?' Lavender asked.

The American said: 'It's a toxin produced from bacterium found virtually everywhere. When crystallised, the toxin is the most lethal substance known to man. Ten milligrams is enough to infect five thousand people if it got into the food supply. Victims would experience crippling nausea, vomiting, and stomach cramps leading to double vision and muscular paralysis. You could expect half the casualties to die.'

Franks stared at him, then turned to Nash. 'Anything else?'

'A larger package was stamped as Bacillus Anthracis and Clostridium botulinum suspended in propylene glycol,' he said, stumbling over the unfamiliar words. 'Our Porton Down people say this is basically an anthrax cocktail.'

Mace said quickly: 'And in that form it's ready to be dispersed – perhaps using that aerosol generator you mentioned the other day. Distributed efficiently, you could expect it to be ingested by tens or hundreds of thousands of people.'

The heavy silence that followed was broken by Franks. 'So now we have confirmation. Iraq's biological weapons are definitely in the hands of some IRA fringe element, courtesy of the 17 November.'

'So simple,' Mace said. 'They could have been posted on to agents in place anywhere in the world.'

Clarissa said slowly: 'I'm afraid Melville may be more

right than he realises.' She turned to Avery. 'Those photographs you took of Gerry Fox's notebook – entries included
a Post Box Number in Canada and the addresses of the six
men activated by Con Moylan. Irish Special Branch has co-
operated with Ralph's people over the past couple of days,
speaking to wives and girlfriends left behind. We know
that at least one man was going to Vancouver.'

'The back door to the United States,' Franks murmured.

Avery seized his moment. 'And Lew Corrigan is the only
one who might just be able to tell you when and where
that stuff is going to be used.'

The CIA man regarded him frostily. 'I'm going to
concede you that point, Max. And it's probably going to
cost me my career. This is just not what the President wants
to hear at this time. I honestly don't see how we stand a
chance of locating Corrigan – let alone mount some rescue
mission – before the war starts. My understanding is that
it's mere days away.'

Ralph Lavender coughed discreetly. 'Um – Willard, it's
just possible there could be a way.'

Just days before the expiry of the United Nations deadline,
Saddam Hussein had called for an Islamic Conference to
be held in Baghdad.

It was a last-ditch public relations exercise to rally reli-
gious support from his Arab neighbours and to persuade
them that any withdrawal from Kuwait should be linked
to Israel's withdrawal from the Occupied Territories.

It had not escaped Ralph Lavender's Middle East Desk

at SIS that many of the Lebanese, Saudi and Jordanian delegates had British bodyguards, several of whom were former special forces soldiers. Through their various security companies, some were primed to become the allies' eyes and ears in the enemy's capital during the run-up to hostilities.

One such was David Carter who worked for InterCon Asset Protection based in the Docklands development area of London. Tall, dark-haired and in his early thirties, he was minder to a Jordanian envoy who was staying at the government-owned Al-Rashid Hotel.

With the conference concluded, Carter could concentrate on fulfilling the last-minute request that had been passed to him by a British Embassy contact just before he had left Amman.

Most of the delegates and journalists were wisely packing to leave, queuing for the endless stream of taxis charging exorbitant fees for the airport run. Others were booked on what was rumoured to be the last flight out of Baghdad the next day – Tuesday the 15th January, twenty-four hours before the UN deadline.

With so many comings and goings, and with an acrimonious debate in the foyer between American CNN and BBC television news teams attracting a large audience, Carter easily slipped the net of plain-clothes secret policemen.

Deliberately dressed in drab jacket and trousers, and with his shoulders hunched in a practised hangdog posture, his dark hair and moustache allowed him to pass easily as just another depressed citizen of Baghdad. Even if challenged by soldiers in the tanks and armoured cars positioned at strategic points, he would give a good verbal account of himself – courtesy of the British Army Language School at Beaconsfield.

He sauntered through the walled gateway and into Yafa Street, making his way towards the old city. No one appeared to be following as he crossed the Shudada Bridge and headed for the carpet souk on the eastern bank of the Tigris.

Normally the market square would have been thronged with early evening shoppers. But as the enormous blood-red sun sank behind the Ottoman tenements on the far bank, the narrow streets were almost empty.

Carter found the shop he was looking for. The owner, dressed in a traditional striped *dishdasha*, was already taking his display of carpets inside. The liquid brown eyes fixed on the unexpected browser.

'I was about to close. There are no customers today. I think everyone has left for the country.'

Carter introduced himself, gave the recognition code.

The old man was not pleased, his concern showing on the bewhiskered face. But then courtesy was a way of life and he invited the stranger into the dark office confines behind the narrow shop.

'You like English whisky?'

'That would be nice.'

A bottle of Teacher's was produced, but for once only a few pleasantries exchanged.

At last the man said: 'There is nothing more I can do now. It is too late. All is in the hands of Allah.'

'Not quite. In the hands of Allah, yes – and you.'

'It is too dangerous.'

'I seek an American. He was brought from Jordan to Baghdad by road a few days ago. Almost certainly he is being held for interrogation.'

'A spy?'

'A friend. His name is Lew Corrigan. The secret he holds will cost the war if we cannot reach him.'

'You talk in riddles.' He sipped delicately at his whisky. 'And this man's secret will stop bombs falling on Baghdad?'

'If he is not found your beloved President will win.'

'I would rather be bombed.'

'Find the whereabouts of Lew Corrigan,' Carter said earnestly, 'and we will bring Saddam to his knees. And, of course, we will be generous.'

'I will need time.'

'There is no time.'

'My family is large. I must find and speak with those who may know such things. Many are at the front or in Kuwait. It will not be easy. Where do you stay?'

'Al-Rashid.'

'I will do what I can. *Inshallah.*'

That night Carter dined with his urbane Jordanian client – a Harrow-educated Anglophile with royal connections – at the Al-wiyah, a former British club now popular with the Iraqi élite.

'I need to stay on,' Carter confided as they ate their

chicken salad, now the only item on the menu.

The Jordanian perfectly understood his King's pragmatic decision to support – albeit without enthusiasm – their intimidating wayward neighbour. Likewise he perfectly understood that Carter's company had the ear of the British Government and that the man himself was former SAS. He knew that at times like these, certain things had to be done.

He said: 'No problem, David. I have business here I can attend to.'

'It will be dangerous.'

A nonchalant laugh. He considered his bodyguard to be a personal friend. 'But I have you to protect me, dear David.'

'Against a bombing raid?'

'Al-Rashid will be safe?'

'So I am told.'

'Then Allah will protect.'

The United Nations' deadline for Iraq to withdraw from Kuwait came and went without incident.

In Baghdad the next night an uneasy calm settled over the city and the population slept on, unaware that the net was already tightening. Unaware that, high over the distant Indian Ocean, wave after wave of lumbering B52 bombers and tanker escorts from the Diego Garcia airbase were inexorably closing in.

As David Carter sat sharing a brandy with the Jordanian envoy on the fifth floor of the Al-Rashid, he was also unaware that two teams of his former SAS compatriots had been lying up for months less than fifteen miles south of the city. Chosen for their dark features and fluency in Arabic they had been stalking the city that very day. Now they were in position to guide in the holocaust that was about to rain from the skies.

It was ten o'clock in London as Max Avery settled down uneasily in the safe apartment in Chelsea Cloisters to watch the late evening news. He had been on edge all day, hoping to hear from Clarissa Royston-Jones. He was not surprised when the call didn't come, but it did nothing for his nerves.

As he poured a whisky too many, over two thousand miles away at the remote American Special Forces base of Al-Jawf in Saudi Arabia, the desert trembled to the deafening sound of six helicopters winding up their power. As their thrashing rotors reached screaming pitch, the two huge blackened MH-53J Pave Low III helicopters swaggered menacingly into the still night air. With their state-of-the-art astro-navigation equipment they would lead the way into enemy territory. Behind them would come four of the US Army's Apache helicopter gunships, heavily laden with pods of Hellfire ground-attack missiles.

By the time Avery fell asleep that night, those helicopters had taken out the key Iraqi warning radars and communications trucks to open up a safe blind corridor in the air-defence network for the hundred Stealth and B52 bombers converging on the country.

Behind them, totally without warning, came the silent air-breathing Tomahawk missiles launched from beneath the deck of USS *Bunker Hill* in the Arabian Gulf.

Even seventy feet below ground, Lew Corrigan was aware when the nearest one struck. The muted sound of its exploding warhead reverberated down through the layers of steel and reinforced concrete. A man-made earthquake. Momentarily the single bulkhead light in his cell flickered and lumps of plaster fell from the ceiling.

He rolled over into a ball on his mattress, nursing his bandaged left hand from which the fingernails had been torn out by the roots.

Attaboys! Bomb the bastards to buggery, he thought savagely and perversely. At least a direct hit would end it all. He'd know nothing about it if thousands of tons of bunker collapsed on top of him.

As it was he knew that he could be facing days more of Dr Hassan's particularly bloody line of questioning. So far he'd stuck to his story. It was good enough and he saw no need to change it. He was resigned to die anyway, so why give his interrogator the satisfaction of breaking him? Funny how you got used to pain. How it hurt more when they stopped than when they were actually doing it. How the anticipation of them starting again was also worse than the pain itself. Then the resignation that your body would never be the same again – the sound and feel of a shattering bone under the thumbscrew, when you just *knew* that no surgeon would ever be able to repair it. When you experienced the thigh wrenched from its socket as the torque wound up remorselessly on the rack.

At least his questioners didn't appear to have access to sodium amytal or any other mind-bending drugs, or perhaps that was too sophisticated for an evil little sadist like Dr Hassan.

Despite the pain and the relentless glare of the light, he found himself drifting towards sleep, his thoughts in Crete and of the girl called Sophie who he knew had wanted him so much.

Con Moylan picked up the portable short-wave radio set and shook it angrily. 'Bloody World Service – you can never get decent reception.'

'Try Voice of America,' O'Hare suggested helpfully.

They were all gathered in Moylan's apartment and all still stunned by the news that the allied air raids on Baghdad had begun – with apparently dazzling success.

Moylan thrust the set at O'Hare. 'You find it.'

'Does this change anything?' Sullivan asked.

Moylan shook his head. 'Not at all. It just makes it more important, more urgent. When Corrigan was here he reckoned any softening-up attacks might go on for weeks before any ground war – not that I should trust anything that bastard said.'

Maggie watched the proceedings with a profound sense of unreality. She was still in shock, traumatised by the utter destruction of her world. For almost two months she had been held in isolation while events in the outside world passed by like a surreal vision, snatched from glimpses of the café television and broadcasts on the World Service. Her life at the hospital, her home and baby in Streatham – it was all just a cruelly happy dream that had never really happened.

Yet reality itself, this huddled group of conspirators in cold, wet Crete, was no less bizarre. She could almost believe that, if she shut her eyes and opened them again, Moylan and the others would have vanished into the ether, and she would find herself alone.

She tried it. But they were still there, gathered around the radio set in earnest discussion.

She focused on Con Moylan. He was reality. Very much so. She could feel the bruises on her arms, as though his fingers still held her as they had the previous night. He had taken her and she had not resisted. She had lain motionless, her brain dulled, as he had violated her. Mesmerised by some small spot on the ceiling she had experienced the pain and rekindled glimmerings of sexual arousal in an abstract sort of way. It was as though her body had been disconnected from her head.

Max. She had tried to hold the fragile picture of his face in her mind. Then Moylan had buggered her as he always had. Drawing her back in time, into the dark excitement of her forbidden world. Swooning in the warmth and fulfilment of being plugged and stoppered, as if a stake had been driven into the very core of her sexual being. Wallowing in the blessed relief of her total subjugation. And her vision of Max had disintegrated like shattered porcelain.

'Maggie.' Moylan's voice startled her.

'Yes?'

He noted with satisfaction her quiet acquiescence. Like the old days of the Magician when she had been his trusted accomplice and night-time comfort.

'How are you getting on with teaching Sophie? Could she pass off as a nurse yet?'

Maggie nodded, still numb, trying to concentrate. 'I've shown her all I can, but we'll need equipment to practise on, hypodermics, oxygen . . . '

'That can be arranged,' Sophie said. She had spent several evenings getting to know off-duty Greek personnel from the Soúda base, and one of the paramedics was keen on her.

Moylan was satisfied; like the rest of the plan, it was all taking shape. O'Hare and Sullivan had almost finished converting the empty gas cylinders into a six-round mortar launcher. Soon it would be fitted to the truck he'd stolen earlier with Corrigan. A suitable test site had been located, deep in an isolated hillside pass, where the landscape resembled that of the US base.

'When will all this be over, Con?' Maggie asked.

The Irishman watched O'Hare absently as he finally found the wavelength for Voice of America. 'The ship is due in ten days. If our weapons trials go well, we'll be ready before that.'

'And I can go back then?'

'Yes, you can go back then.' There was a ghost of a smile on his lips. 'If you still think you've anything to go back for.'

For six nights the bombing of Baghdad had been relentless.

Government offices had been plucked out like extracted teeth from the surrounding buildings with pinpoint accuracy, causing little collateral damage. It had become a ghost town. Most of the bridges across the Tigris were down, together with communications towers and an oil refinery. A few shops remained open, selling provisions at exorbitant prices but there were few people remaining to join the queues for rationed bread and petrol.

The city had no electricity or water supplies, and there was now a stench of sewage in the streets. Telephone contact with the outside world had been lost.

Having spent another night in Al-Rashid's bomb shelter, David Carter washed in the water of the swimming pool before joining his Jordanian client in the glass-strewn lobby. He found the man in heated debate with an Iraqi official.

'What was all that about?'

'They are insisting that we go.'

Carter was not surprised; they had been living on borrowed time. Al-Rashid now resembled a vandalised and deserted mausoleum. The media circus had all been evacuated over the weekend with the exception of a CNN team and one Spanish reporter. Most of the delegates to the Islamic Conference, trapped when the air raids closed down the airport, had already left by road for Jordan.

'How long have we got?' He still had not heard from the carpet merchant.

'We must leave by eleven o'clock this morning. They suspect saboteurs amongst the conference delegates.' The Jordanian could scarcely keep the smile from his face. 'Apparently radio-direction beacons have been found hidden near strategic sites around the city.'

Before Carter could reply he noticed the small boy dressed in dirty and ragged clothes watching them dolefully a few paces away. 'Mr David, please?'

'Yes.'

'I have message from your friend. Please you meet him at the park across the street.'

'When?'

'Now, please, hallo.' And with that he scampered off under the scowl of one of the Iraqi security men.

Carter followed a few minutes later, crossing the road to the Zawra zoo park where he found the carpet merchant seated on one of the benches. He was idly watching a group of civilian militia servicing a multibarrelled AA gun mounted on the back of a Nissan pick-up.

'Do you have news?' Carter asked, sitting at the far end of the bench.

Without looking at the Englishman, and speaking from the corner of his mouth, he said: 'I have a distant nephew who escorted the American in from the Jordan border just over a week ago. My nephew shares my views about our beloved President. He says that the American was taken to a secret interrogation centre which is built during our war with Iran.' He explained the location.

'Does your nephew know how long he will be kept there?'

'No – but there is talk that the American will be kept for bargaining after this war is finished.' He added gloomily: 'If there is anything left of Baghdad to bargain for.'

'Is the American well? Fit to travel?'

'He has been interrogated, but he is alive. A doctor is looking after him. My nephew takes him cigarettes and candies, but it is difficult because it is not allowed.'

'Tell him the allies will not forget his kindness.'

'Is there a message?'

Carter considered for a moment. 'Tell the American that he is missed by the Sports and Social club in England. He is very much in their thoughts.'

'I will tell my nephew. Now I must go.'

'Thank you.'

The man stood and brushed the creases from his *dishdasha*. 'You will thank me by ensuring that our beloved President does not survive this war. There is no other reason that I help you now – I learn yesterday that my son dies in south Iraq. Saddam Hussein must pay for that.'

'I'm sorry.'

Without a further word the carpet dealer walked off towards the old city.

In jubilant mood Carter returned to Al-Rashid to find that his Jordanian client had already persuaded a taxi driver to make the journey by road to the border for three thousand dollars. Apparently the price was so high because several civilian convoys had already been hit by allied war planes.

The highway was deserted as they drove out of Baghdad, passed the battered remains of army camps and anti-aircraft emplacements on the perimeter of the city, and onto the desert road.

Late that evening they arrived at the breeze-block border

station of Trebeil, where Iraqi guards stamped exit visas into their passports before they crossed into Jordan.

The envoy said: 'I understand that you may require some time off.'

'A couple of hours if you don't mind,' Carter replied.

Just long enough to find the SIS station chief in Amman, get him out of bed, and pass on the news.

That welcome information reached London in the early hours of the following morning and was telephoned to the homes of both Clarissa Royston-Jones and Ralph Lavender. In turn the latter called Willard Franks at the London hotel where he was staying. After a hastily arranged breakfast meeting at Gower Street, the American returned to the US Embassy in Grosvenor Square to prepare a secure signal for Red Browning of the National Security Council in Washington.

Such was the paranoia and anticipation of an imminent Iraqi terrorist attack on the White House or Capitol Hill – both now cordoned off with SWAT sharpshooters manning the rooftops – that the President's decision had already been taken. Within the hour Willard Franks had received the go-ahead to mount a rescue operation.

Clarissa told Max Avery the news over lunch at Le Suquet in Draycott Avenue.

'That's wonderful news, Clarry.'

'We got very lucky, Max. A good man on the inside,' she replied. 'It's also an advantage that we have full details of most of Saddam's bunker complexes because they've been built to British specs. The allies have had mixed success in destroying them – now everyone's terrified that the one Lew is in has been badly damaged.'

'When are they going in?'

'Brian reckoned they'd need at least a week of planning, but he was talking off the cuff before returning to Hereford for a feasibility meeting.'

'Brian – is he involved?'

She nodded. 'Schwarzkopf is adamant that his resources are fully stretched already. More likely he's miffed at the distraction and wants nothing to do with it. He smells potential disaster – not to mention political fallout if it goes wrong.'

'He could well be right.'

'So we're going to use the combined SAS/Delta team who've been assigned to this operation all along,' Clarissa explained. 'They've all got to know each other, they work well together and they all feel a personal commitment to Lew Corrigan – so their motivation couldn't be better.'

Avery toyed with his wine, swilling it thoughtfully round his glass. 'I wouldn't mind going along with them.'

She looked at him reproachfully. 'I really don't think that's on, Max.'

'Technically I'm still a member of R Squadron.' That was the shadowy reserve unit whose former regular SAS members were called upon for any particularly controversial or deniable operation.

'But six years out of training,' she pointed out. 'Besides you've your son to think of . . . ' She stopped short of saying 'if we don't get Maggie back.' But he knew what she meant.

He didn't push the matter; the last thing he wanted was a point-blank refusal.

As they parted he said casually: 'My part in all this is over now, Clarry. I'd like to get away for a few days. Maybe a spot of hill-walking – think things out.'

'Of course. But *do* leave a contact number in case I need to speak to you in an emergency.'

He returned alone to Chelsea Cloisters and telephoned Floyd to inform him he was taking a short holiday. Although he had given his manager's telephone number to Clarissa, he had no intention of telling Floyd where he could be found. If there were any developments, he intended to know about them before Clarissa Royston-Jones.

Packing an overnight bag he left the apartment and took a taxi to Victoria station where he hired a car. A little later he was on the M4 out of London, heading west.

He arrived at the county town of Hereford deep in the rural West Country, home of 22 Special Air Service Regiment, in the late afternoon and drove directly to Stirling Lines barracks.

After a brief exchange at the guardhouse he was escorted to the adjutant's office. 'Sergeant Max Avery, R Squadron, reporting for duty.'

The adjutant squinted over his desk. 'Max? Is it you? Long time no see. Christ, you've given us some fun and games over the past months. Until then we thought you'd gone AWOL for six years.'

'I gather there's a party going on. Any chance for a gate-crasher?'

# Twenty-One

For thirty minutes they had been flying high over Iraqi airspace.

Forty-thousand feet. Beyond the reach of any anti-aircraft missile, if the experts were to be believed.

Deeper and deeper. Boring into the blackness of enemy territory, powered by the StarLifter's four massive Pratt and Whitney turbos.

Brian Hunt was unrecognisable apart from the fact that everyone knew he was first in line. Like the rest of Red Element, he was an alien from another planet. A starship trooper with huge shiny bonedome helmet and integrated communications, the wind goggles like bulbous black insect eyes and tentacles of air hoses sprouting from the oxygen mask to the supply bottle. The effect was compounded by the electrically heated oversuit that would protect against the equivalent of a minus-forty Arctic blizzard at high altitude.

He knew what each of the men in the joint American-British team was experiencing, the tension that rose with each second that passed. It shrank the cavernous hold until it became claustrophobic, pushing in on each of the eight

SAS and Delta soldiers who sat facing each other. Together, yet every man alone with his own private fears.

Even now he could feel the unremitting surge of adrenalin and the increasing tattoo of his heartbeat. He winced at the startling pain in his chest as the gases built up in his body, straining for release after the decompression of the C141's hold.

He cursed the discomfort and prayed that it would soon end, willed them on over the enemy's defences.

Then the USAF jump master was on his feet, the signal board in his hand.

Five minutes to go.

Almost at once the massive up-sloping ramp began its maddeningly slow yawn. Inch by inch the magnificent vista was revealed. A swathe of diamanté stars spread across a velvet night that stretched to infinity. The edge of the ramp was bathed in a silver light as the thin crystalline air of near space rushed in to swallow up the anxious men. The sheer beauty of the view and the vastness of the empty sky took the breath away.

Far below and behind them, yellow fireflies of lights arced in the aircraft's wake, dancing patterns over the darker indigo stain that was the landmass of Iraq.

It was a sober reminder. Triple A. Deadly anti-aircraft fire desperately hosing the sky with crisscrossing streaks of tracer. Hunting in vain, their radars blinded by the two escorting EF-111 electronics warfare aircraft which sought out and jammed the Iraqi frequencies and projected false ghost images. Some seventy miles ahead of them lay Baghdad, the enemy heartland, and incarcerated deep within a seemingly impenetrable bunker, Lew Corrigan.

Momentarily it occurred to Hunt that perhaps this was not such a good idea after all.

If he were honest, he was amazed that the operation had got off the ground at all. It must have been a measure of the governments' fears in London and Washington. Even more surprising was the degree of co-operation. In fact such a highly integrated US and British operation appeared to have no precedent. It was essentially an American mission, grafted onto Centcom's vast programme of covert surveillance operations; as such, if it went wrong, its true purpose would never be revealed. Nominally under United States command – it was commonplace for SAS troops to be seconded to the foreign armies for legal reasons of deniability – the man in charge of operations in Riyadh was in fact Major Crispin, OC of the squadron from which the Stalking Horse members were drawn. The operational plans had been pre-agreed with a major from Delta Force who took overall responsibility on behalf of Centcom.

Another signal board from the jump master. Four minutes.

Then Hunt led the way. With a sweating palm, he opened the large plastic valve on the end of his chest-mounted 'walk-about' oxygen bottle and took a deep draught from the black console in the middle of the aircraft. Then he disconnected the supply and switched to his own reserves.

The others followed his example, changing supplies then waddling, heavily laden with main and reserve parachutes and underslung bergens, towards the ramp. Front-to-back checks. Each man inspecting the other's parachute and straps, Luther Dicks and Brad Carver making light of it, Ran Reid and Villiers a little more circumspect. Check, check, check. Oxygen packs, spare chute, weapons securely strapped, twin altimeter units mounted on each man's chest.

One minute.

With gloved hands, Hunt tilted out his bee's-eye goggles to clear the condensation. All set.

This was going to be a combination jump. A combination of a skydiving track for ten thousand feet to defy any enemy radar and to put as much distance as possible between the paratroopers and their aircraft. Open at twenty-five thousand feet for a long controlled descent for pinpoint accuracy, each man steering in over a distance of thirty miles to the outskirts of Baghdad itself.

The red light was suddenly on.

Fifteen seconds. Hunt felt his heartbeat slow. Committed now. No going back.

The macabre dance began, the eight aliens shuffling into a line in readiness for the exit dive, edging towards the lip of the ramp.

Green light on. GO!

Off into the star-spangled void. Arms extended and lower legs tucked back. An unequal human frisbee hurtling into the stratosphere.

For the first twelve seconds they dropped vertically like stones at 172 feet a second, then the StarLifter's slipstream slammed into the fragile formation with the force of a locomotive express. With ice frosting goggles it was difficult for each man to see, eyes straining for a glimpse of his neighbour's dayglo pips or the chemical light-sticks attached to his pack. Bad enough now in the glimmering radiance of the stars high above the ultramarine skyline; worse later when they plummeted into the inky blackness of the landmass.

Someone's gone. Lost it. A spoke of the spinning wheel missing, peeling off like a rocket into orbit, instantly sucked away to be devoured by the aching emptiness of the void.

Hunt thought it was Villiers, but couldn't be sure.

No matter. He was an expert and with the HAHO system he'd stand a good chance of landing in the vicinity of the rest of the team. The formation closed up.

Each man now had a wave of air pressure on which to ride, his speed of descent slowed. Now a steady 120 mph. Almost pleasant, like surfing, calmly concentrating on staying stable, an aeronautical starfish with back arched to centre gravity on the stomach.

Hunt broke away then and, like the lead dancer in an aerial conga, opened the formation into a long snake travelling sideways as the team began its five thousand-foot, semi-horizontal track across the sky towards the drop-zone.

On Hunt's chest pack the figures in his altimeter unwound more slowly, the digits flickering by at a more leisurely rate. He glanced up the line, counting the members. Still seven and still together. No sign of Villiers or whoever it was, despite the fact that his eyes were becoming more accustomed to the sparkling night sky.

But this was no time to lose concentration.

Twenty-seven thousand feet.

Twenty-six.

Twenty-five. That's it. Hunt's free hand jabbed outward, thumb up to confirm to the others.

The line broke, one by one. Each parachutist peeled away, counting up to five before reaching for the ripcord, the sharp crack of the opening canopies unheard in the vastness.

Then only Hunt was left and he deployed his own para-wing canopy, seeing it blossom above his head, feeling the severe and reassuring jolt at his shoulders and crotch. With a practised eye he checked the shrouds. Fine, no twists. Checked his position, pulled on the steering guides and manoeuvred himself onto the top of the stack that stepped down towards the deep shadow of the landmass below.

Already the steady bleep of the far distant radio beacon was intoning in his ear, relaying from the automatic guidance control in the canopy rigging.

He settled in for the thirty-mile cross-country descent, seven phantoms floating purposefully, unnoticed beneath their black silk para-wings, towards their target.

Over the radio someone in Red Element was humming 'Ghost Riders in the Sky'.

A twenty-minute descent, Hunt estimated, allowing for the mild breeze.

On the far horizon he saw the twinkling display of tracer rising in a seemingly endless fountain from the skyline of Baghdad. Occasionally it was interspersed by a meteor of flame as an anti-aircraft missile was launched angrily at a suspected target. Then would follow the intermittent blink of high explosive as another bomb or cruise missile found its mark.

With five minutes to go he became aware of a movement above his head, a shadow cast by the stars. Villiers had rejoined the stack at last, guided in by the beacon's siren call.

The expanse of the heavens was replaced by the darkness of the land as he drifted below the skyline, the others now identified only by their dayglo patches, minuscule sequins travelling through time and space.

Then he saw the pinprick of green light far below. A cluster of chemical light-sticks on the ground to mark the drop-zone. It swirled around tantalisingly, growing in size and brightness.

He braced himself for the ground-rush, pulled on the brakes, flexed his knees. Suddenly he could see it. Rough terrain. Sand and shale, scrub and thorn bushes racing up to meet him. He glimpsed canopies collapsing all around like crushed flowers. Jerking hard on his steering line, he swung to the left, aiming for clear ground.

The impact took his breath away as he missed his chance of a stepping touchdown and crunched heavily into the rocky scree. He began to drag over the rough surface and fought back, gaining his feet and running back around the chute to prevent it refilling with air.

Villiers thudded out of the sky, missing him by inches. Red Element was down.

As Hunt gathered in his chute he saw that the first

members to land were already out of harness and were forming a defensive perimeter, their M16s already unstrapped. He could see now that the glowing bundle of light-sticks was just some thirty metres away. Not bad for a thirty-mile fly-in.

It was with relief that he unfastened his mask and helmet, relishing the fresh air and breeze against his skin. He was aware of the uncanny silence, broken only by the rasp of buckles and straps and whispered curses.

'Something's coming,' an American voice warned hoarsely.

Everyone stopped what they were doing and unleashed their weapons. Expectant.

Again the voice spoke: 'Vehicle. No lights.' A pause. 'Two vehicles. Station wagons.'

Hunt scurried forward and slipped down alongside the man who spoke. It was Brad Carver and he had out his small Spylux night-vision image-intensifier.

'Iraqi?'

'Can't say, chief – civilian, I reckon. A-rabs.'

Hunt was aware of safety catches being eased off, the gentle metallic scrape of rounds fed into the breech. On the slight wind he heard the grumble of the auto engines as the vehicles struggled over the uneven terrain. The first of the four-wheel drive wagons drew to a halt beside the chemical light cluster.

The driver could be seen clearly as he dismounted. A Bedouin tribesman in a white *dishdasha* and *shemagh* headgear.

'Shit,' Hunt growled, 'that's Buster Brown.'

'Sure?'

'Never forget that ugly mug.'

He rose to his feet and walked slowly forward, aware that the rest of the team would be covering in case he had got it wrong. He hadn't.

'Jesus, what do we have here?' Brown said. 'A bloody Martian invasion?'

Hunt shook the man's hand briskly. 'And what's with the Ali Baba costume?'

'I'll explain later, Bri. Get the guys to stow their kit on board, and those chem lights.' He glanced at the others. 'How many are you?'

'Just the eight.'

'Didn't lose anyone then?'

'We tried to lose Villiers, but he insisted on coming with us.'

Brown nodded. 'Right, well speed it up. It's not too healthy around here. If we've lost any pilots tonight Saddam's heroes could be out in force.'

Within five minutes the men had dumped their harnesses and chutes in the back of the wagons and had stripped off the cumbersome jumpsuits. Each carried a Bedouin *dishdasha* in the top of his bergen and quickly pulled the robe over his combat fatigues before climbing aboard.

The vehicles then bounced their way stoically across the desert until they reached a dusty tarmac strip. For five miles they drove towards Baghdad, seeing nothing else on the road. Eventually Buster Brown swung off into the desert again.

'Some of us have been here since September,' he explained as if it were the most natural thing in the world. 'Quite getting to enjoy the nomadic life till they started bombing. Still, all good things . . . We've been busy with the laser designators and all, but it's slackened off a bit now. So this might be an interesting diversion.'

'Where did the trucks come from?'

Brown gave him a curious sideways look. 'Bought 'em in Baghdad, of course. A vehicle auction. Quite a bargain and not bad bits of kit. Two of our lads had a flourishing business in the fruit market before the bombing – reckoned it was bad for trade. Another couple – d'you know Taffy Roberts and Slim Petersfield? They actually joined Saddam's army.'

'Trust them, daft buggers.'

'Ex-REME, you see. We had to get rid of a couple of sentries one night . . . So Taff says what can we do with these two uniforms? British-made, would you believe! Well, to cut it short, once we got the blood out, the two of them just walked into a vehicle repair depot about ten miles from here. They used the dead men's IDs – the photographs were piss poor – and rear echelon security is crap. The point is, even your regular rankers are shit scared of all authority, so if you brass it out you can get away with murder. 'Course Taffy and Slim were brought up in Saudi as kids and speak the language like natives, swear words and all.'

'So what happened?' Hunt asked.

'For a couple of weeks they actually worked at the depot, repairing vehicles. Learnt a helluva lot for the Int boys and managed to accumulate a lot of gash Iraqi kit. Uniforms, helmets and webbing. Well, in the end the two of them drove off with two Iraqi jeeps full of equipment, saying they were going for a test run. That's the last Saddam's heroes saw of them.'

The wagons took one more jolting turn, this time into a dried-up wadi between two rocky outcrops. In the starlight Hunt could clearly see the outline of the Bedouin-style tent encampment. There was even a grazing camel.

'We decided early on to brazen it out,' Brown continued. 'It's excellent cover for any activity that might otherwise raise Iraqi suspicions. Now if they see any vehicles or odd bods they just reckon it's from our camp. In fact the local commander is quite chummy. Even pops in for coffee. The fluent Arab speakers stay at the camp which we move around a ten-mile radius every so often. The Iraqis have got too much on their plate to bother us. The other guys have got a permanent hide never more than five miles from the mobile camp. We've got separate hidden dumps for vehicles, munitions and comms.'

Brown drove on to the hide where most of the troops spent the daylight hours. While the others off-loaded all the parachuting equipment, Hunt went inside with Brown. The entrance was cunningly concealed in a shallow gully which could not be viewed from the surrounding country-side. It was much larger than he'd expected, with a series of rooms and short tunnels hewn out of the sand and shale with picks and shovels. Assorted chunks of timber served as pit props for the low roof.

'That's the benefit of the long run-up to this war,' Brown said absently. 'Gave the lads a chance to make it more homely. The lousy winter weather here was an additional incentive.'

The place was almost deserted, most of the troops apparently engaged in various acts of 'hooliganism' in Baghdad and on the outskirts. To his surprise Hunt discovered a United States F15 pilot playing patience on an upturned oil drum.

'Amazing what you pick-up round here,' Brown laughed. 'He'll have to stay with us for the duration – unless you want to take him back with you.' He took a plastic bottle from the corner. 'Whisky?'

It was incongruous sitting there, six feet under the ground feeling the faint tremors of the bombs falling on Baghdad scarcely ten miles away.

'We've done an eyeball of your bunker like you requested,' Brown said. 'You couldn't have picked a tougher nut to crack, Brian. It's actually set beneath a civilian shelter which Taff visited last night. That wouldn't withstand a direct hit, of course, but the bunker would. All this stuff on the World Service about smart-missiles going right through them is a lot of tosh. Just surface damage to any serious installations. Saddam didn't waste all that money hiring German, Swedish and Swiss engineers, you know. That guy wants to live.'

Hunt nodded grimly. 'I know, Buster, we've seen the

plans and had a mock-up built in Riyadh. We know the place like the back of our hand and there's one conclusion – there's no realistic way to break in. This mother is a three-storey block of eight-foot thick reinforced concrete on gigantic springs set in a foundation of solid rubber to absorb shock waves. It only *begins* forty feet below ground level. Even the two escape hatches are two feet thick with six inches of steel plate so heavy that they have to be opened under hydraulic pressure. You'd need a shaped charge on *both* sides to stand even a chance of a result.'

Brown nodded his agreement. 'That could be a way *out* for you, though. And what about the air ducts? We've seen the concrete mushrooms on the top of the civilian shelter.'

'Quite. First we'd have to blow those off. The bunker's under positive pressure so the shaft drops all the way to the bottom where the filtration plant is set in concrete. To blast a way out of the ducting and into the floor we want would mean at least a fifty-foot abseil down an eighteen-inch shaft, placing a charge, then prussiking out again before the charge went off. Even then the wall is two feet of reinforced concrete. If the charge made any realistic impression, which I doubt, we'd have to abseil back in again one at a time. It's just not on.'

The SAS veteran considered the prospect grimly. 'You haven't come all this way to tell me you don't have an idea.'

'Not much better, I'm afraid. Have you managed to speak to the SIS contact?'

'The carpet merchant? Yeah, he was not too pleased to hear from us again. And he was loath to involve his nephew any more.'

'I think the boy's our only chance, Buster. Is he still in contact with Lew Corrigan?'

'Yes, he's detailed to the security police. Just a lowly squaddie. Like most of them he hates Saddam but they're all terrified of saying or doing anything about it.'

'So it's no go?' Hunt's voice was flat with disappointment.

'I didn't say that. We've got a meet arranged in the souk tomorrow morning.'

'God, Buster, you're a genius.'

'Not me, old son. Thank that sweet-talking Welshman. Taff set it up.'

With the first glimmer of hope buoying his spirits, Hunt slept well that night in the subterranean base until being awoken in the early hours by the SAS teams returning from Baghdad.

As he emerged into the predawn light he saw many familiar faces amongst the men disembarking from their Longline dune buggies before manhandling them into their daytime hides. Nicknamed 'dinkies', the machines were lighter than the American equivalents, although their skeletal frames still weighed up to a ton, including the 1900cc Volkswagen engines. The vehicles were fast finding favour over the traditional accident-prone 'Pinkies' or Pink Panther Land Rovers, so called because of the desert camouflage colour which the Ministry of Defence described as 'grey stone'. Every colour-blind soldier, however, knew pink when he saw it.

After feasting on porridge and appleflakes and dressing in Bedouin attire, Hunt and Brad Carver joined Brown and Taff in one of the station wagons for the journey to Baghdad. It was a nerve-racking but uneventful trip. A handful of private cars were passed leaving the city, filled with passengers and with prized possessions strapped to roof racks. Most of the traffic was military, generally trucks heading south towards the Kuwaiti border with the newest teenage conscripts. Palls· of greasy smoke besmirched the city's skyline after another night of ferocious bombing and few people had ventured onto the streets.

The carpet merchant's shop was closed and shuttered, the rest of the market empty. Feeling conspicuous and vulnerable the SAS men waited for several long minutes before the door was opened to admit them.

A hurricane lamp lit the office area at the far end where a young soldier sat. He was scruffy and unshaven, watching the arrival of the strangers with dark apprehensive eyes.

'There is no electric light any more, I am afraid,' the merchant said. 'This is my nephew Nizar.'

'I am pleased to meet you,' Taff said in Arabic. 'We are most grateful for your help.'

The soldier looked uncertain. 'You are Americanos?' he asked in English.

'American and British.'

'Ah, Mrs Thatcher.' He grinned, unaware that there was now a new Prime Minister. 'She knows you are here to speak to me?'

'She sent us.'

'Yes?' His eyes lit up. 'And Mr Bush?'

'Him too. They both need your help to end this war.'

Nizar looked uncomfortable. 'I do not know what I can do. I am not a general. I am not even an officer.'

'But you are based at the bunker where the American called Corrigan is held?'

He nodded. 'Sometimes. He is a good man. After the war he says I go to visit him at New York. Very nice.'

'Is that what you want to do? Go to America?'

He smiled sheepishly. 'Very much.'

Taff glanced at Carver. 'Tell you what, Nizar. You help us and we'll take you and Corrigan back to New York. How about that?'

'Very good, very good. Thank you very much.'

Two days later, when Nizar's duty roster had him posted once again for guard duty at Bunker NZ2, he took his lunch break with a group of fellow soldiers. They enjoyed playing *chesh-besh*, a type of backgammon, in the seclusion of the lowest level. Here, amongst the paraphernalia of air filtration and sealed sewerage units, electricity generators and water tanks, they were able to relax and forget about the terror that could pour from the skies at any moment. Moreover they could escape the disapproving scowls of officers and senior Ba'athist officialdom.

After one game, Nizar retired to eat his lunch and read the latest defiant headlines of the *al-Thawra* newspaper. When he was confident that the other players were thoroughly engrossed in playing and watching, he wandered surreptitiously between the huge bulk of the main generators and dropped a plastic bag into a dark recess beneath the control housing. That bag contained a small incendiary device that had been given to him that morning by Sergeant Major Brian Hunt of the SAS at a clandestine teahouse meeting. It was set to ignite at two o'clock the following morning.

Exactly twelve hours after Nizar placed the incendiary device, the secure land-line telephone rang at the remote American airbase at Al-Jawf on the Saudi border. The midnight call came from the commander of the US Air Force's top commando unit, the First Special Operations Wing, at Cencom in Riyadh.

Tension had been mounting all evening in the tent allocated to Blue Element of the special Delta/SAS team.

But for one man the waiting was much worse. Max Avery.

Despite the welcome from members of his old Regiment and the overwhelming generosity of the Americans, he still felt like an outsider. He sat alone, unfamiliar with the curious pudding-basin helmet issued to Delta members and complete with chinstraps and patched-in radio earpieces. And the complex-patterned American desert fatigues, he thought, seemed very – American. Only the leather jungle boots with their canvas uppers brought back reassuring memories.

And, while most of the members calmed their nerves by checking and rechecking their equipment, their leader

Jim Buckley ate. He always felt hungry when under pressure and tonight was no exception. He was on his third beefburger with relish when Major Bill Reinhart appeared at the open flap.

All faces turned towards the man in the flying suit.

There was a wide, slightly nervous grin beneath a space-age bonedome. 'Operation Ghostbuster is on, Jimbo – courtesy of the Green Hornets. We take off in ten. Let's go.'

Buckley choked down the last of his beefburger, grabbed his Colt Commando rifle and beckoned the team to follow. But there was no need, they were already on their feet, shouldering packs, weapons and extra equipment.

Outside, the vastness of the glimmering desert sky was filled with the demonic crescendo from the rank of huge blackened monsters as the helicopter pilots ran up their engines, checking and rechecking instruments and controls.

'What's the latest from Hunt's guys?' Buckley asked as he strode with Avery and the major towards the lead helicopter.

'An SAS recce team's had our bunker under surveillance all day,' Reinhart replied, 'and they've confirmed that Red Element have secured LZ Manhattan.'

'And the refuel RV – Nebraska – is secured?'

The airman gave him a sideways grin. 'Stop frettin', Jimbo. If it ain't, it's a long walk back from Baghdad.'

Blue Element climbed aboard the Sikorsky MH-53J Pave Low III, one of two twenty-six million dollar superspook aircraft designed to fly commandos to their target with pinpoint accuracy regardless of whatever weather and terrain can throw at them.

Buckley just prayed they would live up to their awesome reputation as he strapped himself into the hold and nodded across at the row of blackened faces beneath the helmets. Familiar faces, American and British, almost unrecognisable now: Buzz, Monk, Pope and the others. Even Gretchen, who was officially travelling as an observer for Intelligence Support Activity.

He had grown deeply attached to each of the mixed sixteen-person team over the past few months, proud of how they'd handled everything that Stalking Horse had thrown at them. And now they were back doing the sort of mission that they had endlessly trained for.

There was a slight jolt and the Sikorsky was airborne. Behind them three more helicopters would be forming up line astern. Two were empty: one to carry back the snatch team and the second as emergency backup. Following were their protectors, the black shapes of two AH-64 Apache gunships, menacingly dripping with rockets and missiles and each one packing a mighty 30 mm chain gun.

Within minutes Blue Element was hurtling over the border towards its target with instruments reading 150 mph at an altitude of no more than fifty feet.

# Twenty-Two

For Avery it was the stuff of nightmares and he closed his eyes. Tried not to think of the terrain flashing past as they jinked and zigzagged around obstacles and along wadis to avoid the enemy radars.

For Major Reinhart in the cockpit it was 'the fairground ride to end all fairground rides – big dipper and ghost train all in one at ten times the speed!'

At least that was what he joked to Avery. The reality was heart-stoppingly different, demanding immense concentration as he flew entirely on instruments from the infra-red imager, to show him what lay ahead in the darkness, to the ring laser gyros and the rolling map display slaved to the global positioning system which relied on satellites for pinpoint accuracy. Doppler radars warned what lay above and below their path, while electronic black boxes blinded any hostile defence and anti-aircraft missile radars within range.

It was the copilot's task to eyeball anything the high-tech gizmos missed. A task easier said than done. Viewing through his helmet's night-vision goggles had been described as 'looking through a toilet roll tube with a green shade on it'.

Again and again the tiny high-speed air convoy changed direction, jinked its way to avoid towns, villages and main roads and to skirt Iraqi positions. These had been painstakingly plotted from space by Lacrosse, Keyhole and Signet satellites. Twice they even took avoiding action to miss desert Bedouin camps identified only a day earlier by a top-secret Aurora US spy plane overflying at Mach 7 on the very threshold of space itself.

'*LZ Nebraska approaching, Jimbo,*' Reinhart's voice crackled over Buckley's intercom linkup. '*ETA five minutes. Ground Element Green confirm fuelbird has landed.*'

The news brought immense relief to the leader. The refuel problem and final downfall of the Desert One rescue mission to Iran in 1980 still haunted him. Pre-dropped blivets of fuel were prone to burst or to wedge themselves in difficult terrain and it took eight men to shift the huge balloons of avgas. The answer was to land a Hercules EC-130 tanker on a desert strip, secured and marked out by Element Green, SAS team members who'd been in the area for months.

Wheels had scarcely touched at Nebraska before the tanker crews were running out the fuel lines, the area guarded by scruffy, bearded individuals in filthy desert fatigues.

The following minutes seemed like as many hours before the six helicopters were filled up with sufficient fuel to take them on the last hop to LZ Manhattan, then all the way back across the Saudi border. Precisely on schedule the air convoy lifted off again towards the fiery yellow strip on the horizon that was Baghdad.

It was an indirect fifteen-minute flight, a circuitous route making use of every hollow in the terrain and every stand of trees in order to avoid detection by radar or human eye.

LZ Manhattan, just two miles south of Baghdad's last suburban village, had been carefully selected. Its northern perimeter was formed by a steep-sided stream which was crossed at an ancient stone bridge by a southbound road. That watercourse would serve as a natural anti-vehicle ditch in the event of any hot pursuit by the Iraqis. At the centre of the zone was a meteor-created depression of land, providing a perfect hide for the helicopters as they waited for the snatch squad to ride north and, hopefully, return with Lew Corrigan.

Almost as the wheels hit the ground, the hydraulics were lowering the rear ramp and Blue Element was out and running, moving up the embankment sides of the depression to relieve the Red Element team who had been securing the perimeter.

There was a line of vehicles parked to one side: three bare-framed LSVs, one mounted with a GPMG and two with monstrous Mk19 automatic grenade launchers. Next to them was a battered khaki pick-up with Iraqi markings.

Brian Hunt was one of a group, dressed in blue overalls, who waited for them.

'How was the ride, Max?'

'On balance I think I'd have preferred to do the HAHO jump after all! Bloody petrifying. Anyway, how's it going this end?'

'Well, at least we're all here. But listen, I've decided to

take you in with Red Element. Our agent on the inside says Lew's been given a rough time. He might well be disorientated and a friendly face would help – besides which, anything he tells us will mean more to you than the rest of us. There's a chance he won't be fully *compos mentis*.'

'Count me in,' Avery replied.

'It's your decision. I'm not saying this won't be an extremely dangerous stunt. There's no guarantee that any of us will get out.'

Avery nodded. 'What d'you want me to do?'

'You'll find a set of Iraqi army fatigues in the pick-up. Put them over your uniform and get aboard the lead LSV.' He added: 'Remember how to handle a Hockler?'

The 9 mm Heckler and Koch sub-machine-gun with the retractable butt. Known as a Hockler. The siege-buster. How could he ever forget?

The tunic was a tight fit across the chest and the trousers were clearly designed for a much shorter man. Monk, sitting in the front passenger seat of the lead LSV, laughed. 'If we get stopped and anyone asks you about the uniform, just say it shrank in the wash.'

Avery inspected the Longline vehicle with interest; it was a new development since his time in the Regiment.

'A beach buggy on steroids,' was Monk's colourful description.

The one-ton LSV had no bodywork to speak of, it was basically a rollover cage mounted on four massive sand tyres with a spare on the sloping forward bonnet. Next to Monk sat a driver from Buster Brown's team, wearing image-intensifying night goggles. With no third seat available, Avery was obliged to stand on the side bins and hold on to the top rail for dear life.

Pulling away first, the pick-up moved out of the depression and onto the road. Aboard was Able patrol, comprising Hunt, Ran Reid, Brad Carver and Villiers; dressed in blue overalls, they would lead the way into the bunker. The redoubtable Taff was at the wheel, with Buster Brown at his side. Both were fluent in Arabic and were by now fully experienced in the problems likely to be encountered in Baghdad.

Following behind in the three LSVs came the four-man Baker team who, with Avery, would actually conduct the snatch. As the last buggy roared over the hump-backed bridge, a Delta man from Blue Element could be seen preparing an M3A3 shaped charge in case demolition was later required.

Ahead pulses of exploding light could be seen as bomb blasts threw the suburban rooftops into momentary relief against the burning sky; man-made thunder rumbled in an almost continuous barrage.

The high-speed LSV convoy had taken an off-the-road route which meant that they arrived at the target area ahead of the slow-moving pick-up. On time, the lead buggy nosed its way onto the patch of wasteland, the rough ground scattered with bomb-damaged furniture and discarded household appliances.

Ahead of them, through the thick fog of cordite, lay Bunker NZ2.

The slab-sided single-storey building was illuminated in macabre flickering light as a lorry-mounted anti-aircraft unit nearby poured its venom and tracer into the heavens. An eight-foot fence surrounded the civilian shelter, but there was no sign of guards at the gate. No doubt they were keeping their heads down until the raid had finished.

It was now exactly two o'clock, when two things were scheduled to happen. The timed incendiary device in the lower level of the bunker was due to ignite, while simultaneously fighters had been allocated a series of diversionary bombing raids nearby. That, at least, appeared to be running to plan.

The noise all around was tumultuous, the chattering triple-A fire mere percussion to the earth-trembling background detonations of high explosive. Avery felt the thrill of controlled fear as he realised their precarious situation. Although the allied airforce had the co-ordinates of the wasteland from which they watched, it would require only a one digit error to result in their instant annihilation.

Jim Buckley was having to scream into the radio mike to make himself heard above the crashing of the bombs, warning Able team of the triple-A unit's presence and updating Hunt on the situation at the bunker.

He had only just stopped talking when Able's pick-up came into view at the crossroads, passing within feet of the anti-aircraft gun. But the crew were intent on their work and didn't spare the truck a second glance. It jolted to a halt outside the bunker gates, and the four blue-clad service engineers began lifting weighty toolbags from the tailgate. The first man tried the compound gate; it was unlocked.

Then Avery caught sight of a movement in the darkened entrance to the shelter. Spontaneously his finger closed around the trigger of his Hockler as the green-uniformed guard stepped warily forward.

Buckley hissed in his ear: 'Don't shoot the little bastard, Max; he must be our informer, Nizar.'

Across the street Hunt was asking the young soldier what was happening below in the bunker; the moment was critical. An instant decision would have to be made whether to go on or to abort.

'Sure, the bomb goes off,' Nizar explained rapidly, his voice shaking and his eyes darting left and right as though expecting to be caught at any moment. 'There is a small bang and then a fire. The lights go out and there is much panic. But the maintenance crew extinguish the fire and the backup generator comes on.'

'How bad is the damage?' Hunt snapped. Time was of the essence.

'Very bad. The crew cannot repair it. They will need the engineers.'

Damn, Hunt thought, the *real* engineers! Too much explosive. Too late now. Precious seconds were ticking away. He made his decision. 'Right, Nizar, let's go. Just as we planned.'

'Mr Brian, I am afraid.' The Iraqi appeared rooted to the spot.

'So am I, Nizar. Let's go.'

Buckley heard the confirmation over the radio and activated the expendable Racal jammer that would interrupt all signals from the bunker for the next two hours.

Hunt pushed Nizar forward into the dark mouth of the shelter. The first thing that struck the SAS man was the smell. The fetid odour of too many sweating and unwashed bodies crammed together, the hint of urine and excreta from those who could not wait, and the sickly sweet smell of babies' vomit. Three armed guards were sprawled on the step, but paid little interest to the new arrivals who followed Nizar down.

It was like a scene from hell. With the city's power station put out of action by the allies, the shelter was patchily lit by candles. There were people everywhere: soldiers, militiamen, old men and women, mothers with babes-in-arms and screaming toddlers. They wore the forlorn and resigned expressions of those who had come to expect nothing better.

Nizar led the way, stepping over the citizens of Baghdad until he reached a grey-painted steel door marked *Maintenance Staff Only*. A red light glowed above the lintel. He entered his plastic identity card in the security lock and punched in the entry code.

The light changed to green; the door gave a distinct and metallic click. Nizar pushed it open. Inside, steps fell away sharply, the concrete stairwell lit by bulkhead lamps. Hunt sighed with relief – at least they were actually inside.

But his relief was short-lived. Two landings down – Hunt reckoned they'd descended thirty feet – they came across the guards. Three of them, one seated and two others lounging against a functional grey metal desk.

The senior guard recognised Nizar. 'I thought you'd just gone off duty.'

'If you hadn't noticed, there's an air raid going on. It's safer here.'

'And who are these people?'

'Oh, just the engineers for the generator.'

The seated soldier looked surprised. 'Allah be praised – you were quick. It only happened ten minutes ago.' He regarded Nizar with a scowl. 'But you shouldn't have let them in. Have you checked their passes?'

Nizar's face drained of colour. 'Of course.'

One of the other soldiers said: 'I'm the duty officer. That's my job.'

Hunt said quickly in Arabic: 'Please don't waste time. We've been sent on the direct orders of the Revolutionary Command Council. The President himself may be visiting this bunker tonight.'

The sergeant major's mastery of the accent was not normally good, but Taff had helped him practise the few lines.

'You understand, we must be careful.' The soldier had no desire to feel the wrath of the Ba'athist Party chiefs.

Over the previous few months, the SAS teams hidden on the outskirts of Baghdad had collected various items of Iraqi identification documents, permits and passes. The most appropriate of these were now flashed airily by the four SAS men as Hunt strode past. 'C'mon, Nizar,' he called irritably, 'show me the way.'

'Wait a minute!' the duty officer called. 'Do you want to get yourself killed?' He picked up the telephone on his desk and dialled a number. 'Entrance check here. Four engineers and one soldier coming down.' He beckoned Hunt to continue.

As he reached the bottom of the next flight of steps, he saw the machine-gun post. The deadly weapon protruded from a ball-jointed cupola set in a reinforced concrete wall. It made the occupants unassailable from the outside and provided them with a view of both flights of steps through a small periscopic lens.

'They are ordered to shoot anyone who is not first cleared by telephone,' Nizar whispered in his ear. 'Only last week a soldier is drunk, forgets and – pow!'

Hunt exchanged glances with Brad Carver at his side. They'd had a narrow escape.

Two more flights and two more stairwells put them below the two-foot thick detonation slab that covered the entire bunker and was designed to absorb the impact of any direct missile attack. Now they reached the top level and were confronted by a steel door. Again Nizar punched in his ID card and pressed the 'open' button. With a hiss of hydraulics, the door slid wide to admit them into an airlock with another steel door on the far side.

Beyond it was a decontamination chamber and shower stalls. Two Iraqis were playing dominoes at a small table and looked up as the strangers entered.

'The engineers,' Nizar explained simply. The men's concentration returned to the game. As he passed through,

Hunt noted the two escape hatches set in the wall at each end. No more than twenty-eight inches square, they were locked by large wing nuts.

The entrance led into a corridor where a sentry sat in a chair, his legs extended and arms folded, his head nodding as he dozed. Beyond the double doors that he guarded were the staff dormitories, canteen and kitchen. Also the interrogation room and the cell in which Lew Corrigan was held.

But that would come later. First they continued their descent. Another level and another corridor. This time the sentry was alert and standing, guarding the entrance to the communications suite, offices and meeting rooms of top military personnel. There was also a bedroom in which Saddam Hussein himself sometimes slept as he kept on constant move around the city.

Again they passed it by, taking the final flight of stairs to the basement level. The acrid smell of burning was still in the air as they were met by half-a-dozen soldiers. Their grease-splattered fatigues bore the tabs of an engineering unit.

'These are the experts,' Nizar said. 'You'd better show them the damage.'

An older man in his forties shrugged. 'You won't repair it. It needs replacing.'

'We'll see,' Hunt said.

He followed the man and another younger soldier along a passage formed by the water tanks, sewerage units and air-filtration plants until they reached the main generator.

The casing was gnarled and buckled, scorch marks extending to the wall behind it.

'I've no idea what could have caused it,' the older man was saying.

Hunt steeled himself; he was not going to enjoy this. He dumped his toolbag on the tiled floor and opened up the zipper. Reaching inside, his hand closed around the chunky cylindrical silencer of the Hockler. The two Iraqis were watching him absently and did not even react as the silencer barrel came out. Perhaps they were tired, daydreaming. Perhaps they did not immediately recognise the dumpy snout as part of a weapon, but thought it a tool or spare part.

Only at the very last moment did the younger man's eyebrows furrow into a frown and his mouth start to form a protest. But it was too late.

The force of the three rounds grouping into his chest slammed him hard up against the generator side. Immediately the barrel swung towards the older man. Stunned, he made no attempt to release his pistol from its holster, but just began to raise his hands.

I'm sorry, mate, Hunt murmured to himself as the weapon trembled and spluttered in his hands, spitting out its silent seed of death. The victim fell back first, crashing against the generator, then pitched forward with the momentum, dropping on his knees at the SAS man's feet.

Hunt felt sick and kicked the body away. It was bad enough a live man pleading for mercy; he couldn't cope with a corpse doing it.

Turning on his heel he ran back to the others. They, too, had completed their unpleasant business: the four remaining Iraqis lay dead beneath the smoking guns of Carver, Reid and Villiers.

Nizar looked on in disbelief. He grabbed Hunt's arm. 'The other two, the old man – you have killed them too? My friends?'

Villiers wasn't in a sympathetic mood. 'What the hell did you expect? There's a bloody war on.'

Hunt spared the big man a reproachful glare before turning to the grief-stricken Iraqi. 'It had to be done. There was no other way.'

Villiers gave a snort of disgust. 'I'll lay the charge. A five-minute fuse.'

As he disappeared to locate the backup generator, Reid and Brad Carver took up positions to secure the steps. Hunt reopened his toolbag and pulled out two respirator masks with their integrated radio equipment.

He thrust one at Nizar. 'You'll need this. Put it on and after that *don't* speak – I want to keep the net clear. Just listen for my voice. I'll call you by name. Follow any instructions I give you immediately and without question. And when we get to the top, you know what to do . . . '

The young soldier stared numbly at the unfamiliar make of equipment and followed Hunt's example, pulling it over his head and adjusting the tangle of communications wiring and the pressel switch.

Hunt was now conscious of the minutes eating into their tight timeframe. Sweat was building up beneath the rubber mask, his pulse racing. It was rare for him to feel claustro-phobic. But these seconds were critical. If things went wrong now, here they were three storeys down in a concrete bunker and only one way out. Up. Their fate would be as surely sealed as a mummy in a pharaoh's tomb. Moreover, they had no communications with Baker team on the outside because radio signals would not penetrate to ground level. And there was not an exact timetable, because no one knew how long their entry might take. So Baker would have to wait in the escape tunnels. Wait and hope. Vulnerable to discovery.

Villiers was returning from the backup generator. He was sauntering, dammit, bloody sauntering. The man's got nerves of bloody steel, Hunt thought savagely. Then corrected himself. Villiers had no bloody nerves at all.

'All set?' Hunt asked, helping himself to Nizar's side arm. He didn't want the Iraqi changing allegiance halfway through.

Villiers confirmed. 'And the auxiliary battery, Bri. Nearly overlooked that.' He looked at his watch. 'Three minutes to go.'

It was just enough time for Villiers to don his own respi-rator mask and pick up his weapon.

Hunt beckoned. They began edging up the stairwell, backs against the wall. Nizar followed nervously.

On the nearby stairwell, the exploding twin-pack of PE4 sounded like an enormous, muffled belch that shook the steps beneath their feet. Loose chippings shook from the ceiling. And the lights went.

The hum of the air conditioning stopped dead, the silence absolute.

The four powerful beams from the torches fitted to their weapons tore brilliant swathes through the darkness.

Brad Carver was point, powering up the remaining steps with Hunt close behind, both armed with Hocklers. Villiers followed as defence man with another Hockler, then Ran Reid as rearguard with a 12-gauge Winchester pump-action.

As they hit the landing, the corridor sentry was confronted by a dazzling array of torchlights coming towards him. He was confused, having heard the explosion. He assumed that this was the maintenance crew escaping a fire in the basement. He certainly didn't think it was an attack until the short 9 mm burst from Brad Carver blew him off his feet.

They knew the approximate layout of the floor. Some hundred feet square, the double doors opening onto the communications complex with smaller partitioned offices and the President's occasional bedroom suite beyond. Crouching low, Carver kicked in the door and jammed it open with his knee. Momentarily the torch beam revealed the expanse of radio and computer consoles, the soldiers frozen in surprise at their work stations. Then Hunt tossed in the seven-ounce Royal Ordnance G60/09 flash-bang. The mercury fulminate in the grenade went off with an ear-splitting power of one-sixty decibels, repeating the percussion seven times in rapid succession, drowning out the spontaneous squeals of horror. Simultaneously the magnesium charge ignited, a blinding pulse of light the equivalent of three million candelas that seared into the unprotected retinas of the Iraqi troops.

In that moment of total paralysis, Hunt and Carver hurled in explosive grenades. Just as they had rehearsed at the mock-up in Riyadh, they aimed for the far walls and ducked back into the corridor. As both grenades struck the partitioning they blew, blasting their way into the conference room, offices and bedroom beyond. The air was filled with scything steel fragments, dropping bodies like a daisy-cutter, ripping the collapsed walls to shreds, shrapnel studding the wooden doors.

Ran Reid and Villiers followed up, this time tossing in their grenades at those who still sat slumped, dripping blood, at the consoles or crawled on the floor, seeking escape. The twin explosions blew amid the chaos of smoke and debris, the backblast of displaced air expelled out into the corridor like some demonic, evil-smelling hurricane.

Leaving Reid and Villiers to finish off any survivors, Hunt followed Brad Carver and Nizar who were already on their way to the top floor. Because Lew Corrigan was held there, this would be an altogether trickier operation.

The sentry, advancing to investigate the noise from below, was dispatched with a double-tap from the stairwell by Carver's silenced Hockler. Leaving Nizar crouched, bewildered on the top step, the two soldiers raced for the double doors.

Hunt yelled into the throat mike: 'Nizar, now!'

Then Hunt kicked open the door as Carver pitched in

two stun grenades. Through the clamour and dazzling display of pyrotechnics, they followed up with two CS canister rounds fired from the underslung launchers on the Hocklers.

Meanwhile Nizar crossed from his hiding place to one of the emergency exits, a two-foot square slab set in the wall, and began to spin the wheel nut.

Beyond it, the men of Baker team, together with Max Avery, were crouched in the dank concrete shaft that ran down a forty-foot slope from a hatch in the grounds of the civilian shelter above.

The worst aspect was the tightly confined space and discomfort in moving the wrong way down a concrete rabbit hole designed only for escape. Progress had been slow, caused by the need to keep the knees relatively straight and to avoid the hard ladder ridges that scraped painfully on thighs and buttocks.

Now Jim Buckley was seated tight up against the lower exit hatch at the first level, knees bent with the tunnel ceiling forcing his chin down onto his chest. Avery was jammed next to him with Luther Dicks and Monk behind him. Each man strained to hear any sound from the bunker. But the two feet of concrete and steel was totally sealed and soundproofed.

It seemed an age before they heard the rasp of the wing nut as it dislodged an accumulation of rust. It was a nerve-stopping moment.

There was a sudden hiss from the gas bottles as the hydraulic pumps began to flex their muscles. Slowly, maddeningly slowly, the huge steel and concrete block inched open into the bunker.

The beam from Nizar's carelessly aimed torch was blinding and the cacophony of small-arms fire deadened the eardrums after the intense stillness of the tunnel.

Buckley launched himself into the corridor, Avery and the others hard on his heels. The American shoved the Iraqi aside. Ahead of him Hunt and Carver were disappearing into the double doors as smoke and gas belched out. They were starting the dangerous and methodical process of clearing the rooms one by one.

Buckley beckoned the last two men in his team. 'Take the second side of the corridor.' As they rushed forward to assist Hunt and Carver, he turned to Avery. 'Stay back with me, Max. Our objective is Lew – nothing else.'

The clearing operation was moving at breakneck speed. Working in pairs the men tackled two small dormitories at a time. Inside, the occupants, already reeling in incomprehension and incapacitated by the clouds of CS gas, had fragmentation grenades hurled into their midst before being raked with sub-machine-gun fire.

The canteen and kitchen were next – even the chefs were cut down as they cowered beneath their work tables. But progress was necessarily slower now to ensure that Lew Corrigan wasn't accidentally killed by being somewhere that he wasn't expected to be. As a result some Iraqis had escaped the onslaught. Two men, both wounded, were firing back from behind an upturned steel table in one of the dormitories.

As they awaited the all clear, Avery and Buckley heard Hunt's voice in their earpieces. '*Snatch team – in you go!*'

Clearly the sergeant major wasn't prepared to wait any longer. Avery led the way down the corridor, leaping over bodies and around doors hanging off their hinges. Small-arms rounds ricocheted madly from the surviving Iraqis.

He turned a corner, the torchlight from his gun picking out the room he sought. The CS gas had not drifted this far; he had to be ultra cautious now. Buckley backed up against the door jamb, reached out and pushed it open. Avery was in the doorway, Hockler seeking out friend or foe, finding –

'Oh, shit!' he breathed. Wrong room.

Buckley stared in over his shoulder. The deserted room was filled with the instruments of torture. A table-rack, a chair with straps and electrodes dangling. It was all there, hanging neatly on hooks as innocently as tools in a suburban garage. The whole ugly paraphernalia: thumbscrews, tongue wrenches, gougers and pliers; hosepipes and electric cattle probes. There was dried blood on the floor tiles.

Avery spun on his heel, left the awful place and moved on down the short corridor. They went through the same entry procedure at the next door. It was a cell, unlocked and empty. Avery's spirits dipped. Had Corrigan been moved just before they arrived?

The last door. Its steel construction, complete with spyhole, suggested it was another cell. That door too yawned wide.

'WATCH OUT!' an American voice yelled suddenly.

Avery blinked. The voice was Corrigan's.

There followed a curse in Arabic, then in English: 'Keep back, out there! Keep away or I kill this American prisoner! Do you hear me? I have an American here!'

The two masked rescuers looked at each other, hesitant. Buckley held up a grenade. It was a Brock XFS-1. With a single charge it was one of the loudest and brightest makes of stun grenade. Avery nodded. Buckley knelt, pulled the pin, and set it gently rolling through the gap.

The effect was cataclysmic, the shriek of burning mercury fulminate hitting a numbing one eighty decibels and the magnesium flaring like the Second Coming, a single pulsing flux of fifty million candelas.

They moved in together. It was a terror-frozen tableau. A middle-aged Iraqi in tortoiseshell glasses was holding Lew Corrigan around the throat and had a pistol held to his temple. Both men were dazed and disorientated, staggering backwards together.

Buckley grabbed the Iraqi's gun arm, forcing it back against the joint until he heard the ligaments tear. The man's knees gave way on him and he collapsed to the concrete floor as Avery wrenched Corrigan clear. It took several seconds for the American to recover from the shock effects.

The familiar raw grin showed out of ten days' growth of beard. 'Max? What kept you, pal?' He broke off into a racking cough; the CS gas was starting to build up now.

Avery thrust a spare respirator at him. 'Put this on.' The American was still deafened, still not thinking straight. At last he understood and pulled it over his head.

The Englishman's voice came over his radio, ringing irritably in his ear. *'What's with your left hand, Lew? The bandage?'*

'Ask that bastard, Dr Hassan. Took my fingernails for a trophy.'

*'Can you walk?'* Urgent.

'Just.'

*'We've got a stretcher.'*

'Bugger you. I'll manage.'

Avery took the American's arm and shouldered his weight. 'Jimbo – c'mon!'

He turned and just heard the short sharp report of a .45 Colt pistol before Buckley emerged. 'Just saying goodbye.'

Then the two of them began to retrace their footsteps, Corrigan hobbling between them. Through the debris of the dormitory corridors to where the earlier fire fight was over. They passed the rest of the team, who now began their withdrawal, backing up through the body-strewn debris.

On the landing they found Villiers and Ran Reid guarding the downward stairwell. It was only then that Avery became aware of an alarm bell trilling.

'Something's started a fire down there,' Villiers observed, as though it were nothing to do with him.

At that moment Hunt led the last of the men out through the double doors.

'We can't use the escape hatches,' Buckley said. 'Lew's injured. It'll have to be the main entrance.'

Hunt nodded and beckoned Nizar who had been watching the unfolding events with awe. 'Telephone up to the machine-gun post. They'll have heard the alarm bell. Tell them everyone's evacuating – and so must they.'

The young Iraqi ran to the handset by the door. After a couple of seconds he looked back at Hunt. 'There is no reply. They have gone already!' His grin was very wide.

Despite Corrigan's protest, four of the commandos propelled him onto a collapsible stretcher and started running with it up the steps towards the exit. In the upper civilian shelter there were squeals of protest as sleeping bodies were trampled under foot in the group's rush to get through.

They burst out into the open, gulping in the cool night air, oblivious to the continuing *crump* of exploding bombs all around. Fires raged in several government buildings nearby.

Taff still waited with the pick-up at the gates and the anti-aircraft truck was still blasting at the skies from the adjacent crossroads.

Someone in the LSVs lurking on the waste ground across the street decided that the triple-A vehicle was a threat. Without warning the Mk19 grenade-thrower on the support LSV belched into action. Half-a-dozen 40 mm dual-purpose anti-tank rounds struck the triple-A vehicle and it disappeared with its crew in a raging fireball as the ammunition caught.

As the last of the rescuers scrambled aboard the pick-up, the LSVs pulled out to form a convoy and they began moving south through the burning streets of Baghdad.

'God, am I glad to be out of there,' Corrigan said with feeling.

'I'm only sorry it didn't happen sooner,' Avery replied. 'The prospects looked pretty bleak until Nizar offered his services.'

Corrigan grinned at the dejected-looking Iraqi sitting opposite them. 'Big Apple, here we come, eh?' He looked at Avery. 'The lad did his best to make life better for me, but the interrogators weren't going to listen to him. Christ, I swear one of my legs is shorter than the other now.'

'We've got full medical facilities at the LZ.'

Corrigan smiled ruefully. 'A bit late for that, I'm afraid. Some things can't be undone.' He didn't go into specifics. 'So what happened to you? They told me they planned to lure you to Jordan, too. I was expecting you to turn up at that bunker at any time.'

'Oh, I went all right,' Avery replied, 'but with these guys as backup. We thought you'd be there too. We took out the lot of them.'

'Serves them bloody right. Sorry I missed the show. Guess I was already on my way here.'

'So, the sixty-four thousand dollar question, Lew – where the hell are Maggie and Con Moylan?'

Suddenly the pick-up screeched to a faltering halt, the brakes slow to bind. Ahead of them the leading LSV had stopped. Avery climbed to his feet to see what the problem was.

'That's handy,' Reid observed.

An ageing Iraqi T-55 tank from a reserve unit had rumbled into the crossroads of the narrow street. Its massive tracks clanked to a standstill and the turret began a slow swivel until the barrel pointed directly at them. Then a command jeep pulled up beside the tank and soldiers debussed to form a roadblock.

Ran Reid casually picked the cylindrical 94 mm LAW 80 that was part of their reserve equipment stock. He removed the end caps of the latest throw-away anti-tank weapon and extended the HEAT projectile rearwards from the outer casing, locking the extended launch tube into position. As he erected the sight and settled down into an aiming posture, with his elbows on the driver's cab roof, the others silently gathered at his side with an assortment of weapons.

Reid engaged the arming lever and gently squeezed the trigger of the inbuilt 9 mm sighting rifle. There followed a whipcrack and the tracer round sparked as it sang off the turret. The Iraqis at the roadblock began scrambling for cover.

Hunt yelled: 'OPEN FIRE!'

Everything went off at once. The support LSV let rip with its tirade of 40 mm grenades backed up by sustained bursts of heavy machine-gun fire and individual Hocklers. Reid lowered his aim, saw the tracer ricochet off the tank's tracks. Got it! He fired the warhead, the crash of explosive and the tongue of flame adding to the confusion. He barely glimpsed the missile in mid-flight before it buried its nose into the side of the tank. The detonation on impact was dazzling, not penetrating the armour plating, but causing lethal scabs of steel to implode into the crew's compartment.

Taff hit the accelerator and the entire convoy surged forward as one through the wall of flaming wreckage.

Then they were on the open road again, eating up the miles to LZ Manhattan. Yet barely five minutes passed before plumes of steam began rising from the pick-up's front grille and the engine died. An Iraqi round in the previous exchange had done its worst; now the truck was stranded in a shabby suburban high street of locked-up shops.

Buckley was immediately on the radio to Blue Element at LZ Manhattan, which must still have been ten miles distant. Meanwhile Carver was getting a fix on his hand-held Magellan GPS, the global positioning system that consulted the common point on three spheres as viewed by three Navstar satellites miles above them. If the mathematics was elementary geometry, the technology was incredible.

He rotated the side-mounted antenna skyward and pressed the POS button. Immediately the mini-computer began its complex calculations.

Meanwhile Buckley was through to Manhattan. 'We've got a problem with the truck.' He didn't mince words. 'I need the choppers down here pronto to pick us up and gunship support.'

At the other end Major Reinhart could scarcely disguise his enthusiasm at the prospect of action, however cool he tried to sound. *'Willdo, Red. Can you give me your position?'*

The GPS receiver was now giving out its reading, the coordinates accurate to within sixteen metres; they were relayed to Manhattan.

'*Hold on, you guys. The Green Hornets are acomin'!*'

Buckley grimaced at the up-front bravado. It never ceased to amaze him how some people in the military only ever saw action as a game.

Someone called up from the support LSV. 'Looks like we've got company, chaps. I see lights on the road.'

Sure enough, vehicle headlights were showing back down the road towards Baghdad; they were advancing fast.

'Let's get this damn truck unloaded,' Buckley decided. 'We're sitting ducks here.'

Brian Hunt stood up in the cargo hold. 'Get into defensive positions to hold this street,' he shouted.

The LSV drivers waved and began noisily reversing their machines into alleyways and behind jutting concrete walls that offered a measure of protection and a good field-of-fire. While Hunt directed others to occupy some high positions with a commanding view of the street, Avery and Buckley helped Corrigan to the safety of a shopfront doorway.

An Iraqi armoured car had appeared on the main street, a platoon of infantry in its wake. Picking up a Hockler, Avery moved towards the edge of the doorway. A spotlight played from the turret of the armoured car, probing menacingly along one side of the street.

'Get me a gun,' Corrigan demanded.

'You're sick,' Avery replied.

'C'mon, pal. I don't use my left hand anyway. If we're going down, I'll take a few bastards with me.'

Avery relented, and handed over another Hockler. The

American did a three-times roll to bring himself prone alongside his friend. He tried to cock the weapon one-handedly.

'Come here,' Avery said and took the weapon, cocked it and handed it back. Now Corrigan levelled the barrel over his bandaged arm, and settled down.

Suddenly the support LSV let rip. The stuttering percussion of its grenade launcher filled the night air, round after round thundering into the advancing line. The Iraqis broke, some cut down in surprise whilst others rushed to either side of the street for cover. A volley of shots from different positions poured in on top of the explosions. Avery and Corrigan added to the sheer weight of fire power.

Then it stopped. The smoke cleared a little and it was possible to see that the armoured car was unscathed; the grenades had caused only superficial damage.

It must have been clear to the commander that his enemy had given it their best shot – and it wasn't enough. With a crunch of shifting gears, the vehicle inched forward again. Cautious, like a prehistoric beast sniffing the air for signs of danger.

Avery turned to Buckley who was crouched nearby. The American read the unasked question and shook his head sadly. No more anti-tank weapons. Of necessity they had been travelling light and Reid had used the only LAW 80 on the T55 earlier.

There was a crash like thunder. The heavy 75 mm round from the armoured car smashed into the shop front across the street where several Delta men were taking cover. There were cries of agony as the wall collapsed, plumes of mortar dust drifting across the street.

'I don't like the look of this,' Avery thought aloud.

Buckley overheard him, nudged him heavily in the ribs. 'It ain't all over yet, Max. Not till the fat lady sings.'

'What?'

'Listen.' The American had been waiting for the sound, had picked it up first. The steady, menacing downbeat throb of the Apache. Like a distant tom-tom, growing louder by the second. Everyone in the team heard it now, their barrage of fire petering out. The noise of guns gave way to the earth-trembling rumble rushing towards them out of the darkness.

'Christ, the telephone cables!' Reid said.

He needn't have worried. High on adrenalin the pilot of the first Apache came in low behind them, straight down the main street, its pods and weapons clusters hanging just feet from the ground, like some huge evil mosquito. The enormous rotors thrashed, almost touching the buildings on either side. Their world was obscured by a vortex of swirling dust devils.

The engine pitch changed and the massive bulk of the helicopter hovered behind the abandoned pick-up. Two Hellfire missiles erupted simultaneously from the sidepods as the laser found its mark. The streaking meteors of flame were momentarily blinding, and the follow-up explosion was spectacular as the missiles struck the armoured car. Pulsing ripples of white light radiated out of the wreckage as fuel and ammunition caused secondary detonations, the shock waves rocking the street. But even before the noise had subsided the Apache's 30 mm chain gun raked back and forth across the Iraqi positions. Buildings began to crumble onto the pavement, walls and balconies collapsed.

'You two first!' Buckley's voice shouted in Avery's ear.

Corrigan was helped to his feet and the three of them scurried through the maelstrom of the helicopter's rotors towards the bulky black shape of the Sikorsky Pave Low coming down behind.

Avery's last glimpse of the nightmarish scene before the ramp went up, was of the three LSVs scampering fast down the street to be swallowed up by the night.

They still had much work to do before the ground offensive began.

On the flight back to Saudi Arabia, Avery turned to Corrigan. 'Before we were so rudely interrupted, Lew. Where the hell *are* Maggie and Con Moylan?'

'Crete – the Greek island.'

Avery was puzzled. 'Of all places – what the hell is he planning?'

'An anthrax attack on the US base there. We went to the island under cover as orange-pickers. You get the lowlife from all over during the season and, of course, the 17 November has excellent contacts.'

'When is the attack planned?'

'You mean it hasn't happened?'

'Not to my knowledge.'

Corrigan was incredulous. 'I thought that's why my rescue was mounted. In order to stop the other attacks.'

'Others?' This didn't sound good.

'Moylan's planning to hit London and Washington about the same time, but I don't know the details. Soúda Bay in Crete was going to be first. It all depended on when a particular Greek ship put in for refuelling. It's loaded with ammunition for US forces here in Saudi and Moylan has in mind some sort of spectacular.'

Avery was stunned by the news, finding it difficult to assimilate. 'An ammunition ship would certainly do that.'

Corrigan nodded. 'It would vaporise everything within miles. And Moylan intends to video it for the Iraqis. They'll release it to CNN so Washington can't mount a cover-up. But the real purpose is the anthrax attack on the airbase. The Iraqis reckon the threat of a repeat in London and Washington will force Bush to climb down.' He paused. 'But he's planned for those, too, in case Bush doesn't. Neat, don't you think?'

'Christ,' Avery said, 'I reckon we've all underestimated that bastard.' He looked around at the rest of the team as they began to relax, laughing and joking now that their mission appeared to be over – unaware that Saddam's sword was poised over a US base in Crete, in London and Washington. They'd already seen what disregard the Iraqi leader had for the rest of the world. The oil slicks and raging fires in the Kuwaiti oilfields. He was capable of anything. Now hundreds, perhaps thousands of innocent lives could be at risk. 'And Maggie, Lew? What's happened to Maggie?'

'She was okay, Max.' His voice had a slightly hollow ring to it.

Avery picked up the nuance. 'What do you mean? She hasn't been hurt? Why's he keeping her with him?'

'To make sure you didn't rock the boat.'

'But Moylan knows about us both now, Lew. That must mean she's become a liability to him.'

The American didn't know how to put it. Quietly he said: 'Somehow I don't think so, Max.'

# Twenty-Three

Costos Mellas had never killed a man before.

But he had come close to it many years earlier. In 1975, as a rebellious technical student, he had allowed himself to be sucked into an embryonic terrorist organisation which was to become notorious in Greece as the 17 November.

He had played a small part in the reconnaissance for the assassination of the American CIA station chief in Athens.

Afterwards he was shocked at what had occurred. He had known that some sort of protest attack against property was planned, but had not guessed that the organisation would stoop to cold-blooded murder. Hurriedly he had abandoned his education and sought an escape from both his recent past and his conscience by running away to sea.

As the years rolled by, the event in 1975 had become a dimly remembered nightmare; something, he convinced himself, that had never really happened, despite the unwelcome reminders in the press that 17 November was still alive and active. Now approaching early middle age, he had a wife and two children and a good job as a chief engineer aboard a Greek merchantman.

He had certainly not anticipated the untimely arrival of a stranger at his family's apartment in Piraeus, nor the man's thinly disguised threat to reveal his secret history to the Anti-Terrorist Police who were so hungry for a conviction.

The price for his freedom, and for the safety of his wife and children, was made clear. He was to use his position in the shipping company to ensure that he was posted to one of the ships being hired by America for the munitions supply run to Saudi Arabia. It was made to sound simple, as indeed for him as a long-serving senior employee, it was. Only there was one major snag.

If he received the coded signal, he was to prepare himself for the day when the ship the *Corinthian Trader* put in to Soúda Bay on its scheduled refuelling stop. There he was to injure a fellow crewman on board ship so severely that hospitalisation would be required. It should look like an accident and, the stranger added, with a mind to Mellas's nationalistic sensibilities, it would be best if the victim were not a Greek.

Now Mellas sat in his locked cabin, the dreaded signal held in his trembling hands.

It read: *Regret to inform you that your great aunt has died. Her funeral will be at 1200 hours on Friday, 8th February. Signed: Your loving wife.*

The first officer had handed it to him only an hour before, unaware that it told Mellas the time at which he was to commit the terrible act. It did not tell him how.

He took a bottle of Metaxas from his locker and swallowed two mouthfuls. It rasped in his throat and brought tears to his eyes. Tears of shame and self-pity, and tears of fear.

Forty-eight hours to go. In just two days' time, *Corinthian Trader* would be moored alongside the refuelling jetty at Soúda. Just a skeleton crew would be aboard the ship packed tight with artillery shells and missiles destined to kill Iraqi troops in the desert.

The man was in his late twenties, darkly good-looking, despite the day's stubble on his chin.

Although his leather blouson and blue denims were clean, he did not look particularly out of place amongst the dirty and tired orange-pickers who gathered in the Café Neon at the end of another gruelling day in the groves. He got on well with people; his manner was engaging because he actually listened to what they had to say.

'I quite fancy that one,' he said to the local teenager who sat at his table.

The youth followed the direction of the stranger's stare through the fug of cigarette smoke to the far side of the room where two girls sat. Both had dark hair, but one was fresh-faced with a rounded and youthful figure. The other was thinner, her face pale and wan, eyes dark with fatigue. Neither appeared very talkative; they just sat and watched boredly, drinking coffee and chain-smoking.

'You don't mean that old bag?' the youth laughed. Although it was only early evening he'd already had too much to drink.

'I *mean* the younger one. I'm not into grannies.'

'Forget it. She's with an American. A big, mean-looking bastard.' He added: 'Although he's not been around for a week or more.'

'But she is Greek?'

'Sure. There's a group of them got apartments on the shore. Mostly Irish, I think.'

'What are they doing here?'

'Same as everyone's doing here. Orange-picking for my father and other farmers in the district.' He looked again at the stranger. 'Is that why you're here? To work?'

The man gave one of his charming and dismissive smiles. 'No, just some business. Looking for some property to buy.'

He excused himself and left the café. Outside, the uneven pavement was wet but the damp night air was pleasantly mild. Spring wouldn't be long now.

Across the street he found the news kiosk and asked to use the public telephone. He turned his back on the woman as he dialled the Athens number and waited while it rang in the twelfth-floor office of Captain Legakis of the Anti-Terrorist Police.

'Hallo, Nico. I think I've found the girl. She's with a gang of them at a small town called Platanius.' As he listened, his eyes tracked across the street to the café. 'Don't worry, I won't let her out of my sight.'

When the helicopter touched down at the 115th Hellenic Air Force base, the local police chief was there to meet

Nico Legakis and the three other plain-clothes detectives of the Anti-Terrorist Police.

'Your man has put me in the picture,' the local chief said with a nod of acknowledgement to the young detective in the leather blouson and jeans. 'But are you sure it's the 17 November people?'

He could scarcely keep the squeak of excitement from his voice; there had just been four bomb and rocket attacks by the group on mainland Greece in support of Saddam Hussein, and everyone was talking about it.

Legakis's detective showed his boss the photograph he had taken with a zoom lens. 'Is that her?'

It pained the captain to say it. 'There's no doubt.' It opened up the wounds just to see her face again. 'What's the situation?'

'She's with the orange-pickers. Living-in with an American who hasn't been seen for a few days. There's a group of them staying at holiday apartments by the beach. Another couple – Irish – and two other Irishmen.' He gave an apologetic half-smile. 'Forgive me, Captain, but it doesn't seem like a 17 November setup.'

Legakis had to agree. Perhaps she was just making herself scarce until the trail of the murdered policeman in Athens went cold. Perhaps this Irishman was just a casual lover. He said: 'Listen, don't go soft on me. I'm certain this woman was involved in the murder of our fellow officer, so don't be complacent. Pull them all in, and we can sort it out from there. But go easy, I don't want to have to explain a lot of innocent dead foreigners back at headquarters.'

'How can I co-operate?' the local police chief asked.

'Your men can seal off the town at both ends on the coast road. Take two of my men in with you — they can approach the apartment from the front. I'll land by helicopter on the beach at the same time and close the net. But for God's sake, if there's any shooting to be done, leave it to my men.'

It was an hour later when Con Moylan returned from Hania after a secret meeting with Michalis who was in contact with Giorgós and the *Estikhbarat*.

The day had started well. Everything was set. *Corinthian Trader* was on schedule to dock that night and O'Hare and Sullivan had successfully completed the test firings of the mortar.

But the news from Michalis had come as a nasty shock and he was in a sour mood when he arrived back at the apartment to find the two Irishmen waiting for the women to finish cooking the evening meal. The place stank of fish and olive oil, adding to his irritation.

'Have you noticed anyone hanging around?' he demanded.

O'Hare and Sullivan looked at each other and shook their heads. 'No, Con, why?'

He peered out of the curtains. 'It's just there's a lot of police activity up in the town. And I saw several cop cars on the way back from Hania.'

'A roadblock?'

Moylan shook his head. 'No, not as such. More a noticeable presence.'

'No one knows we're here,' Sullivan said. 'It's not possible.'

'Everything's possible, you should know that,' he replied testily. 'Especially after what I heard tonight from Michalis.'

Sophie left the cooking ring. 'What was that?'

The Irishman grimaced. 'That our friend Max Avery and Gerry Fox didn't quite manage to meet with the Iraqis in Amman. Someone intervened – the CIA or British Intelligence – or even Mossad for all I know.'

O'Hare looked perplexed. 'But that was – what – ten days ago? And they only just told you?'

'It's not that easy, Tip. Communications between Iraq and the outside world are very restricted. The first thing they knew was when their team didn't return from Amman. They waited – still nothing. So they sent an agent to investigate. But he couldn't find out anything for sure. Just local rumours that a lot of bodies were taken away by the Jordanian police and their people haven't been heard of since.'

Maggie was aghast. 'What's happened to Max?'

He turned on her. 'Still carrying a candle for your Brit spy, little mouse? Well, I don't know and I don't care, but if Gerry Fox was killed I just hope to hell he didn't get a chance to tell them anything.'

'Did Fox know about this operation?' Sullivan asked.

'Of course not,' Moylan snapped. 'He just received my orders and carried them out. But he might have known *something* that the intelligence people could work on. Put two and two together.'

'You're getting paranoid . . . ' O'Hare began.

'And my paranoia saved you all in the past,' Moylan retorted. 'Remember that.'

Sophie had gone to the window. 'There is a car parked in the lane, behind the bamboo thicket. I cannot be sure, but it may be police.' The air in the room seemed to freeze. 'There are two men walking here. They are not in uniform.'

Moylan turned to her. 'See what they want. It's probably nothing to do with us, just illegal workers or something. You can fob them off.'

'I do not understand.'

'Tell them the rest of us have gone to town and won't be back until late. The rest of you get into the bathroom. We'll get out through the window.'

Sophie was uncertain. She didn't want to be left behind, but then she knew she had a duty to perform. A duty to the downtrodden peasants of Greece whose cause she fought. A duty to destroy the Americans' lackeys who governed in Athens. And the filthy bourgeoisie like her own parents . . . A duty to die if necessary for what she believed in, as Giorgós had so patiently explained on the night he had taken her to his bed. She had always known that it might come to this.

As Moylan ushered Maggie into the bathroom, Sophie became aware that O'Hare and Sullivan had taken out their Vzor pistols, just in case. She reached for her shoulder bag on the bed and slipped the strap over her head, fumbling with the leather flap.

Outside she heard the shuffle of feet on gravel. Still, when the loud knock came it made her jump. The fingers of her right hand closed over the handle of the weapon in her bag as her left reached for the safety chain by the lock. She was aware of the bathroom door closing, followed by the creaking of the window that opened onto the rear court-yard.

She inched open the door. Two men stood there. Mid-twenties, in studied macho pose, wearing sports jackets, jeans and trainers. She could smell them a mile off.

'Yes?' The safety chain went taut, only her eye visible in the gap.

One of them smiled with the vanity of someone who thought he should be in the movies. 'Sorry to disturb you.'

'It's late,' she said quickly. 'And dark.'

'We're police. Making general inquiries.' His voice was easy, coaxing. 'Couldn't you open the door a little?'

'No – come back in the morning.' As she went to close it, the second detective's foot jammed in the gap.

This one was obviously edgy. 'Miss Sophie Papavas?'

Although she had been half expecting it, the sudden use of her name jolted her like an electric shock. It was a spon-taneous reaction. She slammed the door shut, hard, throwing her full weight behind her shoulder. The second detective cried out as she smashed the door again and again until he finally managed to extricate his shattered foot.

Panic overtook her. She didn't wait to throw the bolts, just turned and ran towards the bathroom. Even as she threw open the door she heard the cracking of old timber as the detectives started to break their way in. The volume of the noise suggested they were using a club hammer.

The bathroom was empty, the window thrown wide. In the dim light of the courtyard she could only see Sullivan. He was agitated, anxious to be going. 'Sophie, quick! Get to the boat on the beach!'

In her haste she'd forgotten that Moylan had rented the small speedboat, for just such a contingency as this. As she began to climb, her movement restricted by the tight fit of her denims, she heard the front door collapse.

Too late. She had no time. Turning round, she pulled out the Vzor and threw her bag aside. Then she stepped back into the room.

One stood by the door in classic covering pose, gun held in a double-handed grip, the barrel pointing slightly up. The second detective was racing towards her, pulling up abruptly as she stepped out in front of him.

The blast from the round threw him back into the arms of his colleague. A wild shot sang over her head as she stood rock-steady, suddenly, inexplicably, without fear. Again she squeezed the trigger. The face of the second detective disintegrated before her eyes, exploding in a spume of blood and brain. The bodies of the two men slumped in an untidy pile to block the doorway through which she could see uniformed police approaching.

Feeling strangely calm, she locked the bathroom door and climbed out of the window. The night air was chill but she was flushed with adrenalin, aware now of the noise of a helicopter somewhere in the darkness. She began to run down the concrete crazy-paving path that led through the mimosa trees to the beach.

Abruptly the air was punctured by shouts of alarm and whistle blasts coming from behind her, those noises rapidly swamped by the growing clatter of the helicopter engine. The sound was menacing and she spun in her tracks to pinpoint its position. Pausing, gulping in air, she glimpsed the airborne flashing strobe behind the beachside buildings. As it rose to a crescendo it seemed to fill her head, deafening, maddening.

Along the shoreline all she could see was the ribbon of white surf breaking in the blackness of the night. Then she heard Moylan calling and the urgent whine of an outboard engine.

She began to run again, sinking into the soft sand, muscles screaming as she tried to pluck each foot free. Forcing herself on, her lungs heaving, the din of the helicopter enveloping her completely.

At last she stumbled to her knees, the water lapping around her in probing eddies of froth. The spotlight from the helicopter had her now centre stage like the final tragic act of an opera, her elongated shadow cast over the footprints and keel mark where the speedboat had been dragged into the boiling surf.

From the glass dome of the helicopter cockpit, the pilot and the three Greek detectives were the only witnesses of what was to be a one and only performance. Looking down, Niko Legakis could sense the girl's desperate isolation as she squinted against the spray in the forlorn hope that the vanished speedboat would return for her.

The pilot shifted the pitch lever and the helicopter began

its descent, the searchlight blanching Sophie Papavas's skin tones when she turned towards the blast that tore at her clothes and hair.

She raised the pistol, slow and steady.

Legakis felt she was aiming for him personally. He experienced a mildly burning sensation in his forehead where his eyebrows met, imagined the impact of the bullet. It was with a strange mixture of anger at her betrayal and mild regret that he lifted his own weapon through the open side vent.

The shot was unheard above the engine as though an unseen sword had cut her down. She fell limply into the sand, the advancing tide breaking around her outstretched body.

Without taking his eyes from her, he said to the pilot: 'We must get after the speedboat.'

The man tapped his fuel gauge. 'I am sorry, Captain.'

They hit the deserted beach at full revs, the momentum allowing the speedboat to leap clear of the surf before it ground to a halt on the shingle.

Moylan killed the outboard and in the tense silence that followed the only sound was the barrage of breakers detonating along the shoreline. No voices, no helicopter.

But there was no time to lose. He led the way through the eerily deserted holiday complexes to the coast road. Sullivan broke into a Fiat parked outside a bar and Moylan took the wheel, driving towards Hania until he found a roadside news kiosk. There he put through a call to Michalis on the payphone.

The Greek was relieved to hear from him. 'What has

happened? Giorgós telephoned me earlier – he learns through a well-placed insider that the police come for Sophie. They flew over from the mainland today. I tried to warn you, but the police had sealed off the road.'

Moylan said: 'We escaped by boat but Sophie was shot. I think she's dead.'

There was a brief, stunned silence. Then: 'That is how she would have wanted it. At least she cannot be made to talk. The Athens police wanted her for the murder of that policeman. I do not think they knew about you.'

'Well, they do now, even if they don't know *why* we're here.'

'So what are you going to do?'

'Carry on, of course. *Corinthian Trader* docks some time tonight and we can still strike tomorrow as planned. But I will need your help.'

'The 17 November does not let its fellow revolutionaries down.'

'I'm pleased to hear it. Come to the barn tonight, just as soon as you can. Oh, and get that beard shaved off before you leave.'

It was agreed. Moylan hung up, returned to the others in the car, and headed out of town. Perhaps it was his imagination but there appeared to be a lot of uniformed policemen on the streets.

He took the inland road for several miles before turning off onto a farm track that meandered through orange and olive groves and a series of high passes that led deep into the mountains.

They stopped well short of the barn, first checking for any sign of a police stakeout; the area was deserted.

It had just turned midnight when the headlights of Michalis's car appeared on the track.

Moylan wasted no time in explaining his revised plans.

'With Sophie dead, we need someone else who can speak Greek. You can pose as a doctor to help us get aboard the ship. Maggie will replace Sophie as the nurse.'

'What!' Maggie protested.

He ignored her. 'The Iraqis have arranged for a Valletta-registered yacht owned by a Libyan diplomat to be waiting in Iráklion. We go there after the attack – from there each of us can go to any port in the Med we choose.' He turned to O'Hare and Sullivan. 'It's just a matter of hours to go before the Americans lose their war with Iraq. Take the mortar truck now and get into position well before daybreak.'

It took only a few minutes to remove the tarpaulin from the vehicle. From the outside it looked like one of the numerous battered fruit trucks that plied the roads of Crete in the harvest season. The high canvas sides hid the roll-back aperture in the roof section that would allow the six eight-inch mortars an unhindered exit as they arced into the unsuspecting US base.

Moylan supervised the loading of the tea chest containing the bombs. 'Remember to keep your radio open at all times. If all goes to plan you can expect the attack signal – Blackfire – between twelve noon and one. Whitefly is for an abort – which I do not anticipate. In either case make your way back to Hania and rent one of the letting rooms there for forty-eight hours. Then come on to Iráklion to board the yacht with the rest of us.'

They watched O'Hare start the engine. It coughed a few times in the damp air, finally fired, then trundled slowly away into the darkness.

It was eerily quiet.

Moylan turned to Michalis. 'There are some blankets in the barn; you can sleep in your car. But I'll have the keys.'

The Greek tossed them across. 'You do not trust me?'

Moylan half-smiled. 'As much as I trust anyone.'

'Then you must be a very unhappy man,' Michalis observed darkly. 'But then it is you who have to live with yourself.'

Maggie followed Moylan back to the barn and waited in thoughtful silence as he laid out blankets on a heap of clean dry straw. 'Why are you waiting for two days before we leave? Surely that isn't long enough for the police to lose interest? Not after a major bombing.'

He looked up from the bedding. 'What's this? Starting to think like a terrorist again?' he asked sarcastically. 'I was beginning to give up on you.'

She shook her head. 'I just want to be out of this as soon as possible – to get back to the baby.'

'And Max?'

'I don't know.' Her voice was hoarse, unsure. She'd done a lot of thinking since she had learned the truth about him. But those thoughts just led her round in circles. Still she found it hard to believe that their lives together and Max's love for her had been totally false.

'Anyway, it won't be two days before we leave. That's just what I told O'Hare and Sullivan.'

She lowered herself onto the blankets, almost too exhausted to comprehend what Moylan was saying. 'What do you mean?'

'Those two aren't going anywhere.'

Alarm flickered in her eyes. 'You're not going to . . . ?'

He shook his head as he sat beside her. 'No, sweet mouse, they'll be killing *themselves* during the mortar attack.'

'You mean blow themselves up? Some sort of booby trap?'

'It's not just high explosive. Those mortars contain anthrax spores and some other stuff. Within two days they'll be dead or dying.'

She stared at him and he found her expression of abject horror amusing. 'I don't believe you. Nobody would do such a thing. Even you!' Suddenly she thought of all the news items she had heard on the World Service – the ongoing worry that Saddam Hussein had access to chemical and biological weapons and might actually use them. 'Oh, God, Con, no.'

'Oh, God, Con, no,' he mimicked. 'Oh yes, little mouse. With the funds from the Iraqis I'll be able to revitalise the fight against the Brits back home. Sweep aside those idiots on the Army Council and do things the way they always should have been done.'

She knew now that he meant exactly what he said. His

words came back to her over the years. Sitting in a little back-street café in Derry, his hand clasping hers as she stared into those hypnotic eyes. In awe of the glamour of the freedom fighter. As he told her what he would do if he were running the organisation. Nothing had changed, except that now he would have the power and money to do it.

She could see it clearly, looking back. While she had grown up, he had not. Even when she had first known him he was thirty years old, a maverick even then.

She opened her mouth to speak, then stopped herself. If Moylan didn't trust her completely, he would be capable of anything. Then she would never see Josh again, let alone Max.

Without any hint of disapproval in her voice, she said: 'But why do you want to get rid of O'Hare and Sullivan?'

He looked at her incredulously. 'Because there can't be any independent witnesses; you must realise that. The British Government might know that I was responsible for this – and similar attacks in London and Washington – but not *our* people. They can't be expected to understand. People live in fear of chemical, biological or bacterial weapons. The unseen. No glamour, you see. Bombs and bullets are what the young boyos like. Something to sing about in the bars.'

She said softly: 'You mean no one's going to follow a leader who uses germ warfare?'

He looked at her. And for the first time since she had known him again there was a look of genuine affection in his eyes. 'You understand, little mouse. I knew you would. Power, that's what it's all about. That's what it's always been about. After this, I am going to lead the struggle. From the front. And this time we will have the success we have always deserved.'

She nodded towards the barn doors. 'And Michalis, what about him?'

'When he's served his purpose, I'll deal with him in my own way. It's not something for you to worry about.'

He was very close now. 'I suppose that leaves just me.' There was a slight tremor in her voice.

'I don't think you have anything to fear, sweet mouse.' He stared up at the glow of the hurricane lamp. 'You know, you're the only woman who's ever understood me. Who understood herself, who knew how to submit. There's been no one since you, not really. A girlfriend here and there, but it's never worked like it worked with you. And these last few weeks – well, I can see you've come to recognise that, too. You've nothing to go back for.'

'There's Josh.'

'Max's child.' He almost spat the words.

'He's just a baby, an innocent. It's not his fault. I can't just leave him.'

'Of course not.' Moylan forced a smile. 'As you say, an innocent. He did not choose his father. No, I'll look after both of you.' He looked directly at her. 'You know, when I first saw you and Max together I was jealous. Me, can you believe that? Jealous of that Brit scum! It was almost a relief to discover he'd been planted.'

'But you said it was his idea for the Provies to help the Iraqis. I still don't understand that.'

'Neither did I. But that American bastard has been talking in Baghdad. According to Giorgós, they thought the Provies were the best people to infiltrate the Iraqis and discover what terrorist action was being planned.'

'How?'

'By offering to help do the job – then Max and Lew would have pulled the plug at the last minute. Only I've rather spoiled their plans.'

*A new life.*

Suddenly Max's words rang like a bell in her head. She'd almost forgotten. All that talk about selling the business and moving to Australia. His evasion and excuses so that he could continue for a few months more. Now she saw why. Until his assignment was finished. Until Moylan and his schemes were finished. Would he have lied to her if he hadn't meant it? If she was just being used, then why should he bother? All he had to do was vanish. She would just wake up one morning and find the bed empty.

No, Max had used her and that hurt. But then he had used her to get to the likes of Con Moylan. Perhaps, she realised now as she thought of the deadly anthrax mortars, that wasn't such a bad thing. It could be forgiven. Almost.

She felt Moylan's hand on her arm.

'No, Con, not just now. I'm shattered.'

'I need you.'

'Tomorrow, when it's over. We'll have all the time in the world.'

'Yes?'

She knew what he would like to hear. 'And you can do what you want with me. Anything. Like you always did. It'll be like the old days.'

He found the thrill of her words rush to his loins. The anticipation was almost too much. But she was right; there was a lot to do tomorrow. Ahead was a new and dangerous life. 'Okay. Sleep, little mouse.'

But Maggie O'Malley scarcely slept that night.

Neither did Tip O'Hare and Sullivan. They had driven the mortar truck and the escape car around the deserted streets of Hania and up onto the mountainous knuckle of land that formed the north coast of Soúda Bay. Winding tightly up the narrow road, through the dozy village of Mouzouras, disturbed only by the yapping of some dog with insomnia. Past the roadside olive groves, then diverting up the track.

Sullivan parked the car, hidden from passers-by, then went ahead on foot. O'Hare switched off the truck lights and drove on, following the faint red beam of Sullivan's torch, inching up the precipitous track until the derelict building was reached.

The vehicle was edged into position, the direction bearings and trajectory double-checked. When all was set, the two men settled down with their blankets and binoculars.

A thousand metres away, across the road below them, the compound lights burned fiercely as the steady stream of transport aircraft landed or took off throughout the night.

Working frantically in shifts around the clock, the

American service personnel of Naval Support Activity were blissfully unaware of the invisible terror that lay in wait for the approaching dawn.

The C-5 Galaxy transports of the United States 1st Special Operations Wing touched down at the Royal Air Force base of Akrotiri on the Mediterranean island of Cyprus.

They carried aboard the full complement of the combined Stalking Horse backup team and the array of equipment necessary to cover virtually any eventuality. During the flight Corrigan had discussed at length with Avery, Hunt and Jim Buckley what action would most likely be needed in Crete. Cross-communications between the aircraft broke all the security rules, but it enabled much of the stored kit to be sorted in mid-flight and prepared for possible use.

As Avery and Corrigan walked off the ramp into the rising of the dawn sun, the first thing they saw was the RAF Tristar that had arrived only minutes earlier from London.

Willard Franks and Clarissa Royston-Jones waited patiently for them on the apron.

The CIA man stepped forward first. 'Hi, Lew, how you doin'? I want you to know we're all mighty proud of you. The Agency, the President . . . everyone.'

Corrigan couldn't suppress the moisture gathering in his eyes. There had been times during his life when he had never wanted to see spooks like Franks again. In Baghdad he had faced that very prospect; now he could have kissed the man in gratitude.

'I'm not so bad, Willard. I appreciate what you've done for me.'

Franks indicated the bandaged hand. 'Just sorry we couldn't have got our act together sooner. Now the RAF have kindly laid on a full English breakfast in the mess. Let's go eat while you fill us in on the details.'

As Franks led Corrigan away, Avery came face to face with Clarissa. 'So this is where you decided to have your holiday?' she asked reproachfully as he fell into step beside her.

'Sorry, it was just something I had to do.'

'That's very John Wayne. Still you look good on it.' She meant it. He looked fresher and healthier than he had in months. She guessed it was because he was making the running now, fighting back. She felt more than a little proud of him.

Over a meal of bacon and eggs Corrigan again went over everything he knew about Moylan's plans. When he'd finished, Willard Franks said: 'You asked us about a Greek ship called *Corinthian Trader*. CINCUSNEUR informs us she docked in Soúda Bay last night and there's nothing out of the ordinary to report.'

'Well that's the baby he intends to blow.'

'How? A mine?'

Corrigan shrugged. 'Maybe, but Moylan is no swimmer. The explosives I saw were Semtex. Maybe he's got someone aboard the ship.'

'That's got to be possible, given the 17 November connection.'

Avery had a sudden thought. 'When's the ship due to sail?'

'Midnight tonight.'

'Then it's a tight time-frame. The explosives could already be aboard.'

Corrigan added: 'Tighter than you think, Max. They plan to video the sinking for CNN. That means daylight.'

'Goddammit!' Franks thundered. He had an intelligence man's pathological hatred of the media. 'We gotta move and fast. We can live with that ship goin' up, but not the anthrax attack.'

'I know the location of the mortars for that,' Corrigan said. 'A disused farm building overlooking the airstrip.'

'Thank the Lord for small mercies,' Franks sighed. 'Let's just hope we're in time. If that goes off, then Saddam has won the war and gets to keep Kuwait.'

Corrigan frowned. 'So Bush really would back down?'

'He'd have to, Lew. A demonstration of Saddam's will and ability to use bacterial weapons and the promise to use more . . . He'd show us up to be helpless to defend ourselves. We couldn't let the public know that. And once our allies knew their citizens faced the same threat, you can imagine how long they'd hold together. NBC on the battlefield is one thing, but in our own backyard . . . Oil, nothing – Kuwait might as well be growing carrots. We'd have to back off.'

Corrigan turned to Clarissa. 'Did those names mean anything to you guys? The cell Moylan put together for London and Washington?'

She shook her head. 'We put them through the computer. Only Sullivan showed up for a minor criminal offence many years ago. None of them has any terrorist record. We're running it across Irish Special Branch to see what they come up with.' She turned to Max. 'But at least we have a clue to what methods he intends to use.

'You probably won't have heard, but that mortar attack on Downing Street was mounted by the IRA yesterday. Thankfully no one was hurt. What with snowstorms in London and the media's obsession with the Gulf, it made little impression.

'But the point is, that Thames tug listed on Fox's inventory – well, it wasn't used after the Number Ten bomb. Willard's expert said it would be an ideal way of distributing anthrax around London.'

'And Washington?' Corrigan asked.

'Botulinus toxin is ideal to be used in food or drink,' Franks answered. 'So if Saddam wants to make a political impact, our man Mace reckons he has to go for the centre of government. Capitol Hill itself. I can tell you the President will be gettin' someone else to taste his meals until we nail these bastards.'

'Small clues, I'm afraid,' Clarissa agreed. 'So if we cross swords with Con Moylan on Crete then I hope we can take him alive.'

Brian Hunt and Jim Buckley had been listening intently from the opposite side of the table but, with a soldier's sense of priority, had first finished their food.

Now Buckley said to Franks: 'We've a plan of action for

you now, sir. We worked it out with Lew on the flight from Riyadh. The team is fully briefed and ready to go. If we receive your approval, we can take off just as soon as the aircraft finish refuelling.'

Franks smiled grimly. 'That's what I want to hear, Jim. I've a feeling the sands of time are running out.'

# Twenty-Four

At precisely fifteen minutes to noon, a call was received at the Hellenic Naval Hospital in Soúda.

Speaking in Greek, the member of the public informed the duty officer that one of their base personnel had been involved in a serious road accident at the other end of town. The caller gave the address; within a few minutes the paramedic ambulance was on its way.

When the medics arrived they found a car positioned at an angle across the narrow street and a tall Greek waiting for them. They were annoyed to hear that the victim had been moved, possibly exacerbating any injuries. As they followed the man up the outside steps to an adjacent apartment, neither medic noticed the To Let sign that had been hastily tossed onto the dusty parking space alongside.

A small crowd had gathered around the ambulance when the white-coated medics emerged fifteen minutes later.

The townspeople were too busy trying to see if they recognised the woman on the stretcher to notice that the tunics worn by the medics were made to fit much shorter men.

As the ambulance, its siren wailing, sped out of Soúda town and took the north road onto the peninsula, Lieutenant Commander Valerie Bargellini was jogging along the outer perimeter road of the Naval Support Activity airbase.

She was thirty-two, slim and darkly attractive despite the prominent nose that hinted at her Italian ancestry.

For once the effort of her five-mile run was beginning to tell. As the momentum of the build-up to the impending Desert Storm land battle grew remorselessly, she could find little time to maintain her fitness regime. Day and night aircraft were arriving en route for destinations around Arabia; ships were calling daily at the bay facility to refuel and replenish, to drop stores or take them on, transfer urgent cargoes for forwarding by air or vice versa. In the logistics nightmare of what was to become the biggest armoured assault since World War Two, it seemed that nothing was where it should be.

She stopped now, heaving for breath in her sweat-stained green military vest and civilian jogging pants, and looked up at the rugged hillside as a bird took sudden flight from a derelict farm building.

That's what I'd like to be right now, she thought. A bird. Free and with not a care in the world. No more orders, no more bullshit, no more reams of paper to plough through in a mounting in-tray.

Watery sun reflected on something in the wrecked building, momentarily dazzling her. A peeping Tom with binoculars? It was her first reaction and she chided herself.

Who the hell was going to get his rocks off by watching a sweaty jill tar who wouldn't admit to advancing middle age? No doubt it was an empty bottle of ouzo discarded by some drunken peasant.

She was then distracted by a cloud of dust advancing along the road from the base entrance. Someone was in one hell of a hurry, she thought, and waited, idly checking the tortoiseshell slides that kept her long hair neatly pinned in place.

The driver of the jeep hit the brakes and the vehicle slid to a shuddering halt beside her.

In the passenger seat was the base medical officer.

'Where you off to in such a hurry, Hal?'

'There's been an accident on that Greek ship down the refuel jetty, ma'am. Our liaison officer – Lieutenant Moukaris. In real bad shape.'

She was stunned. Richard Moukaris, the attractive young American, had made a pass at her the night before in the chow hall, and she couldn't bring herself to shoot him down. 'Can you handle it?'

'I dunno till I see, ma'am. If I can't, I'll call up the Greek hospital.'

Valerie Bargellini nodded. 'You do that. And keep me posted.'

'Yes, ma'am.'

The driver hit the accelerator and the incident took her mind from the pain of her aching limbs and struggling lungs, allowing her to reach the camp gate in something resembling her old speed and style. The black Marine guard and his Greek counterpart appeared to be watching her approach with indiscreet interest. But as she neared she saw the look of concern on the men's faces.

She was breathless. 'Okay, soldier, what is it?'

The marine said: 'Your office has got Cyprus on the secure-line, ma'am. Top priority and they's holding. Can I give you a lift?'

Shit, she thought, she should never have left the camp. Not with the CO away at NSA Sigonella. As Executive Officer she was now nominally in charge.

But she hid her anxiety. 'Let's go, soldier.'

He took a civilian car from the guardhouse lot and completed the short journey to the administration block at high speed. She leapt from the car and ran inside.

Her female admin assistant was holding the telephone at her desk. 'It's the CIA, ma'am. Calling from RAF Akrotiri in Cyprus. Some guy called Willard Franks.'

She took the receiver. 'Bargellini speaking.'

'At last!' the voice said in exasperation. 'Listen, Commander, I'm speaking to you direct to save time. I'll get confirmation to you through COMFAIRMED soonest. Meanwhile I want you to put yourself on top-level alert for an imminent terrorist attack.'

'Terrorist, sir? Here?'

'Yes, dammit, woman, there at Soúda Bay!' He could hardly keep the sexist tone from his voice. 'But, listen, you've got to be careful how you handle this. We understand the attack is likely to take the form of high explosive and bacterial agents.'

Jesus Christ, she wasn't hearing this. 'Sir?' Numbly.

'We've got some Delta people coming to help sort this out, but meanwhile it's on a hair-trigger. There's a mortar aimed at your base from the overlooking hill, so any sign that tells the terrorists you know they're there and – well, I hardly have to spell out what the consequences could be. So I want you to do several things. First get everyone inside your strongest building and have them don their NBC gear. Make sure they've all got their anti-anthrax jabs ready. But keep everyone outa sight.'

'Sir.' This was bizarre.

'If nothin's happened by that time, I want you to start an evacuation. Real discreet. Do you have any aircraft on the strip?'

'Sure, sir. Two C130s and a C141.'

'Are they fuelled and ready to go?'

'Just the C130s, sir.'

'Do you have hangars there?'

'Just one hangar, sir.'

'Right, then use it. Get the C130s in and load up with personnel and any top-secret documents you can take. Make sure nothing can be seen from the hillside. Then get them damn birds airborne.'

'Where to, sir?'

'Dammit, woman, who cares? Let the Air Force sort that out.'

'Sir.' Indignant.

'Then there's the refuel facility on the bay. There's three ammo ships in, yes?'

'Yessir. A Greek vessel, *Corinthian Trader*, and two Lyness-class combat stores ships . . . '

'Yes, yes. Get that damn Greek ship out to sea pronto. There is likely an explosive device aboard.'

'Sweet Lord,' she murmured with the sudden vision of an instant apocalypse.

'And keep her separate from the other two – otherwise they'll feel the blast in Baghdad.'

Suddenly she remembered the injured US Navy liaison officer. 'Sir, there's a problem. We've just had a serious accident aboard the Greek ship, sir. I'm waiting to get the injured party evacuated.'

There was an irritable gasp at the other end of the line. 'Very well, but don't pussyfoot about, Commander. Keep this line open and keep me updated.'

Valerie Bargellini puffed out her cheeks at the breathless pace of it all. 'Yessir!'


Athens had been alerted to a supposed intelligence report warning of an impending terrorist attack on Crete by agents of Saddam Hussein. No details were given, but permission was swiftly given for the United States to use all necessary means to defend its base.

The C-5 Galaxy of the 1st Special Operations Wing landed at Iráklion, some miles from Soúda Bay as all other alternatives were downwind of the anticipated anthrax attack. Because their own helicopters would take a further six hours to be flown out of Saudi Arabia, a request for assistance was made to the Hellenic Armed Forces. It was granted immediately.

Two Bell AB 212 helicopters, flown off two Hellenic Navy frigates, awaited their arrival. Designed for anti-submarine warfare, the machines weren't ideal as troop transports, but at least the two eight-man teams were just able to squeeze aboard amongst the array of sonar tracking equipment.

Gretchen, their recruit from Intelligence Support Activity, came into her own, explaining to the pilots in fluent Greek exactly what was required.

The first helicopter took off for the peninsula above Soúda Bay, coming in north of the hillside where Corrigan said the mortar had been concealed. Because the engine noise would be carried on the prevailing north-westerly wind, the helicopter dropped its passengers two miles beyond the hill ridge. The pilot and copilot exchanged uneasy glances as they watched the Delta group pull on respirator masks before moving off on foot.

Meanwhile the team in the second helicopter flew direct to the Hellenic Navy base which was opposite the US Navy refuelling facility on the south side of the bay.

A rubber Gemini dinghy with outboard was waiting for Luther Dicks and Brad Carver who had been travelling in wet suits and carrying their scuba equipment. Their task was to dive beneath *Corinthian Trader* and check that no limpet mines had been placed. If one had and it detonated before they could reach it, then almost certain death awaited them. Armed with HK MP5s and Phrobis fighting knives, they would be guided to their target by the latest state-of-the-art headup displays in the glass of their diving masks.

Corrigan had refused point-blank to submit himself to the tender mercies of the RAF medical officer in Cyprus, pointing out that as a 'non-official cover' operator he was technically a civilian and outside the military's jurisdiction. Nevertheless it had seemed churlish to Willard Franks to prohibit him from travelling to Crete with Max Avery.

The two of them were now transported from the Greek base by road, together with the remaining men of the team. They would stake out the ship with the intention of mounting a stealthy clearing operation. This would commence as soon as the Greek paramedics had evacuated a US Navy officer who had been seriously injured in an engine-room fall.

Dressed in workmen's overalls and carrying toolbags, they travelled by Hellenic Navy truck on a circuitous route around the bay. After passing the British War Cemetery, the vehicle began a laboured climb up onto the peninsula before eventually descending a steep zigzag road to the US Navy's refuel facility.

When the truck halted at the compound gates it was fourteen minutes past noon.

The burly US Marine guard watched on with consternation as the heavily armed team exited from the rear of the truck.

'What's the situation?' Hunt demanded.

'There ain't no situation, sir.' The accent was pure Texan. 'Jest we've been put on maximum alert for some reason and told to get all ships off the refuellin' jetties.'

Corrigan looked down the concrete road that led to the

three jetties with their loading derricks and huge fuel silos. He could see movement between two of them, a slab-sided hull of naval grey.

'That's the last of the two combat stores ships,' the Texan explained, bemused by all the activity.

'Who's on board?' Avery asked.

'Jest a skeleton crew. I gather they've been told to put down their sea anchors once they hit open water.'

'So that's the *Corinthian Trader*?' Hunt assumed.

From where they stood only the rust-streaked white bow showed from behind the silos on the jetty to the far right.

'Yessir.'

'And have any unauthorised personnel been on the base in the past twenty-four hours?' Corrigan asked.

'No, sir.' Indignant.

'Anything unusual happened?' Avery pressed.

'Sir?'

'Anything out of the ordinary?'

'Not unless you count one of our liaison officers breakin' his back.' A smile of black humour. 'That was unusual – and careless. The ambulance has just arrived. That'll be gone soon and we'll be able to get that mother out to sea too.'

A sudden thought occurred to Corrigan. 'Did you check the ID of the ambulance crew?'

The Texan's cheeks reddened. 'Er, no, sir. No need, you see, sir, because we've just called them up. Greek paramedics from the hospital across the bay.'

For a moment Corrigan's eyes met Avery's. Was it possible?

Brian Hunt, standing behind them, had begun directing the rest of the team. Four of them had started converging on the third jetty. Overshadowed by the towering hull of *Corinthian Trader*, they were manning forklifts or pretending to work the fuel-line valves. To the casual eye the men in overalls looked convincing and innocent as depot workers, but each man was armed and in direct radio contact with Hunt.

Avery said: 'I'd like to get a look at that ambulance crew, Brian. There's a possibility it could be Moylan.'

Hunt frowned. From what he knew of the situation it didn't seem likely. There had been a genuine casualty that the Irishman couldn't possibly have known about in advance. Nevertheless he'd always respected his friend's judgement and this was no time to question it, however unlikely. 'Okay, Max, you and Lew go with Big Joe. But keep out of sight and don't get yourself shot. You're not covered by insurance.'

They followed Monk, who was carrying an oddly angular Accuracy International PM sniper rifle, across to one of the enormous fuel silos and rapidly scaled the ladder to the top. From their vantage point they had an uninterrupted view of *Corinthian Trader*, a massive white monolith roped to the jetty. Two gangways ran ashore and the ambulance was parked beside one of them. Two paramedics were unloading boxes of medical equipment, a third was in earnest conversation with an American naval officer with a medical bag and another man in a seaman's sweater and watch cap.

Monk settled down behind the rim of the silo top and handed the PM to Avery. 'Take a look, Max.'

He lifted the 7.62 mm stainless-steel barrel and peered through the Schmidt und Bender telescopic sight. The powerful lenses pulled the scene in tight.

'Taking their time,' Monk observed.

'They'll want to make sure they've everything they need,' Corrigan said. 'It's a long way down to the engine room.'

The paramedics began moving up the gangway carrying equipment and a lightweight stretcher. Avery focused on the leading figure, who was about to enter the open hatchway set high in the hull side. Long black hair splayed against the crisp white material of her coat. She half turned and he glimpsed her profile for a second before she vanished into the dark interior.

His heart tripped. 'Sweet Jesus.'

'What?' Corrigan demanded.

Avery shook his head in slow disbelief. 'It's them. And that was Maggie.'

Monk scowled. 'Your missus, Max? You sure?'

Avery said nothing – just watched. But his mind was reeling in an attempt to grasp the significance of her presence.

'Must have been coerced in some way,' Monk muttered, echoing Avery's own thoughts.

At least she was alive, he consoled himself. He had half expected they'd eventually find her corpse if Moylan suspected she'd known the truth about him. Perhaps she'd realised that and had played along with the Irishman in order to stay alive.

There was just one other possibility. And he did not even want to think about that.

Now the two paramedics followed her onto the ship.

'Well?' Monk demanded.

'That's Moylan,' Avery confirmed, lowering the PM. 'I'm not sure of the other one. It's probably Michalis – if it is, he's shaved off the beard.'

Suddenly Hunt's voice crackled in his earpiece. '*Sunray to Sniper Position, Max, I heard that. How d'you want to play this? We can wait till they come out and try and pick out the bad guys clean, but that's a risk . . .*'

He left the sentence hanging. Avery knew what he meant. Out in the open, it would be textbook stuff. Two snipers to take out two targets. Simultaneously. But that assumed the snipers got a clear field-of-fire at exactly the right moment. And it didn't take into account the close proximity of both Maggie and the American medical officer. Nor the injured man whom they would have to carry away in order to preserve their cover.

It could be a cluttered target area with the added danger of lethal ricochet. And there would be an opportunity for Moylan to seize hostages.

Hunt was talking again. '*There's another thing, Max. I don't know how Moylan pulled this stunt, but it means he must have an accomplice on the inside. Probably a 17 November contact. That means one loose cannon . . . Over.*'

Avery pressed his 'send' button. 'Max to Sunray. Just do

what you think's best, Brian. I'm rusty. Over.'

'Affirmative, Max.' A pause. 'Sunray to all units. Stay in sniper positions as a fail-safe in case targets come off the ship. Aim for the two male medics only – repeat, male medics only. The rest of you make your way aboard in ones and twos. Make it look good and keep all weapons out of sight. Prepare to use flash-bangs and CS when we locate targets. Right, let's move it! Out.'

Avery began edging back from the rim of the fuel silo. Monk grabbed his arm. 'The boss doesn't mean you, Max.'

'Get stuffed, Joe, that's my wife down there.'

Hunt watched Avery and Corrigan go; there was nothing he could do to stop his friend and the American short of ordering another member of the team to shoot them. The sergeant major reasoned that he might have done the same had the situation been reversed. At least neither man was the sort to be foolhardy. In Baghdad Avery had proved he still had his cutting edge; he wasn't as out of touch as he claimed. But then some habits died hard.

There was little he could do now but watch as the two men manhandled a crate of galley stores up the gangway.

Farther down the jetty the boom crane of one of the loading derricks swung out over the ship before lowering a pallet of supplies to the deck. The men clinging precariously to the cargo net were not visible to anyone watching from the ship.

Meanwhile Brad Carver and Luther Dicks had radioed in. Having completed a negative search of the hull, they were now ordered to board. Using hand suction clamps they began their stealthy climb up the blind side of the hull.

'You guys sure got here fast,' the US Navy medical officer commented to the medics as they followed the Greek seaman called Costos Mellas down yet another corridor. 'I'd only just got here myself.'

'Someone called us,' Michalis mumbled absently.

The American recalled his brief meeting on the road with his jogging executive officer. It must have been her. Val Bargellini was one shrewd cookie; it would be typical of her to be one jump ahead.

And when they found the injured liaison officer he was glad she was.

Even from the upper gantry he could see that the man's life was hanging by a thread. He lay in a cramped space at the bottom of a steel ladder. His head was a bloody pulp and one leg was twisted under his body at an unnatural angle.

Moylan affected a Greek accent. 'You can go now. We'll see to this.'

The medical officer demurred. 'Think I'd better stick around, bud. You might need help – besides I might learn something from you guys.'

Moylan hid his irritation. 'It's a small space down there – er?'

'Hal. Call me Hal.'

A thin smile. 'Yes, Hal, there's not room for you.'

'Then I'll wait here. Don't want you falling over me.'

Shit! Moylan forced his smile again. 'Gee, Hal, you are one hell of an obstinate guy . . . '

The American's jaw dropped at hearing the mimicry of his accent by the Greek doctor and he found himself staring into the snout of Moylan's Vzor.

'Michalis!' the Irishman called. The Greek leapt at the American officer, jerking the man's arms behind his back. 'Maggie, get those freezer ties from my bag.'

Stunned, she searched for the thin strips of locking plastic. The American had been her last hope; when he met them on the jetty she had decided to try and speak to him alone, warn him and beg his help. Now that chance, too, had been denied her. As it had the previous night when she would have made a run from the barn – only Moylan had not slept.

Her thoughts turned to the man they had supposedly come to save. While Moylan and Michalis bound and gagged the hapless medical officer, she descended the steep steps. The man was barely conscious and in obvious agony. She had just opened her medical bag when Moylan joined her. 'Christ, Mellas did a thorough job on him – What are you doing?'

'Giving him some morphine.' She lifted the glass phial, filled the syringe.

'Don't try too hard. He'll be easier to handle dead than alive.'

She looked up, met his eyes. 'Bastard,' she hissed.

Michalis joined them at the bottom of the steps. 'What now?' he asked Moylan.

'I need Mellas to show me to the hold – this place is like a bloody rabbit warren and all the direction signs are in Greek.'

Maggie found the vein she was looking for. 'He's in desperate need of hospital attention,' she said.

Moylan's laugh was brittle. 'You must be joking, little mouse. We've got other priorities. You concentrate on getting him bandaged up and secured to the stretcher.' He turned to Michalis. 'You go back up to the next deck and keep a lookout. If anyone comes, persuade them to go away. Think of something. If all else fails shoot the bastard and get the body out of sight. I want to be out of here in fifteen minutes.'

The Greek nodded and began his return climb.

Moylan looked at Maggie as she began to clean up the wounds. 'Fifteen minutes,' he repeated. 'Can you manage that?'

Without looking up she said: 'I guess I'll have to.'

'Atta girl, little mouse.'

He returned up the ladder to collect the Semtex satchel charge secreted in one of the medical boxes. He found Mellas watching the bound American medical officer. He grabbed the Greek's arm and propelled him along the steel-grey corridor.

'Take me to the main hold,' he demanded.

Mellas scurried forward, unnerved by the tall stranger. They passed through two bulkheads, along corridors that led to various storerooms and crew's quarters, then up more ladders until they entered through a small hatchway in one corner of the central hold.

It reminded Moylan of a gigantic warehouse with avenues of stacked pallets denoting various calibres of artillery shell; row after row, like a miniature city of wooden tower blocks, with a grid of intersecting walkways that were wide enough for a forklift to pass.

'Wait here,' he ordered. He had no intention of letting the Greek see where he was placing the explosives.

After a few minutes' hunting he found the ideal location, a narrow gap between two massive stacks of high explosive and incendiary shells.

The haversack held eight two-and-a-half pound slabs of Semtex moulded around and joined by a length of detonating cord which would fire the slug of pentolite booster in each stick. He ran out the separate charges with four under each of four ammunition crates, linking them with additional detonating cord before fitting the instant-action initiator to the small radio receiver control device.

Finally he covered the spaghetti coils of cord with a tarpaulin sheet.

It was all set. Just one press of the button on the radio activator in his pocket and the whole lot would go – the amount of ammunition exploding would be the equivalent of a thermonuclear blast.

He rejoined Mellas and they made their way back to where Michalis was keeping watch through a scuttle which offered a clear view of the jetty.

The Greek took Moylan to one side, out of earshot of Mellas. 'Something is not right,' he warned earnestly. 'I see people on top of the fuel silos. There, on the right.'

Moylan looked through the scuttle. 'I don't see anyone.'

'Yes, there! Maybe a man with a rifle, I think.' He glanced at Moylan. 'I am sure of it.'

The man was clearly convinced and Moylan had no reason to doubt him. Yet how could anyone know what they had planned? It was impossible – unless Sophie had not been killed after all? Or had lived long enough to whisper her secrets to the police who had shot her?

'What are we going to do?' Michalis asked.

Moylan turned to Mellas. 'Is there another way off this ship?'

'Another?' He was visibly trembling; it was all too much for him, he couldn't think straight.

'Yes,' Moylan urged. 'Apart from the jetty itself? Even if we have to swim.'

'Swim?' The idea astonished him. 'There is a crew boat moored on the seaward side. Sometimes it takes the crew across the bay to Soúda town if there is no road transport.'

'Is it there now?'

'I think.' He hesitated, trying to get his brain to function properly. 'Yes, it is.'

Moylan sighed with relief. 'Listen, Mellas, there is a change of plan. I want you and that American to take the injured man out to the ambulance. You drive out through the gates and go to some secluded spot. Tie up the American and leave them both. Make your way to –' he thought for a moment – frankly, it didn't matter where '– to Iráklion. We will pick you up by the Bethlehem Gate at six o'clock tonight. We have a secret way out of the country.'

Mellas was horrified. He had thought his part in this terrible business to be almost over. 'But I stay here. Nobody knows what I have done.'

'The man you hit with the monkey wrench does,' Moylan lied. 'He's already told our nurse. And the American medical officer has witnessed your co-operation with us.' He put a comforting arm around the sailor. 'I'm sorry about this, but it's for your own safety. The 17 November people will look after you.'

Moylan helped Maggie and Michalis to hoist the injured man on the stretcher up to the gantry platform.

Then Mellas was given Maggie's white coat while the American medical officer was lifted to his feet and his blindfold removed. He found himself staring at Moylan's Vzor pistol.

'We're giving you the chance to live, Hal,' the Irishman said. 'The choice is yours, co-operate or die now. Understand?'

A nod of agreement, his fear obvious in the wide eyes. Michalis cut the officer's ties and Moylan gave him his paramedic's coat. 'Let's keep it simple. Put that on and go with this Greek. You just take out your wounded buddy and put him in the ambulance. You drive. Step out of line and the Greek shoots you both. Play along and your buddy might survive too. No heroics.'

'What the hell is all this about?' the American demanded.

'Shut it!' Moylan ordered, and thrust a spare Vzor at Mellas. 'You know how to use this? There's a round in the chamber and the safety's off. If that bastard gives any trouble, blow his fucken head off. Your life depends on it.'

Miserably the seaman stuffed the pistol into his pocket and went to one end of the stretcher. The medical officer picked up the front end. They began walking down the corridor towards the gangway.

Moylan turned to Maggie and Michalis. 'Right, let's go.'

Up on the peninsula airbase Lieutenant Commander Valerie Bargellini heard the thunderous roar of the C130 as it lifted into the air. It was filled to overload with evacuated personnel.

She picked up her telephone and called the hangar. 'How long before the second C130's ready?' she asked.

'Say five minutes, ma'am.'

'I'm just gonna get Marine Taylor off the front gate. Don't leave 'til he's aboard. Got that?'

'Yes, ma'am.'

She hung up and moved to the office window. There was no movement on the hillside. Nothing to suggest that a bunch of terrorists were up there about to launch an anthrax attack. It occurred to her it could all be some kind of exercise. She shrugged, what the hell!

Already wearing an NBC suit, she proceeded to pull on a Marine camo jacket and fatigue trousers, creating the effect of a huge squat dwarf. She secured the webbing harness and pulled the helmet on her head – it came down over her eyes.

On her way out she picked up her respirator case and an M16. She drove furiously to the entrance gate, hitting the brakes late and missing the guardhouse by a fraction of an inch.

The big black Marine and his Greek counterpart stared in surprise as she strode up to them with a manly swagger.

'Ma'am?' Unsure it was her. 'What's this about some terrorist attack?'

'Listen, Taylor, and don't argue. Take our Greek friend here with you, get in the car and drive straight to the hangar. A C130 is about to take off.'

'You're stayin', ma'am?'

'The camp's gotta have a guard, Taylor, else they'll know something's up. Now get the hell outa here.'

'I ain't leavin' you, ma'am.'

'That's an order, Marine. So go unless you want my boot up your ass!'

She was some pint-pot of dynamite, Taylor decided, and led his Greek counterpart to the car.

As Valerie Bargellini watched the dust trail recede towards the hangar she suddenly felt very vulnerable. Very lonely.

Deliberately she strode out to the gate in full view of the hillside. She shoved a round into the breech of the M16, and thumbed off the safety.

It was no consolation to her to recall that she was a hopeless shot.


Two figures in white coats appeared at the top of the gangway, a stretcher between them.

Sergeant Major Brian Hunt, watching from one of the fuel silos, felt a flood of relief. Here was Moylan, after all. Moylan and Michalis.

He spoke into the mike:'Stand by, snipers, stand by. Wait till they put the stretcher in the ambulance.'

Someone asked:'*Any sign of the O'Malley girl, Brian?*'

'Negative,' Hunt replied, wondering what had happened to her. At least it gave the snipers a clear field of fire.

The stretcher-bearers reached the foot of the gangway and turned towards the ambulance where the rear door stood open.

On the next silo Joe Monk settled over his 7.62 mm PM rifle, the long barrel supported by its fixed bipod.'*Sniper Position One,*' he said into his throat mike. '*I have lead bearer. The tallest guy. Over.*'

Farther along the jetty, Len Pope selected his target. '*Sniper Position Two. Roger to that. Confirm I have rear bearer. Stand by.*'

Hunt said: '*Sunray to Snipers. Shoot when ready. Position One leads.*'

'Roger.' Pope.

'Roger. Stand by.' Monk.

The two bearers stood on either side of the stretcher, easing it into the back of the ambulance. Both men took a step back. The taller man closed the door.

'*Now, now!*' Monk called.

The two sharp whipcracks were almost simultaneous, their sound overlapping, reverberating between the silos and the slab sides of the merchantman. Both targets pitched out in different directions, one with a perfect mid-body hit blowing a fist-sized hole into heart and lungs. The second shot had torn into one of Mellas's kidneys, the sledgehammer impact throwing him to the ground.

He squirmed in agony, trying to staunch the blood pumping out from his sodden red coat. Trying, too, to pull free the Vzor that Moylan had given him.

'*Backup Positions – GO!*' Hunt ordered.

Two SAS men leapt from the shadows of the silos, racing to the scene with Browning pistols drawn. A sudden stutter of gunfire shattered the air like firecrackers as half-a-dozen rounds thudded into Mellas's body and the reluctant terrorist fell back, dead.

As the snake of gunsmoke cleared, the two corpses were checked over.

One SAS man spoke into his mike: '*Brian, neither of these are Moylan or Michalis. Repeat not Moylan or Michalis. Over.*'

Hunt groaned. Immediately he had visions of the inquiry that would surely follow; the only consolation was that one of the mystery victims had at least been carrying a gun. Nevertheless it meant that Moylan and the others were still aboard. '*What is the health status of the targets? Over.*'

A brief pause. '*Negative, Brian. Both stone dead. Over.*'

The sergeant major sighed. No information to be gleaned from them. '*Okay, two of you get that ambulance over to the Hellenic Naval Hospital – see if we can't at least save the officer who had the fall. Over.*'

'Roger, out.'

He stared across at the stained white bulk of the ship and wondered just what game Moylan was playing?

Brad Carver and Luther Dicks spotted them first.

The two Delta members had scaled the ship's side, dumped their breathing apparatus and air bottles, and proceeded down through the nearest hatchway, Heckler and Koch MP5s at the ready.

From the head of the stairwell Dicks heard the clatter of feet on steel steps. Dropping to his knees to reduce his exposure, he peered around the side of the bulkhead. Thirty feet below he saw Moylan and the girl, and another man half-obscured by the wall of the stairwell.

'Which way now?' Moylan was demanding.

'This way I think,' said the other man in a Greek accent.

Bingo! Dicks thought, that must be Michalis. He fell back against the bulkhead, indicating to Carver that the enemy was directly below them and the direction in which they were going on the lower deck.

Brad Carver stepped back into the open so that his voice would not be heard by those below and called up Hunt on his personal radio.

He gave his position and that of Moylan's party and added: 'I see there is a lowered gangway to a pontoon and launch on this side of the ship. My hunch is they're making for that. Over.'

'*Can you get there before them? Over.*' Hunt asked.

'No, sir. But we can get down behind them in the corridor. Over.'

'*Go for that,*' Hunt decided. Then: '*All units — is anyone in position to close on that port gangway?*'

In the corridor by the bulwark opening to the gangway, Avery and Corrigan had paused. The American was trying to tighten the support bandage on his injured leg while Avery tried to make sense of the conflicting position reports coming over the radio net.

He heard Hunt's request, suddenly realised where they were, and cut in: '*Avery to Sunray – Lew and I are at that location now . . .*'

His mouth shut, leaving the sentence unfinished. Directly in front of him, where the corridor kinked to allow for pipe ducting, Maggie stepped into view. Moylan and Michalis were right behind her.

It was a moment of total surprise for both sides. The time span must have been less than two seconds, but that instant of paralysis seemed to stretch into eternity. It was like a yawningly slow video replay, each reaction and movement clearly defined, crystal, sequence by sequence, yet it all happened in the blink of an eye.

Maggie's mouth dropped, her expression of astonishment giving way to a smile of relief. 'MAX!'

Avery threw himself to one side, his shoulder hard against the wall as he raised his Browning pistol in a two-handed grip. Corrigan grasped the situation, aimed his own gun.

'Hit the deck!' Avery shouted at Maggie.

She froze in terror, believing he was about to shoot her. It was a fateful delay. Moylan fired the Vzor over her shoulder, the snap shot ranging wildly as it ricocheted down the corridor walls.

'Get down!' Avery yelled, wishing to God he'd been issued with a stun grenade. But it was too late. Moylan had Maggie by the throat, jerking her back with his forearm to form a human shield.

There was a sudden commotion in the corridor behind Michalis. From Avery's position it was difficult to determine the sequence of events that followed.

He was deafened by the short, stammering burst of fire and the muzzle flashes burning through the haze of cordite. Felt the thud as Michalis's stomach was torn apart, his innards dribbling down the walls. Saw the two figures of Dicks and Carver clad in black rubber. Heard the distinctive clatter as the CS gas grenade rolled over the steel rivets on the deck.

Thank Christ! he breathed, preparing to lunge and snatch Maggie from Moylan's arms.

But the Irishman's footwork was quick. As the grenade rolled alongside him, he kicked it hard. Whether it was skill or the devil's own luck, the thing went spinning through the gaping hatchway to spend itself uselessly in the sea below.

Avery wasn't sure the Americans could see Maggie hidden from their view by Moylan's broad shoulders. 'HOLD FIRE!' he bawled.

Dicks and Carver understood, each falling back against the corridor sides, guns still levelled.

Moylan, too, backed against the wall, the girl pulled hard up against his chest. He glanced each way and read the situation, saw his enemies backing off, inching away.

'Keep back, Max, or Maggie gets her brains blown out!'

Brad Carver shrugged his shoulders at Avery in a gesture of apology. Tasked initially to inspect the ship, they had not been issued with stun grenades.

'Drop the weapons – all of you!' Moylan hissed. 'Out of the hatchway, do it now!'

Avery hesitated, trying to see a way out. But if he wanted Maggie to live, he'd reached a dead end. He threw the Browning out to sea and looked at her. 'I'm sorry.'

The pressure on her throat prevented her from speaking, but her eyes watched him with an expression he couldn't quite place. Sorrow? Puzzlement? Perhaps both.

Dicks and Carver removed the magazines from their submachine-guns as they threw them to the deck, mindful not to give Moylan the chance to use them.

It was only when Corrigan tossed his weapon away that Moylan recognised him. His voice betrayed a sense of shock. 'Lew? Christ, what the hell has been going on?'

Avery could only guess at what was going through the man's mind. In just a few seconds his whole world had been turned on its head, his plans rudely shattered. When he was convinced that he was untouchable, the Western security forces had appeared from nowhere. Even the man he knew had been incarcerated in Baghdad was standing in front of him. Like a ghost sent to wreak its vengeance.

But Moylan recovered quickly, his own survival now uppermost in his mind. 'I don't know how you've pulled this stunt, Max, but you're too late to stop it.' He backed towards the hatchway, dragging Maggie with him. Then, keeping the gun at the girl's throat, he reached in his pocket for the two-way radio. He pressed the 'send' button. 'This is the Magician. Confirm Blackfire! Confirm Blackfire!'

'Con, you can't!' Maggie protested.

He ignored her and, with a smug grin of satisfaction, pocketed the radio. 'If any of you make a move until we're away, then it's the last you'll ever see of Maggie, Max, remember that. Even if you managed to get me, I'll take her with me. Understand?' He edged towards the top of the gangway. 'Play it cool and no one gets hurt. I'll let her go once I'm away from here.'

With Moylan's arm free of her neck, Maggie found her voice. 'Please don't worry, Max. I'll be all right.'

He shook his head. 'I should *never* have involved you in all this . . . '

He could see the tears welling in her eyes. 'It was my own fault, Max. If I hadn't once been involved, you couldn't have used me, could you? So I really only have myself to blame.'

'C'mon!' Moylan snapped, jerking her down the gangway with him.

Avery wanted to reassure her, to tell her so much. But there was no time, and the words would have been so inadequate, sounded so crass. All he could think of to say was: 'I love you.'

Momentarily she pulled against Moylan, resisting for a moment in order to stare straight into Max's face, seeing his guilt and his pain. 'A new life?' she asked, irony in her voice. 'Look after Josh until I get back.'

He nodded numbly.

Then she was out of earshot, the buffeting breeze and the splash of water around the pontoon landing stage muffling her words. Moylan dragged her aboard the launch, threw the starter switch.

As the inboard motor burbled into life they all heard the distant thud as the anthrax mortar shells were fired over the airbase.


From the derelict farm building on the hillside, O'Hare had watched with fascination as the second C130 lifted into the sky.

There appeared to have been quite a lot of activity during the previous forty-five minutes, but now it seemed strangely quiet beyond the compound fence.

'Having lunch, I expect,' Sullivan said, his binoculars focused on the lone Marine guard at the gate.

As they waited with growing impatience for Moylan's signal, the stealthy movements through the scrubby, rock-strewn terrain behind them went unnoticed. Inexorably the Delta Force team, led by Jim Buckley, closed in on the neglected building.

O'Hare glanced at his watch again. Moylan was definitely running late.

'*This is the Magician!*'

Although both men had been waiting for it, the abrupt sound of Moylan's voice startled them. This was it. The moment they'd been waiting for. The 'spectacular' to end all spectaculars. The Magician was back, opening up a deadly new chapter in the future of the world's leading terrorist group.

'*Confirm Blackfire! Confirm Blackfire!*'

Both men leapt to their feet, pulling the tarpaulin clear to reveal the dull glint of six mortar tubes.

'Two minutes,' O'Hare said briskly.

'Two minutes,' Sullivan repeated solemnly, setting the clock that would in turn release the electrical charge from the car battery to trigger the sequential timer which would fire the camera flashbulbs in each tube.

'Set self-destruct,' O'Hare said.

'Self-destruct set,' Sullivan confirmed, inserting the time-delay pencil in the small plastic explosive pack which would be sufficient to wreck the remains of the vehicle.

'Right, let's go!'

O'Hare was already on the move, hurrying down the track in long strides. Sullivan rushed to catch up. Together they strode towards the place where their getaway car was hidden, neither sparing a backward glance. Their hearts were thumping with the exhilaration of their greatest triumph. It created a giddy sense of unreality. A feeling that was suddenly compounded as a bush abruptly took on human form in front of them. It was like a bizarre scene from science fiction.

His camouflage fatigues adorned with sprigs of gorse and dry grass, Jim Buckley emerged from the branches of the shrub, his Colt Commando assault rifle wrapped in hessian. Like some nightmarish monster the figure materialised, fixing them with huge doleful black eyes set in a draped respirator hood.

'STOP OR I FIRE!' Buckley yelled.

But the muffled shout sounded like the demented war cry of a lunatic.

O'Hare froze rigid, then turned and began running back up the track.

Sullivan stood his ground. Jerking the Vzor from his jacket, he took aim at the weird apparition. Buckley's Colt shook in his hands, rattling out a controlled burst, raking down the man's chest and stomach. Other troops, whom Sullivan hadn't seen, fired simultaneously from three different directions.

The Irishman was sent spinning by the successive impacts into a spectacular diving roll over the edge of the track. He tumbled to a halt, face down in the loose shale.

From her viewpoint at the base gate Lieutenant Commander Valerie Bargellini saw the events unfold, and watched O'Hare as he stood like a stag at bay, wondering which way to run as more Delta troops descended from the hillside, cutting him off in their attempt to reach the building before the mortar could be fired.

The Irishman realised there was no way back and launched himself off the track, half running and half sliding down the slope in a desperate bid for freedom.

At that moment the derelict building seemed to explode. A massive blink of dazzling light was followed by the guttural belch of explosive as the massive projectiles hurtled skyward in fast succession. She thought she counted six tumbling dark objects against the sky.

Instinctively she ducked, waiting for the airburst and the

flying shrapnel that would rain down death on her and disperse the invisible cloud of anthrax.

She looked up as the first round crashed into the roof of the administration block where she had her office. Twenty pounds of Semtex ignited, the flash pulsed scorching white before her eyes, and the debris scattered in all directions in the maelstrom of displaced air.

The second round hit, a huge fountain of earth spewing skyward from the smouldering crater in the neatly tended garden. Somewhere beyond the collapsed building the third round fell, its earth-shaking detonation making the ground beneath her tremble.

Slowly she uncoiled from her foetal position on the dirt road, tried to shake the ringing sound from her ears and looked up, her large helmet askew. She reached up, pulled it off, and extracted the respirator hood from her side pouch.

Through the haze of the goggle-eyes, she could see the terrorist still running, much closer to her now, and Delta soldiers in hot pursuit.

Suddenly she felt a burning anger at this man who would threaten her and her comrades with such an outrage against humanity. Against the United States. Against her, personally.

She thought momentarily of the deliberate oil spills in the Gulf and the raging fires polluting the planet. Her planet. And now this. She knew little about anthrax, and she had no idea now whether she would die or live to marry and have the child she'd always promised herself.

But with her seething anger came a great sense of calm. She climbed to her feet and slowly, calmly, raised the M16 to her eye in a classic marksman's pose.

She squeezed the trigger. Gently, just once. A single shot. Whether it was sheer skill or just good fortune, she would never know.

O'Hare fell onto the road, shot dead through the head at almost two hundred metres.

Through the smeared lenses of the claustrophobic hood that stank of rubber and charcoal, she stared at the distant body as the Delta soldiers surrounded it. Then a thought occurred to her. She had heard six mortar rounds fired, but had seen only three explode on landing. None, she was sure, had exploded in midair. And an airburst was needed to distribute anthrax effectively.

She frowned. Had the terrorists got it wrong?

Max Avery ran down the gangway to where Brian Hunt waited on the jetty.

'He's made his escape by launch,' he explained breathlessly.

'Yes, Max, I know. It's out of our hands now.'

'What d'you mean?'

Hunt had been in touch with Cyprus via his portable Sky-wave radio. 'Moylan's off-base now, so it's down to the Greek authorities. Apparently they shot dead Sophie Papavas yesterday and they've made the connection with all of this. The 17 November have been very active on Saddam's behalf on the mainland. The Greeks think it's time it was their show.'

'Surely we can do something?' Avery protested, glaring in vain across the bay for sight of the launch.

'We've no helicopter and Delta's Gemini is still over on the island. We've nothing to *do* anything with. But the Greeks have got an Anti-Terrorist unit on the island. Sorry.' He looked up at the ship. 'In the meantime you and Lew had better get back to the truck; I'm trying to get all civilians out of here until we find out if Moylan managed to plant that bomb.'

'No luck so far?'

'Needle in a bloody haystack,' Hunt muttered in disgust.

The launch slapped into the oncoming breakers, fighting its way out to sea.

Maggie sat huddled on the centre thwart, the wind and salt spray whipping at her back through the sodden material of her blouse.

She hadn't spoken since they'd left the ship. Her eyes were fixed on Moylan. He seemed hardly concerned that his plans had been interrupted. Rivulets of water ran down his cheeks as he set his face against the stiff breeze that came in off the sea. His long hair was wild now, his expression the same as the young maverick terrorist who had stirred her mind and her loins all those years before.

It was as though the transformation were complete. Time had gone full circle.

She raised her voice to be heard against the screaming inboard motor. 'Where are we going?'

'Out of the bay!' he yelled back. 'Far enough to blow that ship without taking us with it!'

Her expression was one of horror. 'You can't go ahead with that. Not now!'

His teeth were white against his weather-tanned face. 'Why not, little mouse? They'll have enough on their plate with the airbase and that ship when it blows! Just pray your boyfriend isn't still on board. Anyway, they'll be too busy saving lives and evacuating people to worry about us!' He considered the murky horizon. 'Messier than I planned, but we've done it! By Christ we've done it! We ditch this launch along the coast, then make our way to Iráklion and the Libyan ship. Nothing's really changed! And it's best not to break a pact with the devil!'

She held him in a steady gaze. 'Were you really prepared to shoot me back there?'

He avoided her eyes. 'The threat was enough – it got us away, didn't it?'

'And what about me now?'

He spared her a momentary glance. 'It's up to you, isn't it?'

But it wasn't, she knew that. It never had been. If she defied him now, he'd have nothing to lose by killing her. They both realised that; she simply knew too much.

'You know what I want,' she murmured.

He strained to hear her words.

'You want to come with me? Like the old days.'

A sad half-smile crossed her face. 'A new life.'

'With me?'

She nodded. 'I'll need to have Josh.'

He had never looked more triumphant. 'I'll get him for

you; arrange a snatch. But then we'll have a child of our own – ours. I'd like that.'

Suddenly she felt nauseous, the bile beginning to crawl up into her throat.

They both heard it then. In a lull in the wind came the urgent downbeat thud of a helicopter. Moylan turned in his seat by the wheel.

It was a white blur against the merging grey tones of sea and sky. Coming in low, creating a geyser of spray from its own rotors. It was gaining fast.

Moylan grunted and turned back to her. 'Don't worry, I'll frighten them off.' He raised the Vzor to show her what he meant. 'Now get that video camera out of the bag!'

'You're joking. At a time like this?'

'Do it!' he shouted. 'The Iraqis want proof to show the world. It's all part of the deal.' He'd planned to film it from the quiet British War Cemetery at the head of the bay, but this would have to do.

As she struggled to open the bag, he twisted in his seat and fired three times at the advancing helicopter. Then the rounds ran out.

Nevertheless the helicopter backed off, circling cautiously like a predatory cat.

She had the video camera out now.

'Do you know how to use it?'

Maggie shook her head.

'Give it to me,' he snapped impatiently, 'and take the wheel!'

Awkwardly they changed places in the bucking swell as

they entered more open waters. From his new position he could see the helicopter clearly, starting to advance on them again.

He placed the camera on the thwart and took the small cylindrical transmitter from his pocket, extending its telescopic aerial.

The pilot of the helicopter was getting bolder, lower, creating a mad vortex of water with the machine's downdraught. Moylan could see their plan, guessed they intended to swamp the boat.

He handed the Vzor to Maggie with a handful of bullets. 'Fill the mag, will you? You used to be quick at that, I remember.'

Hurriedly he switched on the camera, checked it was functioning and lifted it with one hand, holding the transmitter in the other. 'It's good to be back with you again, little mouse. I'm glad you haven't forgotten the cause or anything else I ever taught you.'

His thumb edged towards the firing switch on the transmitter.

The noise from the helicopter swelled, the roar of the rotors stupendous, jets of spray gushing into the launch.

'Fire at the fucker!' Moylan ordered, suddenly fearful that they'd left it too late.

Maggie said: 'Max taught me things, too, Con. I realise that now.'

'What?' He couldn't hear her words.

'I realise now what his life must have been like. A life of lies. Devoted to catching bastards like you.' She raised the Vzor. 'And he *did* love me, you bastard. HE DID!'

They didn't hear her screamed words in the helicopter, nor the pumping action of the pistol as she emptied the magazine into Moylan's chest.

The transmitter dropped from his fingers, rolling back and forth in the bilge water.

Through the veil of spume and the jewels of seaspray glistening on the cockpit canopy, Nico Legakis couldn't see the body of the man. Only a woman standing erect at the wheel, a smoking gun in her hand.

He had a clear view now, had to take his chance while he had it. To cut down the accomplice of Sophie Papavas. To cut out the cancer that had been eating away at his country for so many years.

He felt the gun jerk in his hand, saw the plume of cordite whisked away in the slipstream.

And it was over.

As the helicopter circled again, Legakis realised he had somehow managed to kill both occupants of the launch with the single shot.

He felt not a little pride as he watched the boat, still powering out into the Mediterranean as though it had a mind of its own.

Perhaps, he thought, someone might give him a medal for this day's work.

# Epilogue

Fourteen days later, more than a million men were engaged in the desert land battle to free Kuwait from the tyrannical occupation of Saddam Hussein's Iraq.

It lasted just one hundred hours. And resulted in a landslide victory for the allies.

But the two men, listening to the radio news in a limousine on its way from CIA Langley to the White House, knew that the outcome had nearly been very different.

'You should have told me,' Willard Franks said.

Lew Corrigan shrugged and lit his cigar in defiance of the No Smoking sign. 'No point. I couldn't be certain that plugging the propellant feed with plumber's lead would do the trick. And I didn't know Moylan wouldn't have the anthrax rounds checked over again. Guess he was shit scared of the stuff.'

'Nevertheless,' Franks chided.

Another shrug. 'So it worked? Those three rounds hit the deck and didn't explode?'

'One did fracture,' Franks said, 'but on impact at ground-zero. As it was, we had decontamination units flown in the same day. The spores hadn't travelled and concrete is easy to clean. If those airbursts had gone off it would have been a very different story. I can tell you the President was mighty relieved. Even more so after those Irish bastards were caught trying to enter the kitchens at the Senate dining rooms. If you and Avery hadn't alerted us, they'd have got away with it. The kitchens wouldn't otherwise have had that degree of security.' He stared out at the tarmac ribbon of the Capital Beltway. 'It was the same with the Brits. Not many tugboats change hands these days, so Avery's information gave them the lead they needed. The Thames river police caught two of Moylan's men red-handed fitting an aerosol generator to the mast.'

'Nothing reached the media,' Corrigan observed.

'Hell, no, Lew. Everyone kept the lid on real tight. If that news alone had gotten out, public and media pressure could still have forced us to abandon Desert Storm. As I say, the President's real keen to shake your hand personally. He's arranged for you to have a full ten-minute audience with him.'

Corrigan chewed on the end of his cigar. 'He's that grateful, huh?'

The Washington damp was already making his leg ache. It had given him considerable pain since Baghdad and the doctor reckoned it always would.

He lapsed into thoughtful silence, wondering what life would have to offer next. A couple of weeks' holiday perhaps, taking in some fishing off Cape Cod? Or a week of beach, birds and booze down Acapulco? Maybe a few days tramping the Rockies with a rucksack?

But what then? Ireland was out, and that hurt. He'd loved his old home country and most of its people.

There had been envelopes waiting for him on the mat of his apartment on 14th and Q. An offer of a dubious body-guarding job in Colombia. Someone planning a coup in an African republic he'd never even heard of. And there was the offer of a job with Point Four, the secretive agency that policed US aid distribution.

But in all of this there was nothing that appealed. Maybe he was getting too old. And all he had to show for life was a beat-up Thunderbird, a rented apartment and an expensive ex-wife.

He had always been a loner. In a way it was his stock in trade, one of the prime qualities that put him in demand by Willard Franks at the CIA, the Defense Intelligence Agency people and others.

But he realised now he'd been alone too long. Perversely it had been Sophie Papavas who had made him realise it. The only bonus had been working with Max Avery. As alike as chalk and cheese in many ways, but at least they'd rubbed along. He reckoned they'd made quite a team.

Willard Franks said: 'I guess this isn't the time, Lew, but we have a nice one lined up for you. NOC stuff again, right up your street.'

'Yeah?'

'We want to infiltrate these new neo-Fascist movements growing up in Germany. A deep-cover operation. Some of our people feel they could become a real threat to stability in Europe.'

Corrigan nodded sagely and tapped on the window of the car. They were in downtown Washington now, approaching the White House. 'Say, Willard, drop me off here, will you? I need to buy some cigars.'

The CIA man glanced at his watch. 'You're due to see the President in thirty minutes.'

Corrigan grinned. 'Sure, I can walk it. Only a few blocks. I'll catch up with you there.'

The limousine pulled into the sidewalk and Corrigan climbed out. He waited until the vehicle had disappeared before he hailed a passing taxi.

Ten minutes later he was back at his apartment. He picked up the telephone and dialled the airline. 'I want an open-ended ticket to Heathrow, England.'

The voice was velvet but soulless. 'When did you want to travel, sir?'

'Soonest.'

A pause as she looked at her VDU. 'Soonest is actually a cancelled First Class this afternoon, but –'

'I'll take it.'

Some other time, Mr President.


The first crocuses were in bloom in the carefully tended flowerbeds of the bungalow garden in West Kirby, a very respectable middle-class district of Liverpool.

It was a clear bright day and remarkably warm for the time of year. Frank and Vera Avery sat with their son on the wooden patio furniture and watched the child crawl across the lawn.

'He's a lovely boy, Max,' Vera said, dabbing at her running mascara with a handkerchief. 'He's got your face.'

'And his mother's eyes,' Avery added hoarsely.

Vera turned to look at him. 'I'm so sorry to hear that you and Maggie have broken up. And to think we've never even met her.' She found it impossible to hide the disapproval in her tone. 'I suppose there's no chance of you getting back together again?'

He shook his head. 'I wish there was.'

'Is she staying on in South Africa?'

'I think so.' Still, even now, he couldn't escape the lies.

'At least you're home now. How long is it? Since just after you left the army . . . ?'

'Six years.'

Six years of purgatory. Six years of the living lie, during which he had written the letters describing a make-believe life for his controller to post back to his parents, via Johannesburg.

'And you've got custody?' his father said. 'That's unusual.'

'I suppose it is.'

'Are you going to live near here?' his mother asked. 'It would be nice to see Josh grow up – my very own grand-child.'

'I'm afraid I'm taking him to Australia with me.'

'Oh.' Her mouth puckered. Hurt and disapproving.

'Queensland. It's a great place for a kid. A land of opportunity.'

He had put the business up for sale and, with Clarissa Royston-Jones pulling strings, had helped Floyd raise the capital to buy it. Now that Maggie was dead, MI5 had tried to halve the financial settlement he'd been promised; pressure from the Treasury they said. Clarissa had come close to resigning in order to win the battle for him.

But after the successful conclusion of Stalking Horse, her star was in the ascendant. It was even rumoured that she might be in line to become the new Director General of the Security Service.

Avery said: 'You must come and visit.'

His father scowled. 'You never wanted us to come to South Africa,' he said pointedly.

How could he, when he was living a lie in Streatham? 'It was difficult. You know, the job. Me always away.'

Vera didn't want to dwell on such a sore point. 'When do you leave?'

Avery glanced at his watch. 'Any minute. A friend's coming to pick me up. We fly out tomorrow.'

Vera was taken aback. 'This is all such a surprise, and so quick. Couldn't you possibly have stayed a few days – or weeks – before flying off again?'

Not with Danny Grogan at large, Avery thought. He had a lot of tracks to cover.

Ever practical, Frank Avery asked: 'And what are you going to do in Australia? Shear sheep?'

His son looked up at the clear spring sky. 'My friend and I thought we'd set up a security consultancy, draw on our military experience. I've an old friend in London who wants us to open a branch for him somewhere in the Far East.'

'Rob D'Arcy?' His father guessed, remembering his son's old friend, a former SAS major whose company had been in the newspapers a few times.

Avery nodded his reply just as the doorbell rang.

'It must be your friend,' Vera said. 'Is it the Irishman? The one who called here looking for you last week? He didn't leave a name.'

It seemed like a long time before Avery replied. 'No, it's not him – and he's no friend. If he calls again, you haven't seen me. Understand?'

Frank Avery thought he understood.

Half an hour later the hired car was packed and baby Josh safely stowed in his carrycot on the back seat.

As they drove down the tree-lined suburban road and headed towards Heathrow, Lew Corrigan said: 'You know, Max, people are goin' to think we're an odd couple.' He jerked his thumb towards the back seat.

Avery laughed. 'Are you sure you can hack it?'

Corrigan clamped a fresh cigar between his teeth. 'I don't give a toss what folk think, Max. Personally, I'm rather looking forward to it.'

A new life.